THE MACKENZIES
ZACH

THE MACKENZIES ZACH

ANA LEIGH

AVON BOOKS
An Imprint of HarperCollinsPublishers

This is a work of fiction. Names, characters, places, and incidents are products of the author's imagination or are used fictitiously and are not to be construed as real. Any resemblance to actual events, locales, organizations, or persons, living or dead, is entirely coincidental.

AVON BOOKS
An Imprint of HarperCollins*Publishers*
10 East 53rd Street
New York, New York 10022-5299

Printed in the U.S.A.

I dedicate this novel to my editor, Micki Nuding,
who has traveled this long trail
with the MacKenzies and me.

Thanks for turning my garbled words
into novels, Micki. This author couldn't ask
for a better saddle pal.

Chapter 1

Texas 1892

The door suddenly burst open, sending a gritty spray of sand over the newly polished wooden floor. Three men filled the entrance to the restaurant that smelled of fresh paint and baked apple pie. Their glances swept the interior, pausing briefly on Everett Billings standing at the kitchen door, before moving on to fix their stares on Rose Dubois and Kate McDermott. The man in the middle mumbled a lewd remark, and the others snorted in laughter.

"I'm sorry, gentlemen, but the restaurant isn't open," Everett Billings said nervously.

"It is now," the barrel-chested man in the middle said. They entered and headed for a table in the corner. Two more men followed, and another trailed behind.

The last man to enter held Rose's attention. He was tall, his legs long and muscular, and a holstered Colt was tied to his thigh. Unlike the other five men he didn't slouch or shuffle, but crossed the floor in a smooth, loping stride, his broad shoulders squared but relaxed, and his head held high in a way that suggested pride rather than arrogance.

Rose couldn't see what he had to be proud about. He was dressed just as grubbily as the motley crew he accompanied: worn Levi's, shirt, and vest, dusty, run-down-at-the-heels boots, and a battered, sweat-stained Stetson.

Yet he stood out like a peacock amidst a gaggle of geese.

And the gang sounded just as disruptive as the honking fowl, boisterously loud as they scraped chairs across the floor to seat themselves at a table in the corner.

"Why did they have to sit down at one of my tables?" Kate whispered to Rose, as they filled a tray with glasses of ice water.

"Your lucky day, honey," Rose murmured.

"I don't think so." Kate picked up the tray and hurried over to the table.

The Harvey rules required all men to wear suit jackets in the dining room. There wasn't a jacket among this crew, but Rose doubted the manager would insist they don the ones offered to male customers for such emergencies. Billings had made a hasty exit into the kitchen the moment the group sat down.

Just their bad luck that she and Kate had arrived

early; the other three Harvey Girls weren't due for another fifteen minutes.

As Rose continued slicing pies in preparation for the dinner train arriving in an hour, she watched poor Kate taking the men's orders.

Fred Harvey himself had handpicked Rose for this assignment, putting her in charge of the other four girls in the limited crew he'd sent in to "test the waters." Brimstone was still primitive and lawless, so the question was whether it would be advisable to build a larger Harvey House and make the town a scheduled dining stop on this trunk line of the Santa Fe.

The few honest and decent folks in the area had welcomed the possibility. Law and order had always followed after the arrival of Harvey Girls in the other towns along the route of the Santa Fe Railroad where Fred Harvey had established restaurants. It was common knowledge that the fine cuisine he offered, served on fine china and Waterford crystal by the hands of these pretty waitresses of fine moral character, was helping to tame the West as much as the Colt revolvers and Springfield rifles in the hands of courageous lawmen.

Since Rose's quest for a rich husband had proven unsuccessful after two years at the Harvey House in New Mexico, she had welcomed the transfer. A new location offered new faces and new hope.

However, in the week she'd been here, she'd seen that Brimstone offered nothing but sand, scorpions, and shiftless drifters like this gang. The so-called sheriff was as bad as the men he jailed. And her hope of finding a wealthy rancher was slimmer than the town's chance of finding an honest sheriff.

At a sudden outburst of loud laughter, Rose glanced over in time to see a blushing Kate walk away, followed by bawdy remarks and lewd glances. There were tears in the girl's eyes as she passed by Rose.

Why had Harvey sent a sweet girl like Kathleen McDermott to the lawless town of Brimstone? Fresh off a Wisconsin farm, the dark-haired young girl had a naive, wide-eyed innocence that belonged in a drawing room drinking tea with family and friends, not serving coffee to boisterous cowboys in a godforsaken town like Brimstone.

Though these men weren't cowboys any more than Rose was. In the West one fact was undeniable: working cowboys always treated a woman with respect and reverence; no man dared insult a lady in the presence of one of them. These men were ruffians—good-for-nothing drifters. Or even worse, gunslingers.

"Hey, sister, you here to help or just to look at?" one of them called out to her.

The gravel-voiced speaker was a big man whose flesh had begun to slide into bulkiness. Bushy dark brows hovered above gray eyes that were as icy as a morning in January. His cheeks and jaws were covered with a black beard.

"Are you addressing me, sir?" Rose asked coolly.

"Rather be *un*dressing you, sweetheart. Right, boys?"

That brought another round of laughter and ribald comments from the others, except the tall one. He sat silently staring at her.

"Tell your girlfriend to hurry with that grub, and hustle your bustle over here and pour us some coffee."

What a rude excuse for a man! Rose picked up the coffeepot and stalked over to the table, determined to put him in his place.

"You want it in a cup, or should I pour it directly into your big mouth?"

"Hey, Jess, she's sure got your number," one of the men said amidst their guffaws.

Jess appeared to lose his sense of humor when the joke was on him. He turned his cold, gray-eyed glare on the speaker. The laughter ceased instantly, and the men clamped up, exchanging nervous glances with each other.

Belatedly, Rose realized it might have been more prudent to have ignored his crudeness. Maybe she could undo the harm by being pleasant.

"You fellows be sure and save room for a piece of apple pie," she said, circling the table and filling the cups. "It's fresh-baked every day, and it's delicious."

"Humph!" Still disgruntled, Jess glared at her. " 'Pears like we'll have plenty of room for it. Where in hell is that grub? Haul your ass into that kitchen and find out."

That did it—she'd had enough of this bully's crudity. "I have a better idea, sir. Why don't you haul your obscene mouth out of here—and take this pack of laughing hyenas with you. Animals aren't permitted in the restaurant."

She spun on her heel to walk away, but Jess grabbed her arm, yanking her around.

"You little bitch! I oughta—"

His threat ended in a howl as she jerked away, tipping the coffeepot, and a stream of the hot liquid poured onto his lap. Yelping, he released her arm and clutched at his privates.

The men beside him grabbed napkins, but before they could come to his aid Rose picked up a glass of ice water and dumped it over the coffee-stained area between his legs.

"At least it spilled where it can't do any harm," she said and stepped away.

Jess shoved back his chair and tottered to his feet. He balled his fist to strike her, but the tall man put a restraining hand on his arm.

"It was an accident, Tait."

Tait glared at him, jerked his arm out of the man's grasp, and hobbled to the door. He paused at the entrance to look back at Rose. A shiver raced down her spine at the naked malevolence in his eyes.

"I've got a score to settle with you, sister."

Rose knew she had crossed a dangerous line, but it was too late to change it. She raised her head and took the threat without cowering.

They all slammed out except for the tall one, who tossed some coins on the table.

"This should cover the coffee. Save me a piece of that pie."

He ambled over to her. This close, she saw that his eyes were as blue as sapphires and tipped with long, dark lashes. The effect was mesmerizing. He seemed to generate a heat—or was she merely flustered from his nearness? Leaning down, he said softly, "Jess Tait's a dangerous enemy, Redhead. You be careful."

Rose remained motionless as he walked away, her gaze riveted on the door through which he'd disappeared. *You be careful.* Thick with sensual huskiness, his seductive voice had made the warning sound more like . . . like . . . Like he'd just rolled over in bed and kissed her good morning.

She shivered again, but this time fear had nothing to do with it.

Zach MacKenzie paused outside the restaurant. Tait and the others were headed for the Long Horn, where the gang had taken rooms for the night. Obviously the accident had no lasting effect on Tait, because he was moving in a fast clip as he worked his mouth and hands furiously, madder than a cornered rattlesnake in the hot sun—and just as dangerous.

As usual, Pike and Cain were lapping at Tait's heels. Those two butt kissers disgusted him.

When Bull and Joe broke off from the other three, Bull turned his head and shouted, "Hey, MacKenzie, Joe and me's gonna get some ass. You comin'?"

Zach shook his head. "Naw, maybe later."

"Your loss. Ain't too many whores in this town and when I'm finished with 'em, they're gonna be too worn-out to be much good for anything but lay there pinin' fer my return."

"I'll take my chances," Zach said.

Whores and whiskey—that was all those two thought about. Zach was tired of trailing along with this bunch, but for the time being, he had no choice. He glanced over in time to see the other three disappear into the bar. Good. He had an errand to run, and when he got back, he had an appointment with a piece of apple pie—and that redhead.

She intrigued him all right: that hair, those blue eyes, and curves that even her starched apron and black dress couldn't hide. But she was more than just good looking: she had spunk. The way that gal had stood up to Jess Tait may not have been the smartest thing to do—but it took nerve. She had more guts than a lot of men had.

These Harvey Girls were fine, decent women—and some were feisty as hell, like Emily, the Harvey Girl his cousin Josh had married.

He grinned, wondering if the spilled coffee had really been an accident. Then he recalled Tait's threat to the gal. Accident or not, the man was mean and spiteful enough to beat her up—or maybe worse—to get even.

He'd just have to make sure that it didn't happen. If anyone was going to lay hands on that redhead, it was going to be him—and pure pleasure was what he had in mind.

Adjusting his Stetson, Zach headed for the stables.

Chapter 2

⟨∾⟩

Rose was exhausted. There had been forty customers for dinner and only thirty minutes to feed them.

One of the many reasons for the success of the Harvey restaurants was that the meals were ordered in advance on the train and wired ahead, so by the time the train pulled into the depot, the food was prepared and waiting.

Each of the girls had a table of eight and every passenger received a full-course dinner. Normally there would be additional help to fill water glasses and serve the beverages, but since Brimstone was in an experimental stage the only staff was Everett Billings, five Harvey Girls, and a French couple who did the cooking. Although superb chefs, the couple

9

could not speak English; Billings was the only one who could communicate with them in a halting French. They were a far cry from Yen Cheng, the volatile Chinese cook at the New Mexico Harvey House. Rose couldn't help smiling, remembering those days.

But despite the limited personnel, by the time the train departed thirty minutes after arrival, each satisfied customer had been served a cup of hot creamed potato-and-leek soup, a crisp salad of seasoned lettuce leaves garnished with anchovies and strips of red peppers, a succulent beef fillet covered with a *pâté de foi gras*, tiny potatoes boiled in their skins, scalloped onions, and their choice of either meringue shells filled with chocolate truffles or a slice of freshly baked apple pie. Almost all the women had opted for the meringue shells, and the men the apple pie. The offered beverages had been coffee or tea, and those who wished had been served a glass of fine claret as well.

It was after nine o'clock by the time the last piece of crystal and china had been washed and the kettles scrubbed and put away. All had returned to their rented rooms except for Rose and Everett Billings.

Anxious to be on his way, Billings said, "If you have no objection, Miss Dubois, I'll leave now. I've already missed the start of the Bible study."

"Go right ahead, Mr. Billings," Rose said.

"I hate to leave you alone," he replied, putting on his hat. "Particularly since your earlier confrontation with those unpleasant men. Are you sure you don't want me to remain?"

"Really, it's not necessary. I'm almost through here, and it's just a short walk to the boarding-house."

"Well, I've locked the kitchen door, so be sure and lock the front one when you leave. Good night, Miss Dubois."

"Good night, Mr. Billings."

Rose smiled as the manager departed. Billings was a nice man, but too timid for Brimstone—at least until the town became more civilized. But even though the town revolted her, Rose loved the rugged beauty of the land itself. She only wished she could find the rich husband she sought. She could put up with ruggedness as long as there were a few luxuries thrown in—and some respectability.

Born in the slums of New Orleans, Rose had lost her mother early and had been raised by a father who'd constantly been in and out of jail for drunkenness and petty crimes. She'd become streetwise and had learned to survive in the world she moved in. But she wanted a better life.

Back east she could have had the luxury she yearned for, but with her background, the most she could hope for from a rich man would have been an "arrangement." Here, because of the scarcity of women and the desire for heirs, the men—rich or poor alike—offered marriage. They weren't as criti-cal of a woman's background. And because of the high moral standards Fred Harvey imposed, Har-vey Girls were on the top of that preference list.

Rose couldn't have bluffed her way through the Harvey training if it hadn't been for Emily Lawrence, who had taught her the behavior expected of a lady. The thought made her remember the letter in her pocket that she'd received that day from Emily. Between the dinner rush and cleaning up, she hadn't had time to read it. Now, anxious to get back to her room to open the letter, she hurriedly finished folding the last napkin for the morning's breakfast rush.

The bell above the door jingled as she started to turn down the last lamp. "Sorry, we're closed," she called out. "Cook's gone home."

"Who cares about the cook? We have some unfinished business."

A shiver rippled her spine as she recognized the voice. Pivoting, she saw him leaning back against the door, his arms folded across his chest. Cast in shadow, he appeared more dangerous than ever. Definitely more dangerous.

"What unfinished business can we possibly have?"

"A piece of pie."

"I'm afraid you're too late, cowboy; it's all gone. I'm just closing . . . Where are you going?" she asked abruptly when he walked past her and shoved the kitchen door open. "Kindly leave," she demanded, following him.

Ignoring her, he lit a lamp, then hunkered down and peered into the icebox. Turning his head, he gave her a reproachful glance. "Didn't your momma warn you that lying can get you into trouble, Redhead?" He pulled out a pie tin with half a pie remaining. "Care to join me?"

"Just make yourself at home," she sniffed, and stalked out of the room.

He followed, carrying the tin, and forked a bite of

the pie into his mouth. "Don't reckon you have any coffee left?"

Rose glared at him. "You *reckoned* right." Em had once said these Westerners did more reckoning than the Lord would do on judgment day. "Of course, I'm sure you've already checked out the empty coffeepot."

He grinned—a devastating, curl-your-toes grin. The kind that brought an exciting jolt to a young girl's heart. Thank goodness she'd been around enough to recognize it when she saw it and wouldn't let herself be deceived by its appeal.

"You're pretty smart for your age, Redhead."

"Not really. You're just pretty dumb for yours."

"You always have a smart answer, don't you?"

"That's right, cowboy. Tell you what; the pie's on me if you get out now."

"Let's sit. My ma always said that standing up and eating gives you a bellyache."

"Your mother's right. Take the pie with you and sit down and eat it in your room."

"I like the company here." He surprised her by pulling out a chair for her, then waited until she sat down before taking a seat himself. "Bite?" he asked, offering her a piece on the end of the fork.

"No, thank you."

"It's good."

"I know; I had a piece. Will you just hurry up and eat it? I'm tired, and I'd like to leave."

"You been in this town long?" he asked, taking a healthy bite.

"A week too long." She began drumming her fingers on the table.

"So how long have you been in Brimstone?" Another bite passed between his sensual lips.

"A week."

His warm chuckle played a tune on her spine. "I like you, Redhead."

She stared into the sapphire eyes capped with those damn long lashes that women struggled to achieve with mascara or kohl. Even the stubble on his jaw couldn't detract from them.

"I have a name, sir: Dubois. Rose Dubois."

The sapphire gaze remained fixed on hers. "Mine's Zach MacKenzie."

"That's a coincidence," she said, surprised. "I know a Josh MacKenzie. He's a Pinkerton agent—or was, rather. Are you related?"

He didn't bat an eye. "Pinkerton? You have some trouble with the law, Rosie?"

"I just prefer to avoid lawmen. But this one married a close friend of mine."

"Is that right? Well, MacKenzie's a common name out here. What don't you like about lawmen?"

"The ones I've encountered are worse than the outlaws they're chasing." The first, and worst, had been Sheriff Wes Sturges, who'd entered her life when she was seventeen. But she refused to dwell on that.

"So you *have* had some trouble with the law." He popped the last bite of pie into his mouth.

"I didn't say that." She picked up the tin, carried it into the kitchen, and put it on the sinkboard. When she turned, he was there behind her. How could he move so soundlessly on the wooden floors?

He surprised her by slipping an arm around her waist; then he drew her against his hard muscle and flesh. Ordinarily Rose would have repelled the advance with an elbow to his ribs or a knee to his groin.

But for some reason entirely alien to her sense of survival, she didn't do either. There was a heady excitement to being so near him, and she'd been around enough to feel confident she could control the situation.

"What do you think you're doing, MacKenzie?"

"Since I can't have coffee, I'll settle for this." His kiss stopped the words of protest on her lips.

The pleasure was instant, explosive. Realizing she'd underestimated his effect on her, Rose tried to draw away. He cupped her neck with a warm palm to keep her still, and his touch overwhelmed her senses as much as his firm, warm lips—as much as his hard, heated body pressed against hers.

She'd been kissed before, but never felt anything like she was feeling in the arms of Zach MacKenzie. Everything about him excited her, aroused her. How she'd yearned for such a touch—for such a thrill.

But she was playing with fire and it was an insanity she couldn't afford. She groped for the Colt on his hip, drew it out of the holster, then pressed it against his stomach.

He stepped back, but didn't release her. His mouth curved into the barest hint of a smile. "You ever shoot a man before, Rosie?"

"That's for me to know and you to think about."

He dropped his hands away and studied her

with those damn sapphire eyes. "Why, Rosie? You were as curious about this kiss as I was, and you sure as hell were enjoying it as much as I was."

"That's your opinion. And keep calling me Rosie and I *will* pull this trigger."

"Why the act? You're not fooling me for a minute; I know what you want from a man."

"That's good—because you don't have it." She handed the gun to him.

"You sure?" he asked, slipping the Colt back into its holster. "That kiss says otherwise."

"All that kiss will get you is a free piece of pie, MacKenzie. Don't think I don't know *your* kind. I've been fighting off riffraff like you from the time I sprouted breasts. You're all poured from the same mold."

"What's so bad about a couple of kisses between friends, Rosie?"

"Maybe a couple of hot kisses and a roll in the hay is enough for you, but not for me, MacKenzie," she declared, jabbing a thumb at herself. "I've got plans for my future, and they don't include a down-on-his-luck drifter like you."

"Who's talking future? You're wasting your time if you're trying to convince me that you've been saving yourself for the right man. We both know better."

Her fingers itched to scratch the smirk off his face. Granted, she was no virgin, but she was no whore, either. And he was treating her like one. But what did it matter what he thought, anyway? Why should she let it bother her? She'd always shrugged off such looks before.

So why did it hurt this time?

Rose looked up into his eyes, and said softly, "No, Zach MacKenzie, you're the one wasting your time. You see, you don't know me at all."

"But I soon will, Rosie."

For a long moment he stared at her. She returned his gaze in silence, broken only by the sound of her pounding heart hammering in her ears.

He walked to the door, then turned his head and looked at her. "By the way, Rosie, when you're that close to a man, never draw a pistol unless you cock it. Some men might not take too kindly to it and turn it on you." Tipping a finger to the brim of his Stetson, he nodded. "Good night for now."

She stood motionless as he departed, and waited until she heard the bell jingle. With trembling hands she groped behind her for the sinkboard. Leaning back against it, she closed her eyes and drew a deep breath. Her lips still tingled from his kiss—her body still trembled from his touch.

Zach MacKenzie had thrown out a challenge. Did she have the will to meet it? Brimstone had suddenly become more dangerous than she imagined, if a saddle tramp like him had the ability to curl her toes. For the first time in her life she was afraid to trust herself. She could only hope that he and his gang kept moving on. If not, she had to avoid him at all costs.

Zach remained in the shadows when Rose came out and locked the door. There'd been no sign of Tait when he'd returned to town, and that bothered him. Jess Tait swaggered through life making

a lot of threats, and he usually carried them out—
especially with someone smaller or weaker than he.

So the redhead knew his cousin Josh. Well, the
less said about any family connection, the better. He
couldn't keep himself from grinning, though, thinking about Josh and his bride. Rose had said she and
Emily were friends. He'd bet his best pair of boots
that the two gals were too much for any one man to
reckon with. Next time he saw Josh, he'd have to
find out what part Rose had played in his cousin's
courtship.

Hugging the shadows, Zach followed Rose the
short distance to her boardinghouse. A few seconds
after she entered, a light glowed from a rear window.

"Good night for now, Rose Dubois," he murmured. "I'd like nothing better than to tuck you in
bed, so mark my words: one of these days I'll be
saying good morning, as well."

He continued down the street to where loud
laughter carried over the tinny din of a piano. Zach
paused in the entrance of the smoke-filled saloon
and glanced around. Tait and his two minions were
at a corner table. As much as he'd prefer to ignore
the son of a bitch, he didn't have any choice. He
walked over to the table and sat down.

"Where've ya been?" Tait asked. "Ain't seen ya
around." His words were slurred and Zach hoped
he wouldn't get belligerent, like he usually did
when he'd had too much to drink.

"I could ask the same about you. I looked for you
fellas earlier."

"Tait hadda change his pants, then we had somethin' to eat," Pike said.

"What's Bull and Joe up to?" Tait asked.

Zach laughed. "What do you think? Every time we enter a town, Bull has to check out the whorehouse."

"Yeah, and we have to hear about it for a month of Sundays," Cain grumbled. "Hey, Pike, let's go and check out the place for ourselves." The two men got up and headed for the door.

Tait poured himself another shot of whiskey and downed it in a gulp. "Ya tried out these whores yet?" He could barely keep his heavy eyelids open.

Zach shook his head. "Figure I've got plenty of time. I'm guessing we'll be hanging around here for a while."

Tait's bushy brows met in a suspicious frown. "Where'd ya get that idea?"

"You were dead set to come here, Tait. Figure you had a good reason."

Tait thrust out his jaw, his eyes flashing angrily. "Yer too damn smart for yer own good, MacKenzie. It could get ya killed." He shoved back his chair and staggered away.

Zach remained at the table and watched Tait lumber up the stairway. He'd been a Texas Ranger too long—it was a good thing his enlistment would soon be up. He missed the Triple M and wanted to go back to ranching.

It had taken him six months to catch up with this gang. Thanks to his cousin Cole—who'd been riding with the gang before Zach found him and sent him back to Texas—he'd had been able to infiltrate the cattle rustlers two weeks ago. Trouble was, he hadn't found evidence serious enough to arrest them. His instinct told him Tait had brought the gang to Brimstone for a definite reason. But Tait didn't want thinking men in his gang, and if Zach made any more careless slips like he just did, he'd never get the proof he needed. They hadn't done any rustling in the two weeks he'd been with them, but Cole had said they'd done so in Arizona.

Zach was sick and tired of trailing along with this gang; he'd like to ride away and forget they even existed. But if it was the last thing he did before leaving the Rangers, he'd see that bastard Tait dead or behind prison walls.

The only thing that might make this assignment tolerable was that redheaded Harvey Girl. She might add a little spice to the stew. He poured himself a shot of whiskey and thought about that kiss. Yeah, she might help to make this assignment real tolerable.

Chapter 3

After locking her bedroom door, Rose removed the black bow and pins from her hair. It felt good to free her hair, and she shook it out wildly until it hung in unruly dishevelment across her shoulders.

Removing Emily's letter from her pocket, she laid it on the nightstand, then closed the drapes and removed all of her clothing. She loved being unrestrained—her long hair hanging loosely and the feeling of air on her naked body.

Not that she would ever parade nude in front of anyone; she hadn't even undressed completely in front of Em when the two women shared a room in New Mexico. Could it have been out of respect for Emily's modesty rather than her own?

But she'd never stripped in front of Wes, either. And Lord knew he had no modesty to respect. She'd always turned off the lamp or climbed under the sheet to remove her clothing whenever he lay with her.

She paused in front of the cheval mirror in the corner and gazed at her image. So why did she find such pleasure in moments like this? Was there a wanton side to her that she kept contained, hidden from even herself? Was that the reason she presented a woman-of-the-world veneer to others, so afraid of releasing this hidden nature that she was willing to marry for the convenience of money rather than risking the passion of love?

She brought a hand to her lips, which were still swollen from Zach MacKenzie's kiss. Would she hesitate to release her inhibitions to him, too, or could she blatantly stand naked before him as she was doing now? The way she felt right now, it seemed like she wouldn't hesitate.

Leaning forward, she peered more deeply into the mirror as if the answer lay in the reflected image. Tonight, when he had held her in his arms, she'd sensed this hidden nature's urgent cry for release; a clarion call that for a few exquisite seconds had deafened her ears to her own reasoning.

Damn you, Zach MacKenzie. Who are you? Why should you be able to torment me this way?

Seized by a sudden, heated flush, she folded her arms across her naked breasts to conceal the hardening of her nipples.

Oh, how his kiss had excited her. There could be no doubt of that. Dropping her arms to her sides, she saw what the thought of him did to her body. Her nipples were distended, and she felt the draw in her loins. How could just the thought of this stranger cause such an effect on her? No one else had ever been able to do that.

Rose shivered. If just thinking about his kiss could do this to her, what would happen the next time he kissed her? And there *would* be a next time, no doubt about that. His devilish eyes had promised it as much as his words declared it.

And she already yearned for that moment.

Snatching her nightgown from the bed, she hurriedly pulled it over her head, as if blocking out the naked evidence could deny the naked truth.

She turned away, picked up the pearl-handled brush that Em had given her, and began to brush out her long hair. She was angry with herself for even allowing Zach MacKenzie to invade her thoughts. The more she thought of him, the angrier she became, and the harder she stroked. By the time she put aside the brush, her scalp was tingling.

"You see, Rose," she declared aloud, glaring defiantly into the mirror, "unless you keep that man out of your thoughts, he'll always cause you some kind of pain."

She climbed into bed, puffed the pillows up behind her back, and reached for Emily's letter. Smiling with expectation, she opened the envelope.

The strident blast of the alarm jarred Rose out of the sweet euphoria of a delicious dream where Zach MacKenzie was kissing her. She groped to shut it off. Glancing at the clock, she saw that it was only five o'clock. Sleepily, she climbed out of bed.

Within ten minutes she was dressed and had almost finished grooming herself. Rather than take more time to pin up her hair, she brushed it quickly and put on a wide-brimmed hat to protect her face from the sun. She already had enough freckles across the bridge of her nose. A few quick strokes from the fluffy powder puff on the dresser succeeded in covering them.

Rose left her room and tapped on a nearby door. "Good morning," she greeted, when Kate opened the door.

"Good morning. What's wrong?"

"Have you forgotten this morning is our turn to ride out to the Wilson farm?"

Kate groaned. "Oh, dear! I *did* forget."

"I suspected as much when I didn't hear you moving around. Tell you what, I'll go and get the buggy while you get dressed."

"All right. I'll hurry," Kate said, now galvanized into action.

Zach finished saddling his horse and led it outside. As he was about to mount, he saw Rose Dubois. She saw him, too, took a half step as if to halt, but then continued to approach the livery.

The first thing he noticed was that hair of hers, freed from restraint except for the hat that shielded her face. It reminded him of his mother—reminded him of home. Not that one had anything to do with the other; his thoughts of Miss Rose Dubois went straight to his groin.

He doffed his hat. "Good morning, Rosie."

"Good morning."

Her greeting carried considerably less enthusiam than his, but he'd cut her some slack because she was so damn good to look at. She looked as beautiful in sunlight as she had in the moonlight. And despite how well she filled that Harvey Girl uniform, it couldn't compare to seeing her in a bright gown, with her gorgeous red hair hanging to her shoulders. It was enough to make a man's thoughts drift from the work at hand.

"What's got you up with the birds this morning, Rosie?"

"I could ask you the same, MacKenzie. Actually, I'm here to rent a buckboard. Each morning we ride out to the Wilson farm to get fresh eggs."

He glanced skyward. "Looks to be a good day for it. I like early mornings. Everything's still except for the sound of chirping birds."

"Chirping birds generally annoy me by waking me up."

"Yes, but it's a good sound to lie in bed and listen to. Kind of fills a man with a feeling of tranquility."

" 'God's in his Heaven; all's right with the world.' "

"I beg your pardon?"

"It's a line from a poem by Robert Browning."

"Reckon that Browning fellow and I think along the same lines."

"If it's tranquility you're seeking, MacKenzie, your actions last night certainly speak otherwise."

"You mean my kissing you?"

"That's exactly what I mean."

"Come on, Rosie. Don't try to tell me you didn't like it."

"The kiss, or being treated like a whore by some saddle tramp who's too lazy to get an honest job for a living?"

She stepped past him, and a grin curved his mouth as he watched the sway of her hips as she walked away.

He sure liked this gal; she met a man head-on and pulled no punches. Whether she admitted it or not, they had begun a courting dance.

When Rose arrived at the boardinghouse, she shifted over and let Kate drive. A flick of the reins and the team moved into a trot.

The only person stirring was a milkman making his morning deliveries on a creaking wagon drawn by a swaybacked horse. He nodded to them in passing.

"Mornin', ladies."

Kate returned the greeting brightly but Rose's reply was distracted, her mind filled with the encounter at the livery. She had just met the man the day before, and already she was dreaming of him, couldn't get him out of her thoughts, and let him kiss her. But worse—she had enjoyed that kiss! If she didn't put thoughts of Zach MacKenzie aside, she'd be moving around like the walking dead.

After about a mile, Kate broke the silence between them. "You're very quiet this morning, Rose. Is there something bothering you?"

This was the ideal time to really get acquainted with the girl, and Rose decided to use the opportunity. "Kate, have you ever been attracted to a man?"

"Certainly." Kate giggled. "Are you under the impression there's no handsome men in Wisconsin?"

"I don't mean just good-looking; I mean one who's attractive enough that you'd be willing to . . . you know, let him kiss you or even . . . . ah—"

"Rose Dubois, are you asking me if I've ever been intimate with a man?"

"I wasn't, but now that you've said it—well, have you?"

"No, I'm still a virgin—as pure as the day I was born," Kate said, with another delightful giggle that Rose wished she could imitate. "I was raised on a farm, and it seems like the male of any species gets the better of the bargain: he can satisfy his appetite, then trot away. It's the female who ends up carrying the load as the result, and bearing the pain of the birthing. I've seen enough of that to discourage me from considering it."

"So no man's kiss has ever excited you enough to break down that barrier."

"Not yet, at least." Kate turned her head and flashed a dimpled smile. "It would have to be some kiss. Now may I ask you a personal question?"

Rose raised a hand to stop her. "I know what you're going to ask. No, I am not a virgin."

"Well, did you . . . was it . . . Did you enjoy it enough to risk getting pregnant?"

Did I enjoy it? Wes never even attempted to make it pleasant for me; he just satisfied his own carnal pleasures. Even when I'd close my eyes and try to pretend I loved him, it never worked or made it easier to bear. And after he was through, he'd just roll over, blow out the lamp, and go to sleep. Never a word or a good-night kiss. Not that I wanted one; even his kiss repulsed me.

Did I enjoy it? It was a living hell.

She'd learned the hard way that it was foolish to give yourself in love to any man. Love was a naive, wasted expectation of gullible dreamers, because men were all bastards. Yet comparing Wes's kiss to Zach MacKenzie's was like comparing darkness to light—ice to heat. She couldn't help wondering what would have happened last night if she'd allowed him to continue kissing her. A shiver rippled her spine. She sensed his lovemaking would be as intense as his kiss. He had an air about him that made her believe that his pride would demand he bring the woman to satisfaction. And he certainly had the know-how to do it; his kiss revealed that.

"Well, did you?" Kate repeated, intruding on Rose's thoughts.

For a few seconds Rose gazed dumbfounded at Kate, wondering how she knew about Zach, then realized Kate was repeating the question she'd asked about lovemaking.

"No, I never enjoyed it, or loved the man enough to want his child."

"Then why did you ever become intimate with him, Rose?"

"It's very complicated." Rose wasn't ready to tell her about that painful time in her life—so painful she hadn't even told Emily. But she knew that one day she'd have to let it out. If she didn't tell someone, it would continue to fester like a cancer within her.

"What if you had become pregnant?"

"Fortunately, Kate, there are ways to prevent getting pregnant."

"Yes, I've heard, but I don't think I'd ever try one."

Realizing the conversation had become too glum, Rose turned her head and smiled at the young girl. "So what I'm going to do, honey, is marry for money. Luxury can be a strong ally in fighting disillusionment."

"Maybe you're right—but I don't think I could ever be intimate with a man unless I loved him very much." Kate flicked the reins and the horses picked up their pace.

When Kate pulled up in front of the barn, Calvin and Effie Wilson came out of their small home. Now too old to work the surrounding farm, the couple was content to spend their remaining years in the house Calvin had built for his young bride over fifty years before.

Although it was customary for the Harvey organization to ship in fresh meat and produce by rail, Fred Harvey often made arrangements with local residents to furnish these products if they lived up to his high standards.

And although Harvey was a taskmaster who demanded his employees honor his rules to the hilt—he'd even been known to fire a manager who cut back on the size of customers' portions in order to save money—he had a kind heart and had given the egg contract to the Wilsons. He'd even agreed to have the eggs picked up by a Harvey employee so that the old man would not have to make the daily delivery.

"Mornin', ladies," Calvin said. "I'll go get you the eggs."

"You ladies got time for a cup of coffee?" Effie asked. "Just baked corn bread, and I've made apple butter to spread on it. 'Tain't as fancy as the food in that there restaurant of yours, but you're welcome to join us."

Rose knew she and Kate had little time to spare, but she didn't want to disappoint the couple. This was her second trip to the Wilson farm, and she found them to be so like the grandparents she'd always yearned to have.

"We'd love to, Mrs. Wilson," she said. "Wouldn't we, Kate?"

"I'll say," Kate agreed. "I haven't tasted any apple butter since I left my daddy's farm."

Both of the Wilsons grinned broadly, then Effie said, "You gals come right along with me. Coffee's on the hearth."

As soon as Rose stepped inside, she closed her eyes and breathed in the aroma of the tiny house. It reminded her of a country store: a delightful blend of cinnamon, candles, beeswax, apples, and dried flowers.

Crocheted doilies adorned the arms and backs of chairs in the tiny living room, and needlepoint cushions covered the kitchen chairs. An embroidered sampler thanking God for His blessings hung on the wall, and braided cotton rugs were laid strategically on the floor. Pride and effort had gone into the construction of the handmade cabinetry and pieces of furniture.

Rose sighed. It might be a small house, but it was a huge home.

"Did you hear tell about the trouble last night?" Calvin asked when they were seated around the table.

"Trouble?" Rose asked.

"Over at the Lazy R. Steve Rayburn rode past this mornin' on the way into town. He said rustlers drove off part of his herd last night and killed both of his cowpunchers."

"How horrible!" Kate exclaimed.

"Yep. Wonder if it's got somethin' to do with the strange light folks claim to see in the hills. Maybe we got an outlaw gang living up there."

Rose thought of Tait's gang. Could they have rustled the cattle? If so, it must have been either very early or very late, because it'd been almost ten o'clock when Zach MacKenzie had shown up at the restaurant.

"Have there been any other cattle rustled recently?" Rose asked.

Calvin shook his head. "Not that I've heard tell. Guess we've been lucky till now."

Rose asked the question that was foremost on her mind. "What time did this happen?"

"Didn't ask Rayburn, but I reckon durin' the night, 'cause there was only a couple wranglers watchin' the herd he'd rounded up to ship out next week."

"They've got to get some decent law in here," Effie interjected. "That Sheriff Bloom ain't no help."

"I agree with you," Rose said. "The town's full of

unsavory characters, and the streets are wild."

"What is this talk about a mysterious light in the hills?" Kate asked.

"Effie and me ain't seen it, but some folks claim they have. I'm thinkin' of ridin' out and takin' a look at it for myself."

"More 'n likely it's someone minin' or somethin' like that, Cal," Effie said.

"What would he be minin' for, Effie? Ain't nothin' of value up there."

Rose's instinct began racing. She couldn't help thinking that Tait and his gang were involved.

The girls left shortly after, each with a jar of Effie's apple butter. Rose drove the team on the return trip to Brimstone.

"Just think, Cal and Effie have been married for over fifty years. That's so inspiring," Kate gushed.

"So is a mountain, but that doesn't mean I want to climb one for fifty years."

"Oh, you don't fool me for one minute, Rose Dubois. You're not as superficial as you try to make people believe. After meeting Cal and Effie, how can you doubt the importance of marrying for love?"

"I agree the Wilsons are a precious couple, Kate. But the thought of living fifty years with the same man makes me more determined than ever that he'd better be a rich one," Rose countered.

Chapter 4

By the time Rose reined up at the rear of the Harvey House, Brimstone had come to life. As with so many of these lazy Western towns, most of the business activity occurred in the morning before the heat of the day closed in; then the town appeared to slumber in the afternoon, and woke again in the evening, rowdy and boisterous.

Everett Billings hurried out of the kitchen door for the eggs, reminded them that the morning train was due shortly, and went back inside.

"We've only got a half hour to change," Kate said on the way back to the livery.

"I'll drop you off at the boardinghouse; it's on the way. There's no need for both of us to have to rush."

As soon as Kate jumped down, Rose continued

on. The street seemed busier than usual, and she slowed the team for several children crossing in front of her. She glanced over and saw Jess Tait and his gang leaning against a hitching post—Zach MacKenzie wasn't among them.

Rose attempted to speed up, but Tait stepped out and grabbed the bridle of one of the team. "Look what we got here, boys. If it ain't Miss Smarty Ass herself." His fat lips protruded in a smirk from amidst his bushy beard. "I've been meaning to look you up, sister."

"Kindly release the horse, Mr. Tait. I'm in a hurry," Rose said.

"Zat right? Hear that, boys: Miss Smarty Ass is in a hurry."

Zach rode up just in time to hear the end of the conversation. "Let her be, Jess. The whole town's watching you."

Tait snorted. "Like I care. Since you're in such a hurry, sister, I'll give ya a little help."

Before Rose guessed his intent, Tait yanked the reins so hard that she lost her grip on them. Then he drew his Colt and fired several shots in the air. Rose screamed as the team bolted and she fell across the seat. Out of control, the driverless buggy lurched down the street, the reins flapping like a whip at the heels of the horses.

"You damn fool!" Zach shouted at Tait. He goaded his horse and galloped down the road in pursuit of the buggy.

Amidst cries and shouts, people scattered in all directions, trying to avoid being trampled or struck by the careening buggy as the horses raced down the street, trailing a cloud of dust behind them. Another rider had joined the chase by the time Zach caught up.

Tossed and slammed about, Rose struggled to keep from being thrown off the buggy that threatened to overturn any minute. She managed to get a grip on the seat, then watched, horrified, when Zach leaped from his own horse onto the back of one of the team. Within seconds, he succeeded in halting the buggy.

Rose managed to regain her seat and was adjusting her disheveled clothing when the other rider galloped up and dismounted.

"Are you hurt, miss?" he asked worriedly.

"I don't think so." Her trembling legs managed to support her when he assisted her off the vehicle. People began to close in around her, and the solicitous stranger put a firm hand on her elbow and led her over to a bench in front of the general store.

"Sit here and catch your breath," he said in a concerned tone.

"Thank you." Her trembling had ceased, and she drew several deep breaths in an effort to regain her control.

Her gaze swept the crowd and fell on Zach MacKenzie. He was standing alone near the buckboard, looking at her with a strange expression on his face. She remembered the strength in the arms that had held her last night, and at that moment, she wanted more than anything to feel them around her again and draw the comfort of his strength. Zach MacKenzie was the last person she'd ever expect to become her knight in shining armor, but he'd rid-

den to her rescue at the risk of his own life. Had he
fallen, he very well could have been trampled to
death.

It would be hard for her to ignore that truth in
whatever might lie ahead between them.

Zach nodded, touched his finger to the brim of
his hat, then turned away. As he led the horses toward the livery, her gaze continued to follow the tall
figure until he disappeared.

"Are you certain you don't need a doctor?" the
stranger asked.

"No, I'm fine now." Smiling, she added, "Thank
you for your help, Mr. . . ."

"Rayburn. Stephen Rayburn," he said, removing
his hat.

"I'm grateful, Mr. Rayburn. And I'm Rose
Dubois." She stood up. "Now if you'll excuse me, I
have to change my clothes and get to work."

Stephen Rayburn stepped back. "I insist upon es-
corting you to your lodging, Miss Dubois." He
grasped her by the elbow again.

As they walked back to her boardinghouse, Rose
tried to remember where she'd heard his name before, then she recalled that Cal Wilson had mentioned it earlier.

"I understand you had a misfortune earlier as
well, Mr. Rayburn."

"Yes, cattle rustlers killed two of my men."

"How tragic. Did they leave families behind?"

"No." He smiled slightly to soften his words.
"Most cowpunchers don't have families, Miss
Dubois. You must be new to the West."

"Just to Brimstone. I'm a Harvey Girl. I've been in

New Mexico for the past two years, but I admit I still have a great deal to learn about the West."

"A Harvey Girl. No wonder I don't recall seeing you before."

Rose took a long look at Stephen Rayburn. He didn't have Zach MacKenzie's devastating handsomeness, but he wasn't unpleasant-looking, either.

He appeared to be in his late thirties, with light hair and green eyes. His face was on the rugged side: aquiline nose, clean-shaven angular jaw, and a neatly trimmed mustache above narrow lips.

She stood almost eye to eye with him, which would make him just slightly taller than her own five feet eight inches, and he had a lithe, trim build which he carried with a sense of authority. Stephen Rayburn was clearly a man used to giving orders— not taking them. But his demeanor was gentlemanly. And she didn't fail to notice that he was very well dressed—no dusty jeans or worn boots. His clothes looked tailor-made, his boots and Stetson expensive.

Rayburn must have sensed her interest, because he turned his green-eyed gaze on her. "And where are you from, Miss Dubois?"

"New Orleans."

His smile flashed whitely against his deep tan. "A fabulous city. Whatever would tempt you to leave it for a town like Brimstone?"

"It must be my adventuresome spirit, Mr. Rayburn."

"If you permit me saying, that makes for a very intriguing combination with that red hair and those lovely blue eyes of yours, Miss Dubois."

Rose would have to be blind not to see the interest in his eyes. Could it be she had finally met her rich rancher? With her luck, he was probably married already. However, this was neither the time nor place to ask.

"Here we are," she said lightly, having reached the boardinghouse. "Thank you again, Mr. Rayburn."

"The pleasure was all mine, Miss Dubois." He tipped his hat and walked away.

Her curiosity continued to dwell on him as she changed hurriedly into her uniform. But by the time she started to pin up her hair, she'd slipped back into thoughts of Zach MacKenzie and the look in his eyes as he'd watched her with Stephen Rayburn. What was behind that look? It couldn't have been jealousy. Zach MacKenzie didn't look like he'd have a jealous bone in his whole body—his whole manly body.

A train whistle reminded her of the need for haste. She pinned the bow to the back of her hair and hurried out the door. Hooting and puffing steam, the morning train had just rolled into town.

By the time Rose rushed through the kitchen door, the train's passengers were already seated. Everett Billings gave her a disapproving glance.

"I'm sorry, Mr. Billings. I had an accident."

"Apparently not a serious one, Miss Dubois, since you appear to be uninjured. We will discuss it later," he said, and handed her the two plates he was about to carry into the dining room.

Kate had already filled the coffee cups at Rose's

tables and had served them compotes of fresh fruit. Rose gave her a grateful smile, put the plates of egg soufflé and chicken livers down in front of two of the customers, then hurried back to the kitchen for more.

Until the advent of the Harvey Houses, an unfortunate traveler had been subjected to a box lunch, bitter coffee, and such fare as salt pork and beans or a tasteless stew served on a tin plate at way stations. After paying for a meal in advance, he'd often had to rush back onto the train before even being served.

Fred Harvey had changed all that. Since opening his Harvey restaurants along the route of the Santa Fe, he'd made it the preferred railroad for travelers. Now for a mere seventy-five cents a meal, a passenger was offered fine cuisine served in the style of gracious dining.

For the next thirty minutes, Rose didn't have time to think of rich husbands or dark-eyed cowboys, as she made certain all her customers were fed and satisfied before the train departed.

She heaved a sigh of relief and sank down on a chair when the train finally pulled out of the station.

"You look tired, Rose," Kate said, and took a chair next to her.

"I am. I didn't sleep well last night." She'd tossed and turned, thinking about Zach MacKenzie. "And this day's already been exhausting though it's not even halfway over."

The other girls joined them as Rose began to relate her harrowing experience with the runaway team.

"Jess Tait should be arrested," Aubrey Jeffreys declared.

"My goodness, you could have been killed," Melanie Clemens said indignantly, her blond curls bouncing with every word.

"Not only Rose, but some innocent bystander as well," Kate added.

"If there is an innocent bystander in this town," Andrea Reynolds challenged. The dark-haired waitress from Chicago was a little more worldly than the other three girls.

"Well, the important thing is nobody was injured," Kate said, patting Rose's hand.

"Ladies, ladies, this is no time for a kaffeeklatsch," Everett Billings reminded them, entering the room. "The eastbound train will be coming through in three hours." He clapped his hands to get them moving. "There's work to be done."

"Mr. Billings, Rose was almost killed this morning," Aubrey stated, her bright blue eyes still wide with shock.

"Killed! Oh, dear, Miss Dubois, was that the accident you mentioned?"

"That horrible Jess Tait's responsible," Melanie informed him, shaking her head so severely that her blond curls threatened to bounce off her head.

Talking all at once, Andrea, Melanie, and Aubrey proceeded to tell Billings of the incident. When they finished, the manager looked contritely at Rose.

"Miss Dubois, I have no objection if you'd like to take the rest of the day off to recover."

"That's very kind of you, Mr. Billings, but I'm fine now."

"I still say that Jess Tait belongs behind bars," Aubrey reiterated.

The bell tinkled as the door opened, and the women jumped to their feet. Rose stared, appalled, as Jess Tait crossed the floor trailed by his gang, and they all sat down at one of the tables.

"The nerve of that man!" Andrea hissed through clenched teeth. "I'm going over there right now and tell him what I think of him."

"No." Rose's hand on the young girl's arm stopped Andrea from doing so. "It's my table, honey, and I have a few words to say to that bully."

Rose picked up the coffeepot and walked over to the table. The men quieted, as if waiting to hear whatever she intended to say.

She filled their coffee cups and when she got to Jess, he warned, "You try that same trick with that coffee that ya did yesterday, and you'll get more than a fast ride in a wagon. How'd ya like that little ride I gave you, sister?"

"Mr. Tait, I consider you a dangerous man, and if there was any decent lawman in this town, you'd probably be long dead by now. As it is, it's just a matter of time before you end up in that condition."

"Oh-h-h, I'm so scared," Tait said. "Hear that, boys? Sounds like the bitch is threatenin' me."

Rose smiled sweetly. "Not at all. I can wait. I'm the patient type."

"Well, I'm not," Zach said. "So how about some breakfast, Redhead? What's on the menu today?"

"An egg soufflé and chicken livers."

"Sounds good," Zach said.

Jess and the others ordered the same. Rose went

into the kitchen to place their orders, and when she came out, she saw Stephen Rayburn seated at one of her tables.

"Good morning again," she said.

Rayburn smiled up at her. "I'm told this restaurant serves the best food in town."

"You heard right, Mr. Rayburn."

"If the food is half as sweet as the waitresses who serve it, it must be true."

"Why, Mr. Rayburn, how nice of you to say so."

"Looks like I'll have to hire a beautiful waitress in my diner, so you don't run me out of business."

"You own the diner in town?" she said, surprised. "I thought you were a rancher."

"I am, but I have other investments."

"Are you going to order our breakfast and find out for yourself how good the food is here?"

"I certainly am," he said.

"Then I'm sure you'll like it."

His gaze lingered on her. "I'm sure I will, Miss Dubois."

As she walked away, she glanced at Tait's table and caught Zach MacKenzie staring at her. He had the same bemused expression she'd seen in his eyes after the accident.

After serving Tait's gang their breakfasts, Rose began changing the linen tablecloths and placing clean china and crystal on the empty tables in preparation for the luncheon arrivals.

When the gang finished eating, they stood up to leave. Zach threw down a dollar, but the others continued to the door.

"Just a minute, gentlemen," Rose said, "you can't leave without paying for your breakfasts. Seventy-five cents apiece."

"You gonna stop us, sister?" Jess asked. "Let's go, boys."

"I insist you pay for your meal, Mr. Tait."

She flinched when he approached and his fingers bit into her arm. "I don't give a damn what you *insist*, sister. And don't forget, I ain't finished with you. This mornin' wuz just a taste of what's to come. By the time I'm through with you, you'll be on your knees beggin' for mercy." His mouth curled into a malicious grin, and he shoved her away. "See you later, bitch."

"I believe you owe the lady an apology, Mr. Tait." The soft command had come from Stephen Rayburn.

Oh, dear God, no, Rose prayed. Tait would probably shoot the gentleman right on the spot.

"This ain't your fight, Mr. Rayburn," Jess said.

Surprisingly, Tait's statement lacked his usual threatening bluster. In fact, it had an undertone of supplication.

Everyone stared speechless as Rayburn picked up a napkin, dabbed lightly at each corner of his mouth, then laid the napkin aside.

"Mr. Tait, if you intend to work for me, I never want to hear again of your threatening this young lady or any of the other women in this town. If you do, you'll have me to deal with. Have I made myself clear?"

Tait opened his mouth as if to speak, then spun

on his heel and slammed out the door. His gang followed.

Unable to believe what she'd just witnessed, Rose hurried over to the rancher's table.

"Mr. Rayburn, do you realize what you've done? Jess Tait is an out-of-control bully who carries a grudge toward anyone who crosses him."

"I hardly think he'd do so with me, if he and his companions wish to remain in my employment."

"You mean that gang of hoodlums works for you!"

"As of this morning, Miss Dubois."

"Why would you ever hire the likes of them?" Rose asked, astonished.

"I haven't much of a choice. Two of my crew are dead, and the other two left me this morning. For all I know, those rustlers will return to run off the rest of my herd. I don't want to be caught shorthanded again."

"It's likely *they* are the ones who rustled your cattle, Mr. Rayburn."

"No, I caught sight of that gang. These men were not among them."

Rose shook her head. "I still feel you've made a serious mistake."

He chuckled. "It wouldn't be the first one I've ever made. Now, I insist you call me Stephen."

"Why, Mr. Rayburn, I hardly know you. It would be very improper of me to do so."

"Then I think we should remedy that at once by becoming better acquainted, Miss Dubois. Will you permit me to call on you tomorrow?"

Rose couldn't have been more pleased. Then she realized—*Drat, I have to work!*

"I'm sorry, Mr. Rayburn, but I'm a working girl, you know."

"Surely you have a day off."

"No, a Harvey Girl's duties are seven days a week. But we do have some rest time in the afternoons between the lunch and dinner hours."

"Then how about tomorrow afternoon?" he said.

"I'd like that." Indeed, she liked it very much, and hoped she wasn't making that fact too obvious.

He laid some coins on the table, then stood up. "This should cover their bill, and I will count the hours until tomorrow, Miss . . . Rose."

"*Who* was that?" Kate asked as soon as Rayburn had cleared the door.

"His name is Stephen Rayburn, and he's a *rich* rancher. It was he and Zach MacKenzie who came to my rescue this morning."

"Zach MacKenzie? You didn't tell me Zach MacKenzie was one of your rescuers. Isn't he one of Tait's gang?"

"Yes, he is. Strange, isn't it?" Rose replied, with a lingering smile.

For a morning that had begun so disastrously, it had certainly taken an interesting turn. The rest of the day turned out to be very routine. When she wasn't waiting on customers, Rose was busy preparing salads for the next meal. It was then she could think about the following day's date with Stephen Rayburn. The trouble was that Zach

MacKenzie's face kept invading those thoughts.

To Rose's relief there was no sign of him when she and Billings closed the restaurant that evening, but as she walked back to her boardinghouse, she couldn't help but feel slightly disappointed. She quickly chastised herself for being a fool. MacKenzie undoubtedly had moved out to the Lazy R Ranch; it was unlikely she'd see much of him again. And that was just fine. Good riddance, and *adios*. With the prospect of a relationship with Stephen Rayburn, she certainly didn't need a saddle tramp like Zach MacKenzie muddying the waters.

Rose undressed for bed, then turned off her lamp and opened the window. As she sat down on the edge of the bed, she thought about the two men. They were complete opposites: one was fair, the other dark; one short, the other tall; one a successful rancher, the other a no-good bum—who was too exciting for his own good!

"Rosie." The sound had come from outside the window. "Call for Rosie to come out and play." Only one person called her by that ridiculous name.

Rose pulled on her robe, then went to the window and parted the drapes. Zach MacKenzie grinned at her. She opened the window wider, and said in a loud whisper, "Will you please be quiet before you wake the whole household? Just what do you want at this time of night?"

"Come on outside," he whispered. "It's a beautiful night."

"Go away! I'm about to go to bed."

"We could do that, too."

"MacKenzie, I don't know what else I can say that will convince you I'm not interested in anything you have to say or do." She started to close the window.

"Wait, Rosie."

"What now?" Exasperated, she puffed at a strand of hair on her forehead.

"I thought maybe you'd like to thank me for riding to your rescue this morning."

Guiltily, she realized, in all the earlier excitement, she hadn't thanked him. Rose softened her tone. "I *am* grateful for what you did, Zach."

"That's better." He hoisted himself up and sat on the windowsill.

"What do you think you're doing? If you don't get out of this window, I'm going to start screaming!"

"Why would you do that, when all I'm looking for is a quiet talk with a lovely lady?"

He was incorrigible. Rose's sense of humor prevailed, and she couldn't help laughing. "Now, why do I doubt that, MacKenzie?"

"Because you have a suspicious mind, Rosie Dubois."

"You're right. Why ever should I be suspicious of a down-on-his-heels drifter just because he's riding with a gang of no-gooders?"

"My argument exactly."

His grin was so persuasive that she couldn't help laughing again. Shaking her head, she folded her arms across her chest and lowered herself to the sill. They now sat side by side, but faced in opposite directions that forced them to turn their heads to look at each other. Strangely enough, she found the proximity of their positions exciting, and the expression in his eyes led her to suspect that he felt the same awareness.

"I thought you and your gang were working for Mr. Rayburn."

"We are. I just felt like a ride."

"This time of night?"

"I like riding at night. I—"

"Let me guess; you like the the sound of coyotes howling at the moon."

"Wolves howl. Coyotes are scavengers; they just wail."

Her light laughter joined with his chuckle. "So where did you learn so much about coyotes?" she asked.

"I'm Texas-born and-bred, Rosie."

"Are your parents still alive?"

"Yeah. They're good people." His engaging grin tugged at her heart strings. "Nothing like me."

"How long have you been riding with Jess Tait?"

"Met up with him a couple weeks ago." For a long moment he stared at her. "What about you, Rose? I figure you for a city gal."

"That's right. I was born in New Orleans."

"Your folks still there?"

"No. I was seven when my mother died, but even before that I never had a normal childhood. When my father wasn't drunk, he spent his time cheating at cards or swindling people out of their money. I can't ever remember a time he tried to earn an honest dollar, so there were times when there wasn't even bread to eat. But it didn't matter to him; he drank his meals."

"Didn't you have any kin to go to?"

"No. Other than my father, I was on my own."

"Where is he now, honey?"

"One night he tried to rob the wrong man, and ended up with a knife in his stomach."

"I'm sorry. How old were you when it happened?" His voice was husky with compassion.

"Almost seventeen." She had allowed herself to become seduced by the compassion in his compelling dark eyes and had already said too much. She didn't want his sympathy, much less his prying into her life.

"And what brought you to Texas?"

"What do you think?" she asked flippantly. "The Atchinson, Topeka, and Santa Fe."

"Come on, Rosie, why are you afraid to lower that shield you hide behind?"

"That shield's gotten me this far, MacKenzie. Since you've got a problem with it, feel free to leave."

"Can't you just drop it for once and relax, Rosie?"

She shot to her feet. "Don't try to get into my head, MacKenzie—or my bed. Both are off-limits to you. Now, get out of this window; I'd like to go to bed."

"Good night, Rosie," he said, stepping down. "Sleep well."

She slammed down the window and closed the drapes.

Chapter 5

The following morning, Zach MacKenzie was still on Rose's mind as she dressed for work. She enjoyed talking to him, but he intimidated her—not by what he said, but his nearness excited her. It was a complication she didn't need, especially with Stephen Rayburn showing an interest in her. She would not let any silly heart-fluttering jeopardize that opportunity.

Rose went through breakfast and lunch by rote, waiting for her afternoon outing with Stephen Rayburn.

As she hurried back to her room to change her clothes afterward, she caught a glimpse of Rayburn riding into town with several of his crew—Zach MacKenzie among them.

She barely had time to dress before Mrs. White, the housekeeper, knocked on the door to inform Rose that she had a caller waiting in the drawing room.

Stephen Rayburn stood up when she entered the room. Approval gleamed in his eyes as he kissed her hand, and Rose was glad she had donned a simple white dimity gown with a bertha flounce for the occasion. She'd brushed out her hair and put on a wide-brimmed picture hat, which Emily had left behind after she married Josh MacKenzie.

"You do the South honor, my dear Miss Dubois," Rayburn said. "You belong on the portico of a gracious Southern mansion surrounded by honeysuckle and—"

"Mint juleps," Rose teased.

It was hardly a memory she carried of the life she'd led, but she wasn't about to change his impression.

"I thought a carriage ride would be a pleasant outing. Is that satisfactory with you?"

"It sounds divine," she said. "Let me get my parasol."

As they rode through town in the open carriage, she saw Jess Tait and Zach MacKenzie lounging against the wall of the saloon. Unable to ignore the temptation, she stole a quick glance back after they rode past and saw that Tait had turned to enter the saloon, but Zach MacKenzie's gaze was still fixed on the moving carriage.

For a traitorous moment, she thought of how exciting it would be if Zach was beside her instead of Rayburn—then she reminded herself what a fool she was and smiled at Stephen Rayburn. He returned her smile. *Actually, he's very sweet*, she thought, and vowed she would not allow any more thoughts of Zach MacKenzie to intrude on this afternoon.

Zach watched with mixed emotions as Rose rode past with Rayburn. As much as he wanted to bed the gal, he liked her enough not to foul up her life. As soon as they were safely out of sight, he walked to his horse. With all of the gang in town, he now had a chance to get away without being seen. They wouldn't miss him, because he'd set up a story that he had a girl in town. They all believed him except that bastard Tait; he was the one to worry about.

Zach deliberately headed south when he rode out of Brimstone in case he was spotted. But once clear of the town's limits he turned back, skirted the town, and headed north back to the Lazy R. He'd seen some tracks the day before that had made him curious, but before he could follow them, Bull and Joe had ridden up.

Zach had no problem picking up the tracks again, and after following the trail for thirty minutes, they ended at a tangled wall of mesquite and sagebrush. His instinct told him something wasn't right.

A closer inspection revealed barbed wire under the piled brush, and he was able to peer through it enough to see that it appeared to be the entrance to a box canyon.

He'd been a Ranger too long to be fool enough to ride into a box canyon without knowing what he'd find. Dismounting, he tied his horse to a shrub and began to work his way on foot up the rocks.

Once at the top, he had a good view of the whole canyon floor. Milling below were at least a couple hundred head of cattle.

His gaze swept the rocks and crannies at the base of the canyon. Upon seeing no sign of anyone, he climbed back down, opened the entrance, and rode into the canyon.

Dismounting, he examined several of the cows. They wore the Lazy R brand.

"Well, boy," he murmured to his horse, "these cattle sure as hell didn't just stray into this canyon. The question now: did rustlers hide them here, is Rayburn behind it, or does Mr. Jess Tait have himself a little business on the side?"

He glanced up and saw a lone horseman on the rim above. Zach mounted quickly and rode out of the canyon.

"Well, tell me about it," Kate whispered that evening, as they stood at the entrance to the Harvey House waiting to greet the passengers disembarking from the train. It was the first opportunity the two women had time to chat with each other since Rose had returned from her outing with Stephen Rayburn.

"He took me for a carriage ride, and told me about his life. He was raised in Missouri and moved to Texas ten years ago after the death of his wife."

"Does he have any children?"

Rose shook her head. "He said he's unable to have children."

"And he's never remarried?"

"No. Between grieving and building a successful and very *profitable* ranch, Stephen just didn't have time to think about remarrying ..." Rose flashed a fanciful smile. "Until now."

"Oh, Rose, he said that!" Kate enthused, squeezing Rose's hand. "I'd say that's very encouraging."

"I'll say," Rose said. The two girls giggled.

Then there wasn't time for any further conversation as they greeted the stream of customers.

The rest of the evening passed swiftly, and before Rose knew it they were through for the evening. Mr. Billings bade them all good night and sent them on their way.

"So, did Mr. Rayburn ask to see you again?" Kate asked, picking up the conversation where they'd left off earlier.

"Yes, the next time he comes to town."

"That's very encouraging, too," Kate commented with a dimpled smile.

"I know I'm being foolish, but I hope so. Oh, Kate, Stephen Rayburn more than fills my expectations for a husband. Not only is he rich, but he's very handsome and a gentleman, too." Rose drew a deep breath. "Kate, do you think I'm reading too much into a simple afternoon carriage ride?"

"I'm sure he wouldn't have asked you out if he weren't interested, Rose. And the fact that he wants to see you again is even more positive."

"I thought so, too, but I'm afraid to trust my own judgment because I want so much for it to be true."

"I especially admired how he stood up to that horrible bully, Jess Tait," Kate said.

Rose's eyes widened. "Yes, wasn't it wonderful! And did you notice how Tait backed down, too?"

"I sure did. Thanks to Mr. Rayburn, we don't have to worry about Tait bothering us anymore. Mr. Rayburn's obviously very influential, even in this lawless town. How old is he, Rose?"

"Forty-two. That's actually very young."

"Rose, it's twice as old as you are."

"I wouldn't care if he was three times older," Rose said with a saucy grin.

They reached the boardinghouse and started to climb the porch stairs when Rose suddenly halted. "Drat! I left my apron at the restaurant. It got badly stained and must be washed. I'll have to go back for it."

"I'll come with you," Kate said.

"Nonsense, it will only take me a couple minutes to run back and get it."

Rose quickly returned back to the restaurant. The light still glowed in the dining room, so she knew Billings was still there.

She rapped on the front door and called out to him, but he didn't respond. She repeated it several times, and when he still didn't hear her she figured he was in the kitchen, so she hurried around to the rear of the building.

The kitchen was dark. Rose tried the door, and it swung open. She looked around uneasily, aware that the whole area was in darkness except for a faint glow from a lantern on the nearby platform of the train depot.

"Mr. Billings," she called out, "it's Rose." She stepped into the black kitchen and took a few seconds to adjust her eyes to the darkness. "Mr. Billings?"

When he failed to answer, she crossed the room. He would never be negligent enough to leave the kitchen door unlocked or a light burning in the dining room. Something had to be wrong. Had he taken ill?

Rose pushed the kitchen door open and peered into the dining room, then gasped with alarm when she saw him lying on the floor. Rushing over to him, she saw he was unconscious, and put an ear to his chest. To her relief, he was breathing normally. Fearing he'd fallen or had a heart attack, she was about to run for a doctor when he groaned and opened his eyes.

"Mr. Billings, what happened?"

Billings sat up. "I don't know. Someone struck me from behind." He felt his head. "Oh my, I have a lump on my head."

"I'll get some ice. It will help to reduce the swelling."

He suddenly gasped. "Today's receipts! Where are they?" He began to crawl around on his knees looking for them. "They're gone! I was just preparing to put them in the safe." He looked up at her, aghast. "We've been robbed, Miss Dubois." He got to his feet. "I must report this to the sheriff before the thief gets out of town."

Rose doubted the sheriff would be of any help, but Billings had already unlocked the front door to leave.

"If you insist, go ahead. I'll finish locking up here."

"Thank you; expediency is important at times like this. By the way, why did you come back, Miss Dubois?"

"I forgot my apron," she said.

"I see. Well, be sure and turn off the light." He rushed out the door and down the street.

Rose went into the kitchen and locked the door, then grabbed her apron off a wall peg in the cloakroom and returned to the dining room. In the whole two years she'd worked at the Harvey House in New Mexico, there had never been an attempt to rob it. In her opinion, Mr. Harvey would be well advised to forget attempting to establish a restaurant here until there was a better effort to maintain some law and order.

She turned off the light and started to the door. Suddenly a hand clamped over her mouth and she was pulled back against a hard body.

"Don't scream, Rosie." When she nodded, Zach MacKenzie released her.

Eyes glaring, she spun on her heel to face him. "So you're the one who robbed us."

"It wasn't me," he said. "I saw you come in, so I followed you. Then when I heard you talking to Billings, I stayed in the kitchen until he left."

"Do you expect me to believe that ridiculous story, MacKenzie?"

"I've no reason to lie to you."

"Other than staying out of jail."

"If I'd robbed this place, do you think I'd stick around to get caught?"

"I wouldn't put anything past you, MacKenzie. Exactly what *are* you doing here?"

"I came for this."

He wrapped an arm around her waist and drew her against him. Cupping her neck, he tilted back her head and captured her mouth with his own. His lips were as firm and warm as she remembered—and more exciting than her body could resist. His tongue stroked and plundered until she moaned with pleasure, even as she told herself she must stop. She couldn't allow the exquisite thrill of his kiss to continue blinding out her reasoning.

Pressing her hands to his chest, she shoved him away, but he kept his hold on her. Her body trembled, and she could only stare breathlessly up at him as his sapphire gaze remained fixed on her flushed face. She waited, transfixed, when he raised his other hand and pulled the pins out of her hair. Weaving his fingers into its thickness, he lowered his head and traced the outline of her lips with his tongue, the day's stubble on his jaw an arousing scrape against her smooth cheek.

"Let me kiss you like you want me to, Rosie. Stop putting up a defense when you want this as much as I do."

He covered her mouth again, and from the first contact she knew that this time there was no hope for any further resistance. Their lips melded together as the kiss deepened, filling her entire being with such exquisite heat that she thought surely they both would be consumed by the fire. Oh, but it felt so good—burned so brightly. She'd never felt so alive. She reveled in the wanton pleasure of it, molding herself to the muscular warmth of his body.

"What did I tell you, Rosie? You love it," he murmured against her lips.

As his words penetrated her senses, she realized he'd slipped his hand to her breast. She became rigid. What was she doing? She was a pawn in his hands, and he knew it.

Anger cut through, and she broke away. He took her slap to his face without even blinking, which only increased her fury.

"I won't stand for any more of this, MacKenzie."

"Then let's take it to a bed, where it belongs."

"I'm grateful to you for saving my life, so I won't mention that you were here tonight—but I'm telling you for the last time to stay away from me."

"Why are you afraid of me, Rose?"

"I told you, there's no place in my future plans for a saddle tramp like you."

"Your kiss says otherwise, so who are you trying to convince: me or yourself?"

"Your arrogance is pathetic. What makes you think you're different from any other man I've ever known?"

"I think you've figured that out for yourself."

"Whether you believe it or not, I'm not going to let you spoil my plans. I told you my future—"

"Does not include a saddle tramp like me," he said scornfully.

"That's exactly right. I think I've finally met that man who can make my plans come true."

"You talking about Rayburn?"

"You bet I am. He's interested in me, and I'm not going to let a drifter like you spoil it for me. So why don't you return the money you stole, and get out of here? I'll tell Mr. Billings that I found it on the floor."

"I've already told you that I didn't steal the money."

"Get out of here, Zach. Get out and leave me alone."

She opened the door, and he followed her out. After locking the door, she walked away hurriedly.

He closed the gap between them. "I'll walk you back to your rooming house. The street's not safe."

"Not as long as you're around," she sniped. "And who's going to protect me from you?"

"I'm no threat, Rosie. I'd say the only one you need protection from is yourself. I figure you're gonna lose that battle."

They'd reached the boardinghouse. "If I do, it won't be with you, MacKenzie."

He grasped her by the arms, his gaze intense as he looked down into her eyes. "You and I are alike, Rosie. We both know what we want when we see it. I can feel you trembling now, fighting what your body is crying out for. You're too much woman to keep all that passion contained much longer."

"We'll see about that." She made no effort to conceal her contempt. "By the way, why are you still in town? Did Mr. Rayburn get wise to you already and kick you off his ranch?"

"Why should you care, Rosie?" he taunted.

"I don't. I'm just curious why you didn't go back to the ranch with Mr. Rayburn today. If he hasn't fired you, could it be you remained here because you had a restaurant to rob?"

"Rayburn didn't go back to the ranch."

His statement took her by surprise. She was sure

when Stephen Rayburn left her earlier that he'd mentioned he was returning there. "Really? And what kept him in town?"

"Her name is Rita. She's a wh . . . ah, local resident."

Rose wanted to cry, seeing all her expectations draining away. If Rayburn really cared about her, how could he leave her to go and spend the evening with a whore? Then again, why should that surprise her? Just when you let your guard down long enough to trust a man, he showed his true colors. Men thought of nothing but satisfying their lust; she'd been naive enough to think that Rayburn might be different. Well, the one person to whom she'd never reveal her disappointment was Zach MacKenzie.

She looked him squarely in the eyes and smiled broadly. "Well, since I intend to marry him, I'm glad to hear that he's a healthy, virile male. It should make our marriage considerably more pleasurable. Wouldn't you say, MacKenzie?"

Then she marched up the porch stairs.

Chapter 6

To everyone's relief the breakfast and lunch meals passed swiftly the next day, since the Tait gang didn't appear for the second day in a row. The consensus among the girls was that Stephen Rayburn's warning must have made some impression on the lawless bully.

Now with lunch out of the way, the next three hours were free. With high spirits Rose left the restaurant, planning to answer Emily's letter. As she neared her rooming house a buggy rolled up alongside her.

Rose glanced up and discovered Zach MacKenzie at the reins. A saddled horse was tied to the rear of the buggy.

"I thought after your experience the other day, you could use some lessons."

"I had that team under control until your friend intentionally spooked the horses."

"Rose, it's not only Tait who can spook a horse. There's a dozen things that can do it: a tumbleweed, thunder . . ."

She debated briefly. "All right, Mr. MacKenzie, I'll take you up on that offer. If we don't have a repeat of what happened last night."

He grinned wickedly. "Who can make that kind of guarantee, Rosie? Do you have a split skirt?"

"Yes, I do. Why?"

"You'll need that to learn how to ride a horse."

"I have no desire to learn how to ride horseback. I thought you meant a carriage or wagon."

"How do you expect to live out here without knowing how to ride?"

"That's what buggies are for," she sniffed.

"Rose, not all trails are wide enough for a buggy."

"I see no reason why I'd be traveling on such trails; therefore, I have no need to climb on the back of a horse."

"This is the West, Rosie. There aren't always carriages and railroads for transportation. Texas is full of narrow trails and ravines. You'll find a horse is your best friend out here."

What he said made sense. And since it appeared horses were the main means of getting around out here, if Zach MacKenzie was willing to take the time to teach her, she could only profit from it.

"Okay. It'll take me a couple minutes to change my clothes."

"I can wait; I'm the patient type." His wicked

grin indicated the innuendo referred to more than a change of clothing.

Rose changed quickly into a split skirt, riding blouse, and boots, and hurried out to the buggy.

By the time Zach drove to a spot on the outskirts of town where they'd have more privacy, Rose had begun to lose her nerve and wasn't sure if she still wanted to go through with climbing onto the back of a horse.

She was convinced of it when she stood beside the horse. The animal seemed as big as an elephant to her.

"The important thing is to get as close to the horse as you can," he said.

"But it's so big, Zach. How can I ever control it?"

"This is a mare, Rose. They're much smaller than stallions."

She was so conscious of his nearness as he stood close behind her that she had to force herself to concentrate on what he was saying.

"Rule Number One is that you always mount from the left side of the horse."

"Why is that?"

"Because you have to swing your right leg over the saddle."

She turned her head and their faces were only inches apart. "Why can't I swing my left leg?"

"Because you have more control of your right leg." He nudged her nearer to the mare with his hips. "Gather both reins in your left hand and grasp the saddle horn, or the horse might shy away from you when you try to mount it. Then comes the tricky part. You have to step up into the stirrup with your left foot and swing your right leg over the saddle."

Tricky was grossly understated; impossible was more realistic. He literally had to put his hands on her bottom to swing her over.

After several attempts, he said patiently, "Rose, try to do it all in one motion. Hop and swing. It's kind of like a square dance, honey. You pick up the gal and swing her around in the same motion without losing the rhythm. This would be the same. Think of the beat of a tune. Om-pah-pah. Om-pah-pah. Hop, left foot, right leg."

"Maybe we should have brought along a tuba player to mark the rhythm," she said.

His grin crinkled the corners of his eyes. "Try it again. I'll hold the mare still while you mount her."

Grasping the reins and saddle horn as he had taught her, Rose om-pah-pahed herself onto the mare's back. Now, astride the horse, she felt as if she'd be pitched forward over the horse's head.

"Let me adjust those stirrups so that they fit your legs."

"You mean you're going to let go of the horse!" She felt the rise of panic.

"Relax, honey. The mare's not going anywhere until you tell it to."

Rose clutched the saddle horn with both hands, and by the time he made the adjustment her legs were resting comfortably and her feet had a good foothold in the stirrups. She felt a little more relaxed.

"Maybe this isn't so bad after all," she conceded.

"The rest is easy, Rosie. Now you talk to the

horse—and I don't mean 'giddup' or 'whoa.' You talk to it with the reins and the pressure of your knees. So let go of that saddle horn, and hold the reins lightly in your hand. Don't jerk or pull on them."

"Which hand?" She was feeling the flutter of butterflies in her stomach.

"Your left. Always keep your right hand free—in case you have to draw your Colt, for instance."

"Oh, yes. I expect to do a lot of that," she said nervously.

"Out here, a man needs two things to stay alive: a fast horse and a faster gun."

"And what does a woman need?" she asked.

He grinned. "A man with a fast horse and a faster gun."

"Are you suggesting a woman can't exist out here without a man to protect her?"

"She can in a larger city, but there are too many towns like Brimstone that still have a lot of taming to do."

"I won't argue about that."

"That's refreshing. Now, gently nudge the horse with both knees."

"Oh-h-h," she shouted, when the mare took several steps forward.

"Now suppose you want the horse to turn right: tighten up on the right rein and nudge the mare with your right knee." She tried it, and, miraculously, the mare turned right. "Now do the same with the left rein and knee."

"I think you've got this horse trained, MacKenzie," she said when the horse obeyed.

The more she experimented, the more confident she became. In no time, she lost her fear of falling off, and soon Zach had her trotting away a short distance, turning the horse, and returning to him.

"I never realized how easy this is," she said.

"Just remember: the harder you nudge the horse, the faster it will run."

"You needn't worry about that. I have no intentions of running any races."

"But it also applies to the reins. The tighter the rein, the sharper the turn, and if you rein up suddenly, the horse will come to a quick stop and you could get thrown."

"I understand. Now how do I get down from here?"

"Same way you got up. Shift forward a little, put your weight on the left stirrup, and swing your right leg back over the saddle."

She did it effortlessly and smoothly. "You're a good teacher, Zach."

"Just don't get overconfident," he warned. "This is a docile mare who's used to being ridden often. Not all horses are that predictable, so don't take any chances on an animal you're not familiar with."

Rose felt quite confident by the time they returned to her boardinghouse. After she said good-bye to Zach and stepped inside, Mrs. White handed her an envelope.

"Rose, dear, while you were gone, Mr. Rayburn came to see you. He left you this note."

"Thank you, Mrs. White."

Dismayed, Rose hurried to her room. She had missed an opportunity to see Stephen because of that stupid riding lesson. And even worse, if he should ask, how would she explain her absence?

She tore open the envelope. The short note said he regretted having missed her and hoped she would be available the following afternoon if he came to call.

It was a relief to know that Stephen hadn't given up on her; but in the future she would be wise to avoid any future contact with Zach MacKenzie. She put aside the note, and changed into her uniform.

Rose was halfway through serving the dinner meal when the pain set in. Muscles that she didn't even realize she had ached from her knees up. Even the cheeks of her rear end were sore, and the simple movement of taking a step caused excruciating pain.

She pushed herself to get through the dinner hour, and as soon as the shift ended Rose went back to the boardinghouse and soaked in a tub of hot water, despite the day's ninety-degree temperature.

As she sat in the tub with vapor steaming the mirror, Rose vowed that in the future she'd stick to stagecoaches and buggies. Leave the narrow trails to the more intrepid. She'd never climb on the back of a horse again.

Surprisingly enough, she slept peacefully.

As promised, Stephen called on her in the afternoon, and they went for another carriage ride. He was his usual pleasant self, but she discovered he lacked a sense of humor—far different from Zach MacKenzie, who often succeeded in making her laugh.

And when Rose went to bed that night, she lay and thought about the outing with Stephen. He had begun to ask her questions about her past. She had hedged most of the answers. Somehow it had been easier to tell Zach the truth about her childhood than it had been Stephen. She'd merely told him she'd been orphaned at seventeen.

You're trying too hard to please him, she told herself, just before she fell asleep.

By the time they parted after the next day's carriage ride, she could tell Stephen had more than a casual interest in her, though he had made no attempt to kiss her.

Yet somehow, Rose found herself wondering what Zach MacKenzie had been up to. There'd been no sign of him for two days.

Zach hugged the shadows as he waited for Will Grainger. Tait had kept him busy for the last two nights, and this was the first chance he'd had to slip away to meet Will in their usual spot.

Will suddenly appeared like a specter out of the darkness.

"I was beginning to think I'd have to come looking for you," Will said.

"These past two days Tait's had me doctoring the brands on those cattle in that box canyon."

"I went to Zanesville," Will said, "and you were right. There's been a lot of cattle shipped out of there lately."

"Was it a Lazy B brand? That's how we've been doctoring those cows."

"Yeah. Looked up the brand in the Stockgrowers'

Book. It's a brand registered to an S. Breakman. A month ago, five hundred head of Lazy B were shipped to Kansas City. Last week, another five hundred. But none of the locals are familiar with this brand, or with any Mr. S. Breakman."

"And you can bet that now that we've finished venting those brands, there'll soon be another five hundred shipped. Tait won't say who he's taking orders from, but Rayburn's leaving town tomorrow. That'll give me a chance to get into his house, and maybe I can find some evidence. But I'd better get back now. Take care of yourself, old man," Zach said in parting. "Things are beginning to heat up here."

"You don't have to worry about me, sonny," Will replied. "I've forgotten more about being a lawman than you'll ever hope to know."

As Zach rode back to the bunkhouse, he thought of Rose's hope of marrying Rayburn. Zach hoped that for her sake, Rayburn wasn't involved in this rustling.

To Rose's surprise, Stephen appeared at the restaurant during the breakfast hour the following morning. She had little time to talk to him while serving her tables, but they did manage to exchange a few words. He told her he was leaving on the morning train and would be gone for several days.

Sadly, she waved good-bye to him as the train pulled out. The next day Brimstone was holding a Fourth of July celebration, and Fred Harvey had ordered the restaurant closed for the day. Rose had been looking forward to spending the holiday with Stephen; now that wasn't going to happen.

Chapter 7

When Rose left work after the lunch train pulled out, Zach was waiting for her, a horse tied again to the back of the buggy. He smiled and doffed his hat. "Hi, Rosie, may I offer you a ride?"

"If you think I'm taking any more riding lessons, you're mistaken."

"I rented this buggy hoping you would enjoy a relaxing ride."

"That was very presumptuous of you, MacKenzie."

"I know where there's a quiet, shady grove of elm and willow with a cool spring. Wouldn't you like to get away from this dusty town for a short while?"

"I'd like to get away from this dusty town for a *long* while—forever to be exact," she declared. "I haven't seen you and your gang around for a couple days. I thought Stephen might have sent you all packing."

"You missed me!"

"That's not what I said." She continued on her way, but he followed.

"Think of it, *querida*, just the two of us. Cool . . . shady . . . peaceful . . ."

"Groping . . . panting . . . kissing. I'm not stupid, MacKenzie."

"Rosie!" he exclaimed, feigning indignation. "You do me an injustice. I swear I won't touch you." Then his warm chuckle caused her to smile. "Unless, of course, you insist."

"In your dreams, MacKenzie!" she said, trying not to laugh. Why did he have to be so darned engaging? For several seconds she tottered between going with him and telling him to drive on. With the relationship between her and Stephen growing, she'd be wise to avoid Zach. But the thought of getting away from the town was too tempting to refuse. Besides, what harm could come from a buggy ride? "You promise to keep your distance?"

He raised a hand. "On my honor."

"All right, I'll take you at your word."

"That's my girl!"

He reined up and she climbed into the buggy. "But I have to be back in two hours."

Rose didn't quite know what to think about Zach MacKenzie. He certainly seemed to be a cut above the gang he rode with, and for some bizarre reason she trusted him. Was it intuition or just wishful thinking?

After about thirty minutes, she wondered if she'd put her trust in the wrong man. The area had become very rugged, with rocky cliffs and deep chasms. Then suddenly the copse he'd described appeared out of nowhere, like an oasis.

Zach's strong hands encircled her waist as he lifted her out of the buggy. She liked the feel of his touch too much. Hurrying away, Rose sat down in the shade of the spreading branches of an elm tree while he filled a canteen with the cool water from the spring.

"I thought you'd become a working cowboy, MacKenzie. What are you doing in town?" she asked, after a refreshing drink.

"Rayburn went to Dallas to buy some stock. With no cattle left, there's not that much to do on the ranch. So Tait, Pike, and Cain stayed back there, and the rest of us came to town with Rayburn. He told us to remain here until he returns."

She leaned back against the tree trunk and he plopped down beside her. "Have you worked on a ranch before, Zach?"

He cocked his head in amusement. "Lady, I was born and raised on a ranch." He glanced at the cool stream. "You have any objections if I take a bath in that water?"

"I certainly do. I didn't come here to watch you bathe, MacKenzie."

"Then join me?" He started to pull off his boots.

She felt a rise of disappointment. "Why did I believe you'd honor your word? Is this why you brought me out here: to get me to take off my clothes? You're insulting my intelligence."

"Now don't go getting all puckered up, Rosie.

Where's the harm? You must be wearing a combination or bloomers. I see them in store windows."

"And that's not the only place, I'm sure."

"Do as you want. I've brought along a bar of soap and I'm going to jump in, wash off the dust, and cool off. I'll keep my drawers on, if that will make you happy."

"You're such a gentleman, MacKenzie," she said tartly.

He quickly stripped down to his underwear and dived into the water. "Rosie, come in and play," he crooned.

After five minutes of watching him soaping himself and diving under the water, she began to envy him. The urge to rid herself of her hot layers of clothing and join him became overwhelming. But that was just what he wanted, of course. Instead, she removed her apron. Folded it carefully and put it aside. Removing her shoes and stockings, she spread out his shirt on the riverbank and sat down on it, dangling her feet in the water.

The cool water felt exquisite, and she sat enjoying the moment as she watched him soaping and rinsing his hair.

"You could use a haircut, MacKenzie."

"I've got a pair of scissors in my saddlebags, if you know how to cut hair," he said, climbing out of the water.

"A woman has to know how, MacKenzie. A hairdresser is not always as conveniently available as a barber is for a man."

He grabbed his jeans, ducked behind a shrub, and came out with his pants on and carrying his wet underwear. After wringing them out, he spread them out on the ground.

Rose moved back to the shade of the tree and waited while Zach got several items out of his saddlebags.

"I'm not making any promises," she said, when he handed them to her.

"I trust you, Rosie." He sat down beside her, and she knelt to trim his hair. It was thick and silky, almost sensual to the touch. Before she realized, she'd lost herself in the task.

After sitting down, Zach had closed his eyes and let his thoughts drift. As usual they were about Rose—which had been the case since the moment he'd seen her.

He'd never met a woman like Rose Dubois before. Her lovely face, that red hair of hers, and those damn blue eyes all combined to challenge him to just try and ignore her. She knew the effect she had on him, and she made no attempt to pretend she didn't know.

But he couldn't help grinning, because she was right. Trouble was besides having that gorgeous face, that incredible red hair, those irresistible blue eyes, the most kissable mouth he'd ever encountered, and the most delicious kiss he'd ever tasted, she'd also had the most desirable body he'd ever lusted for, and the most seductive fragrance.

"I could find you in the dark."

"What? she asked.

"Your perfume. I could find you in the dark, Rosie."

"That's comforting to know in the event I'm ever lost," she said lightly. "There, all done. You look much better." She handed him the comb and scissors, then brushed the hair off his shouders.

Her touch on his bare flesh roped through him and knotted his insides. "You gonna shave me, too?"

"Are you sure you want to trust me with a razor that close to your throat?" she teased.

"I think I'm a pretty good judge of character, Miz Rose." He soaped up his shaving cup and handed it to her.

"Is that why you're riding with Jess Tait?" She smeared shaving soap all over his chin and cheeks.

"Where did you learn to shave a man, Rosie?"

She hesitated for an instant, then replied, "My father. Now tip your head back a little and don't move." She began to scrape away the soap and whiskers.

He couldn't speak while she shaved his chin, but he enjoyed her leaning over him. Her lips were parted slightly, and her tongue toyed with her upper lip as she concentrated on the razor strokes. Her luscious lips were mere inches from his, and her hair hung down loosely, screening their faces behind a silken curtain.

What the hell, his body was already on fire. He might as well go out in a big blaze instead of a slow burn. As soon as she lowered the razor, he pulled her head to his.

Memories were sweet to savor, but were mere appetizers compared to the reality of kissing Rose Dubois. He would never tire of that taste.

When the kiss ended, she pulled away. "Why did

you have to go and do that, MacKenzie? You've spoiled everything."

"Rosie, there's no way of spoiling a kiss between us."

A patch of shaving soap was smeared on her cheek, and he wiped it away with a finger.

"But there mustn't be any more. I like being with you, Zach. We have fun together. But I don't want you to think I'm looking for anything other than friendship."

"I think we are friends, Rose." He wiped off his face and took the shaving cup from her and put it aside.

"Then why did you kiss me?"

"I guess I'm fated to be the moth to your flame. Now, answer my question. Who taught you how to shave a man? And don't try to tell me it was your father."

For a long moment she hesitated, then she leaned back against the tree.

"Only someone with a weak mind would refer to Wes Sturges as a man."

"Who's Wes Sturges?"

She swallowed hard, and he saw the bitterness in her eyes. "I told you how my father died. Well, that was the night I met Sheriff Wes Sturges. He brought the news about my father, and implied that a witness had claimed my father had a female accomplice. I was implicated. Apparently he liked what he saw, because he told me he wouldn't involve me in the robbery if I took up with him. I had nothing to do with the robbery, but I had no way of proving it—so I was guilty by association.

"I didn't want to go to jail. Wes was big and handsome, and the only man who'd shown me any kindness. I fell hard for him, and moved in with him." Her face hardened. "I soon found out how naive I'd been. He was a brutal animal who enjoyed inflicting pain—on me and his unfortunate prisoners. For the next two years, my life became a living hell."

"Why didn't you leave him?" he asked quietly.

"At first there was the fear of prison. Then I began to feel prison couldn't be any worse than being with him, so I tried to run away. He always caught up to me. It wasn't that he loved me—Lord knows he had plenty of other women, even then. Wes kept me for the enjoyment of his power over me. In or out of bed."

"How'd you finally get away?" A muscle flicked in his jaw as his gaze remained on her face.

"He was cruel once too often, and one of the prisoners strangled him to death with his bare hands. I couldn't get away from Louisiana fast enough."

"So Sturges is why you distrust all lawmen?"

"He was the worst, I guess. But the others I've encountered weren't much better: they either were as crooked as Sheriff Bloom, or made up their minds about me because of my circumstances. When I read the ad for Harvey Girls, I saw it as an opportunity to leave my past behind. Of course, with my background, I'd never have made it through the training if it hadn't been for my friend Emily. She taught me the manners I needed to know, and I taught her how to survive in a tougher environment than she was used to."

"Was this Sturges your first?"

"My first what?" she asked.

"The first man who—"

"The first and *only* man. Thank you for asking, MacKenzie," she said angrily.

"I wasn't trying to be critical, honey." He wondered if she would ever get over that bitterness. She had too much to offer a man to allow herself to be marred by those scars.

"I don't know why I've told you all this. I didn't even tell Em about Wes, and she's my best friend. I was too ashamed."

"You can't blame yourself for the hand you were dealt."

She looked at him with a half smile. "Zach, I know you mean well, but all the bromides in the world can't change a thing. So what about you, MacKenzie? How did you lose your virginity?"

"I'm not the kind who kisses and tells."

"I told you things I've never even told my best friend."

"Okay, you win. Her name was Bobbie Jo Dawson. She was three years older than I was when she talked me into playing Mama and Papa in the Dawsons' hayloft."

"Talked you into it?" Rose said cynically.

"Okay, seduced me. I was only fourteen."

"So innocent little Zach MacKenzie got seduced by an older woman."

He chuckled. "I never said I was little."

She laughed. "Male ego never ceases to amaze me."

"And as pleasant as it was, my mom and dad

weren't too happy when they heard about it—much less amused. Matter of fact, they were downright angry. It was the only time Dad had ever struck me, and Mom did worse—she didn't talk to me for a whole week." He grinned. "My parents never said another word about the incident, but the rest of my family never let me forget it."

"And what happened to Bobbie Jo?"

"Well, it seems after trying out every young fellow in the county, Bobbie Jo packed her bag and headed out for greener pastures."

"Do you ever think about her?"

"Not until now. You can't live in the past, Rose. It's best to put it behind you."

"That's easier said than done, Zach." She jumped to her feet. "We'd better get back. I have to change my uniform and return to work."

He finished dressing while she put on her shoes and stockings. As they walked to the buggy, he heard a rifle blast and a bullet kicked up a puff of dust near Rose's feet.

"Get down," he yelled, and dived for her, knocking her down. "Stay down and don't move," he ordered, drawing his Colt.

"Who would be shooting at us?"

"My guess is whoever it is, you're the target. It sounded like a rifle shot, so I figure the shooter is probably over on that bluff."

"Who would want to shoot me?"

"I can think of one guy for sure. Jess Tait hates the sight of you."

"But Mr. Rayburn ordered him to leave me alone."

"Rayburn doesn't know Tait as well as I do. He carries grudges. Lie still, and for God's sake, keep your head down. My Colt's useless at this distance. I'm going to try and get closer."

"No, don't do it, Zach! It's too risky."

"Honey, I don't take kindly to people who take shots in my direction. Besides, he's either just putting a scare into you, or he's not that good with a rifle. Otherwise, he'd have picked you off with one of those shots. But if he keeps getting off shots, he might hit the horse. Then we *will* have a problem. So just do as I told you and keep your head down."

Zach dashed toward the cover of a tree as bullets whizzed past him. Rose's heart pounded in her chest as she watched him work from tree to tree until he was out of sight.

She soon lost track of time until she suddenly realized Zach had been gone for a long time, and she hadn't heard any gunshots for some time as well. Fear swept through her. What if he'd been wounded?

A deadening silence hung over the countryside. Not a leaf stirred on the trees, and her own breathing sounded like a drum in her ears. Dare she disobey his orders? He'd said not to move, but what if he needed help?

"Zach," she shouted past the lump in her throat. When there was no answer, she raised her head and shouted again.

"Here I am." He came walking through the trees as if he were out for a Sunday stroll.

She stood up, then grabbed the buggy for support when her trembling legs almost buckled. "Are you okay?"

"Yeah. Whoever was doing the shooting took off."

"Did you see who it was?"

"No, he was too far away. Let's get back to town."

He appeared deep in thought, and as she studied his ruggedly handsome profile Rose realized that try as she might, she couldn't dislike Zach MacKenzie.

They had gone barely a mile when a rider approached the wagon. Zach stopped, then handed her the reins. Climbing down, he said, "Stay here, Rose."

"Do you know him?" she asked.

"No."

"Maybe he's the one who was shooting at us."

He shook his head. "No, the shots had come from the other direction, so the shooter couldn't have gotten here so quickly. I'll talk to him."

She watched them intently but they were speaking in such low tones that she couldn't overhear what they were saying. Rose was certain she'd never seen the man before. He was tall and lean, his face lined from wind and sand. When he removed a battered and soiled hat she saw that his hair was thick and gray.

As they talked, he wiped out the inside of his hat. Then, nodding, the stranger rode away. Zach returned to the buggy.

"Who was he, Zach?" she asked as they continued on.

"Just some old-timer asking directions."

"And you're sure he had nothing to do with the shooting."

"Yeah, I'm sure," he said.

"Are you going to report the incident to the sheriff?"

Zach snorted. "That would be a waste of words."

Feeling indignation rise, she asked, "Are you just going to forget it ever happened?"

"No, I don't take lightly to someone trying to bushwhack me." He slipped into deep concentration and was quiet the rest of the ride.

"Thank you for the ride, Zach," she said when he drew up in front of her boardinghouse.

He smiled. "I'd like to try it again with a happier ending."

"I enjoyed it while it lasted. Besides, it's not every day a girl gets to be shot at." She grinned.

His chuckle was engaging. "You're a good sport, Rosie."

The smile eased from his face as he studied her thoughtfully for a long moment. She thought he intended to kiss her again, but to her surprise he reached out a hand and gently ran his knuckles along her cheek. "Watch your back, Rosie," he said softly. Then he climbed onto the buggy and flicked the reins.

With confused emotions, Rose stood at the gate and watched the buggy go down the street. Zach MacKenzie was the most appealing and exciting man she had ever known. But why did she suspect there was a lot more to him than he was willing to reveal?

Chapter 8

The evening meal was in progress when the Tait gang showed up at the restaurant. Seeing there was no empty table, four of them sat down at a table occupied by a couple and their two children. Zach and Joe took seats at the counter.

"Hey, sister, get your ass over here," Tait shouted to Rose.

"As soon as I'm able," she said, and continued to serve the previous customers.

Tait continued to grumble expletives loudly above the conversation of the other diners. After a troubled glance at his wife, the man at Tait's table said, "Excuse me, sir, but I would appreciate your not using that indelicate language in front of my wife and children."

Tait picked up a roll from one of the young girl's plate and took a bite. "That's too bad. Tell 'em not to listen if it bothers 'em."

"It bothers me, sir," the man persisted.

"And *you* bother me, mister." Tait took another bite of the roll, then smirked at the man. "Come to think of it, you're spoilin' my appetite." He tossed the roll back onto the girl's plate.

The woman put a hand on her husband's arm. "Please, Joseph, let's leave before there's any trouble."

"Joseph's got trouble already, lady," Tait said, "Less he wants to pay for my meal so's I won't wipe the floor up with him."

The man leaped to his feet. "I am not paying for your meal, you foul-mouthed bully."

The two young girls started to cry, and Tait glared at the woman. "Lady, tell 'em gals of yers to stop that wailin', or I'll give 'em somethin' to cry about."

"Don't you dare threaten my family, or I'll—"

"You'll what?" Tail asked ominously. He put a hand on the butt of the pistol at his hip. "Hope yer packin' iron to back up that threat."

"I do not carry a weapon, sir," Joseph said.

"Joseph, please let's get out of here," his wife pleaded.

Rose came out of the kitchen carrying a tray in time to see several of the customers hurrying out of the restaurant without finishing their meals. After a quick glance at Tait, it wasn't difficult for her to guess the reason for their hasty exit.

She slammed down the tray and strode angrily over to the table. "Mr. Tait, you are disturbing the other customers. Either quiet down or get out of here."

"You gonna make me, sister?"

"If I were a man I certainly would," she said, with a quick glare in Zach's direction. "Didn't Mr. Rayburn warn you about causing a disturbance in here?"

"Oh, don't tell him, girlie. He'll spank me," Tait whined mockingly. That provoked laughter from his three companions, and an actual giggle from Joe at the counter.

"Well, I intend to inform your boss as soon as he returns."

She knew she was getting nowhere with the man, but it distracted Tait's attention long enough for the couple and their children to leave.

"We have orders from Mr. Harvey not to serve you or your gang unless you pay for your meal in advance. I'll be glad to take your orders as soon as I see your money."

"Ain't you heard, sister? That fella over there said he'd pay for my dinner." He walked over to a nearby table and pounded it with a balled fist. "Ain't that right, mister?"

"Oh, yes. Yes, of course," the hapless man said. Quaking, he put the money on the table and then hurried out.

"You know, Tait, someday there's going to be a man who'll stand up to your bullying. I hope I'm around to see it."

Tait snorted in amusement. "You ain't gonna be around for nothin' if I don't get some food real quick, bitch."

"You'll just have to wait until we finish with our other customers. They have a train to catch."

"I'm tired of waitin'." Tait kicked a chair and it skimmed across the floor and crashed into the wall.

It was enough to start a mass exodus out the door until only Tait and his gang remained.

Tait's lips curled in a taunting smirk. "Looks like you gals got plenty of time to serve us now."

She trembled with rage but cloaked it with indifference. "Thanks to you, Mr. Tait, there's plenty of food left on the plates. That ought to be ample for swine like you." She pivoted and walked away, pausing only long enough to glare at Zach. "All of you."

The girls went into the kitchen and listened to the string of threats and expletives coming from the dining room until the gang finally stormed out. Surprisingly, they didn't break any of the dishes.

Billings locked the front door, and within the hour the dishes had been washed and everyone was ready to leave for the night.

Zach was waiting outside the restaurant.

"This is getting to be a habit, MacKenzie. What do you want now?"

"I need to talk to you, Rose."

"I don't think we have anything to say to each other."

"Please, Rose. There's something I'd like to tell you."

"All right." She nodded to Kate. "You girls go on."

"Are you sure you'll be okay?" Kate asked, with a derogatory glance at Zach.

"I have no intention of hurting her, Miss McDermott," Zach said. "And I'll have her home by ten o'-clock." He gave Kate one of his "melting on the spot" grins, which produced a round of giggles from everyone but Rose and Kate.

"See that you do, sir," Kate declared. "Come on, girls."

"Where are your cohorts in crime?" Rose asked when the girls walked away.

"Down at the Long Horn."

When he led her over to a buggy, she stopped short. "What's this? I have no intention of riding anywhere."

"It's such a hot night; I thought you might enjoy a ride before going back to your room."

"Whatever you have to say, I can listen to right here."

"Come on, Rose. It will cool you off."

Against her better judgment, she let him help her into the buggy. "The last time you took me for a ride, I wound up getting shot at." She removed her apron and released a couple of the dress's top buttons to try and cool off.

Flicking the reins, he turned his head and glanced at her. "I'm sure whoever took those shots at us isn't still hanging around."

"I'm not so sure. Whoever it was is probably watching us right now." She glanced back. The other girls had reached the rooming house, and the sound of the door slamming as they entered it carried to her ears in the still night.

Zach was right about the heat. It lay heavily on the night air, extinguishing any hope of a breeze.

Paralleling the railroad track, he kept the horse at a slow trot, skirting the town before he turned off and headed toward higher ground.

Rose relaxed, leaned back, and closed her eyes. As they moved away from the town an occasional breeze fanned her face, but not enough to stir a hair on her head. Regardless, she had to admit it was better than returning to a hot, stuffy room. The quiet night soon became a soothing balm, and the trotting horse's hooffalls dulled into a rhythmic lullaby.

Her face was in shadows as she slept.

Zach reined in and climbed out of the buggy. Gently, so as not to wake her, he lifted her out and carried her beneath a cottonwood. They were high enough to catch a breeze now, and his gaze roamed her face as she slept, her head in his lap. The soft glow of moonlight had deepened her hair and the provocative fragrance of her perfume embraced him.

He was a fool. He'd allowed himself to let his emotions get involved in this flirtation with her. Lord, how she fired his blood! All he could think about was making love to her. Trouble was, as much as he didn't want to admit it, his feelings for her were beginning to go beyond just wanting her physically.

It had taken him a while to figure out what there was about her that fascinated him so, that put her above any woman he'd kissed and ridden away from before. That one element he hadn't been able to identify until today, when she'd spoken about Wes Sturges. It was her vulnerability. Underneath all that feistiness, grit, and toughness lay a sensitive little girl who'd been knocked down so often it was a wonder how she could keep picking herself up.

And he wanted her so badly, he ached. Yet he knew he'd end up hurting her, just like her father and that bastard Sturges had done. If he had any decency, he'd stay away from her and give her a chance to get on with her life.

But the die had been cast from the moment he'd walked into that Harvey restaurant and looked into her eyes. He could tell she realized it, too. The chemistry between them was undeniable—on the verge of boiling over. It no longer was *if*, it had become *when*.

Rose opened her eyes and for a long moment stared up at him.

"You're so beautiful, Rose." With passion-filled eyes he gazed down at her. The air was charged with a hushed expectancy.

"What's happening between us, Zach?"

The warmth of his smile carried to his eyes, and he tenderly cupped her cheek. "Don't you know, honey?" he asked in a husky whisper.

She closed her eyes when he lowered his head. Their mouths fit perfectly to one another's. He increased the pressure and felt her hand on his neck, holding him. Her lips were soft, moist, and tasted delicious. She parted her lips and he slipped his tongue between them. As their tongues coupled and dueled, hot passion surged through him like a brushfire out of control. He was so hard and aching he thought he'd explode.

Zach slid his hand down the column of her neck

and found the opened neckline of her gown. Her skin felt like satin, and he dipped his head and licked it with his tongue. It was warm, sweet, soft; it tasted like Rose. He had to taste more of her.

Opening more of the buttons, he parted the front of her gown, then slid his hand under her chemise and cupped her breast. It was firm and full, and the nub hardened to a peak.

Lord, she felt good. Hot blood pounded at his temples. Lowering his head, he rasped the nipple with his tongue, then sucked it into his mouth. She moaned and arched her back. The pressure of her hand on his nape encouraged him further, and he shoved up the chemise and caressed her breasts with his hand, mouth, and tongue until she clutched at his shoulders, moaning and writhing.

Raising his head, he reclaimed the divine taste of her lips.

"Don't stop, Zach. For a few moments, make me forget everything but you and me."

Her words froze him. Tears were glistening in her eyes, and she looked helpless, *vulnerable*. Dammit!

He'd never wanted any woman as much as he wanted her at that moment—but he couldn't do it. He'd be damned if he'd use her like Sturges or her father, for whatever suited their purpose.

He pulled her dress together, then kissed her on the tip of her nose. "I'm not going to take advantage of you. I promised, remember? I apologize, Rose."

Even in the dark he could tell she was blushing. "I guess we kind of got carried away. That kiss of yours is very potent," she said lightly. "I apologize for my part in it, too."

Watching her try to appear nonchalant as she buttoned her gown and tucked strands of loose hair back in place, Zach felt himself get hard again. He had to be the biggest damn fool that ever walked on God's good, green earth.

Shifting her off his lap, he stood up. "How old are you, Rose?"

"Twenty-one. What about you?"

"Twenty-two."

"Have you ever been in love?" she asked seriously.

"No. I never let myself. Love means being tied down, babies, working a ranch. I don't like ropes—not even long ones."

"You mean you don't like commitment."

"Call it what you want. I'm not interested in marriage."

"That's why I decided I would marry a rich man. I don't need love, either."

"I always heard you were supposed to be in love to marry."

"If I endured Wes Sturges, I can bear any man—as long as he's rich."

"You're not on the street anymore, Rose, so there's no excuse to marry a man just for money. That's not much better than prostitution."

He must have hit a nerve, because she came back at him with anger.

"I've had to look out for myself since I was seven years old! I want someone to look after me—take care of me. You know what that would mean to me, Zach? Do you have any idea? No more fighting off sadistic lawmen or saddle tramps. No worrying where my next meal is coming from. No more taking orders from people who aren't even half as smart as I am. And all I have to do is be someone's wife. You can call it prostitution or any other name you want, but how can you believe for a moment that I wouldn't grow to love the man who gave me this peace of mind?"

He sympathized with her hardships, but her view made a mockery of his parents' marriage, and his uncles' and aunts'.

"If security is all you want, any man who loved you would look after you. It wouldn't have to be a rich man. But maybe you want more than love and security. Are you sure it's not luxuries and the social status and approval that goes with that position that you want?"

"I want respectability," she lashed out. "Rich or poor, a man can lie, steal, or even abuse a woman, and he's still a man—but one false move from a woman, and she's a tramp or a whore. So a girl raised in a New Orleans slum isn't worthy of a prestigous marriage, is she, MacKenzie? Even a saddle tramp like you thinks she's got to settle for whatever she can get."

Rose felt betrayed. She'd thought that since he was down and out himself, he'd understand. For a few foolish moments she'd let her guard down, fooled herself into believing he was different. But he was just like all the other no-goods she'd encountered in her life: if they didn't have it, they didn't want anybody else to have it, either.

She stood up and brushed herself off. "I'd like to go back now. It's getting very late."

Once again, they rode back in silence. When they reached her boardinghouse, he jumped down and helped her off.

She didn't want to part with the quarrel between them, so she swallowed her anger and tried to show some graciousness.

"Thank you, Zach. It was very thoughtful of you to suggest the ride."

"I'm sorry, Rose. Considering the life I lead, I've no right to criticize your choices. And I'm sorry how the guys messed up the restaurant tonight."

"What are you doing with those men, Zach? Deep down I feel there's good in you, but if you keep running with that pack of jackals you're going to end up at the wrong end of a rope."

"What does it matter to you if I die from hanging or old age?"

She was glad the darkness hid her face. "I guess I just don't want to see you hurt."

He stepped closer and lifted a strand of her hair. Rolling it between his fingers, he stroked the silken strands with his thumb. His nearness was like an aphrodisiac, exciting her senses even as it lulled her into submission.

"Is this red hair of yours the real thing, Rosie?" he asked.

The awed huskiness in his voice made the question sound like a declaration of love. She chastised herself for allowing girlish fantasies to enter her mind.

"The hair's real, but I paint on the freckles."

Her attempt at flippancy failed miserably, because he released her hair and ran a finger across her nose. The tender touch unnerved her more. "I think they're cute. They reveal the little girl who's hiding behind the tough woman you try to appear." His dark-eyed gaze conveyed more than his teasing words. He kissed her on the forehead. "Good night, Rose."

As Rose watched him drive away, she bit her lip to keep herself from calling him back.

Rose had no sooner entered her room than Kate tapped on her door and came in. "Rose, the Fourth of July celebration's tomorrow. We need a schedule of when we have to work the Harvey booth."

"Mr. Billings has worked it all out. He said he'll post it at the booth. I have the first shift."

"It sounds like it's going to be fun," Kate said.

"I agree. But I was under the impression these Texans only celebrated their independence from Mexico," Rose replied, tongue in cheek.

"Not this time; Brimstone's made big plans. There'll be fireworks, and the Behling Brothers Circus will be here for the occasion."

"I don't know which I'm looking forward to more," Rose said. "The celebration itself, or having most of the day off."

Kate stretched out on the bed as Rose began to undress. "So what was so important that Mr. MacKenzie had to say tonight?" Kate asked.

Rose shrugged. "I honestly don't know; I fell asleep. He did apologize for the way his gang caused a disturbance in the restaurant. That must have been it."

But was it? Rose wondered. They hadn't really discussed anything before their argument, and she doubted that was what he'd had in mind when he took her riding. Had he planned all along to make love to her? If so, she certainly hadn't tried to stop him, so why had he broken it off?

Zach MacKenzie was the most confusing man she'd ever met. Whenever she was convinced of his intentions, he'd do just the opposite. There was an innate honesty to him, so why was he riding with that gang? Even though he didn't want to be tied down with a wife and children, that didn't mean he couldn't get an honest job.

And why did he have to be so irresistible? Why did he have to have a grin that curled her toes; a warm chuckle that stroked her spine, and a touch that fired her blood? Rose sighed deeply. And a kiss that—

"Hey, that was a pretty deep sigh, Rose," Kate said.

"I was thinking about Zach MacKenzie."

Kate giggled. "That would explain it, then. He's enough to make any girl sigh."

Rose grimaced. "Trouble is, he knows it. But I've got other plans, and they don't include a down-on-his-heels drifter like Zach MacKenzie."

Rose had hoped she sounded more convincing than she felt, but apparently not so.

Grinning, Kate glanced at her. "Nice try, honey, but he's the one you have to convince."

Rose knew she had to tell someone or she'd burst. "Kate, Zach and I had a big argument tonight over marriage."

Mouth agape, Kate sat up. "You mean he asked you to marry him and you refused?"

"No, nothing like that. He's adamant about not being tied down, *no matter how long the rope*. He as much as called me a whore when I told him I intended to marry for money."

"I'm sorry, Rose," Kate said. Her brown eyes were warm with compassion. "But there's more to it than him calling you a name, isn't there?"

Fraught with confusion, she turned to Kate, and the truth poured out of her like a pot boiling over. "Kate, I almost let him make love to me tonight. We went far beyond a kiss."

"At least you had the sense to stop."

"He stopped—I didn't stop him. I wanted him to, Kate. I was willing to let him do anything that he wanted to me." Her voice trailed off in a sob. "I don't know what to do."

Kate rushed over and hugged her. "Oh, Rose honey, I'm so sorry. Are you in love with him?"

"I hardly know him, but each time I see him, I want to be with him more. Even arguing with him is exciting." Tears slid down her cheeks as she looked at Kate. "But when we aren't arguing, he makes me laugh, Kate. He warms my heart."

"He's trouble, Rose."

"I know, Kate, but soon he'll be out of my life. I intend to marry Stephen Rayburn."

"In the meantime you're playing with fire, honey. You can get burned. Though maybe you *should* have an affair with him."

Rose gasped in surprise. "What are you saying?"

"Maybe once he makes love to you, you'll be able to get over him."

"No, I don't think so. I think it would just make

me want him more, and my heart would break when he rode away. And someday he *will* ride away." Rose squared her shoulders, and said resolutely, "It's insanity! I've planned my future. Stephen Rayburn's on the verge of asking me to marry him and fulfill my dream. I'm not going to let Zach MacKenzie spoil it when everything I've ever hoped for is within arm's reach."

Kate walked to the door. "If you're certain that's what you really want, Rose, then I hope for your sake you get it. Good night."

Rose gave Kate a quizzical glance. Had she been mistaken, or did Kate's words sound more ominous than supportive?

Troubled, she undressed and went to bed. There was no relief from the heat and she would have loved to remove her nightgown and lie naked, but that would mean closing the window, thus eliminating any hope of a breeze. Finally, after a couple of hours of tossing and turning, she managed to doze off.

Chapter 9

A more pleasant day couldn't have dawned for Brimstone's Fourth of July. Fluffy white clouds drifted lazily across a bright blue sky as a light breeze stirred the air.

The ladies' church auxiliary had been preparing food and wares for weeks. Tables displayed crocheted doilies, needlepoint samplers, and knitted afghans for sale. There were booths offering roasted ears of corn dripping with butter, slices of decorated cakes, and mouth-watering pies. The aromas of popping corn, beef roasting on a spit, and baking rolls whetted the appetite.

Normally the town rarely attracted visitors from neighboring communities, but people had been arriving since early morning from as far as fifty miles.

The main attraction was the Behling Brothers Circus. In the wee hours of the morning, their colorful, ornate wagons and carts had rolled into town and they'd raised their big tent. Now the blare of the brass band, wearing bright red-and-gold uniforms, rose above the shouts of excited children, the occasional trumpet of an elephant, or the roar from a lion or tiger during the performances offered every two hours.

The Harvey booth was having phenomenal success selling strawberry-filled crêpes. These tasty French pancakes were a rarity to most of the crowd. Andre and Colette Chevalier had risen at dawn, fried and stacked several hundred of the basic crêpes, and with smiling Harvey Girls manning the booth in shifts, Colette filled and rolled them, and Andre popped them into an outside oven until they were lightly brown, then topped them off with a dusting of confectioners' sugar.

Having just been relieved from booth duty by Aubrey, Rose went in search of Kate and found her watching a baseball game between Brimstone and the neighboring town of Scottsville.

"Who's winning?" Rose asked, taking a seat beside her.

"We are," Kate replied, absorbed by the activity on the field.

"Speak for yourself." Rose felt no loyalty toward the accursed town. Seeing horses among the players, she asked, "What are those horses for?"

"If a player gets a hit, he climbs on the horse and rides to the base."

"That's the dumbest thing I've ever heard," Rose

declared. "Whoever heard of playing baseball on horseback?"

"They only get on horseback when they have to run the bases."

"That's exactly what I mean. The *players* are supposed to run the bases—not horses."

"I don't think cowboys *can* run," Kate said consideringly. "I've never seen one run. Must be those boots they wear. Anyway, the batter hits the ball, climbs on a horse, and rides around the bases. If the ball reaches the base before the player does, he's out."

"Who's dumb enough to stand on a base to catch a ball while a horse is bearing down on him?"

"They aren't quite bases as we think of them. First base is that big oak tree, second is that elm out there, and third base is the pine tree. An outline for the home plate is drawn in the mud. Other than that, the rules are the same as any baseball game."

"How do you know so much about baseball, Kate?"

"I've got two brothers. We played it often on the farm—without horses, of course. Right now we've got a man on second base."

"You mean a horse and a horse's ass," Rose commented with a droll look at her excited friend.

"Uh-oh, he struck out." Kate sighed. "One more out and the game's over." Kate suddenly poked her in the arm. "Look, Rose. Zach's up to bat."

Rose looked up to see Zach approaching home plate, carrying a bat in one hand and leading his horse by the reins with the other.

Kate put two fingers in her mouth and let out a

loud whistle. Amazed, Rose looked at her. "Kate McDermott, wherever did you learn to do that?"

"I told you, I have two brothers. Come on, Zach, hit a homer," Kate shouted.

Rose glared in disgust at Jess Tait and Bull, who hooted loudly when Zach let two strikes get past him.

"Aren't those two animals supposed to cheer on a teammate?"

Kate snorted. "Why would you expect anything better from that pair? Both of them have struck out every time they've been at bat."

On the third pitch, Zach connected with the ball and it sailed far out to left field. Kate jumped to her feet. "Whoopee! Ride 'im, cowboy."

Zach leaped onto his horse and galloped down the would-be baseline, circled the oak, and raced toward the elm tree as his teammate crossed home plate. He headed for the pine tree and appeared to reach it at the same time as the ball did.

The umpire called him out.

Rose jumped to her feet in indignation. "He was safe by a mile," she shouted angrily. "Get yourself a pair of glasses so you can see what you're doing."

The umpire turned around and to her dismay it was the Reverend Downing, the local pastor. Shamefully, she sank back down on the bench.

The game ended with the visiting team winning by a run. Desolate, Rose sat with her elbows on her knees and her chin in her hands. "Too bad it wasn't robbing a bank instead of baseball; the Brimstone team could probably have won hands down."

"Come on, Rose. Let's go and get something to eat."

After having sandwiches, the two women ventured to order small mugs of cold beer. Giggling like mischievous children, they sat down in the shade of a tree and sipped the beer, enjoying the restful moment as they watched the people passing by.

"I can't say I like beer," Kate said. "Do you?"

"I think it stinks—literally. I feel like holding my nose before I bring the mug up to my mouth. It's just another nothing that men make a big to-do over."

"Cheers," Kate declared as they clanged their mugs together and broke into giggles again.

Suddenly two women in flashy dresses paused before them. Their flamboyant clothing and overly made-up faces marked them as members of the oldest profession.

"Look at that, Flora, two of them high-falutin' Harvey gals drinkin' beer. Disgustin', ain't it," the blonde said.

Raised on the streets, Rose had encountered many prostitutes and had found most of them likable and easy to get along with. But these two women clearly had an axe to grind.

"Yeah, Rita, that oughta get 'em booted out of their sainted girl union," the other said.

Rose glanced up with curiosity at the blonde. So this was Rita—the woman whom Stephen Rayburn visited when he came to town. Whatever beauty she possessed was marred by the cynical draw at the corners of her mouth.

"Was there something you wanted, ladies?" Kate asked with bored tolerance.

Rita snickered. "Yeah, for you Harvey bitches to get out of town. Come on, Flora, we're wastin' time here."

"That's right, Miss Rita," Rose said. "Some of those fellows are spending their money so fast you two could end up out of business."

"Bitch!" Rita snarled as they moved on.

"Enjoy the holiday," Rose countered. Eyes brimming with merriment, she looked at Kate.

"Another nothing that men make a big to-do over," Kate murmured. They broke into peals of laughter.

As they returned the mugs, Zach was getting a sandwich from the booth nearby. "Hey, Rosie, are you game to be my partner?" he called out to her.

"If you mean through life, the answer is a definite no, MacKenzie," she yelled back, which brought laughs from those in earshot.

He came over. "The games are about to begin. There are four events, and the rules say each team has to consist of a male and female, no younger than sixteen years old. The winners get front-row tickets to the circus. What about it?"

"I'll tell you after I hear what we have to do in those events."

Zach read from a printed flyer. "The first is a mule race, which begins at one o'clock; the next one's a shooting competition at two."

"I have no idea how to shoot a gun."

"Just point it at the target and pull the trigger, Rosie. The third event's at three o'clock and involves the team's female member only. It has something to do with greased pigs."

She eyed him suspiciously. "What does that mean?"

"I have no idea," he said. "Since it involves women only, it's probably something to do with cooking or roasting pigs."

"You mean on a spit?"

"That would be my guess," he said.

"Well, I suppose I could do that, as long as the pig's already dressed. I don't want to have anything to do with skinning one."

"Oh, Rose, I'm sure they wouldn't have the women slaughtering pigs," Kate said. "I agree with Zach; it probably means preparing pork some way."

"What's the last event?" Rose asked.

"It's a hunt and doesn't start until eight o'clock tonight. Each couple has to find the items indicated by clues. Sounds easy, so what do you think, Redhead?"

Rose hesitated. "I don't know, Zach. I'm not so sure about that greased pig one."

"Oh, go ahead, Rose," Kate said. "I'm going to do it, too. I promised Mr. Billings I'd be his partner."

Rose's eyes almost popped out of her head. "You and Mr. Billings are going to enter these contests?"

"I'm afraid so."

"But, Kate, if I enter, we'll be competing against each other."

Kate arched a curved brow. "I don't think it'll be much of a competition. Are you forgetting Billings is going to be my partner?"

"Well, I've got to think about this some more. I'll let you know later," she said to Zach.

Kate left to do her shift at the booth, and Rose continued to explore the rest of the sights. When she finished browsing, she returned to the booth in time to witness Jess Tait doing what he did best—harassing people. He'd bump into them and "accidentally" knock the crêpes out of their hands.

When she saw him frighten a little boy into dropping the one the youngster had been eating, Rose exploded. "You are loathsome, Mr. Tait. Must you even terrorize children with your bullying? Don't you have any conscience?"

"Come here, sweetheart; I'll give you another one," Kate said to the lad, who had begun sobbing.

The scene had attracted a large crowd that now stood around listening. A voice from the crowd yelled, "Hey, mister, it was your fault. You oughta pay for the new one."

Many of the bystanders, who were not local and thus unaware of Tait's reputation, nodded and murmured their agreement.

"The bully should pay. The bully should pay," began as a murmur and soon rose to a chant.

Rose smiled smugly. "It appears the people have spoken, Mr. Tait. Looks like you're not getting away with your bullying this time."

"You think so, sister?" Tait snickered. "All I have to do is draw my Colt, and this crowd'll scatter like chickens with a fox in the coop."

Zach appeared out of the crowd and moved to Rose's side. "If I were you, I wouldn't try putting that theory to a test."

Tait's eyes gleamed with malice. "You pickin' a side, MacKenzie?"

"Just trying to keep you out of trouble," Zach said good-naturedly.

"I don't need you to blow my nose or wipe my ass, MacKenzie."

"No sense in anyone getting hurt, Jess."

"If I wuz you, MacKenzie, I'd be worryin' more about keepin' yerself from gettin' hurt. 'Specially when ya stick yer nose into somethin' that ain't yer business."

"Sounds to me like the young man's talking sense, Mr. Tait."

The man who'd spoken stepped forward. In his early forties, he carried himself with an air of assurance, which, to a discerning observer, was more intimidating than Tait's swagger.

"Who in hell asked you?" Tait snarled.

"That's of no importance. What is, is that you buy that youngster another of those fancy pancakes."

"Zat so." Tait snorted. "Do I look like Santa Claus? If the kid can't hold on to what he's eatin', it ain't my problem."

"I think it is, Mr. Tait."

There wasn't a sound from the crowd as they backed away. Like Rose, everyone was holding their breath waiting to see what would follow.

Rose stole a glance at Zach and saw he wasn't watching Tait. His eyes were on the rest of Tait's gang, who were slowly moving in behind the man.

"Back off, fellas," the man said, without turning his head.

Obviously Tait began to realize he wasn't facing

someone who'd back down easily. "You a lawman, stranger?"

"Used to be." His gaze never wavered from Tait.

"Around these parts?"

"New Mexico."

"You got a name?" Tait asked.

"Name's Garrett."

Tait blanched, and a low murmur spread through the crowd as others recognized the name.

"Pat Garrett? The sheriff that gunned down Billy the Kid up there in Lincoln County?" The bluster had fizzed out of Tait like air out of a balloon.

"That was some time ago, Mr. Tait."

Tait hesitated for a moment, then he turned around and slapped a coin on the table. "Give the kid another one of those damn things." He stomped away, followed by his minions.

With the crisis past, the crowd dispersed. Zach took Rose's hand and led her over to Garrett.

"Mr. Garrett, I'm Zach MacKenzie. My dad's often told me stories of when the two of you were fighting the Comanches. It's a pleasure to finally meet you, sir."

"Who's your dad, son?" Garrett asked.

"Flint MacKenzie."

Garrett broke into a wide grin. "You're Flint MacKenzie's son! How's that ornery son of a mule doing?"

"He's fine—probably just as ornery, though."

Garrett laughed. "Thought for sure somebody would have shot him by now. Reckon I wasn't much older than you at the time, but to this day, I've never met a man who could follow a trail like your pa. He's one hell of a man."

"I'll tell him that, sir, the next time I see him." Zach turned to Rose. "Mr. Garrett, this is Miss Dubois."

Garrett doffed his hat. "Pleasure to meet you, ma'am."

"The pleasure's mine, Mr. Garrett," Rose said. "I was raised in the South, but even I've heard of the legendary sheriff who killed Billy the Kid."

"Reckon Billy's the legend, ma'am, not me." He shook Zach's hand. "You be sure and give my regards to your dad, Zach."

"Thank you, sir, I will."

"And, son, watch your back. That Tait's got a mean streak in him as wide as the stripe on a skunk's back." He tipped his hat. "Miss Dubois."

Once Garrett walked away, Zach grabbed her hand. "We'd better get going; the contest's about to start. We're signed up already."

Rose stopped short. "You registered us before I even agreed to do it?"

"I knew you would; you're a good sport, Rosie." He gave her one of his irresistible grins. "Just one of your many endearing qualities."

"You're hopeless, MacKenzie. Utterly, totally, completely, out-of-control hopeless."

He squeezed her hand. "Rosie, honey, we're gonna win those circus tickets."

Chapter 10

Spectators were lined up on each side of the two long blocks that comprised Brimstone's main street, the site of the mule race.

Rose stood with her arms folded across her chest as she listened to the Reverend Downing explain the rules of the contest to the five teams participating. She really was not competitive when it came to games, and wondered how she let Zach once again talk her into doing something.

"Points are awarded according to the position in which a team finishes," the pastor said. "When all the events are completed, the team that has accumulated the most points wins the prize. In this event, the winning team earns five points on down and the last team earns one point. Points will be adjusted according to the number of teams remaining, because any team that fails to finish an event is disqualified from continuing on to the next one."

"That sounds like temptation knocking," Rose murmured to Kate.

"The rules of this first event are quite simple," the pastor continued. "Each man must ride a mule down to those five men you can see near the railroad tracks. He must then dismount, give the reins to the man with his corresponding number, and then run back here. Once he crosses the finish line, he hands the baton to his partner. The woman must run down there, climb on the mule, and ride it back here. The first woman back is the winner. Is that clear to all?"

When all nodded, Reverend Downing shouted, "Gentlemen, mount your mules."

Grinning, Zach asked, "Do I get a kiss for luck, Rosie?"

"Did you say a *kick*, MacKenzie?" she asked.

He sighed. "At least wish me luck."

"Luck," she said.

A gunshot announced the official start of the race, and the shouting began as the men prodded the mules down the road. Now that the time was almost upon her, the thought of climbing on a mule became less and less appealing. Zach looked ridiculous: his long legs dangled over the sides of the mule and his feet almost touched the ground. The whole thing was dumb.

"Did you ever ride a mule?" she asked Kate, who was standing next to her.

"Sure, plenty of times. Just don't whip it, Rose.

Mules are stubborn, and it might balk. Use your knees and lightly prod it; that will keep it at a steady pace. And remember, a mule's not a horse, so don't expect too much speed."

"Speaking of horses, it's kind of ironic that these same cowboys who couldn't run bases in the ballgame, are now going to run two blocks in a mule race."

"Or try, anyway."

Still skeptical, Rose said, "Kate, you actually don't think Mr. Billings will be able to run two blocks?"

"Honey, I don't think he'll be able to ride that mule for two blocks. I have great expectations of being eliminated in this first event." She grinned at Rose. "I don't think you're going to be that lucky."

"Probably. Zach's a driven man, Kate. It would have cost him less just to buy the circus tickets."

"You're missing the point, Rose. We're all doing this for charity."

"I guess you're right. I must be the only one who can't get into the spirit of it. Even those two seem to be enjoying it," Rose said, looking down the line to where Rita and Flora were cheering on their partners.

"Yeah, but did you see who they have for partners? Bull and Joe."

Both girls broke into laughter.

The cheering increased as the men ran back. A young man who appeared to be not a day over sixteen was in the lead; Zach was a couple yards behind him. Everett Billings had a firm hold on last place.

"I think that young couple has this race in the bag," Kate said. "That girlfriend of his looks like one of those Amazon warriors in mythology."

"I visualize her in a horned helmet at the helm of a Viking ship."

"She'll probably make us all look like old ladies. All I can hope is that Billings cries uncle before he can finish."

"Oh, this is going to be so embarrassing," Rose groaned as Zach neared the finish line.

As soon as her partner handed the baton to her, the young Amazon took off in a spurt of speed. Rose chased after her.

She had covered about half the distance to the mules when she approached Mr. Billings, still on his way back. He was running with a high-stepping motion: knees high and his elbows bent and hugging his sides. He appeared to be running in place, rather than advancing. She nodded as she passed him.

Her lungs felt near to bursting when she reached the mules at the same time that Rita did. The young Viking had just mounted her mule when a train racing through the depot tooted a whistle in passing.

Spooked by the shrill blast, the mule kicked up its hind legs and began braying. Its discordant hee-haws rent the air as the animal pivoted and bucked in circles like an unbroken mustang.

Taken by surprise, the young girl was tossed off right onto Rita. Rita lay bare-bottomed in the street, her head buried under yards of gown and tulle petticoat, cursing a blue streak as her legs and red-laced boots wiggled in the air.

A high voice, more shrill than the train whistle, came from under the skirt. "Get off me, ya clumsy bitch," Rita screeched at the young girl.

Awed by the spectacle, the goggle-eyed mule tenders flocked to the aid of the fallen women. Shoving the girl aside, Rita sat up and glared at the men.

"Get your hands off me or I'll start chargin' ya."

No one paid any attention to Rose, who climbed on her mule and headed back to the finish line while Rita crawled around on the dusty street shouting, "Where in hell is that baton?"

Flora, who had ignored the fracas as well, was a short distance behind Rose.

Rose crossed the finish line to cheers and applause, and as Zach swung her off the mule, she savored the sweet taste of victory.

The second loudest cheer of the event came when Kate crossed the finish line.

In a show of bruised pride and lack of sportsmanship, the tearful young Amazon refused to finish and wanted the race to be rerun. The Reverend Downing saw no reason for doing so, declared the accident the hand of Fate, and the young couple were disqualified.

So the first event ended with Rose and Zach having four points, Flora and Joe with three, Rita and Bull with two, and Kate and Everett Billings earning one point. They all moved on to the shooting range.

A shooting contest always attracted people's attention, and Rose discovered that today's event wasn't any exception.

She peered at the four targets, their centers painted with round red circles four inches in diameter, erected about two hundred feet away. "I don't understand what people find so fascinating about pointing a gun at a standing target."

Kate said, "Of course a moving target would be harder to hit, but it still takes a good eye and steady hand to hit a standing one."

"So what am I doing in this contest?" Rose asked.

"You felt the same way about the last event and look what happened," Zach said. "We won, didn't we?"

"Because of a fluke! That young couple deserved to win that race."

"Rosie, you'll do great," Zach assured her.

She continued to stare at him. "I'm trying to understand why I continue to let you talk me into embarrassing myself."

He regarded her solemnly. "I don't think there's anything either of us can deny each other anymore, except the one thing we both want the most."

"How can you think about sex at a time like this?"

She watched his appealing grin dawn. "What makes you think I meant sex, Rosie?"

"You know darn well that's what you meant, Zach MacKenzie."

He was kept from replying when the Reverend Downing shouted, "All right, gentlemen, take your positions. Each pistol you've been given has six bullets. A team's hits will be combined to determine the winning scores."

Zach glanced at her. "Are you going to wish me—"

"Luck," she murmured.

Joe shot first and hit the mark four times, then Bull followed with five hits. Everett Billings surprised everyone by matching Joe's score.

Zach was the last to compete. Without hesitation, he stepped up, aimed, and rapidly fired all six shots into the center of the red circle.

"See, honey, nothing to it," he said as he rejoined her. "We're in the lead."

"Not for long," she grumbled, and stepped up to the line.

Flora and Rita each managed to hit the bull's-eye three times, then Kate surprised Rose by making five out of the six shots.

As Rose moved in place, Zach called out, "Just take your time and gently squeeze the trigger. Don't jerk it."

Following Zach's example, she took careful aim, then rapidly fired all six shots. Not only did she miss the bull's-eye, but she completely failed to even hit the target.

Zach looked appalled.

Now she knew exactly how the young Viking felt. "I told you I can't hit anything."

Even worse, she had wiped out their lead. The four teams were tied with five points each.

Vowing to redeem herself in the next competition, Rose fortified herself for the mysterious greased pig contest.

The mystery increased when she saw the knee-high rubber boots, long-sleeved flannel shirt, and bib overalls that each woman was given. The Reverend Downing had wisely provided a tent for them to change into the ensemble.

"These are strange costumes to cook in," Rose murmured softly to Kate when they had completed the change. The sleeves of the shirt hung past her hands, and she rolled them up to her elbows.

"Yes, I can see now that this is not what we thought it would be."

"What did ya think it was gonna be?" Rita asked from where she and Flora were changing.

"Oh, we had several ideas in mind," Rose said nonchalantly, indicating with an eye signal to Kate not to say anything. The last thing she wanted was for these two prostitutes to know the mistaken impression Kate and she had had about the event.

"I hope one of 'em was catching a greased pig."

"*Catching* a greased pig!" Kate exclaimed, shocked.

Rose hurriedly shoved Kate ahead of her out of the tent.

"Come along, ladies," the pastor said.

Rose clopped along behind him, curling her toes to try and hold the boots on by suction. He led them over to an area enclosed by a slatted fence. Four piglets were rooting within the enclosure.

"Ladies, your task is a simple one. The first woman who climbs out holding a pig is the winner. To make the attempt a tad more difficult, the little piggies have been greased. Good luck to you all."

Trying not to trip, Rose waddled over to Zach and glared at him.

"I now am expected to wallow in the dirt not only like a pig—but with a pig! I *will* get even with you for this, Zach Mackenzie."

He spread his arms wide in a gesture of innocence. "I swear, Rosie, I had no idea. You and Kate should feel free to drop out of the contest," he said earnestly.

"And let *them* win?" she declared, glancing at Rita and Flora smirking at her. "Not on your life."

Rita snickered. "Listen to Miss High-and-Mighty Harvey Girl. You two better haul your royal asses out of here before you get 'em dirty."

Rose and Kate exchanged a determined look, then crawled over the fence.

"Here, piggy, piggy, piggy," Rose cooed as she approached one of the tiny pigs. The little pig's round black eyes regarded her with curiosity. She made a grab for it. Squealing and wiggling, the greasy animal slipped right through her hands.

Kate succeeded in holding on to one of the tiny pigs and headed for the fence, but Flora gave Kate a shove, and Kate landed on her backside. The squealing pig wiggled out of her grasp. Flora raised her arms above her head in a gesture of victory.

Kate stood up and put her hands on her hips. "Reverend Downing, she should be disqualified."

"For what? Nobody said anything about rules," Rita shouted. Screeching like a banshee, Rita dived at Rose, but she stepped aside adroitly, and the prostitute flopped to the ground amidst the pigs, sending the four frightened animals scurrying in all directions.

Amused, Kate looked down at the two women in the dirt. "Have you ladies had enough?" she asked.

"Not on your life, ya skinny-ass biscuit pusher," Rita yelled.

"Oh, my," the Reverend said, shocked. "Dear ladies, we must not get profane."

The spectators were hooting and hollering. Some had begun making bets as to the outcome.

A gaping Everett Billings said, "Miss Dubois, Miss McDermott. This is no way for a lady to act."

"You're telling me," Rose declared. She glared at Zach. "I've had just about enough of making a spectacle of myself. If you want to win those stupid tickets, you can very well climb in here and catch one of these pigs yourself!"

"But that's not in the rules, Miss Dubois," the Reverend said.

"Didn't you hear, Reverend Downing, there aren't any rules," Rose declared.

Kate went over to the fence. "Souee-e-e-e," she called.

Grunting, the four piglets scurried over to her. Kate bent down, picked up one of them, and handed it to Rose. "Be my guest."

"How did you do that?"

"That's a pig's feeding call." Kate picked up another pig. "After you, my dear."

Rose crawled through the fence, and Kate followed. The other two pigs scattered when Rita and Flora made a grab for them.

The crowd broke into laughter as the two women continued to pursue the pigs, sputtering expletives as they crawled on their hands and knees in the dirt. Disgusted, they finally stood up and trudged over to the fence.

Zach gallantly stepped forward and put out his hands. "May I offer you ladies some assistance?"

"Ya sure can," Rita said.

They each took one of his hands, and he helped them over the fence. Then they turned around, gave him a shove, and sent him sprawling on his backside. Shaking their fists at the crowd, they stormed away.

Rose looked at Zach, then at the the two women striding away.

"You know, Kate, there might be some truth in that old adage that no good deed goes unpunished."

Chapter 11

Rose and Kate went back to the boardinghouse to wash up. It was nearing sunset by the time they returned to the site of the celebration.

"I don't remember seeing that before," Rose said, pointing to a brightly painted wagon set in the shade of a tree. "Let's take a closer look."

A gypsy woman with a gold loop dangling from one ear and a bright red scarf tied around her long, dark hair leaned against the wagon smoking a cigarette.

She called out to them. "Hey, young beauties, you vant Celina to predict zour futures?"

"Let's do it," Rose said.

Kate hung back. "I'm not so sure I want to know my future."

"It'll be fun, Kate. Besides, she'll probably just tell us we'll marry, have a dozen children, and live long lives."

"But Rose, take a good look at her; I don't think she's bathed in months."

Rose grabbed Kate's hand and tugged her toward the wagon. "Oh, don't be such a spoilsport."

"All right, but I'll make a prediction right now: we'll probably catch her fleas."

"How much do you charge, Celina?" Rose asked.

"Celina vill read both of zour palms for vun dollar," she said in a thick accent. She motioned for them to follow her into the wagon.

"Za cards for anozher fifty centz."

"Why would our futures be different if we pay more for the reading?" Kate asked as Rose dug out the necessary coins.

The gypsy tucked the money in her pocket, then closed the door behind them. The windowless wagon was cast into darkness except for a single candle flickering on the table. A punguent mix of garlic and stale air blended with the sweet scent of incense, stinging the nostrils.

"I think I'm going to throw up," Kate whispered.

"Shhh," Rose warned. "She'll hear you."

"Celina hears all and knoz all," the gypsy said. "So vhich of you to be firzt?"

"I do not intend to have my fortune read," Kate said.

"Zhen vhy you come? You vait outside."

"We prefer to remain together," Rose added quickly.

There were only two chairs in the wagon, and the

gypsy pointed to one. "You zit," she said to Rose. Nodding toward a cot in the corner, she said to Kate, "And you vait there."

Kate held her ground. "If you don't mind, I'll just stand."

Celina gave Kate a disgruntled look. "Iz okay. But you muzt remain quiet or vill chase avay za spirits."

"I understand," Kate replied. She winked at Rose.

Sitting down opposite her, the gypsy picked up Rose's hand. Pulling it closer to the candle, she peered at it intently. After a series of hmmms, humphs, and uh-huhs, she released it and stared at Rose.

"You've had a hard life, little vun," she said. She picked up a deck of cards.

"I certainly don't need you to tell me that," Rose said, amused.

The woman stared unwaveringly as she slowly shuffled the cards, then pushed the deck toward Rose. "Cut zhem."

Celina's ambivalent stare was making her so nervous that Rose wished she'd listened to Kate and not been so impulsive. This whole thing was a mistake.

Celina laid out a row of cards on the table, and after several seconds glanced up with a wily smile. "Aha! You're a sly vun, my lovely. I zee two men in your life: vun iz dark and za other iz light."

The dark man had to be Zach. Could the light one be Stephen Rayburn? She hoped that Celina was even half as good as she claimed to be, because Rose certainly was interested in hearing the outcome.

Celina laid down another row of cards and studied them. Her glance shifted up to meet Rose's inquisitive look.

"I zee treachery and deceit by zhose you trust." She turned over another card. "And danger. Beware, my lovely."

Rose glanced furtively at Kate and saw that her friend was glaring indignantly at the gypsy.

A chilling silence engulfed the interior of the wagon as Celina dealt out another row of cards. Rose held her breath, waiting to hear the next disturbing message. Celina's expressive face sobered into a grim line and her eyes darkened with distress. Suddenly she brushed aside the cards. "Zhat is all. Celina tires now, she can do no more."

A warning voice pounded in Rose's head. *Don't ask. Don't ask. Get out of here before it's too late . . . before you hear something that you don't want to know.*

But curiosity overcame caution. Swallowing the lump that had risen in her throat, Rose asked, "What is it, Celina? What did you see that you aren't telling me?"

The gypsy's hands were trembling as she gathered up the cards. "Vaz nothin'." She lowered her head. "Celina haz told you all zat she zaw."

"No, you're concealing something. Look at me, Celina. What did you see in those last cards?"

Celina slowly raised her head. "I zaw za face of death."

Rose felt a chilling shiver down her spine. "Whose death? Mine?"

"Celina haz told you all she knoz. You go now."

"You have no business scaring her like this with

your falsehoods," Kate lashed out angrily. "Come on, honey." She helped Rose to her feet. "You'll feel better once we're out of here."

Celina stared blankly at them, then spoke slowly and ominously. "Perhapz she vill feel better outzide, but vhereever she goez, zhere iz no ezcape from deztiny."

Too dazed to offer any resistance, Rose let Kate lead her to the door. Her mind spun with frightening visions. Once outside she took a deep breath, and her trembling began to lessen. But the warning was too haunting to ignore. The day had been ruined for her.

"Kate, I'm not in the mood for any more *fun*. I think I'll go back to my room."

"Nonsense, Rose, we just came from there. The evening activities are just beginning. You aren't going to let that fake clairvoyant spoil the rest of the night, are you?"

"She appeared to be genuinely upset, Kate."

"So what? That just means she's a better actress than fortune-teller, honey."

"Kate, do you think people can really predict the future?"

Kate linked her arm through Rose's. "Only God knows people's destinies, Rose. You can't put any stock in what that old woman said. Besides, every fortune-teller predicts life and death. It's a safe subject, because everyone has experienced it within their own families."

"More of that Midwestern logic of yours, I suppose," Rose chided.

"But I will admit that some of what she said is

true—especially the part about a dark man in your life. Here he comes now."

Rose looked up. Looking fresh and clean in a change of clothing, Zach MacKenzie was headed straight for them.

"There you are; I've been looking for you ladies." He took a longer look at Rose. "You don't look too good, Rose. Aren't you feeling well?"

"She just had her fortune told, and that fake clairvoyant upset her," Kate declared.

"Told you that you wouldn't marry a rich man, did she, Rosie?"

Rose glared at him. "I do not intend to discuss it with you, MacKenzie. And, Kate, I'd appreciate it if you would do the same." She spun on her heel and walked away.

"Rosie, I was only teasing," Zach said as he and Kate followed her. "I'm sorry that whatever she said upset you, but you ought to have more sense than to put any stock in what such people have to say."

Kate nodded. "That's exactly what I've been trying to tell her."

"They're as crooked as bank robbers," Zach said.

Rose stopped abruptly. "I'm sure you'd know more about that profession than I do."

"I think I'll let you two battle this out alone," Kate said. "I see the other girls over at the circus tent. 'Bye." She left before Rose could utter a protest.

"See what you've done now, MacKenzie?"

He looked at her with utter astonishment. "Me! What did I do?"

"You've chased Kate away."

"Kate is a discreet woman. And her sound judgment has never been more prudent than now: two's company; three's a crowd."

"Then take your own advice and leave. Goodbye." She headed for the circle of Harvey Girls.

Rose hadn't taken more than two steps when he caught up with her and grabbed her hand. "Come on, Rosie. We're here to have fun. The final event of the contest is due to start in an hour. We've gotten this far, so why drop out now?"

"Don't talk to me about any more contests, Zach."

"This one's nothing like the last one. We're given clues, and all we have to do is find the items within a specified time. Kate and Billings are the only couple besides us still in the running."

"Free tickets to a circus are not worth it, MacKenzie."

"How about a free chicken dinner?"

"What would I have to do to get that? Wring its neck?"

He grinned. "No, I'll buy. We have time to eat before the contest begins." He watched with amused anticipation as she considered.

"Well, all right."

"Then let's go, honey." He tucked her arm in his and led her to a booth serving fried chicken and potato salad.

As much as she hated to admit it, Zach could make everything fun, even drinking mugs of foamy root beer while eating cold chicken and warm potato salad. Too soon, it was time for the contest.

When they reached the booth, Kate and Everett

Billings were waiting. The other two couples had been disqualified as a result of Rita and Flora leaving without catching a pig. Each remaining couple was given a pink slip of paper by the Reverend Downing.

"There are three parts to this contest," he said. "In honor of the holiday, each clue is given on red, white, or blue paper. You have to stretch your imaginations and think of this pink as being red." The remark brought some polite tittering. "Of course," the pastor continued, "you're going to have to stretch your imaginations even more to be the winner. When you solve this clue, bring the item back here and I'll give you the next one, then the third in the same way. The contest is officially over at ten o'-clock. Is that clear to everyone?"

Amidst nods of agreement from the men, Pastor Downing said, "As you're all aware, the circus has donated front-row tickets to the wining couple, and Mrs. Downing has graciously offered jars of her spiced apples as consolation prizes to the losers. Good luck to all of you."

With heads together, Rose and Zach read the pink slip.

To send all our heads into a whirl,
Bring us a picture of an All-American girl.

"That's easy, Rosie. You're an All-American girl. Do you have a picture of yourself?"

"I think that's a little too easy, Zach. I'm sure they have something more difficult in mind."

"Hmmm." He thought for a minute, as did Rose.

"I bet I know what it means!" he said. "When I was in the barbershop the other day, I was paging through *Life* magazine. There was a picture of a woman painted by some artist named Gibson."

"Oh, I've heard of that: the Gibson Girl. He's painted other pictures of her," Rose said.

"Yeah. The article said she's considered the 'All-American Girl,' and that must be where the preacher got the idea. He probably read the magazine, too. Don't suppose you or the other gals have a copy of *Life*?"

Rose shook her head. "No, we pass around our magazines, and *Life* wasn't among them."

"I know where there's one for sure," he said.

"You mean the barbershop? We can't just break into that barbershop and steal a magazine," she said, scandalized.

"We aren't going to *steal* the magazine; we're just going to remove a page from it."

"You're splitting hairs, MacKenzie."

"Come on, Rosie, it's the difference between circus tickets and spiced apples."

"You don't even know if you're right," she argued. "Reverend Downing may have had someone else in mind."

"No. It's that Gibson Girl; I'm sure of it. Let's get to the barbershop. I'll figure out a way to break in."

"That's just what I'm afraid of, MacKenzie."

He took her hand and hurried down the street to the barbershop. "Dammit," he cursed, after he tried the door and found it locked.

"What did you expect?" Rose said. She folded

her arms across her chest and leaned against the building. "What now?"

"We've got to get in there." He looked around in desperation.

"What do you mean *we*, MacKenzie? Considering your profession, I'd think you'd be an expert at illegally breaking into buildings and banks."

He glanced askance at her. "I don't rob banks." Glancing above them, he suddenly smiled. "There's an open window up there. I'll hoist you up, and you can climb in the window and then go downstairs and get the picture. It's in about the middle of the magazine."

"Do you actually believe I'd enter someone's house illegally just to win a silly contest?"

"It's all good, clean fun, Rosie. No one will think the worse of it."

"Has it occurred to you that someone may be sleeping in that room upstairs?"

"You know as well as I that everyone is at that celebration waiting for the fireworks to start."

"They'll start, all right, if we're caught breaking into this house."

"No one will even know."

Rose couldn't believe she let him hoist her to his shoulders. Before she could find a logical explanation, she found herself sitting on his shoulders and stretching her arms to reach the windowsill.

"I'm not high enough to climb in," she said.

"I'll fix that." He pulled off her shoes.

"What are you doing?"

"Now you can stand on my shoulders."

Rose grinned. "You should have gotten one of

those circus acrobats to be your partner. I'm going to end up killing myself over these darn tickets."

"If so, Rosie, I'll think of you while I'm enjoying the show . . . Ouch!" he yelled, when her knee dug into his shoulder blade as she shifted her position. Unfortunately, her gown was now bunched under her knee and she couldn't stand up. After several seconds struggling to free her foot out from beneath her gown, she managed to get her foot on his shoulder and hoist herself through the window.

Moonlight enabled her to see a doorway opposite, and a cat eyed her curiously as she passed it on her way downstairs. "Sure glad you're not a dog, kitty. I don't think MacKenzie took that possibility into consideration when he planned this heist."

The cat hissed at her.

After trying several doors, she finally found the one that opened into the barbershop. Rose located the magazines and carried them over to a large window to enable her to read the titles. She found the one she was looking for, flipped it open, and lo and behold, there was a picture of the Gibson Girl, just as Zach had said. She pulled out the page, folded it carefully, and put it into her pocket. Then Rose replaced the magazines on the table just as she'd found them and hurried back upstairs. The cat hadn't budged, and its yellow eyes glowed in the dark like beacons, following her every move.

"I won't tell anyone if you don't," she murmured as she passed by.

It hissed again.

Leaning out the window, she called, "Okay, what now, MacKenzie? How do I get down?"

"Just drop down. I'll catch you."

Rose had climbed out plenty of windows in her youth to evade paying rent, but she had her doubts about Zach catching her. However, she heard voices and the sound of laughter and knew someone was approaching.

Quickly climbing out, she lowered her legs and clung by her fingertips for several seconds. Then, closing her eyes, she let go. A strong pair of arms closed around her before she hit the ground.

"Did you get it?" Zach asked.

She opened her eyes. "Got it!"

He hugged her and gave her a big kiss on the cheek. "I knew you could do it, Rosie."

No doubt about it: she was beginning to enjoy this contest.

Chapter 12

❦❦❦

"**M**iss Dubois and Mr. MacKenzie, you are the first couple to figure out the correct answer," the Reverend Downing said when they returned with the picture. "Isn't that right, Grace?"

Beaming, his wife nodded. "Reverend Downing thought the clue was too easy, but I knew it would be a challenge."

Rose couldn't believe Zach could look them in the eye when he said innocently, "We were fortunate enough to have access to a *Life* magazine."

"Good luck on this one," the Reverend Downing said, and handed Zach the white slip of paper.

They walked over to a bench and sat down to read it.

An exceptional value, worth one's salt.
Even the parrot shouts it out.

"Oh, this is simple!" Rose exclaimed. "Polly wants a cracker."

"What?"

"Polly wants a cracker," she repeated. "That's what the parrot is saying on the box of Premium Saltines."

"I'll take your word for it. Does this mean we'll have to break into the general store?"

"Not this time." She dug into her pocket and held up a key. "This is the key to the solution of the second clue. The key to my boardinghouse, where in turn I have a key to the restaurant, where I know we can find a box of Premium Saltines."

"Then what are we waiting for, Rosie?"

"For you to tell me what a smart partner you picked for this contest."

He stood up and pulled her to her feet, then tucked her arm through his. "Miss Dubois, did I mention how smart I am for picking such a smart partner for this contest?"

Laughing like children, they hurried to her boardinghouse.

Ten minutes later, a box of Premium Saltines in hand, they hurried back to the booth. "I can't believe how easy this one was," Rose said. "I do hope Reverend Downing will return the crackers, though, or Andre and Colette will be very surprised to find them gone when they go to serve the soup tomorrow—not to mention what Mr. Billings will say."

"Can't you explain it to them?"

"Andre and Colette don't speak a word of English, and I can't speak French."

"Yet you were raised in New Orleans."

"Not everyone there speaks French, MacKenzie. Especially in the section that I was raised in."

"Too bad they aren't Mexican. I speak that real well."

"In addition to your ability to speak Horse, and some Snake, no doubt, since you could talk one out of its skin. But that doesn't help my situation, does it?"

"Maybe not, but it might come in handy if you want a pair of fancy snakeskin boots," he teased.

"I'll keep it in mind."

The Downings were surprised to see them back so soon.

"I told you, Matthew, that clue was too easy," Grace Downing said.

"I'm afraid you were right, my dear. I thought it was so clever, too," the Reverend said desolately.

Rose spoke up quickly. "Actually, it was very clever, Reverend Downing. I had the advantage of working in a restaurant that serves that brand of crackers."

"That's right, sir. I never heard of them before, so I never would have guessed the clue."

The minister's spirits clearly lifted immediately, and he said, "I am sure you young people won't find this final clue so easily solved. Once again, good luck."

"And win or lose, Mr. MacKenzie, I shall give you a jar of my spiced apples," Grace Downing said.

"That's mighty generous of you, ma'am. I was tempted to lose just to get a jar. From the time I rode into Brimstone, I've heard about the preacher's wife's sweet-tasting spiced apples."

"Thank you, young man," Grace Downing said, flustered with pleasure. "I shall make certain you get a jar."

"My cup runneth over, ma'am," Zach replied, tipping a finger to his hat.

Rose yanked him away. "Zach MacKenzie, you should be ashamed of yourself," she hissed. "You truly are a snake charmer. You ought to join this circus."

"I *do* like spiced apples, Rose. Only trouble is, no one makes them as good as my ma."

"Of course. An unbiased opinion, Mackenzie. Let's read the clue."

He unfolded the blue slip.

It has shimmering gems and shorter hems.
Golden watches and velvet sacks.
"Satisfaction or Your Money Back."

Rose regarded it reflectively. "This is much harder. Hmmm, shortened hems, velvet sacks."

"What in hell is a velvet sack?" he asked.

"I believe it's a man's jacket?"

"A velvet jacket!" He shoved his Stetson to the top of his forehead. "Not in Texas, honey."

"I'm sure that shortened hems refers to women's gowns and that velvet sacks refers to men's jackets."

"Sounds like something to do with a tailor, then?"

"A fancy dressmaker might put gems or beads on a gown, but what about the golden watch?"

"That last line is in quotation marks. That would mean it's a direct quote," Zach said.

" 'Satisfaction or Your Money Back.' I know I've read that before. Now, where was it?" Rose repeated the line over and over again, searching for one of the many trivial facts that one tucks away in memory, never expecting to draw upon it again. Suddenly it came to her. "A catalog! I read it last year in an old catalog that Em had."

"Which one?"

"Let me think—she had several. It was a . . . Sears catalog. That's it, Zach," she cried out excitedly. "That's the Sears motto."

"Do you still have the catalog?"

"Heavens, no. It was a couple years old. And you know where old catalogs usually end up."

"In outhouses. So let's go."

Rose looked at him with revulsion. "You don't mean—"

"That's right, honey. Looks like we're going to have to make the rounds of the latrines in town."

"I'll come with you, but you can check them out yourself. You're the one who wants the circus tickets."

He grasped her by the shoulders and looked down at her. "It's gone beyond circus tickets, Rose. It's all about winning now." He looked so serious, she could hardly keep from laughing. He released her and grabbed her hand. "Let's find us a Sears catalog."

In a short time, they'd searched every outhouse

in Brimstone. Zach found one catalog from Montgomery Ward, a half dozen grain and seed ones, and even an early catalog from a Harrods in London, England. But no Sears catalog.

Emerging from the latest outhouse, Zach shook his head. "No luck."

"This is ridiculous, Zach. Let's forget about it."

"No, I remember seeing another outhouse on the south end of town that looked abandoned. We'll give that one a try."

"If we don't have any luck there, I'm giving up. We're missing the celebration by doing this, and it must almost be time for the fireworks. If you want to keep on, that's your business, but after the next one I'm through."

"Okay, Rosie. One more, then we'll go back and enjoy the celebration."

The outhouse was set on the top of a hill near an abandoned, broken-down shack. Exposed to wind, rain, and sandstorms, its boards were rotting, and several slats were missing. The door of the latrine clung as precariously to its hinges as the structure did to the hillside.

"I wouldn't go into that dirty old thing," Rose warned. "Who knows what might have crawled into there since it was abandoned?"

"The door's hooked shut," Zach said. "Nothing could get in."

"A hook on a door isn't going to keep out spiders and bugs, and Lord only knows what else might have crawled through those missing slats. Don't say I didn't warn you," she said, stepping away as Zach proceeded to unhook the clasp and enter.

He emerged seconds later waving a catalog.

"Is it a Sears?" she asked hopefully.

"It was too dark in there to see."

Just then they heard men's voices raised in argument. Zach recognized them at once. "Sounds like Tait and Bull."

"Let's get out of here," she said. "I don't want any scene with them."

He grabbed her hand and they ran over to conceal themselves in some nearby bushes.

The two men stopped in front of the outhouse. Tait's speech was slurred in drunkenness. "Do ya hear me?"

"Yeah, yeah, I hear ya," Bull grumbled. "We'll get it done before Rayburn gets back."

"Then get goin'. Where's MacKenzie?"

Rose glanced up at Zach. He put his finger to his lips, cautioning her to remain silent.

"Ain't seen him," Bull said.

"Find him and take him with you."

"Okay." Bull started to leave.

"Wait up. I gotta piss," Tait said.

"Ya don't need my help for that," Bull said, and walked on.

Grumbling, Tait staggered into the outhouse.

Zach grinned down at her, his eyes gleaming with mischief. "This is too good to pass up," he whispered.

Guessing his intent, Rose nodded.

He handed her the catalog. "Wait here."

Zach sped over to the outhouse, slammed the door, and hooked it shut.

"Hey, what in hell's goin' on?" Tait bellowed as

Zach raced back to her. "Bull, is that you? Open this damn door." The whole structure began to shake as Tait kicked at the door to get out. Rose clamped her hand over her mouth to stifle the sound of her laughter.

Just as the door broke loose from the hinges, the latrine broke loose from the hilltop. Amidst the sound of splintering wood and vile curses, Tait and the outhouse tumbled down the hill and ended in a heap several yards below. Snorting like a maddened bull, vowing vengeance on whoever had done it, Tait emerged from the pile of rubble, pulled up his pants, and stomped up over the hill.

Zach grabbed Rose's hand and they raced away, laughing so hard they could barely run. Finally, safely out of sight and earshot, they stumbled to a stop, sank down on the ground, and lay side by side, gasping for breath.

"I haven't laughed so hard in my life," Rose finally managed to say.

"I wish we could have seen his face," Zach said.

"I saw enough of him as it was." Rose started to laugh again. "You think he saw us?"

Zach shook his head. "He couldn't have. The bushes concealed us."

"What a glorious moment." Several giggles escaped her, then unable to hold it back, she burst into laughter again.

Zach rolled over and smiled down at her, and as their gazes met, the laughter in his eyes slowly gave way to the stirring of arousal.

"You smell wonderful, Rosie. Like a flower garden."

She swallowed hard, as aware of his masculinity as he was of her femininity. "I suspect you've been sniffing too many outhouses lately, MacKenzie."

He drew a deep breath and buried his head in the thickness of her hair. "No, honey. You're wearing my favorite fragrance." He raised his head and smiled tenderly at her. "It's called Rosie."

The next move was inevitable. He lowered his head; she parted her lips. As always, his kiss sent sweet shocks of passion racing through her.

"You know this is a mistake, Zach," she murmured when breathlessness forced them apart.

"Sure it is—but what's a few kisses between friends?"

His next kiss was more demanding.

Both of them were succumbing to the danger that always threatened when they were together, but he was right. It *did* feel so good. It always felt so good. Rose wanted to let him go on kissing her forever, but one of them had to look beyond the moment.

She broke off the kiss. "The catalog, Zach. I thought you wanted to win those circus tickets," she said breathlessly.

"To hell with the tickets," he said, and slid a trail of moist, warm kisses along her neck before settling his lips into the hollow of her throat. Instinctively, her body arched against him.

Rose knew if she didn't stop him right now, there'd be no stopping him from taking her right there in the grass. She wanted it so badly, but she'd regret it the rest of her life. He'd broken off such a dangerous moment between them once before; it was up to her this time.

Rallying all her will, she put her hands on his chest and shoved him off her. Sitting up, she said, "Let's see that catalog."

Groaning, Zach lay back. "You're a heartless woman, Rosie. A beautiful, redheaded, heartless woman."

He sat up and handed her the catalog.

She flipped open the cover. "This is it, Zach! See, 'Satisfaction or Your Money Back,' " she read aloud.

"Great." He flopped down on his back, his arms outstretched at his sides. "Give me strength, Lord."

Rose stood up and brushed herself off. "Come on, Zach. There's a time limit, remember? And the fireworks will start soon."

"Seen fireworks once, seen them all," he said.

"What about those circus tickets? You were the one who wanted them."

"We know we won; that's all that matters. Besides, seen one circus—"

"You've seen them all," she finished. "Let's go, MacKenzie." She reached out a hand to help him to his feet.

"All right, you merciless minx, we'll go and collect our prize."

"Congratulations, you're the undisputed winner," the Reverend Downing said when they gave him the Sears catalog. "Dear Miss McDermott and Mr. Billings failed to solve even the first clue."

I bet! Rose thought. *Kate just figured out a way of not having to go on with the contest. Wait until I see her!*

"And I do hope you enjoy the circus," the pastor said, handing Zach the tickets.

Zach tucked them into his shirt pocket. "Thank you, sir, I'm sure we will."

"And the best news is that between the contest and the sale of Mrs. Downing's spiced apples, we raised over a hundred dollars for charity from this booth alone."

"That's wonderful—and we certainly enjoyed the contest," Rose said.

Grace Downing handed Zach a jar of the apples. "Here you are, Mr. MacKenzie. I hope you'll enjoy them."

"I know I will, ma'am."

As they searched for a good spot to enjoy the aerial display, Zach said, "Rose, wait here. I want to put this jar in my saddlebags. I'll be right back."

She watched him stop and speak to an older man, and recognized him as the man they had met on the trail. They spoke for a few minutes and then, to her surprise, they walked away together.

After waiting several minutes, Rose spied Kate and the other girls across the fairground and decided to join them. Zach could find her easily if he tried. Seeking a shortcut, she cut through the darkened area near the circus tent where the wagons and animal cages were kept.

A resounding boom split the air. Luminous streamers of Roman candles soared heavenward and burst into a shimmering glow of incandescent brilliance against the dark sky. A chorus of oohs and ahs—and scattered wails from startled babies—rose from the throng of spectators.

And then Rose heard a low, feral growl.

Chapter 13

Rose spun around, and by the luminous radiance of the fireworks she saw a tiger leap with fearsome agility from its cage to the bed of a wagon mere yards away from where she stood. Its eyes glittered with an amber glow.

Her scream of terror was swallowed by the roar of the crowd as another burst of color illuminated the sky. Another low growl emanated from the huge cat, a sound so savage the hair on her arms stood on end.

Rose stared transfixed at the huge cat, her heart hammering at her chest. Her instinct was to bolt, but her legs were trembling too much to move. It was a nightmare. One second she'd be in darkness, and the next the animal would appear in a misty glow swirling around its head. The odor of sulfur stung her nostrils, the explosive sound of the fireworks thundered in her ears, and flashes of the jungle beast poised to spring paralyzed her. She knew if she attempted to move, the tiger would spring.

Suddenly Zach's voice cut through her frozen state. "Rose, don't move. I'm right behind you, but I'm not sure my Colt will bring down a cat that size before it could reach you. I need a perfect shot, so I have to get a better angle for it."

"I'm so scared, Zach," she quavered

"I know, honey, but you're doing fine. Just stay calm."

Her head began to spin, and the cat became a blurred image. "I think I'm going to faint."

"You're not going to faint. Take a couple of deep breaths and think of that cat as Jess Tait with his pants down."

"Stop it, Zach, or you'll start me laughing."

She heard the cock of his pistol and knew he was getting ready to take his shot.

Suddenly a man shouted, "Don't shoot! Don't shoot!" Rose didn't dare turn her head to see who it was. "Back, Sinbad! Back, boy."

Two men appeared in her periphery and moved slowly toward the animal. The tiger snarled in protest and bared its fangs.

"Back, boy. Back, Sinbad." The men passed Rose, carrying long poles, and the tiger's amber gaze shifted to them.

When a firm pair of hands grasped her shoulders, her knees buckled, but Zach prevented her from collapsing. She slumped against him and he slipped an arm down to her waist, keeping his pistol trained on the tiger.

The cat gave another defiant snarl, then leaped back into its cage and stretched out in the corner. One of the men slammed the door shut.

"Who in hell left that cage unlocked?" the other man demanded.

"I swear I locked it up after the last show, boss," the roustabout said. "Hey, look at this: the padlock's broken. How do ya figure that happened?"

"You okay, Rosie?" Zach asked.

Rose nodded. "I will be, as soon as my knees stop shaking."

"Take deep breaths. I'll be right back—I want to take a closer look at that padlock."

"You can be sure I'm not going anywhere near that cage."

"Will you look at this lock?" the trainer said when Zach joined them. "The hinge is still attached to the wood; this padlock was broken open from the outside. Looks to me like somebody with a rotten sense of humor broke the lock, then took off."

"Has the cat ever gotten loose and harmed anyone before?" Zach asked.

"Nope. I think those fireworks spooked him. Sinbad's pretty docile; I've raised him from a cub. He's gotten loose a time or two when someone left his cage unlocked, but he's never harmed anyone."

"Let's not mention your suspicions to Miss Dubois. She's had a big enough scare already."

"Gotcha," the man said, nodding. He walked over to where Rose was leaning against a building. "Sorry about the accident, miss. Thank goodness there was no harm done." He pulled two tickets out of his pocket and handed them to her. "Here's front-row tickets to the performance. It's about to start, now that the fireworks have ended."

Rose stared at the tickets, then at Zach, then back to the tickets. "I'll take them," Zach said. "Here come Kate and the other girls. Maybe they'd like to see the show."

"Oh, Rose, weren't those fireworks beautiful," Kate said. Upon seeing Rose's stricken face, she exclaimed, "What's wrong? You look like you've just seen a ghost."

Zach handed the four tickets to Kate. "Show's about to start; hope you gals like the performance. I think Rose has seen all the circus she wants to for one night."

She stood numbly as he ushered the confused women toward the circus tent.

Zach tried to cheer her up as they walked back to her boardinghouse, but Rose still felt too shaken. They stopped at the front door.

"This has been a fun day, Rosie. I'm sorry it ended on such a bad note."

"Somehow, being with you always ends in trouble." She shook her head. "I'll probably have nightmares tonight."

He grinned mischievously. "I'll be glad to stay and make sure you have sweet dreams."

"I'm not that naive, MacKenzie."

He kissed her on the forehead. "Can't blame me for trying. Good night, Rose."

She opened the door, and then looked back. "Zach, thanks. It *was* a fun day."

He smiled at her. "You're great company, Rosie."

And so are you, Zach. So are you.

She was still smiling when she climbed into bed. Today *had* been fun, except for the fortune-teller and that jungle cat. She felt like a cat herself—using up her nine lives. With the many narrow escapes she'd had in the short time she'd been in Brimstone, those lives were slipping by swiftly.

From the time Zach had joined her that evening, she hadn't given any thought to the gypsy's words. She didn't know if the warning referred to her death or someone else's. *Heck, Rose, you don't even know if you can believe anything she said. Kate was right: life and death occur in everyone's life.*

And what about Zach? She could no longer tell herself that when the time came, she would forget him. Not when the sight of him made her heart skip a beat. She had always scoffed at that silly expression, but it was true. Every time she saw him, for an instant she'd hold her breath. And when he kissed her, it was so easy to forget everything but the excitement of his kiss.

She turned off the lamp, rolled over, and closed her eyes. *Face it, Rose: Zach MacKenzie is a bigger threat to you than that jungle cat could ever be.*

From the shadows outside Rose's window, Zach saw her bedroom light extinguished. He didn't believe in coincidence; whoever had broken the padlock on that cage had intended for Rose to be harmed. It had to have been Jess Tait. The drunken madman was crazy enough to endanger other women and children to satisfy his desire for revenge. He had to be stopped.

So Zach decided to stay around for a while, in case Tait had any other crazy ideas.

Early the next morning, Rose was wakened by Mrs. White rapping on her door.

"You better get to the drawing room, Rose," she said. "Someone shot at Andrea and Melanie on their way to the Wilson farm this morning."

"Oh, good Lord! Are they hurt?"

"No, but they're pretty well shaken up. I've got a pot of tea brewing."

Snatching her robe from the bed, Rose entered the drawing room to find Melanie sobbing and a pale and shaken Andrea. When Rose put her arms around the sobbing young girl, Melanie buried her head against Rose's shoulder.

"There, there, honey. You're safe now."

"For how long?" Melanie cried out between sobs.

"What happened, Andrea?" Rose continued to pat Melanie in an effort to soothe her.

"I was driving and we were on our way to the farm when suddenly someone began shooting at us. I tried my best to keep control of the buggy." It was easy to see the poor girl was on the verge of breaking down. Rose passed Melanie over to Kate, who'd entered with Aubrey, and went over to Andrea and held her hands.

"Were either of you hurt?"

"Just scared."

"Why are we even here in this town?" Melanie cried out, tears streaking her cheeks. "This is a horrible place, and most people don't even want us here."

"She's right, Rose," Aubrey said. "I didn't become a Harvey Girl to live in a place where there's no law. You can count the respectable people in this town on one hand."

"All the town needs is an honest sheriff and deputy," Kate said. "That would drive the lawless element out of Brimstone."

"Well, if there's no change by the time my six months' service is completed, I'm leaving," Aubrey declared.

"So am I," Melanie said. "Mr. Harvey has a responsibility to station us in a town where it's safe to walk the streets."

Mrs. White came in carrying a tea tray. "I've sent for the sheriff."

"What good will he do?" Aubrey grumbled. "He probably wants us out of here as much as anyone."

"Maybe we'd be smart to hire our own protection," Kate suggested.

"Why should we have to?" Aubrey questioned. "I think it's Mr. Harvey's responsibility to do that."

Andrea stood up and walked to the door. "I think he should just forget Brimstone and move on to a different town. If the decent people here had any sense, they'd all move out, too."

Melanie and Aubrey got up to leave with Andrea. "We're sorry, Rose," Aubrey said, "but we've talked about this before. Another incident, and the three of us are leaving."

"Is that how you feel too, Kate?" Rose asked,

when the three girls left to return to their rooms.

"I haven't made up my mind. But you must admit it's time to leave when it goes beyond harassment and they start shooting at you." She left on that note.

"Or time to start shooting back," Rose murmured.

By the time the girls dressed and were ready to leave for work, the sheriff still had not arrived on the scene.

There were no smiles on the girls' faces as they served the morning meal; all were preoccupied with the danger.

Rose had to talk to Zach. There was no doubt in her mind that Jess Tait was the culprit behind the shooting, but she knew Zach would help her despite his association with the gang. If she had to, she'd even ride out to the Lazy R to see him. It would be difficult to manage, but somehow she'd figure out something.

She'd intended to go out to the ranch in the afternoon, but Mr. Billings detained her to discuss the threat of the girls leaving Brimstone. She couldn't offer him any solution at the moment, and by the time they finished talking, it was too late to consider driving out to the ranch.

The tension eased slightly among the girls by the time they'd finished serving dinner; however, they all departed the restaurant together.

When they stepped outside, Rose saw Zach. She couldn't believe the good fortune. Excusing herself, she hurried over to him.

"Zach, I need a favor."

"What is it?"

"Will you teach me how to shoot a gun? This morning on the way to the Wilson farm, someone shot at Andrea and Melanie."

He looked shocked. "Were they hurt?"

"Just shaken up. The horses bolted, but Andrea managed to keep the buggy from tipping over."

"Did they see who did it?"

She shook her head. "No. Apparently it happened too quickly. She managed to turn the buggy and come back to town. I doubt they even had a chance to look behind them."

He folded his arms across his chest. "And what do you expect to do with a gun?"

"Shoot back."

"Uh-huh. That's a good way to get yourself killed."

"You shot back when it happened to us," she argued.

"Rose, that's a ridiculous comparison."

"What are we supposed to do, just let whoever this is pick us off like fish in a barrel? He wants us out of town, and he'll get what he wants if we let him get away with it. You're the only one I can turn to. I thought you were my friend, Zach."

"I am your friend, Rose—so I'll do it. But it's against my better judgment."

Uh-oh! He had his arms folded across his chest and had called her Rose twice in a row.

She pushed her luck. "Could we do it now?" He looked reluctant, but said, "I'll get you a mount, and we'll ride out where we'll have more privacy."

"Thank you, Zach. But . . . will you make that a

buggy? My body's just stopped aching from the riding lesson."

"All right. I'll be right back."

She hoped her smile looked as grateful as she felt. "I'll wait for you at my boardinghouse." He nodded and left her. Rose ran down to the house and quickly changed her clothes. She was waiting for him when he came back with a buggy.

They rode a safe distance from town, then Zach reined up. "It'll soon be dark, so this lesson will have to be brief." He pulled out his pistol. "This is a Colt .45," he said, and spun the chamber. "As you can see, it holds six cartridges. You cock the hammer and the chamber will revolve as you squeeze the trigger."

"Hammer?" she asked.

"This metal head that looks like the head of a hammer." When she nodded, he emptied the shells out of the gun and handed it to her. "The first thing to remember is that a gun is a dangerous tool, Rose, so treat it like one. Get the feel of it. Test its weight in your hand."

Still puzzled by his continued hostility, she slapped the pistol from hand to hand, surprised to discover how heavy the weapon actually was.

"Okay, now cock the gun by pressing the hammer back with your thumb until you feel it lock."

She found that was easier said than done. It took her several attempts before she succeeded in locking it.

"Remember, Rose, once you cock that gun, it can go off easily. Now release the hammer so that the weapon isn't ready to fire, because you're about to load it."

Putting cartridges into the chamber turned it into a lethal weapon. Rose determinedly swallowed the lump in her throat when he handed her six cartridges.

"Just slide one into each empty chamber. You should always be aware of how many bullets are in the gun. And I'll give you the same advice my father gave to me when he taught me how to shoot: never point a gun at anyone unless you're prepared to fire it, and always reload your pistol after you've used it. A half-empty chamber can leave you one bullet short when you need it the most."

"I shall keep that advice foremost in my mind."

"Now, to make the weapon useful, you have to have a good eye and steady hand. Aim at that tree trunk and see if you can hit it. It's a lot larger than the red circle on the target."

"Will you cut me some slack, MacKenzie?" she snapped. "We won that darn contest, didn't we?"

She cocked the gun, took careful aim, and fired. The bullet hit the ground at the base of the tree next to the one she was aiming at.

The corners of his lips twitched. "You're going to have to work on this. Try it again."

He moved behind her, and she sensed his nearness even before he put his arms around her. "Now, hold your arm steady and point the pistol at the tree." He closed his hand over hers to steady her aim.

She loved feeling the warmth and strength of his hands. Blushing, she remembered the touch of them on her breasts. Then he stooped enough to help her line up the shot, and their cheeks touched. She was tempted to turn in the circle of his arms and—

"Go ahead, Rose."

His voice jolted her out of her musing. "I'm sorry. What did you say?"

"I said just gently squeeze the trigger."

This time her bullet zipped past the tree. By her sixth try, she managed to hit some leaves on the tree she'd aimed at.

After another six shots, she managed to hit the tree. She sat down with a sense of accomplishment. Zach sat down beside her and took the pistol. He reloaded it, then returned it to its holster.

After a lengthy silence Rose said, "I can't thank you enough, Zach. I don't know why we can't get help from the decent people in the town."

"Ever think they might want to stay alive?"

"Why are you so angry with me, Zach? What did I do?"

"You've got the crazy notion that you and your girlfriends have a chance against gunfighters and outlaws. And how come it doesn't bother you that your fancy boyfriend's not doing anything about it?"

"It *does* bother me. I don't understand how Stephen can ignore the problem. With his position, his influence could help make a big difference in bringing law and order to Brimstone."

"Maybe he has a good reason for not riding to your aid," Zach suggested darkly.

"What reason could he possibly have?"

"Maybe he doesn't have a white horse." Disgusted, he got up and walked over to the buggy. "Or maybe he's not all you think he is."

She jumped to her feet. "What is that supposed to mean?"

"You ever stop to consider that Tait would have been long gone if Rayburn hadn't hired him to hang around here?"

"Stephen was desperate. He had no choice."

"There are plenty of honest cowpokes looking for jobs, Rose."

"You're just jealous, Zach. You're justifying your life by criticizing his."

"And maybe denying the truth is your way of justifying marrying a rich man instead of a poor one."

Rose angrily climbed into the buggy. "Thank you again, Zach. I'm sorry I put you to so much trouble," she said stiffly.

They didn't speak to each other on the way back. He stopped at the boardinghouse and before she climbed out, Rose turned to him.

"I'm sorry we quarreled, Zach."

"So am I. Listen, Rose, while I'm in town I'm staying in Room Four at the Long Horn. If you need me, you can find me there."

"That would start a nice scandal if I walked into the Long Horn looking for you."

"Take the back road—nobody's ever on it—and go to the rear door. It opens into a storage room. Opposite that room is a stairway, and my room's at the end of the hall upstairs."

"Thanks for your offer of help, but I don't think I'll need to sneak into the back doors of saloons, Zach."

"You never know. Take care, Redhead. And remember what I told you: watch your back. Looks like things are starting to heat up around here."

She started up the porch stairs, stopped, and looked back. He was waiting until she reached the door.

Strangely enough, she felt as if it was their final good-bye.

Chapter 14

Early the next morning, Rose got up to make the trip to the Wilson farm. She was not looking forward to the ride. Melanie and Andrea's experience yesterday made her edgy, and she jumped when there was a tap at her window. Anticipating who it might be, she parted the drapes.

"What are you doing here this time of morning, MacKenzie?" she asked.

"Who's riding out for the eggs this morning?"

"Kate and I."

"You gals stay here. I'll do it for you," he said.

"You'll do nothing of the kind, Zach. This is our problem, and we can't run from it. We'll always be intimidated if we do."

"That's a noble attitude, but it can get you

killed. Just once, will you do as I say, Rosie?"

"That's ludicrous—I *always* end up doing what you say. If you insist again on having it your way, I'll tell Kate not to come. But I'm going with you."

"Well, there's no sense in arguing. Let's go, I've got the buggy in the front."

"I'll tell Kate and be right out," she said.

Zach walked back to the buggy. Once Rose got an idea in her head, there was no getting it out. Normally, he liked that about her, because it always led to an exchange between them. But this time he was concerned about her safety. His dad was right: women had to be told the right way about something, or they balked. And the right way was to put the idea in their heads so that they believed they'd thought of it first—especially feisty redheads like Rose.

After last night, they had a lot to talk out. He figured he still held something of an upper hand—even if that hand was getting a little weak to lift. He couldn't believe she'd go through with a crazy scheme like trying to outshoot outlaws.

She came out the door looking as fresh as a morning glory, and wearing that big hat she liked to wear, her hair loose down her back. The more he saw her, the more he wanted her. Like it or not, they were involved, all right. No use in crying over spilled milk.

"It's a shame an armed guard is necessary to get a few eggs," she complained as they rode along.

Ordinarily he'd enjoy the ride sitting next to her, but wondering if any moment someone would take a shot at them kept him on the edge of his seat.

"I'm sure those outlaws you associate with are behind these incidents. Matter of fact, I don't know why I should trust you, since you're one of them."

"Rosie, I am not an outlaw."

"You're the next best thing to one—a drifter."

"Are you going to carp the whole damn trip?" he asked. "Why don't you just relax and listen to the birds chirping?"

"Are you always so crotchety in the mornings, MacKenzie?"

"I *love* mornings!"

She shut up. He knew her grousing was just trying to cover up her nervousness. And if Tait was behind the shootings, she had every right to be nervous. He had it in for these Harvey Girls—particularly Rose. And if Rayburn was linked to Tait in this cattle rustling, as he suspected, Rose would be in even greater danger.

He fretted on that thought until they reached the Wilson farm. The barn doors were closed and barred when they drove up.

"I'm surprised Calvin and Effie didn't come out to greet us," Rose exclaimed. She climbed down from the wagon and walked up to the house. "Mr. Wilson? Mrs. Wilson?" She knocked on the door. When there was no answer, she looked at Zach and shrugged. "They must be gone."

"Would they go away without telling you?" he asked.

"Not likely; they know we come every morning. Come to think of it, I didn't see them at the celebration, either."

Zach began to feel uneasy. He climbed down

from the wagon. "Maybe they simply forgot to tell you they were going away."

"I don't think so. They're too considerate to make us ride out here on a wild-goose chase."

"There's no smoke coming out of the chimney."

Rose looked up at the roof and nodded. "You're right. Do you suppose they're ill?"

"Let's find out." Zach turned the doorknob, and when the door opened, he stepped in. He recognized the stench at once. Lord knows he'd smelled it enough times. "Dear God," he murmured. The old man was in a chair, his head slumped on the table. He'd been shot in the back. His wife lay on the floor in front of the fireplace. "Don't come in here, Rose."

His warning came too late. She'd already entered behind him. "Oh, no-o-o," she shrieked, and raised her hands to her mouth in horror. He put his arms around her and tried to shield her from the sight.

Zach led her outside and held her for a long moment. "Can you stay here, honey, while I examine them?" She nodded, sobbing softly.

He went through the useless task of checking their pulses, but knew by the dried bloodstains on the floor that they'd been dead for a while.

"Wha-what should we do?" she asked when he rejoined her.

"There's nothing we can do for them, Rose, except go back to town and report it."

"You mean just leave them like this?"

He slipped his arm around her shoulders and led her to the buggy. "Honey, we can't do anything now. It's a matter for the sheriff."

Rose was desolate with grief. "I don't understand how anyone could do such a heinous thing to those two dear people. Do you think it was Indians?"

"The Indian wars have been over for years out here."

"Then who, Zach?"

The image of Jess Tait's face sprang to his mind. "Evil's not exclusive to a particular skin color, Rose."

"I just don't understand such evil. How can anyone be that merciless?"

"Some people are just born that way. None of us has the luxury of determining what course our life will take."

Appalled, she asked, "Are you defending the likes of anyone who would commit such an act?"

"Of course not. But there will always be men like that—the Jess Taits of the world."

"Do you think Tait did this?"

"I don't know, Rose," he said soberly.

She turned on him angrily. "But knowing how he is, you're still willing to associate with him. That makes you as guilty as he is."

"Guilt by association? Be fair. Sometimes the circumstances in a person's life lead him to make choices that aren't always the best. You chose Sturges, didn't you? I chose Tait. We end up having to live with the results of those choices for a long time."

They rode in wretched silence the rest of the way back to Brimstone.

* * *

Sheriff Bloom and his deputy, Jed Wringer, were seated in front of the jailhouse when Zach pulled up; neither of them got to their feet when he told them of the deaths of the Wilsons.

Bloom was a squatty, bowlegged man with a belly that bulged over his gunbelt, owing to a preference for food and cold beer and an aversion to physical activity.

Jed Wringer, who happened to be the nephew of Bloom's wife, was physically the opposite: tall and skinny, he looked like a good wind could blow him away.

It was safe to assume that neither man would ever die in the line of duty.

"Me and Jed'll have a ride out to take a look," Bloom said.

"And just when do you intend to do that, Sheriff?" Rose asked, exasperated that neither one had moved since informed of the deaths.

"Well, since Cal and Effie are dead, there ain't much I can do 'cept bury 'em. We'll ride out there after lunch."

"Aren't you going to form a posse, Sheriff, and try to track down whoever murdered them?" Zach asked.

"You said they looked to have been dead for some time. Reckon whoever killed them is long gone. Most likely that gang of cattle rustlers."

"The Wilsons didn't have any cattle to rustle, Sheriff Bloom. They raised chickens!"

"I knowed they raised chickens, Miz Dubois," he replied with a disgruntled look. "That don't mean them rustlers couldn't have killed them."

"Or maybe a fox stealing into the coop did it," Rose said sarcastically.

"Sheriff Bloom, you have a responsibility to this community. Two law-abiding citizens have been brutally murdered, and you aren't making any attempt to pursue the culprit."

"Told you, Miz Dubois, they wuz most likely killed by cattle rustlers. Every rancher around these parts been out lookin' for 'em. If Rayburn and his crew can't track 'em down, what makes you think I can?"

"Because I don't think they were killed by cattle rustlers!"

He gave her a condescending look. "Now, now, Missy, no call to get worked up. You go back to slinging hash and leave this kind of work to men."

Seething with anger and frustration, Rose clenched her teeth to keep from screaming as Zach drove to the livery. "I can't believe the ignorance of those men! They didn't seem the least bit disturbed about the Wilsons' deaths. I intend to tell Mr. Harvey that Brimstone is no place for a Harvey restaurant."

When informed of the Wilsons' deaths Everett Billings expressed his regrets, but Rose thought he seemed more concerned that they didn't have any fresh eggs for breakfast. Or maybe the events of the past few days had just driven her over the edge. Regardless, his attitude only added to her irritation.

Word of the murders spread through the community and throughout the day, the few law-abiding citizens stopped by to hear the story firsthand from Rose.

* * *

The next morning the Harvey Girls trudged to work, more leery of Brimstone than ever before.

Zach had disappeared shortly after they'd returned to town yesterday, and as much as Rose yearned to speak to him, she was relieved when the gang didn't show up for breakfast.

However, she was pleasantly surprised when Stephen Rayburn arrived on the lunch train. Rose was reminded of how handsome and distinguished the rancher was when he came in and sat down at one of the tables. Since they had to get the customers fed and out of the restaurant in thirty minutes, she didn't have time to do much more than say hello.

Stephen remained behind when the other customers departed, and Rose sat down at his table. "Welcome back, Stephen."

"It's good to be back, Rose. I missed you."

With a guilty start, she realized she hadn't missed him at all. Zach had monopolized her free time.

"I came to an important decision, Rose. Unfortunately, I must get to the ranch, but may I call on you Saturday? I have a question to ask you that will affect both of our lives."

"I'd like that, Stephen."

He was going to ask her to marry him—her hopes had finally come true. But oddly, rather than feeling jubilant, she was struck with depression.

"Then I'll call for you Saturday afternoon at two o'clock," he said. "Until then, my dear." He kissed her hand and hurried away.

Rose walked to the door and saw Stephen ride away with the Lazy R riders. Zach was among them.

Chapter 15

The following day seemed like eternity before two o'clock finally arrived. Rose knew Stephen would propose to her; whether or not to accept his proposal was the most important decision she'd ever make in her life.

Though once she would have rushed gladly to meet this moment, her steps slowed as she neared the boardinghouse's drawing room. Forcing a smile, she entered.

Stephen rose to his feet. "Rose, my dear, you look as lovely as ever."

"Thank you, Stephen."

"The minutes passed like hours since last we met."

"For me as well."

At least her reply was an honest one, even though their reasons differed.

"I thought a carriage ride would be pleasant and allow us some privacy."

"That's fine with me, Stephen. And the good news is that because of a breakdown, the dinner train has been delayed two hours. I don't have to rush back so quickly."

She regretted her words the moment they slipped past her lips. They indicated more encourgement than she felt.

"Then this would be a good time to show you the Lazy R. We have plenty of time to drive out to the ranch and get you back in time to go to work."

Rose remained quiet on the ride out, merely nodding and smiling as Stephen kept up a light conversation.

The ranch house was white with black shutters. Well kept, it was comfortably furnished, but clearly inhabited by a bachelor.

"Your home is very nice, Stephen," she remarked, when he finished showing her around.

"I have a Mexican woman who comes in and cleans once a week, but the house needs a woman's touch to make it a home. And that's what I want to talk to you about Rose. Since my wife's death, I've been a lonely man. I've devoted my time to becoming successful and have accumulated a great deal of wealth, but it doesn't mean anything if one doesn't have anyone to share it with. I want to travel and see more of the world, but I need a companion, Rose. I'm not getting any younger."

She still wasn't ready for this! "Nonsense, Stephen. You're still a handsome figure of a man. I'm sure any woman would—"

"I don't want just any woman, Rose. I want you. From the moment I saw you, I knew you were the woman I want to share the rest of my life with. Will you marry me, Rose?"

Rose took a deep breath. "I'm flattered, Stephen, but we barely know one another. Other than casual meetings in town, this is only the second time we've spent time together."

"I didn't become successful by being indecisive, Rose. I know what I want when I see it. And I want you." He withdrew a ring from his vest pocket. "I know this was presumptuous of me, but I bought this ring for you when I was in Dallas."

Astounded, Rose stared at the gold band circled with diamonds.

"Marry me, Rose, and make me the happiest man in Texas."

"I don't know what to say," she replied honestly, her heart pounding. "I'll need time to think about it before giving you an answer."

"Of course," he said, returning the ring to his pocket. "But please spare me the anguish of too long a wait."

"I promise, Stephen."

Rose wasn't being coy or playing the coquette; thanks to Zach, she was no longer certain she could marry just for money.

Stephen reached for her hand. "Come, my dear, we still have time for me to show you a little of the ranch."

Hand in hand, they strolled down to the barn. There were several horses in stalls, and a few more in a corral outside. Both barn and corral were neatly painted with whitewash, as were the bunkhouse and other outbuildings.

"How old is this ranch, Stephen?"

"Two years."

"I'm very impressed. Everything looks barely used."

"I take pride in appearances, Rose."

"How big is the ranch?"

"A hundred thousand acres."

"My goodness. Do you raise anything other than cattle?"

"No, just cattle, my dear." He changed the subject. "Rose, do you like to travel?"

"I haven't done much, so I really can't say."

"When we marry, I'd like to sell the Lazy R and travel abroad for a few years, see the foreign capitals of the world. Would you like that, Rose?"

"It sounds wonderful."

Forced to eke out an existence her whole life, Rose couldn't imagine what it would be like not to have to work from sunrise to sunset. To visit the mysterious places she'd only seen pictures of or read about in books. How easy it would be simply to say yes to him.

Instead she said, "I think we'd better get back to town, Stephen."

"Of course."

They returned to the carriage and were just pulling away when Tait and his gang rode up.

"Did you move those cattle, Tait?" Stephen asked.

"Yeah, it's done," he said, with his usual unpleasant manner.

"I'm taking Miss Dubois back to town. After I return there are some matters I'd like to go over with you, so stay close. Boys, you're the first to know: I've asked Miss Dubois to become my wife."

Her gaze sought out Zach; his expression was inscrutable. Tait, on the other hand, looked fit to kill.

One by one the men nodded and congratulated Rayburn, except for Zach.

When it was his turn, he said, "Congratulations, Miss Dubois."

"It's customary to congratulate the groom, Zach," Stephen said. "You wish the bride happiness."

"Is that so?" Zach shoved his hat to the top of his forehead and looked at Rose. "I'd say in this case, congratulations are due all around." He wheeled his horse and rode to the bunkhouse. The other men followed.

Zach's remark stung as much as the salty tears Rose held back. Dammit, what had *he* ever offered her? "Stephen, I've made up my mind," she said suddenly. "I will marry you."

"Rose, I'm so happy." He pulled the jeweler's box out of his pocket and slipped the ring on her finger. "Saturday, I'll give a party in town to announce our engagement."

Then he took her in his arms and kissed her hungrily. His lips were firm and warm, but his kiss failed to curl her toes, to set her heart to hammering, or send excitement spiraling through her body.

As they rode away, she glanced over to the bunkhouse. The lone figure of Zach stood in the doorway watching them.

In the week since she'd agreed to marry him, Stephen had spared no expense in making arrangements for the party, including renting the Harvey restaurant to announce their engagement. Once the dinner hour had ended that evening, Billings had begun the preparations for the party.

Kate pulled the curtain aside and glanced out the front window of the boardinghouse. "Well, your future husband's just arrived, so I guess we better leave."

Rose walked over to see that Stephen Rayburn and the Tait gang were tying their mounts to a hitching post near the Harvey House.

Her gaze immediately sought and found Zach MacKenzie. He looked handsomer than ever in a black vest and pants, his tanned face a devastating contrast against the white shirt tied at the neck with a black string tie.

She turned her gaze to Stephen Rayburn, remorsefully realizing she should have done that first. He wore a light gray suit that looked very expensive, tailored to his broad shoulders and well-muscled body. Then her glance swung back to Zach. She hadn't seen him since the day she agreed to marry Stephen. It seemed like a lifetime ago.

"I wonder who's watching the ranch?" Kate said.

"What do you mean?"

"With this current streak of cattle rustling, I'd have thought Mr. Rayburn would leave that gang behind to guard his herd. Isn't that why he hired them?"

"Maybe he figures by bringing that motley crew with him, the cattle will be safer." With a shrug, Rose turned away from the window. She took a final glance in the mirror, then stretched out her arms and spun around. "Well, do you think I'll pass inspection?"

Not only had she and Kate taken extra pains with her hair, but Rose had spent practically all she'd saved in the past two years on the dress all the girls had been working on every free minute.

Appliquéd with beaded lace, the bodice of the ruby gown of silk organza had a fitted waist, a low, ruffled neckline, and cap sleeves set off her shoulders. The small train of the skirt was appliquéd in matching lace.

Stepping back, Kate tapped her chin in deep cogitation. "Hmmm, it still needs something. Perhaps your apron would help." Laughing, she linked her arm through Rose's. "You look gorgeous. Poor Mr. Rayburn—he's at his wit's end to begin with. Wait until he sees you in that dress."

Giggling like schoolgirls with a shared secret, they left the house and walked the short distance to the restaurant.

As soon as they entered the room, Stephen walked over and clasped Rose's hands. He stepped closer, admiration gleaming in his eyes. "Rose, you look exquisite."

"Thank you, Stephen. I'm glad you're pleased."

And she meant it sincerely. At least Stephen could take pride in her appearance, which wouldn't have been possible two years ago. Red had always been Rose's favorite color, and Emily Lawrence, in her sweet fashion, had not only taught her good taste in clothing, but also how the flashier red dresses that Rose had worn in the past clashed with her hair. The rich tone of the gown she wore tonight deepened her hair to auburn, and Rose said a silent prayer of thanks to her dear friend.

Stephen pulled her closer and kissed her cheek. "You fire my blood, my love. I don't know how much longer I can keep from ravishing you. How will I ever wait another week to wed you?"

She smiled flirtatiously and batted her lashes. "Shame on you, Stephen Rayburn. People are watchin' and listenin'." Then laughing, she slipped her arm through his. "Seriously, I'm just as anxious to get married as you are."

She glanced over his shoulder and saw that, indeed, several people had overheard his passionate confession—Zach MacKenzie among them. Her eyes met his mocking stare, and she blushed and looked away.

The guests consisted primarily of ranchers, their families, and the few honest citizens in town. Between the engagement congratulations and questions about their future nuptials, talk always gravitated back to the cattle rustling, the Wilson murders, and the mysterious sightings in the hills. There were few ranches that had not been hit by the rustlers.

And through it all, Rose was aware that Zach had not come near her even to say hello.

After several hours, she'd had enough. Her jaw

actually ached from holding a smile on her face. Looking for some fresh air, she slipped out the door. She was tempted to go back to the boarding-house and not return, but that would cause embar-rassment to Stephen. Instead, she strolled along the platform of the depot.

At that time of night the station was deserted, and she welcomed the quietness. The night breeze gently caressed her throbbing temples as she leaned back against a post and wondered why, with every-thing she'd ever hoped for now within arm's reach, she should feel so low.

"You ought to be called Ruby instead of Rose."

She spun around at the sound of Zach's voice. "Must you always lurk in the shadows?"

"That dress, alabaster skin, moonlight gleaming on auburn hair . . ." He shook his head. "It's enough to rob a man of his breath."

"Poetry from your tongue, MacKenzie! I think I'm going to faint."

"Okay, just say the sight is enough to drive a man to want to ravish you."

"And talk like that can get you into trouble. I don't think your boss would appreciate you mock-ing him."

"Mocking him? I agree with him. It's been on my mind from the first time I saw you."

"The feeling isn't mutual."

"So, you figure you've finally found what you've been looking for. Gotta hand it to you, Rosie. When you see what you want, you don't waste any time."

"Sour grapes, MacKenzie?" Irritated by his sarcasm, she started to walk away, but he took her arm.

"Why don't you admit you've played this game long enough?"

Damn him! Her guilt manifested in an outburst of anger. "And why don't you accept the fact that it's not a game? Next week at this time I'll be Mrs. Stephen Rayburn, and nothing you can do or say will change my mind."

He pulled her against him. "Then one more kiss won't matter, will it, Rosie?"

"Let me *go*, Zach."

She struggled to free herself from the muscled vise of his arms, but his mouth closed over hers, his lips and tongue stoking the familiar fires he ignited so easily. This time she fought it, though, and when she failed to respond, he released her.

"Don't be a bigger fool than you have been," she said. "You're taking foolish risks—anyone could see us out here. I don't think Stephen would take kindly to one of his hired hands taking liberties with his future wife."

"So you're really going through with it? I figured by now, you'd have come to your senses."

"This is the chance I've been waiting for, Zach. I'm not going to let you spoil it for me. As Mrs. Stephen Rayburn, I'll be treated with respect in this territory, and saddle tramps like you will have to think twice before putting a hand on me."

"Respect? Respect is earned; you don't get it by marrying a man for his money."

Anger throbbed at her temples. "Stephen will get

his money's worth; you can be sure of that. I'll be as good a wife to him as any other woman he could marry. So don't let it trouble you, MacKenzie. It's not your problem."

"You ever think that maybe I don't want to see you get hurt?"

Her head shot up in astonishment. "Good! Then leave me alone."

He didn't want her hurt? The damage had been done already. Her waking moments were haunted by the reminder of how much she wanted him, and the more her mind tried to deny it, the greater the truth was driven into her heart with every beat.

Her lips quivered, and moonlight glittered on the tears glistening in her eyes. "Can't you be happy for me, Zach?"

"I wish I could, Rosie," he said sadly. "I wish I could."

"Then just leave me alone. That's all I ask."

"Yeah, I'll leave you alone," he murmured. "I wish I'd never met you, Rosie. I know I'll never forget you."

Zach clenched his hands into fists as she sped away. Why did he always end up hurting her? He wanted to chase after her, to hold her in his arms, to kiss away her tears and tell her he was sorry. But if he did that, he'd have to tell her so much more, and he couldn't do that now—for her safety as well as his own.

Dammit! He was a fool for letting the situation between them get out of control, just because he couldn't keep his hands off her. She was right: he should have left her alone. But he'd let his dick do his thinking for him—and now his heart. Lord knows his body ached for her, but his senses wanted just as much: the sight of her face, the sound of her laughter, the sweet scent of her.

Watching her tonight with Rayburn had tied his gut in a knot. Even if he did tell her the truth about himself, she'd made it clear she wanted no part of him. He didn't measure up to her future plans. How in hell had he ever let the mercenary little redhead burrow so deeply under his skin? Next he'd be making excuses for why she was willing to sell herself.

He'd be glad when the time came to saddle up and ride away for good. And there was no reason for him to stick around there any longer tonight; he'd had enough.

Rose paused outside the door to wipe her eyes and get control of herself. Why didn't Zack go away, ride out of her life? He didn't have to remind her what she was doing; nobody knew that better than she. She'd had to make compromises her whole lifetime; now she had the chance to put her past behind her once and for all, and she wouldn't let Zach MacKenzie spoil it.

Her head was throbbing, so she leaned back against the wall and closed her eyes for a few quiet moments before rejoining the others.

She'd so wanted this evening to be the joyous beginning of a new life, but instead, it was miserable. She wished it was over and she could go back to the privacy of her room.

The door was flung open and a blaze of light and drone of voices shattered the silence. Rose shrank back and hugged the shadows as Jess Tait lumbered out. He looked inebriated—and he was the last person she wished to encounter, especially in his current state. Despite Stephen's orders to him, she still distrusted Tait and felt uneasy in his presence.

Tait closed the door, shutting off the noise and light, and much to her relief staggered to the opposite end of the building, where he began speaking in low tones to someone around the corner. His back was to her so she started toward the door, but stopped when she overheard Tait mention Zach's name. The fact that they were speaking in whispers made it appear sinister.

Curious, she stepped back into the shadows to listen, but only bits of the conversation carried to her ears. "Yeah, yeah . . . hate that MacKenzie bastard . . . sure it'll look like an accident . . . soon." Then she heard nothing more as they walked away. A wave of apprehension coursed through her. If she'd heard correctly, they were planning to harm Zach.

Rose hurried to the corner and peeked around in time to see Tait go back inside through the kitchen door. He was alone, and there was no sign of anyone else. She raced down the side of the building, rounded the corner, and saw a ring of men smoking cigars. Seeing Stephen among them, she hurried over to them and forced a smile.

"Excuse me, gentlemen. Stephen, may I speak to you for a moment?"

"Of course, my dear." He left the group and came over to her. Upon seeing her pallor, he looked concerned and put his arm around her shoulder. "What is it, darling? Are you ill?"

She clutched his hand, drawing comfort from his support. She had intended to tell him about the conversation she'd overheard, but as her panic subsided, she thought better of it: the person she should inform was Zach.

Picking up on the excuse he'd offered, Rose nodded. "I'm afraid so. I'm sorry to spoil the party, but I have a beastly headache."

"I understand, my dear. We'll leave at once."

Stephen was so kind and understanding. It ripped at her conscience that she didn't try to tough it out instead of lying to him.

"There's no need for you to leave your guests, Stephen."

"Nonsense. I think it's time for our guests to leave anyway."

They went back inside, and he thanked everyone for coming. Rose was on tenterhooks as the guests said their good-byes. She had to find Zach and warn him he was in danger!

Finally, Stephen escorted her to the boarding-house. "I hope you feel better in the morning, my dear."

"I'm sure I will." Filled with guilt for deceiving him, she smiled at him. "Thank you, Stephen. You're a wonderful person. I'm so grateful for everything, and I'm sorry I spoiled the party."

"Rose dear, this is just good night, not good-bye. There'll be other parties. We have a whole future together." He kissed her gently. "Now get some sleep."

For a long moment, she stood on the porch and watched him proceed down the street. He deserved a woman who would come to him with love, not for her self-serving reasons.

Then she slipped down the stairs and into the darkness to find Zach. He'd never returned to the party, so she figured the best place to find him would be his room. Thank goodness he'd told her how to reach it without being seen.

Hugging the shadows, she worked her way down the street until she reached the rear of the Long Horn. She listened at the back door and when she didn't hear anything, she turned the doorknob and peeked in. To her relief, the room was empty, but as soon as she closed the door the room was pitched into total darkness. As impatient as she was to reach Zach, she took time to adjust her eyes to the dark, then made her way across the room, occasionally stumbling or bumping into empty beer kegs. By the time she reached the hallway door she was certain her legs were black-and-blue, and the worst was still ahead—she had to cross the hall to the stairway.

Drawing a deep breath, she cracked the door open. Shouts and laughter carried down the hallway from the barroom; Tait's guffawing was the loudest. Peeking around the door, she saw that the hallway was empty.

It's now or never, Rose. She dashed across the hall to the stairs, climbed them rapidly, and sped down the dim hallway to Zach's door.

When the door opposite suddenly opened, she spun around in startlement. Rita came out of the room and stopped in surprise. Rose was too alarmed to do anything except stare dumbfounded at her.

The blonde arched a brow and smirked nastily. "Comin' or goin', honey?"

Was it so dark that Rita didn't recognize her? That would be too much to hope for.

Rita continued down the hall, paused briefly to glance back at her, then went down the front stairway.

Rose sagged in despair, tempted to get out of there as fast as her legs could carry her. As she reached again for the doorknob, she was struck with a dismal thought.

What if Zach isn't even here?

Chapter 16

After Rose opened the door she peered into the darkened room, lit only by the moonlight that glittered through the open window, then gasped in shock when she found herself staring at a cocked pistol.

"Well, this is an unexpected surprise, Miss Soon-To-Be-Mrs. Rayburn." Zach uncocked the pistol and slipped it back into the holster. Barefoot and dressed only in jeans that hugged his hips and long muscular legs, he moved toward her, a black panther on the prowl.

The door closed behind her as she backed into it. Zach stopped in front of her and leaned forward, supported by his outstretched arms that boxed her. Instantly she was enveloped in the provocative scent of his male muskiness. He pressed closer, and she felt his hardened arousal against her stomach. The sensation sent an electrifying shock to her loins as her own female drive responded to it.

His breath became a seductive warmth at her ear when he said in a husky murmur, "I hope this visit means what I think it does."

"I—I came to warn you," she stuttered, forcing the words past her constricted throat.

She tried to shrink back farther when he leaned forward. "About what?" he said, more mocking than curious.

"I overheard Tait and another man plotting to kill you."

"Is that right? Who was this other man?"

"I don't know. They spoke in low tones, and I was too far away to recognize the voice."

"I'll keep it in mind." Raising his arm, he began picking the pins out of her hair. His mouth curled into a pleased smile when her hair dropped past her shoulders.

Rose's heart pounded at her ribs so hard she thought they would surely break. The click of the key in the lock sounded as loud to her as the cock of a pistol. "What do you think you're doing?" she said in weak protest.

He grinned so near she could barely resist the temptation to capture his mouth with her own. She had tasted those lips and knew the devastating pleasure they afforded. "What you knew I'd do when you stepped through the door."

It was clear he didn't believe her—or didn't much care one way or another. His mind was on one thing, and one thing only. "I was a fool to come here. I thought we were friends, and I didn't want to see you hurt." To her horror, she began to sob. "Now, I don't know why I even bothered."

She turned and fumbled with the key, but his hand closed over hers. Turning her to face him, he drew her into his embrace.

"I'm sorry, honey." The mockery had left his voice, and his eyes were tender with compassion. "We *are* friends." His arms tightened around her and he held her in his embrace and let her cry.

She couldn't understand what caused this sudden emotional breakdown. Was it exhaustion? His accusations? Her feeling of guilt? All she knew was that his arms were warm and reassuring, and she felt an incredible sense of security—a feeling she hadn't known since her mother had rocked her as a child.

As her tears waned, she became conscious of a different awareness: the male scent of him, the firmness and warmth of the bare chest her cheek rested against, the softness of the curled hair on it that tickled her nose, and the vitality of his muscled body.

She lifted her head and met the tenderest eyes she had ever gazed into. Zach lowered his head and tenderly kissed away each tear sliding down her cheeks. Then he cupped her cheeks between his hands, and his mouth closed over hers.

It had been meant as a gentle, comforting kiss, but from the first touch, passion replaced tenderness. Hot blood pounded at her temples, pelted her pulses, and filled her veins with an exquisite heat. Lord knows he'd kissed her enough times before that she should have been prepared, but she wasn't. She doubted she would ever be . . . could ever be.

His tongue teased at her lips until she parted them. Then he plundered her mouth, flicking, sweeping, his tongue twining with hers until breathlessness forced them apart.

For a long moment, neither spoke. Zach's gaze probed hers and found the answer he sought. He slid the bodice of her gown off her shoulders, trapping her arms in its folds.

Rose's hands ached to touch him, to feel his warm flesh. She wriggled in an attempt to free them, and the movement created a dangerous friction between her stomach and the heated bulge pressing against it. Now her body yearned to feel that friction lower, in the place that tingled for its touch. Instinctively, she parted her legs.

He didn't miss the move on her part. They communicated wordlessly. She knew they both had thought of this moment too long, the wait too lengthy, the anticipation too intense.

He grasped her camisole and, as if it were paper, ripped it down the middle and freed her breasts. He cupped them in his palms, and her body flooded with sweet rapture when he rubbed his thumbs across the nipples already rigid with arousal. Lifting her under her bound arms, he slid her up the door, pressing her to it with his hips, and his seeking mouth found one of the taut peaks. Then his mouth closed around it and he began to suckle. She gasped, closed her eyes and threw back her head, and reveled in ecstasy at the erotic sensation.

When he lowered her to the floor her legs were

trembling, and she slumped against him as he fumbled with his jeans. His pants swiftly dropped to the floor. Shoving up her skirt, he yanked her bloomers past her hips and guided his hard arousal to its eager nesting place between her legs. Now freed from restraint, his swollen penis was a throbbing, tantalizing heat at her core.

Breath was too limited, control too tenuous—she felt her own moistness and knew she was ready for him. She arched her hips to receive him and he drove into her, pumping in and out.

Her eyes, so heavy with passion she could barely raise the lids, saw that his head was thrown back, his neck rigid with taut cords. Perspiration dotted his brow. The tempo of the love dance increased, the intensity escalated, and the coil within her wound ever tighter. It built and built to a blinding eruption that sent waves of rapture through her. He stiffened, groaned as her tremors took him, and then his climax filled her. When his shuddering ceased, she could only slump her head against his sweat-slickened shoulder.

It was all a blur to her when Zach removed her gown and torn camisole, when he released her petticoat and slid her bloomers and stockings off her legs. She had a hazy recollection of him kicking his jeans aside, scooping her up in his arms, and carrying her to the bed. There he entwined his long legs around hers.

"I've thought about this from the first moment I walked into that restaurant and saw you looking all prim and proper in that black dress and white apron."

"I have, too," she said softly.

"I spent a lot of time imagining what you looked like under those prim and proper clothes." Her stomach tightened when he palmed one of her breasts. "You're everything I'd thought you'd be, and more." He dipped his head and teased the nipple with his tongue, then took it between his teeth and gave it a little tug. She arched against him as his warm, moist mouth closed over the nipple and began to suckle.

"I take it I've just been complimented." She had reached arousal already, and her voice was throaty. "I'll try not to let such flattery go to my head."

He raised his head and grinned. "Better we direct it to mine."

She couldn't help smiling. There was too much devilment in his eyes to miss his meaning. God help her, but his bawdy innuendo excited her more. Sliding her hand down, she grasped the subject of his joke and gave it a playful tug. "You're right, MacKenzie. Feels like it needs all the direction it can get."

That hidden side of her she'd always feared existed had materialized. She'd never been this bold with Wes, but somehow she was shameless where Zach was concerned.

Naturally it was too much of a challenge for him to ignore. Chuckling, he leered down at her. "Oh, lady, before this night's over, you're going to eat those words—and a lot more."

She closed her eyes, her head swirling in an overwhelming tide of passion. She felt free. It was a glorious feeling, and she could no longer keep up the pretense of denial—no longer wanted to. This night had been inevitable from the first time she had looked into his mesmerizing sapphire eyes and saw how much he wanted her. And she knew his eyes must have mirrored her own.

The hours passed too swiftly as they explored one another with hands and mouth, sometimes intensely, other times gently. Often laughing or teasing, moaning or sighing. He'd whisper bawdy promises into her ear. She'd dare him to try, and end up whimpering with ecstasy. He'd challenge that she couldn't break his control; and he'd end up groaning with lust when she'd prove otherwise.

She felt so much. Excitement, yes. Anticipation, yes. Arousal, beyond control. Every touch, every slide of his lips became a rapturous reminder of how much she had yearned for such a moment, and it was more exciting than anything she had ever imagined secretly and denied fervently.

Still, the haunting realization that it would not go on forever crept into her thoughts. He wanted her for the same reason that Wes had wanted her, to satisfy his own bodily cravings, and she couldn't help wondering if the moment would be even greater if they'd come together in love—not lust.

So for this one night, she'd pretend that they were *true* lovers. She'd let herself believe that he cherished her, adored her, loved her—as she did him.

And she confessed this love with her own response. Her every movement, every caress, every heated kiss, sigh, or groan of pleasure cried out, *I love you, Zach*. Words she feared—dared not—say aloud or he'd only laugh. And if he laughed, the illusion would shatter—and crush her heart into bits.

She clung to him, molding her soft curves into his hardened flesh, and reveled in being in the arms of the man she loved.

Then, finally exhausted, they slept.

Zach awoke slowly. He felt drugged: his body too sapped to move, his hands too heavy to lift a finger. Morning sunlight streamed through the open window, hitting him squarely in the face. He managed to roll over on his stomach and muffle his groan in the pillow. Fully awake now, the first thing that popped into his head was last night. There was no sign of Rose. Had it actually happened, or had it just been the dream of every man's greatest fantasy?

He shifted his head to the other pillow to get out of the sun, and the faint aroma of jasmine tantalized his nostrils.

So it hadn't been a dream.

Zach rolled over to his back and lay thinking about Rose, last night—and the greatest sex he'd ever had.

What a woman! Hadn't he known she would be? That red hair and that luscious mouth that warned him to stand clear, even as her blue eyes dared him to go ahead and try. Once she dropped that control of hers, the sky was the limit. She became a wild vixen—the most sensual, uninhibited female he'd ever bedded. He could thank his lucky stars that he even survived last night—although he sure as hell was ready and willing to take her on again.

Recalling the way her eyes deepened with passion, remembering her touch, his blood heated again and he grew hard. Why had she run off without waking him? They had a lot to settle. Next time, he'd make sure she wouldn't run away.

But was she thinking about next time? Was she still planning on going through with her marriage to Rayburn? Maybe that's why she'd left.

He was a damn fool. He was spinning cobwebs over a woman who openly admitted she intended to marry for money—to sell out for a shot at an easy life. But who was he to criticize? He knew damn well she was engaged when she walked into his room last night. So what did that make him? Maybe he should check the dresser to see if she'd left him two bucks on her way out. It'd be just like her.

Disgusted, he looked down his naked body at his erection.

"Shit, MacKenzie!" he grumbled. "You just need to pee." He crawled out of bed.

Chapter 17

When Zach went downstairs he saw no sign of the gang, so he headed for the Harvey House. After last night, he couldn't stand aside and let her marry Rayburn. He doubted he would have even if she *hadn't* come to him last night. Just the thought of her made him hot and hard. Lord, she was under his skin! He had never let any woman get that kind of upper hand with him before.

The hot bath he'd taken had rejuvenated him and succeeded in washing the scent of her from his body, but somehow he still smelled the jasmine as though she were standing beside him.

The bell tingled overhead when he entered the Harvey restaurant and paused to look around. The morning train had come and gone, and now only a few locals were eating. He saw Bull and Joe sitting at a table in the corner. There was no sign of Tait, Pike, or Cain. Good. The last thing he needed this morning was those three. He'd have liked to avoid Bull and Joe, too, but it'd be too noticeable, so he sauntered over to them and pulled out a chair.

"Where's Tait?" If Tait was out to kill him, he sure as hell wanted to know where the bastard was. He also wanted to know who Tait had been talking to last night. It looked like things were starting to move faster, and he had to warn Will.

"Ain't you heard?" Bull asked.

"Heard what?"

"The sheriff locked him up. Last night Jess got drunker 'an hell and started to slap around one of the whores at the Long Horn. When the bartender tried to stop him, Jess knocked the fella out and started to bust up the joint."

"What're Pike and Cain doing—sitting in Tait's cell holding his hand?"

"They rode out somewhere early this mornin'," Bull replied. "Said they had an errand to run for Jess."

"What kind of errand?"

"Didn't ask. Weren't none of my business," Bull said pointedly.

Joe joined the conversation, his eyes glowing. He thrived on bedlam. "Can't believe you didn't hear that ruckus last night."

"I was occupied."

Bull and Joe exchanged lewd grins.

"Bet I know with what." Bull's beefy face twisted

into a smirk. "She must've been damn good for ya to miss hearin'."

"She was."

"Then don't be greedy, MacKenzie," Bull pursued. "Let Joe and me in on some of that action. Who is she?"

"Not a chance. You'd wear her out, Bull, and I'd be out in the cold," Zach said lightly, knowing how the man considered himself to be a great stud. Truth was, Bull's testicles were huge, which was how he had earned the moniker. He took great pride in them, confusing their size with sexual prowess.

"Betcha it wuz that skinny-ass blonde at the Long Horn," Joe said. "The one who said we'd have to take a bath afore she'd climb into bed with us."

"Betcha yer right, Joe. Wuz it her, MacKenzie?"

"Fellas, you're wasting your breath."

Joe poked Bull in the arm. "See, wha'd I tell ya. It wuz her, all right."

Zach saw Rose come out of the kitchen and carry plates over to two cowboys at a nearby table. She looked bright-eyed and bushy-tailed. Even her step had a spring to it. He was amazed, considering how she'd spent most of the night.

When she remained at the table laughing and joking with the cowboys, he began to feel resentment. Was this her way of telling him that last night hadn't meant anything other than a good romp? Or was she trying to make him jealous?

With a belligerent glare, he decided it was the latter. Well, she was wasting her time if she thought Andrew Zachary MacKenzie was the type to get jealous over anything or anyone. From now on, he only wanted one thing from her—and he knew now how to get it: just light her fuse and she blasted off like a Roman candle. He cast another annoyed glance in her direction.

"Can we have some service here?" he called out.

Rose patted one of the cowboys on the shoulder and walked over to them. "Good morning, gentlemen. I thought you were waiting for your other cohorts. Do you wish to order now?"

Joe scratched his balding head. "What's a cohort?"

"A colleague in crime. Your glorious leader," she said.

"Ya mean Jess? He's in the calaboose right now."

"Now, why doesn't that surprise me?" Rose said.

"Yeah, he busted up the Long Horn last night. You mean you ain't heard about it?"

"Not a word."

Bull poked Joe. "She mustta been *occupied* same as MacKenzie." The two men snorted with laughter.

Rose gave Zach a scathing look. "If you gentlemen intend to order breakfast, that'll be seventy-five cents in advance from each of you."

"Dammit, Rose, how long is this going to go on?" Zach declared, tossing down a silver dollar. "I've always paid for what I ate."

"Blame your friends, not me. I have my orders. Mr. Harvey isn't running a charity house for riffraff and petty outlaws."

"You talk too smart, lady," Bull said.

"It's not too *smart* of you to speak so nastily to your boss's future wife, Mr. Bull." She smiled at him. "Fortunately, I don't hold a grudge."

Bull threw down his money and offered no comeback.

Joe slowly counted out his coins and added them to the pile. " 'Sides, Miz Rose, weren't our idea not to pay before. Jess's the one who thought of it."

Rose picked up the money. "I'm afraid the specialty is all gone by now, but I can offer you ham and eggs."

"Sure. From what MacKenzie's been tellin' us," Bull said, "sounds like after last night he could use some lead in his pencil." That elicited another snort from Joe.

Rose's eyes clouded with anger. "What about you two?"

"Yeah, bring me some eggs for sure," Bull declared, "but Little Joe here don't need none—he don't know how to write." Bellowing with laughter at his own joke, he slammed the table several times with the palm of his hand.

After a disgusted look at Zach, Rose spun on her heel and walked away.

"Bull, can't you swallow that filth in front of ladies?" Zach groused. "And like she said, she's gonna marry the boss. I'd watch what I say in front of her."

His gaze was drawn magnetically to the sway of Rose's hips. Recalling the feel of those hips in his hands, the satin-smooth texture of those rounded cheeks, he clenched his hands into fists to curb the itch that had begun in his fingers. Adding to his discomfort, he could smell the faint aroma of jasmine. His blood heated up and he moved his chair closer to the table to conceal the growing erection straining at his jeans. Dammit! He was as disgusted with himself as he was with Bull.

Zach purposely avoided any further conversation with Bull and Joe, who were making comments about the physical attributes of the other Harvey Girls who were scurrying to finish up the breakfast trade before the luncheon train's arrival in three hours.

When Rose returned with a tray of food, she placed heaping plates of ham and eggs in front of Bull and Joe, then slammed Zach's plate down in front of him.

She was pissed with him, all right. What in hell had he done, other than give her the best sex she'd probably ever had? If he lived to be a hundred, he'd never understand women.

As Zach ate, he concentrated on how he could get back to being on the good side of her—or any side of her, for that matter. Recalling the delights of last night, he'd take her any way she wanted.

Rose put down the dishes she'd carried into the kitchen and, closing her eyes, she leaned back against the wall. How could he have done this to her? From Bull's lewd remarks, she could imagine what he'd told them. Hadn't last night meant anything to him other than something to boast about to those animals?

Tears slipped from under her eyelids and trickled down her cheeks. How she'd wanted to believe he was different from them, but he wasn't.

Yet could she resist the temptation to see him again? She trembled, recalling the thrill of his kiss, his touch. For her own welfare and her plans for the future, she knew she mustn't ever make the mistake she had last night. Zach MacKenzie was a drifter running with a gang of no-goods. You couldn't pick your relatives, but you could your friends—and Zach had chosen these men. One day he'd end up the way they would: in prison, or dangling from the end of a rope.

Her tears increased at the thought of Zach's endearing grin erased, his mesmerizing sapphire eyes closed forever, or the warmth of his laughter stilled in death. She could never remain immune to whatever Fate had in store for him. Last night had linked more than her body to him; it had linked her soul.

When she had wakened that morning in Zach's bed, she'd felt guilty and ashamed for her actions. And despite all her former hopes, she'd planned to tell Stephen she couldn't marry him. Until last night she'd always believed she could be a good wife to him, but now she had betrayed him. And she knew, despite the heartache she now felt, that as long as Zach MacKenzie was near, she'd do it again—and Stephen deserved much better than a cheating wife.

Yet her attraction for Zach was hopeless, and could only end in tragedy. She'd wire Mr. Harvey today and ask to be transferred out of Brimstone.

Rose felt a gentle touch on her arm and opened her eyes.

Kate's brown eyes were filled with compassion. "Rose, what is it?"

Wiping away her tears with a napkin, Rose forced a smile. "Nothing, really. I just have a headache."

"Is there anything I can do?"

Although Rose usually faced trouble head-on, she needed some time alone to collect her thoughts.

"Would you mind finishing up my tables? Perhaps if I go back to my room and lie down, I can get rid of this headache. I'll come back in time for lunch."

"Of course I will." Kate put her hand on Rose's elbow and led her to the rear door. "You get some rest, dear, and I'll explain to Mr. Billings."

The fresh air felt good on Rose's flushed cheeks. She hated not being entirely truthful with Kate. Although the two women were becoming closer every day, there hadn't been time to form the type of relationship Rose had had with Emily Lawrence. How she wished Em were here now!

Inside her small room, the walls seemed to close in on her immediately and she opened the window. Then she plopped down on the bed, pulled the bow and pins out of her hair, and shook it out. As she lay back, she thought of Emily again. At least it had all ended happily for Em—Josh and she were crazy in love.

Rose's smile slowly dissolved. "Crazy" was right. A person would have to be crazy to become vulnerable enough to fall in love.

Her last conscious thought before drifting into slumber was that there was no way her relationship with Zach could ever have the same happy ending.

"More coffee, gentlemen?"

Zach looked up to see Kate McDermott holding a coffeepot. For the past fifteen minutes there'd been no sign of Rose, and absorbed with his thoughts about her, he'd been unaware of Kate's approach.

"Yeah, cutie," Bull said, holding up his cup.

"What happened to Rose?" Zach asked. "She give up on us?"

"Rose is feeling under the weather, so she went back to her room. Last night's party totally exhausted her."

Kate was a good-natured woman, Zach thought. And besides having a pretty face, her body was just as appealing—which unfortunately made her a target for some of Bull's and Joe's crude remarks.

As Kate refilled his cup, his thoughts returned to Rose. If she'd gone back to her boardinghouse, it would be a good time to catch her alone and find out what had made her angry with him.

He took a gulp of the coffee, then shoved back his chair. "I've gotta go. See you fellas back at the Long Horn."

"Yeah," Bull grunted, "you don't want that gal of yours to cool off."

"That's right, Bull," Zach said, and headed for the door.

Hoping Rose had left her window unlocked, he went to the rear of the boardinghouse. His luck was better than he expected: the window was open. After a glance around to make certain he wasn't observed, Zach climbed into the room.

He sucked in a breath when he saw her lying on the bed asleep, that gorgeous red hair fanned out on the pillow. She looked so peaceful. Somehow, in the course of their chaotic relationship, he'd always associated some tension with her. But last night he'd discovered another side to her nature that she'd kept disguised with all her talk about marrying for money. She had made love as if she was in love with him; she hadn't even realized she'd cried it out once at the height of her passion.

Seeing her now, deep in slumber, she looked so different—serene and utterly beautiful. The same way she'd looked last night in the moonlight. This was the Rose he wanted to know better. The kind of woman who would love a man as deeply and intensely as the passion she brought to the bed. That same kind of love his parents felt for each other.

Rayburn was getting more woman than he deserved—more than any man deserved.

He yearned to lie down beside her, slip her hand into his, and smell the sweet jasmine of her scent until he, too, fell asleep. But waking up to find him beside her would probably just anger her more.

No, he'd let her sleep undisturbed. There'd be other times.

Leaning over, he pressed a light kiss to her lips. "Next time, Rosie love."

Then he climbed back out the window.

Chapter 18

She cried aloud when she saw Zach lying in a bloody heap.

Rose awoke with a start and sat up in bed. The nightmare had reminded her of the threat on his life, which last night's lovemaking had shoved to the back of her mind. Glancing at the clock, she saw that she'd been sleeping for several hours and the luncheon train was due soon. Within minutes she was dressed in her uniform and headed for the Harvey House.

"How are you feeling?" Kate asked as soon as Rose entered. The tables were all set and ready for the train's arrival.

"The nap really helped, Kate. Have you seen any of Stephen's crew?"

"Not since they left after breakfast."

"Did Jess Tait ever show up?"

"No, thank goodness."

That was good to hear. At least if Tait wasn't around, and Zach was in town, Rose felt he was safe. "What about Zach MacKenzie?"

"He left before the other two did. I haven't seen him since." Her curiosity clearly piqued, Kate asked, "Is there a problem, Rose?"

Rose pulled her aside and said in a low voice, "I must speak to Zach. If you see him, will you tell him that? But do it quietly; I don't want anyone to know."

"All right. What's going on, Rose?"

"I don't have time to tell you now. I'm going to see if I can find Zach in town." Rose rushed out the door before Kate could question her further.

She ventured a peek into the Long Horn and saw Bull and Joe, but no sign of Zach. Joe caught sight of her and she beckoned to him to come outside. Bull followed him.

"Have you men seen Zach MacKenzie?"

Rolling his eyes, Joe poked Bull. "Not for a couple hours."

The little weasel knew something, but it was obvious he wasn't about to tell her. "Is Mr. Rayburn in town?"

"No. He went back to the ranch last night," Joe said.

"What about Jess Tait? Is he still in jail?"

"No, he sobered up and the sheriff released him. He went back to the ranch, too," Bull replied.

"Are you expecting them back?"

"Reckon not," Joe said, scratching his head. "Mr. Rayburn said it made no sense fer us to ride back to the ranch, so he gave us off till Monday. Don't sound to me like he'll be comin' back too soon."

"Then why didn't Tait stay with you fellows?" she asked.

Bull frowned. "Yud have to ask Jess. Whatta ya want with him?"

"I suppose it will have to wait until I see Mr. Rayburn. Thank you, boys."

Well, that hadn't gotten her far, she thought on her way back to the restaurant. She didn't dare attempt to try sneaking up to Zach's room in broad daylight, but at least she'd found out that he was probably still in town.

She helped serve lunch, and for the rest of the day, every time the bell tinkled over the door, she looked up hopefully.

Where was Zach? Had something happened to him? What if Tait already had . . . No, she wouldn't let herself believe anything had happened to him. Zach had been warned and could take care of himself.

By closing time, there still was no sign of him. Since she'd be leaving town soon, she had nothing to lose. Throwing caution to the wind, she went into the Long Horn saloon, ignoring the surprised glances when she walked boldly up the stairs, and rapped on the door of his room.

When there was no answer, she opened the door. Her gaze fell on the bed, remembering the glorious hours they had spent there. She forced aside the tender memory and looked around for a clue to explain his disappearance. But his clothes were all gone. The room was stripped of any sign that Zach MacKenzie had ever been there.

Rose went downstairs to see what she could find out from the bartender. "Excuse me. Can you tell me if Mr. MacKenzie is still registered?"

He looked perplexed. "Registered for what?"

"Room Four at the end of the hallway. Has he checked out?"

"Lady, this ain't no fancy hotel," he said. "Far as I know, he's still got the room."

"But it's empty; his saddlebags are gone."

His leer was insulting. "Tell you what, lady, why don't you try lookin' for him down the street at Rita's. She runs the—"

"I know what she runs," Rose snapped. Zach had made a point of letting her know that fact when Stephen had gone there. "Thank you."

She returned to her room, more confused than ever as she undressed and put on her nightgown. She couldn't believe he'd go to another woman so soon after making love to her. But what about those smirks and remarks on Bull and Joe's faces that morning? It all must have been a joke to Zach—and his leering friends. And to think she had wasted a moment's worry about him, when all the time he was with a whore!

Rose squared her shoulders. She must stop this self-pity and get a grasp on her emotions. The worst was still ahead: saying good-bye to Stephen. This was no time to turn into a quivering heap of jelly.

Moving to the dresser, she pulled the pins out of her hair and began to brush it vigorously, staring at her reflection in the mirror. "It's all his fault, Rose. I keep telling you: Zach MacKenzie can only cause you pain."

"You always talk to yourself, Rosie?"

Startled, she dropped the brush and turned her head. Zach climbed in the window. "Heard you've been asking around town for me."

She closed her eyes and thanked God Zach was okay. "What's the matter, Rita kick you out?"

"Rita? Rosie, my taste runs toward long-legged redheads." He sauntered over to the bed and picked up a piece of the lingerie she had tossed there. "Hmmm. Seems like I've seen this before."

She snatched her underwear out of his hands. "If you weren't with Rita, then where were you?"

"If I'd known you were that concerned, I'd have hurried back."

"Oh, don't sound so damn cocky, MacKenzie. And close those drapes before someone sees you in here. It's bad enough I jeopardized my reputation chasing all over town looking for you."

He closed the drapes, then came back and reached for her.

She slapped his arms away. "Answer me, Zach: where have you been? I've been worried sick."

"Why? What's wrong?"

"What do you think? I warned you that Tait's going to try to kill you."

He slid his hands up her back and drew her closer. "He can try," he whispered, nibbling at her ear.

He clearly wasn't the least bit concerned, trailing kisses along the column of her neck. When he added his tongue the sensation became erotic, and she had to concentrate on her words.

Pressing her hands against his chest, she held him away at arms' length. "Dammit, MacKenzie, aren't you the least bit worried?"

"Rosie, I can handle Tait anytime I choose."

"All day, I've been worried sick, and now you come here—most likely from the bed of a whore—intending to get into mine. I want to know where you've been, Zach."

He stepped away and she dropped her arms. "Why is it so important to you? I wasn't with Rita, if that's what you're thinking."

"Then why won't you tell me?"

"I guess I just don't like to be prodded. I'm not the guy you're engaged to, remember?"

"You don't have to remind me of that," she lashed out angrily. "Knowing how I betrayed Stephen last night, I feel guilty enough as it is."

He stared at her as if she'd struck him in the face. "So that's it. You're feeling guilty that *Stephen* will find out about your indiscretion." He reached out and picked up a thick strand of her hair. For a long moment he rolled it with his fingers, as though it were so fragile it'd break off.

"You know, Rosie, when I first came in here, I thought you were actually worried about me."

The sadness in his voice wrenched at her heart. She looked up at him and felt the sting of salty tears.

"I-I *was* worried," she stammered. "It's just . . . I mean, you disappeared so suddenly I feared that Tait had carried out his scheme. Then when I looked for you, the bartender said you were probably with Rita."

"And you resented the thought of me going from your arms to those of a whore."

"That, added to the lewd innuendos your friends made in the restaurant this morning—"

"You thought I'd bragged to them about last night. Thank you for your high opinion of me. I've told you before, Rose, I don't kiss and tell."

Though he spoke softly, his voice sounded like a roar in her head. She put her hands over her ears to shut out the sound, but he didn't stop.

"And whether you believe it or not, I thought last night was pretty special."

She had hurt him deeply. "Zach, please, don't make this any harder than it is. I'm sorry I misjudged you. I swear I was worried about you, until I went to your room and your clothes were gone. I knew you hadn't gone back to the ranch with Stephen and Tait, and when the bartender said you probably—" She wiped her eyes, then drew a shuddering breath. "You're right. I resented it. It was a stupid, silly mistake on my part."

"So having said that and cleared your conscience, you now want a no-good bastard like me to get out of here and leave you alone to agonize about your guilt over Rayburn."

No, that wasn't it at all. Her heart swelled with the aching realization that she was in love with Zach. Leaving him would be the most difficult trial she'd ever faced, because the memory of him would haunt her the rest of her life. She could never love any other man again—much less marry one. Her dream of marrying a rich man had dissolved the first time Zach kissed her. She'd tried to deny it, but it hadn't worked. She would never be able to abide any other man's kiss. And now, with the realization of this love, she also knew she could never actually face him and say good-bye.

Common sense told her to tell him to leave, but her treacherous heart reminded her that she would never see him again—that this would be the last time they'd be together. Even though she was merely postponing the inevitable, she couldn't let this moment pass. Moving closer, she slipped her arms around his neck.

"No, I don't want you to leave, Zach. I want you to make love to me." She closed her eyes and parted her lips.

The kiss was hot and passionate, deepening with every heartbeat. She had opened Pandora's box, and there was no closing it now—as if she wanted to. No man's kiss had the effect on her that Zach's did, and she felt bereft when he broke it.

"I've never known a woman like you, Rose," he murmured, trailing kisses to her eyes and cheeks. The whispered words fueled a fire already raging out of control.

"Am I so different?" She needed the feel of his hands on her, his flesh against hers, and she wanted him to take her now—the way he had the first time. She lifted the Stetson off his head and tossed it aside.

Cupping her face between his hands, he stared into her eyes as if probing her soul.

"What?" she asked, confused by this delay. Why wasn't he as eager as she?

"You're so much woman, Rosie love. Wild. Uninhibited. Not ashamed to let a man know what you want from him. And you give what he wants right back."

"I've never been so with any other man," she said softly.

"I'm glad." He traced her lips with his tongue. "And grateful you saved all that passion for me."

His mouth reclaimed hers, and their tongues dueled until she moaned with arousal—and anticipation. Now, she knew what lay ahead. She knew how the thrill of his kiss would make her head reel, how his tongue would make her flesh come alive. And she knew how his hands could play her body like a master musician—the scent of him, taste of him, warmth of him, all added notes to this passionate rhapsody.

They undressed each other and at last they were on the bed, face-to-face, flesh on flesh—her soft curves molded to his hard angles in a perfect fit. They now breathed as one, their hearts beat as one, and their passion blended as the warmth of each body coursed into the other. They kissed, tasted, stroked, explored; dragging precious breaths into their lungs in gasps and exhaling it in sighs and moans. And when she could no longer stand it lest her body explode, it did—in ecstatic tremors that sent her whole being whirling in blinding, swirling sensation.

They lay together side by side, as their ragged breathing slowed to an even rise and fall—until temptation became demand, and they reached out to touch each other. And then it began again. Entwined, they kissed, they caressed, they stroked, and once more ascended to that rapturous peak that only true lovers can scale.

And it all felt new again.

Throughout the night they made love over and over.

Toward dawn, Zach fell asleep. Rose turned on her side, propped up an elbow, and cradled her head in her hand to gaze down at him, gently tracing his jaw with a finger as she memorized every line of his beloved face.

I love you, my darling. I'll never forget you.

He opened his eyes and softly smiled. Her heart turned over. How could she leave him without her heart breaking into bits?

He wove his fingers into her hair and pulled her head down to him. "I can't get enough of you, Rosie." Then he kissed her tenderly.

It was a bittersweet moment: poignant with the tenderness of his lovemaking, but unbearably painful, knowing this would be the last time he'd ever hold her.

Her heart shattered.

Each time Zach saw her, it was harder to leave her. This time was the worst. Something just wasn't right. She hadn't disappointed him last night; she'd been all he remembered. She'd driven him wild. Yet he'd sensed she was holding something back.

He kicked at a stone in his path. What in hell did it matter? Unless he told her everything, soon she'd be married to Rayburn. Maybe it was meant to be. Maybe it would be better to forget her.

But that wouldn't be easy, because the redhead was not that easy to forget.

Truth was, he wanted to be with her out of bed as much as in. There was a damn sight more to Rose Dubois than just good sex. The defiant way she'd thrust up that pert little chin when she was toughing it out, even as her eyes filled with the tears she refused to shed. And he liked the sound of her laughter—that mellow throatiness when she was laughing with him. Nothing got to him as much as that sound. Well, maybe that perfume she wore, or those blue eyes smoking in anger at him. Lord, she excited him when she looked at him that way. That was probably why he'd deliberately baited her so much. Funny though, despite all their squabbling, they had spent a lot of time laughing together.

He frowned, troubled by a nagging uneasiness— last night she hadn't laughed. She was holding back something, all right—something she didn't want to tell him.

There were many puzzling parts to her, but he was running out of time before he had a chance to put all the pieces together. For her own good, he had to tell her some of what he'd discovered—or it would be too late.

He headed for the livery. Rose's warning indicated the gang might be on to him. He'd ridden out yesterday to warn Will, and now he'd return to the Lazy R. If Jess Tait planned on killing him, he'd make it convenient for the son of a bitch to try.

Chapter 19

After Zach left that morning, Rose knew she had to leave Brimstone immediately. She'd go back to Chicago to personally tell Fred Harvey that Brimstone was no place to bring in unprotected young ladies. And then she hoped he would reassign her somewhere as far from Texas as she could get. Maybe California: the Santa Fe had completed its line all the way to the Pacific Ocean. But she knew no matter where she went, Zach would haunt her forever.

Her heart was heavy as she finished dressing. She had a lot to do before the eastbound train came through tonight—*and she slinked away like a thief in the night.*

The first thing she must do was tell Billings she

212

was leaving, and then ride out to the Lazy R ranch and tell Stephen Rayburn she couldn't marry him. Then she'd leave Zach forever.

When Rose informed Everett Billings of her intention to leave, he threw up his hands in frustration.

"Why are you doing this to me, Miss Dubois?"

"My decision to leave Brimstone has nothing to do with you, Mr. Billings."

"But you just got engaged to a local resident."

"I know. I hope to depart on the train tonight, and I must resolve that problem with Stephen before I can do so."

"So you are going to just take off and leave me shorthanded, Miss Dubois."

"I wouldn't, Mr. Billings, if I thought the other girls weren't capable of handling the service. Frankly, I wish all of you were getting on that train with me tonight. Please understand I have some insurmountable problems, or I'd never consider this drastic action."

For a moment he stared at her, appalled, then his expression softened. "You've always been a very dependable employee. I'm sorry you are having problems, Miss Dubois. Is there anything I can do to help?"

Compassion was the last thing she ever expected to hear from Everett Billings, and his concern made her want to break down and cry. But the only way she could hold onto her resolve was by not giving in to self-pity. She alone was responsible for the mess in which she found herself, and it was up to her alone to settle it.

"Thank you, Mr. Billings, but it's something I must do myself."

"Then I wish you good luck, Miss Dubois."

Thanking him for his kindness, Rose ran out the door. She would say good-bye to Kate and the other girls later that evening, before departing. Once on the train, there'd be plenty of time for tears. The thoughts of what might have been—love, marriage, friendship—would be painful memories from which there never *would* be an escape.

The heartache threatened to suffocate her. She had to get it out, but the only person she could bare her heart and soul to was Emily.

Returning to her room, she sat down and wrote Emily a long letter telling her the whole story of her love for Zach MacKenzie (though she didn't mention him by name), the engagement to Stephen Rayburn, and her reason for leaving Brimstone. After posting the letter, she rented a buggy for the next unpleasant task she had to face.

As she drove out to the Lazy R, Rose struggled with the anxiety of telling Stephen she couldn't marry him. She was ashamed of how she had misled him, and brokenhearted to think that her love for Zach had been the source of that shame. It was painful enough to know Zach didn't love her, without knowing how her love for him had caused pain to others.

Arriving at the ranch, Rose reined up sharply when she saw Jess Tait astride a horse near the bunkhouse. Bull and Joe joined him, and her heart thudded when she heard one mention Zach's name.

Had Tait succeeded in harming him? She had to know the truth. Rose got down from the buggy and moved closer.

"There ain't no sign of him in town, boss," Bull said. "Nobody's seen him since the night of that party."

"Well, keep lookin'. Maybe he's around here. And make sure you bring him to me when you find him."

"What if he don't wanna come?" Joe asked. "He don't strike me as the kind who's gonna do what he don't want to."

"Yeah, and he's a fast draw, boss," Bull added. "He can clear leather faster than anyone I've ever seen."

Tait snorted in disgust. "I ain't plannin' on tryin' to outdraw him. That'd make me as dumb as you guys. Just find him. Where's Cain and Pike?"

"They rode out on the range lookin' for him," Bull said.

"Why in hell wud they think he's out on the range? Ain't nobody got no brains?"

"Pike said he thought he saw MacKenzie one day out on the range ridin' alone, and he weren't workin' cattle."

"More'n likely it wuz that old man Wilson snoopin' around. Get movin'. Rayburn's chewin' my ass."

Relieved to learn that Zach had not fallen victim to Tait's foul play, Rose started back to the buggy just as Tait turned around and saw her.

"Hey!"

Ignoring his outcry, Rose continued on to her buggy. Hoofbeats drew near and Tait caught up with her before she reached it. He jumped down from his horse and grabbed her arm.

"Whatta ya doin' snoopin' around here?"

"Take your hand off me, Mr. Tait," she ordered in a show of bravado.

"I think Rayburn's gonna be interested in hearin' how ya been snoopin' around here." He tightened his grasp on her arm and forced her toward the house.

"Who is it?" Stephen shouted in an irritated tone when Tait rapped on the door.

"Tait." He opened the door.

"What in hell do you want? I told you not to bother me when—" Stephen choked off his words and gaped in surprise when Tait shoved her in ahead of him.

Stephen's shock couldn't compare to her own at the sight of Rita sitting on Stephen's lap. Had the woman already told him that she'd seen her in the Long Horn? Stephen nearly dumped the blonde on the floor in his haste to stand up.

"Rose! What a pleasant surprise. What are you doing here?" Although his tone was welcoming, he was clearly uneasy at being caught with his hand in the cookie jar.

Rose felt a sense of relief. Catching Stephen in an act of infidelity eased the guilt of her own perfidy.

"Snooping around. That's what she's doin' here," Tait declared with his usual snarl.

"I asked *her*, Tait." Annoyance had replaced the surprise in his green eyes. "Get out of here and leave us alone."

"She—"

Stephen's glare silenced Tait's protest. "I said get out."

Tait paused at the doorway for another resentful glare, then left the house, slamming the door behind him. Stephen turned to the blonde. "You, too, Rita. I'd prefer to speak to my fiancée alone."

"*That's* the gal you're marryin'!" Rita stared at Rose. "Seems like we meet again, Miss High-and-Mighty."

Rose lowered her head, trying not to make eye contact with the woman.

"You two have met?" Stephen asked, his surprise evident.

"At the Fourth of July celebration," Rose said.

"That ain't the only place. I've got a good memory for fancy gowns." Rita started laughing.

"What's so funny, Rita?" Stephen asked.

"All this time you've been worryin' that your fine fiancée would get wind of us. The joke's on you, sugar. She's the gal I saw sneakin' out of MacKenzie's room the same night of your big engagement party." She started laughing again. "While you were with me, the future Mrs. Rayburn was right across the hallway mixin' it up with one of your hired hands."

"Get out of here, Rita. Get back to town and keep your mouth shut."

"Haven't I always, sugar?" She smirked at Rose. "Better luck next time, honey."

As soon as the door closed, Stephen turned to her, his lips a harsh line of anger, fury burning in his eyes. "You little tramp!"

She drew back in surprise, unprepared for his raw fury. "Stephen, let me explain."

Surprise became fear when he lashed out; the blow to her jaw caught her unexpectedly. Rose stumbled backward and crashed into a table. Her cheek stung from his blow and before she could regain her footing, he grabbed her by the shoulders. His fingers cut into her flesh like talons. Wincing from the painful pressure, she cowered under the force of his fury.

"How dare you deceive me! I was going to give you the honor of becoming my wife, and all this time you were making a fool of me."

His rage seemed to be out of control and she looked around desperately for a way to escape. How could she have misjudged this man so miserably? Zach had tried to warn her of the other side to Stephen, but she had scoffed at his warning. "Please, listen to me, Stephen!"

"Shut up!" He shook her until she couldn't speak. With each jolt hairpins flew in all directions and it felt like her head would bounce off her shoulders if he didn't stop.

"You cheating little whore!" By the time he shoved her away, she was dizzy and felt as if her brain was rattling.

In a feeble voice, she managed to gasp out an apology. "I'm sorry. I'm not proud of it. I came here to tell you I couldn't marry you because of what I did."

"No one makes a fool of me."

Rose screamed as he hit her again and then again. "You and MacKenzie will both pay for this." His next blow knocked her to the floor, and she huddled in a heap, sobbing. Hot tears scalded her cheeks, and pain shot through her head like flashes of lightning as the beckoning blackness of unconsciousness called to her.

"Zach," she cried out before finally slipping into oblivion.

Shouting. Pain. More shouting. More pain.

Rose tried to open her eyes. One of them felt swollen shut, so she gave up trying. The floor was hard beneath her, and she tried to move. Her aching body refused to, so she lay there and tried to assemble her thoughts, but her head ached even more than her body and the loud shouting coming from across the room was making it worse. She forced her eyes open and in a hazy blur recognized Stephen and Jess Tait. The effort was too painful to sustain, so she closed her eyes and listened.

"I looked in the bunkhouse and the barn," Tait said. "There ain't no sign of him."

"Where in hell can he be? Get the hell out of here and find him."

"I've got the boys lookin' for him, boss."

"Those idiots are dumber than you are. I told you to get rid of him, but now I want him found and brought to me. Mr. MacKenzie's death is going to be slow and painful. He made a big mistake in touching the woman I intended to marry. Nobody does that to me."

"And what about your girlfriend over there?" Tait asked.

"Get rid of her—make it look like an accident. See

that you don't pull what you did when you knocked off that old couple. You've got the whole town talking about it."

Tait snorted in amusement. "So what? They think it's rustlers. And besides, whatta you grousin' about? Nobody's figured you're behind the rustling. If that old man Wilson hadn't come upon us driving that rustled herd, he'd still be alive."

"Just the same, her death's got to look like an accident. I don't want anyone connecting it to the Lazy R." Stephen poured himself a drink and stared into the glass of brandy. "I shall play the role of the bereaved fiancé as convincingly as I have an upright citizen of the community."

Rose almost gasped aloud. She had to get out of there, but how?

Stephen drank the liquid in one gulp and slammed the glass down. "It's no thanks to you that nobody suspects me. It's because I was smart enough to pretend my cattle had been rustled first. You're stupid, Tait. As stupid as that gang of yours." He poured himself another drink.

"Well, we wuzn't too stupid to do your dirty work for ya, Rayburn. I'm sick of you and your stinkin' orders. Give us the money we've got comin' to us and me and the boys'll move on."

"You're not going anywhere until you get rid of the girl and MacKenzie."

"That's what you think." Tait pulled out his pistol. "Open that safe. I've taken all I'm gonna from ya."

"Fine—go ahead and run out on me; I don't need you. I can finish this job myself." Rose lost sight of

Stephen when he knelt at the safe. After several seconds, he stood up. "Here's the money I promised you."

"All of it, Rayburn."

"I gave you what I said I would."

"And I'm takin' the rest," Tait said, motioning toward the safe with his pistol.

Stephen threw down a stack of bills. "You're not going to get away with this. I don't care what it costs me: I'll see that you're tracked down and dealt with."

"Wish you hadn't said that, Mr. Rayburn, 'cause now that little gal is gonna have to kill ya. Reckon she didn't take too kindly to that beating ya gave her. Good thing you wuz able to put a bullet into her before you died." He laughed loudly. "Ya sure gave me a good alibi. After we deliver your bodies to the sheriff an' tell them what happened, me and the boys can ride away without havin' the law on our trail."

"Wait, Tait, don't do it. I'll—"

Rose swallowed her scream when Tait fired several shots into Stephen. He knelt over Stephen's body, then headed over to her. She held her breath, fighting her panic when she felt his nearness and knew he was standing above her.

"I told ya I'd get even with ya, bitch."

Horrified, she waited for the shot. Suddenly, the door opened.

"What's goin' on here? We heard shootin'."

"I shot Rayburn. Pike, you harness up a wagon. We're gonna take his body and his girlfriend's into town."

"Is she dead?" Cain asked.

"She's gonna be. Rayburn beat the hell out of her. I'm gonna tell the sheriff that they shot each other, then we're pullin' out of here. Pack up our gear, and as soon as Cain and Pike get back, we'll take the bodies into town."

"What about MacKenzie?" Cain asked. "Ain't no sign of him."

"Forget him—he must've taken off. Rayburn was the one who wanted him dead, anyway. Get goin'."

Rose heard the door close, and then Tait cocked his pistol. "Too bad you ain't awake, bitch, so'd yud know that Jess Tait always gets even."

Her heart started pounding so rapidly that it made her head spin. The pounding at her temples and head drove her into blackness. A gun blast sounded, and she slipped into oblivion once more.

Chapter 20

Tait grabbed his hand in pain, his pistol falling to the floor. He blanched as he looked at the drawn Colt in Zach's hand. "MacKenzie! What the hell are you doing? You coulda killed me."

"And I would have, if I wanted to."

Zach walked over and examined Rose. She'd passed out, but her breathing was steady. He stood up. "Hope you weren't really thinking about shooting her, Tait."

"She killed Rayburn. Damn it, MacKenzie, my hand's bleeding."

"I just grazed it. Wrap a handkerchief around it and it'll be fine. Why'd she shoot Rayburn?"

" 'Cause he didn't want nothin' more to do with her when he found out you wuz humpin' her. They

had a big fight. He slapped her around a little, and she
shot him."

"So you were going to do your civic duty and kill
Rayburn's killer."

"Sure, that's all what I wuz doin', MacKenzie."

"Why wouldn't you just take her to the sheriff?"

"I ah . . . wuz afraid she'd get away."

Zach nodded. "Makes sense. That way, if you
killed her she'd pay for the crime without wasting
time on a trial."

"Yeah," Tait said, noticeably relieved. "Figured
it'd save a lot of people's time."

"There's just one thing wrong with that plan,
Tait: I don't like it. I enjoy her company."

"Ah, come on, MacKenzie. World's full of wim-
min. Why wud ya wanna strap yerself down with a
murderin' one? Ya cud end up being her next victim."

"I like living dangerously."

"It's your funeral—don't say I didn't warn you.
As soon as Pike and Cain get back, me and the boys
wuz figurin' on taking Rayburn's body to town,
then headin' out. There ain't no reason for hangin'
around here any longer. Ya comin' with us?"

"Where are you heading?"

"Most likely north. Hear they run a lot of cattle in
Wyoming and Montana."

"They *run* cattle, not rustle them, Tait. That kind
of leaves you boys out in the cold, doesn't it?"

Tait smirked. "There's always ranchers like Rayburn who're lookin' for gunfighters."

"I think I'll go my own way and take the girl with
me."

"Go ahead. We'll tell the sheriff the same rustlers that killed that old couple killed Rayburn."

"Think I'll ride into town with you just to make sure you do, or I'm afraid Rose and I might end up with a posse on our tails."

"Ya don't think I'd double-cross ya, do ya?"

"You double-cross me! Of course not, Tait. I just don't want anybody wondering why I didn't show up with you. And Rose needs to see a doctor, then pack up her things."

"How do ya know if she's even willin' to go with ya?"

"Because that's what she came here to tell Rayburn." His tone hardened. "That's why I know she didn't shoot him, Tait. You did. So it appears we're at an impasse."

"What in hell is that?"

"A Mexican standoff: I'll keep my mouth shut, and you do the same. Now get that wagon hitched. Rose isn't in any condition to ride."

"Sure thing." Tait bent down to pick up his gun.

"Slow and easy, Jess," Zach warned.

"I ain't no fool, MacKenzie." He picked up the pistol and eased it back into the holster. "I'll get that wagon like ya asked, but me and the boys are gonna wait for Pike and Cain to get back."

Zach couldn't have asked for a better break. With Pike and Cain not there, he'd only have to worry about the other three. "Rose needs a doctor. Pike and Cain's got enough sense to ride into town when they don't find you here. Let's get the hell out of here."

Zach had arrived back at the ranch in time to see

Rita driving away. When Tait went into the house, he had sneaked in the back door and listened to the conversation between Tait and Rayburn. It confirmed his suspicions—Tait had killed the old couple and Rayburn was behind the cattle rustling. He hadn't been surprised to hear that the rancher was out to get him because of his affair with Rose; the shock was seeing her in a heap on the floor. He hadn't known she was there until after Tait shot Rayburn and walked over to her. As soon as she was safe, he'd take care of Tait. He now had a personal score to settle with him, and hoped the bastard would try to draw on him.

When Zach was sure Tait was headed for the barn, he picked Rose up, and carried her to the couch. The whole time he was stringing Tait along, all he could think about was her lying unconscious on the floor. If he didn't need the bastard alive, he would have shot him on the spot.

"Rosie, can you hear me?" he said.

She moaned slightly, and opened her eyes.

"Zach, is it really you?" She tried to sit up.

"Just stay still, honey, until I can get you to a doctor."

He ran his finger lightly over her bruised cheeks. Rayburn had done a real job on her, but her nose and her cheekbones didn't appear to be broken.

He heard the wagon pull up outside, and Tait came in. "Wagon's ready."

"Call in the boys to cart out Rayburn's body. You carry Rose outside—and handle her gently."

Tait gave him a scathing glance. "Ya sure like to

give orders, MacKenzie. Why in hell don't ya do it yerself?"

"Not that I don't trust you, fellas, but I prefer to keep both hands free."

"Ya sure goin' to a lot of trouble to keep her alive."

Zach casually rested his hand on the butt of his Colt. "That's right. So remember, if I have a choice between you or her, she has the edge."

Soon they were under way. Tait and Bull rode ahead, with Joe driving the wagon. Zach rode behind, where he could watch all three.

They hadn't traveled more than a couple miles when Cain and Pike rode up to them, leading a mustang with a body slung over it. Zach's stomach knotted the moment he recognized the horse. He forced himself to remain impassive when Pike dumped the lifeless body of Will Grainger on the ground.

"Who in hell is he?" Tait asked.

"We caught him snoopin' around the ranch," Pike said. "I had to shoot him when he tried to ride off."

"What do ya want us to do with him, boss?" Cain asked.

"Why'd you even bring him? Toss him into the chasm and let the scavengers have him," Tait grumbled.

Zach drew his Colt. "Put him in the wagon."

Startled, the five men looked at him. Seeing the drawn Colt in his hand, they backed away.

"Whatta you up to now, MacKenzie?" Tait asked. "This another friend of yours?"

"Matter of fact, he is. His name's Will Grainger—and we're taking him into town with us. Pike, you and Cain put him in the wagon."

Puzzled, Pike looked at Tait. "Is that what ya want, boss?"

"You heard me!" Zach could barely keep from shooting them all on the spot.

"Do what he says, Pike. MacKenzie's got the gun."

Cain and Pike picked up Grainger's body and carried it over to the wagon.

"Hey, what's goin' on? Ain't that Rayburn and his gal?" Cain asked when he looked in the bed.

"Yeah, Rayburn's been killed. We're taking the gal to the doc in town."

"What happened, boss?"

"One of them rustlers shot him."

Cain looked bewildered. "Boss, there ain't no rustlers 'ceptin' us."

Tait snorted. "Reckon one of us must have shot him then, huh?" Bull and Joe burst into laughter.

With the arrival of Pike and Cain, Zach knew it would be impossible to keep an eye on all five of them. He'd have to take their weapons.

"Okay, boys, time to shuck those gunbelts."

"Like hell I will!" Bull declared.

"What's he talkin' about, boss?" Cain asked.

"I'm not partial to getting shot in the back, the way Will was. I want to see those gunbelts hit the dirt *now*." Tait started laughing and unbuckled his belt. "What's so funny, Tait?" Zach was suspicious that Tait gave in so easily; it was unnatural.

"You're playing right into my hands, MacKenzie.

You take off with that gal, and our deal's off."

"Then what's keeping me from putting a bullet into you right now, Tait?"

He laughed. " 'Cause ya ain't the kind to shoot an unarmed man, MacKenzie." His statement seemed to get through to the other four men. They couldn't remove their gunbelts fast enough.

"Gather them up and put them on the wagon, Joe," Zach ordered. "And no tricks. Not one of these guys is worth you dying for."

Zach backed over to the tethered horses, untied his saddlebags, and tossed them into the back of the wagon. Then he released all the horses. Climbing up on the wagon seat, he sat down and picked up the reins. "Sorry, fellas, but I have to slow you down a bit." He fired several shots in the air and the horses bolted, trailing clouds of dust.

Whipping the reins, Zach shouted to Rose, "Hang on, honey. This is going to be a bumpy ride, but we have to get to town as fast as possible."

"Zach, who is this man they killed? He's the same man we met that day on the trail, and I remember seeing you talking to him at the fair."

"He's an old friend, Rose."

He whipped the horses to a faster gait, and the wagon bounced behind on the rough terrain. After several miles, he reined up and jumped down from the box.

"What's wrong?" Rose asked.

"Time to switch." He'd already begun to unhitch the team.

"What are you doing?" she asked when he put the reins on one of the horses.

"If we ride into Brimstone in a wagon, we're sure to be seen. The best way to get in unobserved is on horseback. I don't think you're well enough to ride alone, so we'll ride double. As soon as Tait finds this wagon, he won't know if we headed for Brimstone or Zanesville."

He weighted down the other horse with the gang's gunbelts, then smacked it on the rump. The horse galloped off.

"Hope it runs far enough to keep them occupied for a while looking for their weapons. They won't take the chance of riding into Brimstone without packing iron, if they think that's where I headed."

He picked up Rose and lifted her onto the back of the horse. Then he returned to the wagon and grabbed his saddlebags. For a long moment he gazed at the body of Will Grainger. "I'm sorry, old-timer. I'm going to have to leave you behind."

"Rose, you'll have to hold these." He handed her the saddlebags. Then he swung up behind her, pulled her back against his chest, and reached for the reins. He prodded the horse to a gallop.

Zach almost wished Rose was still unconscious, because the ride would be hard on her. She was probably hurting like hell, but she had a lot of grit. And if this ploy worked, he could get her in and out of the doctor's by the time the gang rounded up their horses and got to town.

He had some explaining to do to her, too, but at least it would soon be over. Jess Tait was a merciless killer and had to be stopped.

His jaw hardened. Yep, once he had Rose safely

tucked away, he had a score to settle with Mr. Jess Tait.

When they reached Brimstone Rose refused to go to the doctor, insisting instead on returning to her boardinghouse.

Zach avoided the main street and used the rear window again to get into her room. Once he had Rose tucked away safely, he needed to send a telegram.

Rose groaned when she looked at herself in the mirror. "Oh, my!" Her left eye was swollen and blackened and her cheeks bore the bruises from Stephen's beating.

"I suspect Tait and his gang will be showing up here very soon, Rose, so I want you to do exactly what I tell you. If Tait sees you, he'll kill you to prevent you from telling your side of the story."

"Stop speaking to me as if I'm a child, Zach. I know Tait intends to kill me, but he can hardly try to do that now in front of the whole town."

"There's no law in this town, so what's to stop him?"

She turned around and, despite the pain of the effort, managed a soft smile. "You." The trust in her eyes shone through the bruises that had been inflicted upon her.

And in that moment, he realized just how deeply he loved her.

He opened his arms and she walked into them. For a long moment, he held her and knew she was right. He'd go to any means to protect her. She was *his* woman.

So he held her, wanting to kiss her but knowing it would hurt her—and Lord knows she'd been hurt enough.

"I was so frightened," she whispered.

He gently cupped her bruised cheeks in his hands. "Honey, what were you doing out there alone?" He brushed aside a tear sliding down her cheek and thought of how close he'd come to losing her forever.

"I went there to tell Stephen I couldn't marry him."

"How'd you come to that decision?" He found himself holding his breath waiting for her reply.

"You know the answer to that. We're not fooling ourselves anymore, are we? I could never have married Stephen knowing what's between us. And when he found out about you and me, he began hitting me. Zach, Stephen was behind the cattle rustling, and Tait was the one who murdered the Wilsons."

"How long have you known?"

"I overheard him and Tait discussing it today."

He felt relieved. There'd be time to talk about it later; now it was a grim reminder that he still had work to do. He kissed her on the top of her head, then forced himself to step back and release her. His arms suddenly felt so empty that he wanted to pull her back. "I have to get to the telegraph office."

"Why?"

"I could use some help to get out of this mess."

Her lips trembled as she looked up at him. "Zach, were . . . were you involved in any of it?"

"I knew about the rustling, Rose. I even helped to

change some of the brands. We'd do it at night. That was the light people saw. But I didn't know about the Wilsons, or I'd have tried to stop it."

Her shoulders slumped in despair. "Then you really are an outlaw. I held out the foolish hope you weren't a part of it. What about those shootings? Was it Tait?"

"I don't know. He'd hardly admit it to me, because I was with you at one of the times."

"Well, what about the time Melanie and Andrea were shot at?"

"If he did that, he never admitted it. I'm convinced he did, though."

"What about the robbery at the restaurant?"

"I don't think he's the one who did it. Tait was a braggart; he'd have said something. It was probably some drifter. This town's full of them. Tait was the one who set that tiger loose, though. The bastard had a big laugh about that."

"Zach, we've got to get out of here now. When the truth gets out, you could be hanged for cattle rustling."

"Don't worry. It's a long story, honey, but I'll explain everything later. Right now I have to get to that telegraph office, but I'm afraid to leave you here. This is the first place they'll look for you."

"I'll go next door into Kate's room. She'll help me."

"Okay. Stay out of sight. There's a good chance Tait might think this is the last place we'd show up, so the fewer who know we're here, the better."

"Kate can be trusted."

"Have her put something on that eye of yours."

"I will. Be careful, Zach."

He grinned. "Don't worry, Rosie, I can take care of myself. Now go on—I want to know you're safe before I leave."

She nodded and left the room. In a few seconds, Kate came to the door. "Don't worry, Zach. She'll be safe with me."

"Thanks, Kate. Take care of her. I'll get back as quickly as I can."

Kate nodded and went back to her room. Zach closed the door and climbed out the window.

As Zach came out of the telegraph office, Tait and his gang rode into Brimstone with the bodies of Stephen Rayburn and Will Grainger in the wagon. Their arrival and the news that Rayburn had been murdered attracted a crowd immediately.

"Who shot Rayburn?" the sheriff asked.

"That gal he was gonna marry. They had a big fight and she killed him."

"Who's the old guy?"

"One of the rustlers. Him and MacKenzie wuz in it together. We wuz bringin' the bodies to town when MacKenzie caught up with us. He drove off our mounts and rode off with that gal. By the time we rounded up our mounts, we figured we oughta get the bodies into town."

An angry murmuring rumbled through the crowd.

"That Miz Dubois was a nice gal," one of the men said. "Don't seem like she'd be the kind to kill a man."

Tait snorted. "Women are all whores. Ya can't trust any of 'em."

"What was Mr. Rayburn and her fightin' about, Tait?" Sheriff Bloom asked.

"He found out she wuz cheatin' on him with MacKenzie."

"She was cheatin' on him, all right," Rita confirmed, her mouth curved with a smug smile. "I saw her one night sneakin' into the Long Horn to meet her lover. And I was out at the Lazy R today when she showed up there."

"Sounds to me like Mr. Rayburn was doing some cheating himself," the storekeeper's wife said with a disparaging look at Rita.

Rita giggled. "He weren't the only man in this town cheatin' on his woman, lady."

"A man's got needs," the sheriff grumbled, "and there's no call to be shot for it. Did you hear what MacKenzie and this fella argued about?"

"Splittin' up the take. Heard him say they killed them Wilsons, too. Sounded like the old guy didn't like the idea of the gal ridin' along with 'em. He wanted to split up the take, and go their separate ways." Tait smirked. "Reckon MacKenzie had a different idea of what the old guy meant by 'separate ways.' "

Just then Bull and Joe came hurrying up to the crowd. "The doc ain't seen Miz Dubois, and she ain't at her rooming house or the restaurant," Bull said. "Her clothes are still in her room, but them other gals said they ain't seen her since mornin', and her boss told us she quit her job this mornin' and told him she wuz leavin' on the train tonight."

"Dammit!" Tait cursed. "They musta headed for Zanesville, or are hidin' out waitin' to catch that train tonight. Whatta ya gonna do about them, Sheriff?"

"Reckon I'll have to swear in some of you men for a posse and ride out to look for them."

"Me and the boys'll ride with you," Tait said.

When several other men volunteered as well, the sheriff swore them all in as deputies. "We got a better chance of finding them if we split up into two groups. Tait, you and the other Lazy R riders can be one, and all you other fellas come with me."

Zach couldn't have been more pleased. With the posse headed out of town it would buy him some time. He could only hope for a quick response to his telegram.

As soon as they rode away, the undertaker drove off with the two bodies, and the crowd dispersed, Zach stealthily returned to the boardinghouse. He paused when he saw the Harvey Girls come out of the house and head for the restaurant. Kate was among them. When he was certain the coast was clear, he climbed in the window of Rose's empty room and tapped lightly on Kate's door.

"Rose, it's me," he said softly. She opened the door and he stepped in and closed it. "Anyone else in the house?" She shook her head. "What about the housekeeper?"

"Mrs. White went to Albuquerque yesterday. Andre and Colette don't come back until after the dinner hour. Mr. Billings rents a room at the minister's house."

"Good. That gives us a little freedom, but we still have to keep out of sight."

"What's happening in town?"

"It's not good. Tait and the boys rode in with Rayburn's body and convinced the sheriff that you shot Rayburn in a lover's quarrel. The sheriff formed a posse and just rode out."

Her shoulders slumped in despair. "So now not only Tait's after me, but the sheriff, too."

"He's after both of us. They claimed I'm one of the rustlers who committed the Wilson murders, and then killed Will Grainger. Tait's gang rode out with the posse, but when they get back they're sure to check out this place again. We've got to figure out where to hide until I can prove Tait killed Rayburn."

"And how are you going to do that?"

"I'm waiting for an answer to my telegram, but that can take hours. Why don't you try and get some rest?"

Her head snapped up in surprise. "Rest! How do you expect me to rest, knowing there's a madman out to kill me and a posse searching for us?"

She was right. He walked over to her and tucked a finger under her chin, tilting her face up to look at him. Whatever Kate had done to Rose's eye had helped. It still was discolored, but the swelling was down. Time would heal the bruises on her cheeks, too.

"Rosie, you've had a rough time. A rest would do you good. How are you feeling?"

She tried unsuccessfully to smile. "Like I've been socked in the jaw."

He lightly traced the bruises on her cheek.

"Could have been worse. At least there are no bones broken."

Suddenly her expression changed back to desperation. "Zach, why don't we get out of here while we have the chance?"

"If we run now, every bounty hunter in the territory will be tracking us. The thing to do is clear our names once and for all."

"How can we do that? You said yourself that Tait has convinced everyone that we're both murderers. It's our word against theirs."

"Leave that to me."

"Zach, you're only one man. There's five of them! The sheriff thinks we're murderers—the town, too—so you can't expect anyone to help us." She turned away from him. "I don't want your death on my conscience, too." There was mounting hysteria in her voice.

He moved closer and put his hands on her shoulders. Her body was trembling. "Hey, honey, don't worry. I've gotten out of worse spots than this." He slipped his hands down her arms and pulled her back against him. Lord knows there'd been plenty of close calls that he'd escaped by the skin of his teeth. But this time Rose was in danger, too. His arms tightened around her. Despite everything, he had fallen in love with this woman. And as long as there was breath in him, nobody was going to hurt her again.

Not even him.

Chapter 21

The day passed slowly. Kate returned to change into her black uniform for the evening meal and thoughtfully brought them sandwiches and fruit. As they ate, she filled them in with the local gossip: Stephen Rayburn had been well thought of, and the citizenry was anxious to see that his murderer was punished.

As soon as she left, Rose slumped down on the bed. "How can anyone believe Tait's story?" Sighing, she lay back with her head on a pillow. "He's so evil."

Zach joined her on the bed. Stretching out on his side, he propped up his head in his palm and smiled tenderly at her.

"Because you're not there to defend yourself."

"Maybe it's a mistake for me to remain in hiding," she said, sounding demoralized and uncertain.

"Not if you want to stay alive. Have you forgotten Tait was on the verge of killing you? Show yourself now, and he'll finish the job. That damn sheriff won't try to stop him."

"Oh, Zach, how are we ever going to get out of this mess?"

She looked so sad and vulnerable that he wanted to hold her, but he knew he'd want more once she was in his arms. Instead, he lightly brushed aside the hair clinging to her bruised cheek. "Nothing's going to happen to you, Rosie. I promise you. As soon as I get an answer to my telegram, we'll get the help we need."

"I'm afraid we'll need a troop of cavalry to get out of here." She rolled over on her side, tucked a hand under her cheek, and closed her eyes.

For a long moment, he gazed at her. The trouble was, he didn't feel as confident as he implied. It was unlikely they could remain hidden much longer. His hope rested on a speedy response to his telegram.

He saw that Rose had fallen asleep. To avoid waking her, he stood up and went over to the window. Damn! Tait and his gang had returned to town and were at the depot checking the eastbound train that had just pulled in. Obviously in search of them, the gang boarded the train. They finally climbed off and began checking the passengers returning to board. Zach decided this would be the best chance to avoid being seen. He woke Rose.

"Honey, Tait and his gang are back. I'm going to

the telegraph office to see if the reply to my telegram has come in. Stay away from the window and don't open the door to anyone except me or Kate."

"But if Tait's in town, he might see you, Zach!"

"They're occupied checking the train so they must figure if we're in town, we'll try and leave on it. I should be able to get to the telegraph office and back before they're through."

As he started to climb out Kate's window, Rose came over to him and put a hand on his arm.

"Be careful, Zach. He wants to kill you, too."

He grinned at her. "Tait's on borrowed time, Rosie. Trust me. Now lock the door. I'll tap three times when I get back." Seeing her worried frown, he kissed her lightly on the nose. "Hey, Rosie, didn't I tell you I won't let anything happen to you?"

Zach succeeded in reaching the telegraph office without incident, only to get the bad news that there was still no response to his wire. Leaving the office, he saw a large crowd had gathered. To his further dismay, Tait was in the center of it elaborating on his lies about Rose's involvement in Rayburn's death. Maybe rather than remaining hidden, he should go on the offensive, Zach thought. He drew his Colt and spun the chamber. Satisfied, he sauntered over to the crowd.

"Tait, I understand you've been shooting your mouth off about me."

Tait's forced smile didn't fool Zach for a minute. He knew the man was itching to kill him. "You helped Rayburn's killer escape, didn't ya? Where ya got her hidden, MacKenzie?"

"Where you can't hurt her until she can prove her innocence. Maybe you should have checked those passengers more carefully before that train pulled out."

"What did I tell you, folks? He helped that killer get away."

"You're a damn liar, Tait. Rose Dubois didn't kill Rayburn—*you* did!"

As Zach had anticipated, the crowd swiftly backed away. They'd witnessed enough such confrontations to know what followed such an accusation. Now only Tait and his gang remained facing Zach.

Tait's thick lips curled in amusement, but his dark eyes glared blatant hatred. He slipped his hand to his holster. "Did I hear you call me a liar, MacKenzie?"

"Nothing wrong with your hearing, Tait."

"And I suppose she ain't the kind to cheat on Rayburn with you either, huh, MacKenzie?"

"That doesn't make her a murderer."

Cain and Pike started to sidle behind Zach. Not shifting his fixed stare from Tait, Zach said, "Rather have you boys stay where you are. Same goes for you and Joe, Bull."

"You don't see me movin', do ya?" Bull grumbled.

"You figure you can take us all, MacKenzie?" Tait asked.

"Can't say— but *you* won't live to find out. I'm not as easy to kill as Rayburn and that old couple you murdered."

"That's damn fool talk even from you, MacKenzie. Ya ready to back it up?"

"Anytime you feel lucky, Tait."

Pandemonium broke loose when Tait started to draw. Shouting men and screaming women scampered in all directions to get out of the line of fire. Tait's shot went astray, but Zach's bullet found its mark, and the outlaw was dead before he even hit the ground.

In a hail of bullets, Zach dived behind a horse trough as the gang scattered and ducked for cover. Water squirted like a fountain through the dozen bullet holes in the trough. A bullet ripped into his shoulder, and he looked around for better cover. The closest place was a run-down barn. He had to risk it, so he fired several rounds at the gang to make them keep their heads down, then crouched and dashed for the safety of the barn a few feet away. A bullet ripped into his leg just as he dived through the doors and closed them. Bullets splintered the wood as he shoved the bar in place to prevent anyone from entering, then he crawled away from the door.

Zach pulled off his bandanna and tied it around his thigh, then took a look around him. A loft, no window, and empty stalls. At least there'd be no way anyone could get in. The bad part was that he'd have to wait until dark to slip out of there, and time was running out: the sheriff and his posse might return before nightfall.

Several shots slammed into the door again, as if to remind him just how desperate his situation was. When he peered out through a crack he couldn't see anybody, but he knew there were at least four men out there hoping to gun him down. He was safe for the time being, though: none of the four were the kind to risk their hides by rushing him.

His shoulder was stinging and his leg hurt like hell. He reached behind and touched the back of his shoulder, then wiped his bloody hand on his pants leg. At least the bullet had gone right through him. The rip in his jeans at front and back showed the same was true of the wound in his thigh. Good.

Once again, bullets riddled the door. How long would those idiots continue to waste ammunition? At least he'd taken down Tait; the bastard couldn't hurt Rose now.

Grimacing with pain, he sat down, reloaded his pistol, then leaned back against a post and began to work out his strategy. He figured the loft door offered a better escape route than trying to pull out some rotted slats.

He knew damn well he'd get no help from the town. "You gotta admit, MacKenzie, this sure isn't the smartest move you've ever made," he said with self-deprecation. *What would you do in this spot, Dad? Uncle Luke? Uncle Cleve?* He wracked his brain, trying to remember their countless stories of narrow escapes.

Rose bolted to her feet the moment she heard the gunfire. Certain Zach was in the center of the shooting, her heart began pounding so hard it felt like her chest would burst. Ignoring his warning, she went to the window, but all she could see was the train depot. The shots were coming from the other end of town.

Frustrated, she began to pace the floor. Was Zach

still alive? Was he wounded? Maybe it was just a drunken cowboy shooting up the town. When the gunfire stopped suddenly she froze, unconsciously holding her breath. Her anxiety built to an over-whelming panic. She couldn't remain hidden in the room; Zach might be out there fighting for his life! Or lying dead in the middle of the street! She rushed to the door, then paused when the gunfire resumed. Relieved sobs burst from her throat. As long as the firing continued, it meant he was still alive. She had to go to him.

Just as she reached to turn the key in the lock, there was a rap on the door. Startled, she jumped back.

"Rose, it's Kate."

Her hand was trembling so much she could barely turn the key in the lock. Kate came in and at the sight of her grim expression, Rose's previous fear returned. Tears blinded her eyes and the knot in her throat burst into a wail of despair. "Zach's dead, isn't he?"

"No, Rose! No." Kate's eyes glistened with tears of compassion as she clasped Rose's hand. "He killed Jess Tait, and the rest of the gang's got him trapped in a barn."

Joy surged through Rose in a floodtide. "Then he's still alive, or they wouldn't be shooting. I've got to help him."

Kate pulled her back into the room and closed the door. "Rose, what help can you be to Zach if you rush out there half-cocked and possibly get yourself killed?"

Hot, salty tears stung her eyes and choked her

words into sobs. "Don't you understand? I love him, Kate. It's my fault he's even in this fix. I can't stand by and not try to help him."

"I understand, honey," Kate said, trying to soothe her. "But we've got to think this out."

"And while we're doing that, Zach could be killed! No, I'm going to him." Rose tried to leave but Kate's grasp held firmly.

"Listen to me, Rose. If you really want to help Zach, you'll take time to think what would be the best way to do so. He's safe in the barn for the time being. The sheriff and his posse haven't returned yet, and you can be sure those four fools aren't about to risk getting themselves killed by trying to go in after him. We've just got to think of a way to divert their attention so Zach can escape."

The wisdom of Kate's practicality began to cut a swath through Rose's panic. Little by little she felt warmth creep through her body, which had been cold with despair.

"I guess you're right—I've been too upset to use my head."

"That's right." Kate led Rose over to the bed. "So let's sit down and think this out. Surely the two of us can outsmart those four idiots."

"Well, we certainly can't start a fire, or we're liable to burn down the whole town."

"That's for sure," Kate agreed. "From what I've seen of that Bull, though, any woman can divert his attention."

Rose lifted her head. "Well, we're women, aren't we?"

"Sure, but you can't show your face, because

Tait's convinced everyone in town that you murdered Stephen Rayburn. And Bull wouldn't trust you anyway, even though he knows you didn't kill Stephen."

"I realize that, but he'd have no reason to distrust the rest of you." Rose jumped to her feet as an idea entered her head. "You girls could appear sympathetic and offer something like . . . ah—"

"Like what?" Kate asked, feigning indignation. "Just what do you have in mind, Rose Dubois? You know as well as I do what's always on Bull's mind."

"I was thinking more along the lines of a cup of coffee and pie, or cake."

"That's not a bad idea. We had a couple of apple pies left over from dinner. Maybe we can lure them into the restaurant with that offer."

"And when you do, I'll get to Zach."

"But I doubt they'd all just walk away from the barn and not leave someone behind to guard it."

"Right, but that will probably be Joe, because he's the dumbest. And Joe always does whatever Bull says. My guess is that probably makes Bull the leader now that Tait's dead."

Kate smiled with satisfaction. "And we all know that Bull only has one thing on his mind. A smile and an offer of coffee and pie from a gal is sure to give him even bigger ideas. It will be easy to get him away. And where Bull goes—"

"So go the others," Rose said.

"Rose, we can do it!" Kate exclaimed.

Rose felt there still was another obstacle to consider. "What about the people in town?"

"The decent people have returned to their homes.

They want nothing to do with it. The ones I talked to said Zach goaded Tait into drawing by calling him a liar, but at the same time, he let Tait make the first move."

"Then why don't they help Zach?" Rose cried, feeling the return of her frustration.

"Honey, nobody's going to put their lives on the line against four armed outlaws, unless it personally affects their own families. Remember, they consider Zach as bad as the rest of the gang, so what do they care who shoots who? As for the no-gooders in town, they don't much care who ends up on Boot Hill. So let's get this done before the sheriff gets back."

"Do you think the other girls will be willing to help?"

"I'm sure they will. None of them believed for a minute that you killed Stephen Rayburn."

Within minutes, the other Harvey girls had joined them in Kate's room. All three were appalled to see how Stephen had beaten Rose and were eager to help in whatever way they could.

Kate laid out the plan, and the girls hurried to their rooms to put their uniforms back on.

Kate paused before leaving. "I know this will work. Zach will be okay, honey."

"I'll be going with him, Kate," Rose said.

"I know." She smiled softly. "I'll miss you."

They reached for each other, and Rose hugged her tightly. In a world that had turned chaotic, she clung to Kate for solace.

"I'll never forget you, or what you and the girls are doing for Zach."

"When this is all over, come back to us, Rose," Kate whispered. Then she turned and left.

Rose changed quickly into her split skirt and blouse, exchanged her shoes for a pair of boots, then stuffed a few of her items into Zach's saddlebags.

Tears glistened in her eyes as she stood by the window and watched the small, white-aproned army march down the road to do battle. After they passed, she climbed out, praying it wouldn't be too late to save the man she loved.

Chapter 22

Rose hurried down the back street, darkened now under the mantle of a night heavy with the smell of a coming rain. Distant flashes of lightning and the faint rumble of thunder heralded the approaching storm, and she quickened her step.

The street was deserted, the doors and windows of the houses closed and bolted, as if sealing out the sights and sounds of the grievous injustice occurring at the barn would shut it out of the occupants' consciences.

She passed behind the Long Horn. Laughter rose above the discordant pounding of a piano, the only sound other than the sporadic gunfire that echoed through the night.

An amber light glowed dimly from the telegraph

office—a painful reminder to her of what had brought Zach to the spot. And as she passed the office, she caught a glimpse of the outline of the barn. Her heart leaped to her throat.

Rose's jagged nerves were jarred by the sudden screeching of two cats fighting in the shadows. She jumped back in alarm when one dashed across her path, followed by a larger black one.

She wasn't superstitious, but why did this sign of bad luck happen now—when so much was at stake? A wave of apprehension washed through her as she remembered the gypsy's foreboding message. *I zaw za face of death.*

She reached the barn and slinked along the side of it, hugging the shadows and hoping no one would spot her.

"Hey, pretty lady, whatta you doin' here?"

Distressed, she recognized Bull's voice. She'd been discovered already—and now there was little she could do to help Zach.

"This ain't no place for you gals. You could get yerselves shot."

Oh, thank God. He wasn't talking to her. Her spirits rose as she heard Kate reply, "We felt so sorry for you fellows, Bull, that we thought perhaps you'd all like a cup of coffee and piece of apple pie."

Peering through the darkness, Rose located the small group clustered in a circle about a hundred feet away.

"Uh-huh!" Joe exclaimed." That sure would be pleasin'. My mouth's waterin' just thinkin' about it."

Flashing a dimpled smile, Melanie tilted her

curly head at a captivating angle. "And there's no charge for it, Joey."

"How come you gals are being so nice to us?" Bull asked. "You never even wanted us in your restaurant before."

"We were only following orders, Bull," Kate said. "Why, in our eyes you fellows are heroes, the only ones protecting us from that ruthless killer in that barn."

"I'm afraid to even lie down and close my eyes until that killer's behind bars," Aubrey added with a shudder.

"And if I had my say-so, you men would never have to pay for another meal again in a Harvey restaurant." Andrea's remark appeared to please them, because they hooted with approval.

"Gotta admit, hot coffee, apple pie, and the pleasure of good company is mighty temptin'. But we've got a desperado holed up in that barn. We all jest can't up and leave."

Rose felt like screaming. Bull was taking his newly found leadership role more seriously than she'd anticipated, and they were running out of time.

"Oh, fiddle-faddle!" Melanie exclaimed, grasping Cain's hand. "You all don't have to stay back to guard one li'l ole prisoner, do you?"

Cain nodded. "Reckon, she's right, Bull."

"Yeah, Bull, it'd be a shame to let that pie go to waste," Pike added hopefully.

Kate linked her arm through their leader's. "Oh, come on, Bull," she coaxed. "Don't be such a spoil-sport. Coffee's on the stove."

"Hmmm, this calls for some ponderin'," he said, stroking his chin. "Reckon it don't make no sense for all of us to stay here—MacKenzie won't even know we're gone. Joe, you stay put. There's only one way out of that there barn. If MacKenzie so much as sticks his head out that door, get off three quick shots as a signal and we'll come arunnin'."

"That ain't fair, Bull. Why do I have to stay behind? I like apple pie same as the rest of yuh."

"Tell you what, Joe. I'll bring you back a piece myself. How about that?" Kate said.

"Reckon that'll have to do," he said with a pout. " 'Pears like I ain't got no say in it."

The minutes felt like hours as Rose waited for Kate's return. The sheriff and his posse could ride in at any minute.

As soon as she saw Kate coming down the street, Rose picked up Zach's saddlebags. Now that the time had come to execute the most difficult part of the plan, she was suddenly calm and in complete control.

Plate in hand, Kate reached Joe, and Rose began to move cautiously closer to them. As she sneaked up behind him, Rose heard Joe say, "This sure is fine-tastin' pie."

"I'm glad you like it, Joe," Kate said, watching Rose's approach.

Rose drew a deep breath and with all her might swung the saddlebags at Joe's head. The plate slipped out of his hands and he fell unconscious to the ground.

"Good heavens, did you kill him?" Kate put her

head to Joe's chest, then looked up, relieved. "He's still breathing."

"He'll be okay; it just knocked him out." Rose opened the saddlebags and dug out bandannas and the pieces of rope they had cut earlier. "Hurry and tie up Joe while I get Zach."

Rose ran to the barn door and called out, "Zach, it's Rose." She knew if she tried opening it without warning, he'd likely shoot her by mistake.

"Rose! What in hell are you doing down here?"

"Open the door; it's safe to come out."

She wanted to fling herself into his arms when he slipped the bar and stepped outside. "What happened? Where are the others?" he asked.

"I'll explain it all later. Right now we've got to get out of here." She ran back to Kate, who had bound and gagged Joe, and was now sitting against a tree in the process of binding her own ankles together. Rose knelt beside her. "I hate to do this to you, Kate."

"Just go ahead and get out of here." She thrust up her arms and Rose quickly tied her wrists together. "Good luck, you two."

Rose and Kate exchanged a long look, then Rose tied the gag on her mouth. "Can you breathe okay?" Kate nodded. "Thank you for everything." She kissed Kate on the forehead, then turned away.

"What next, General Lee?" Zach asked.

"Grab those saddlebags and come with me. I passed a hitching post that had some horses tied to it. We can take two of them and get out of here."

"They hang horse thieves you know," he said lightly.

"Have you got a better idea?"

"Not at the moment." He picked up the saddle-bags. "Let's go, Rosie."

As they hurried away, Rose noticed that he was limping. "What's wrong with your leg?"

"It's nothing."

When they reached the hitching post, Zach recognized the horses. "These are Lazy R mounts. That's the sorrel Tait always rode. Take that black; it's a better horse than the other three," he said as he climbed up on Tait's sorrel.

"Where are we headed?" she asked.

"West."

They galloped out of Brimstone and within seconds were swallowed up by darkness.

Shifting to get more comfortable, Kate glanced over at Joe. He'd regained consciousness in time to see Rose and Zach ride away, and was now struggling to free himself. Kate did the same to keep up appearances.

After about fifteen minutes Joe succeeded in freeing his hands, and he'd just finished untying Kate when the rest of the gang returned from the restaurant.

Bull's lips narrowed in a disgusted line when Joe told him of Zach's escape. "How could he have gotten out of that barn without you seein' him?"

"He had help, Bull—two people rode off on the west road. I only got a glance, but it looked to be a woman with him."

"Most likely that Dubois gal," Pike said.

"Them two's been together all this time. You

dumb idiot! Why wasn't ya watchin' like ya wuz supposed to be doin'?"

"I wuz till I set down to eat my pie." Joe looked around and picked the pie up off the ground, brushed it off, then proceeded to eat it.

Bull tramped over to Kate. "I suppose yer gonna tell me you didn't see who wuz with him either."

"It all happened so quickly, Bull, I really don't know."

"I think ya do. Yer coverin' up for your murderin' girlfriend, ain't ya?"

"Bull, you knowed as well as I that gal never killed—"

Bull smacked him across the mouth. "Shut up, Joe."

"Hey, Bull," Cain said, running up to them. " 'Pears like MacKenzie rode off on Tait's sorrel. And the black that Pike wuz riding's gone, too."

"Shit!" Bull looked furious and turned his wrath on Kate. "Ya know more than yer tellin' me, so start talkin' or that face of yours ain't gonna look so pretty when I'm done with ya. Where are they headed for?"

Fear rose in Kate, as chilling as a blast of northern air in winter. These men were murderers—and she had angered the worst one of them.

"I've told you everything I know, Bull. This all has been very distressing to me. I'm going back to the restaurant." Kate turned to leave, but Bull grabbed her arm.

"Ya gonna be more *distressed*, sister, if ya don't tell me where they're headed."

She cried out in pain when he twisted her arm,

forcing her to her knees. "I swear I don't know. They didn't say. Please stop, you're hurting me."

"I'll break your damn arm if you don't tell me."

"Let her go, Bull. Can't you tell she's tellin' the truth?" Joe yelled. "Who cares about MacKenzie anyway? He don't mean nothin' to us."

"He killed Tait," Cain said.

"So what? I never liked Tait either," Joe argued. " 'Sides, Tait was a damn fool to think he could out-draw MacKenzie. We all seen how fast he is."

"Yeah, well, MacKenzie prodded him into drawin'," Pike declared in defense of his dead leader.

Snarling, Bull shoved Kate to the ground. "This is wastin' time. Let's get movin'. MacKenzie's got a big enough head start on us as it is."

Kate lay still, too petrified to move as they continued to argue.

"Why risk our asses goin' after him?" Joe asked. "Let's just clear out like we planned."

"You ain't figured it out yet, have ya? The money Tait took from Rayburn's safe wuz in the saddle-bags on the sorrel MacKenzie rode off on. We gotta find him."

"But you ain't got no horse, Bull," Joe said.

"No, *you* ain't; 'cause I'm takin' yours."

"What am *I* gonna do?"

"Steal one, if yur comin' with us."

Relieved that Bull hadn't put a bullet into her, Kate got to her feet as the gang hurried to their horses. If she was any judge of human nature, Zach MacKenzie would have no problem evading this gang. But Bull had raised a good question: just where *was* he headed when he and Rose rode away? He could have chosen any direction, so why west?

She brushed herself off and was on her way back to the restaurant when the sheriff and his posse rode up.

"Howdy, ma'am," the sheriff said. "Ain't it pretty late for you to be out walkin' the streets, Miz Mc-Dermott? Especially with the recent murders."

She considered the sheriff not much better than the gang that had just left. "It's a lot safer now that Tait's gang of outlaws have left."

"What gang?"

"That other *posse* you deputized. Sheriff Bloom, how could you give Jess Tait and his gang of outlaws a legal right to shoot innocent people!" Her eyes blazed with indignation. "They admitted that Tait killed Stephen Rayburn and stole money from his safe." She put her hands on her hips and stamped her foot in the dust. "And you . . . you've been out trying to hunt down an innocent man and woman. While you were gone, Tait tried to kill Zach MacKenzie: the only man in this town willing to stand up against that lying bully, and accuse the real murderer. Fortunately Tait failed, and Zach shot him before he had a chance to try it again. Then, thanks to your blunder, your *deputies* tried to shoot Zach, but he managed to take cover in that old barn down the street. Are you following me?" she asked, making no attempt to conceal her anger. She paused to take a breath.

"Reckon so. MacKenzie's down in the barn now," he said.

"I didn't say that. He escaped, and those

scoundrels took off after him because he rode off on Tait's horse."

"They were just doing their duty. Horse thieving's a serious crime in these parts, Miz McDermott."

"Oh-h-h, you're impossible!" She was so angry she shook her fist at him. "You don't seem to care about murder or cattle rustling, but stealing a horse is a major crime. For your information, Sheriff Bloom, duty had nothing to do with it. Those cutthroats rode after him because Tait left the money he stole from Rayburn in his saddlebags. Now, just what do you intend to do about it?"

"Go down to the Long Horn and have a drink. Me and the boys have been riding most of the day. We're hungry, thirsty, and tired."

Kate was on the verge of screaming with frustration when Charlie Jenkins, the telegraph operator, ran up to them.

"Sheriff, have you seen Zach MacKenzie? He's been waiting for this telegram all day." Jenkins held up the paper clutched in his hand.

"Nope. Understand he rode out of here."

"Pursued by a bunch of outlaws trying to kill him," Kate spoke up, with a derogatory glance at the sheriff.

Jenkins chuckled. "They best hope they don't succeed. He ain't no outlaw. Zach MacKenzie's a Texas Ranger."

Chapter 23

Despite the need to put distance between them and Brimstone as quickly as possible, Zach followed the road at a moderate speed. It would be foolhardy to gallop across the rugged terrain at night; one of the horses might step in a pothole and break a leg. Right now a healthy horse was more necessary than his Colt. His shoulder ached, his leg felt like it was on fire, and the ride wasn't doing either of the wounds any good. He was still losing blood. Eventually they'd have to stop to treat the wounds, or he wouldn't be worth spit in the wind.

Zach turned his head and glanced at the silent rider behind him. Conversation was impossible at the moment, but Rose appeared to be doing fine. She had a lot of grit. Fiery and feisty, willing to challenge him even about the time of day, but in a crisis she trusted his judgment.

There was so much he had to tell her. He couldn't help but worry how Rose would take the news that he was a Texas Ranger. She made no secret about how she hated lawmen, and probably would be more upset that he was a Ranger than a lowdown drifter. Yeah, she'd hit the roof for sure.

But he couldn't have told her sooner. He'd been working undercover; then she'd become engaged to the very man he suspected.

Zach grimaced in pain, thinking of Will Grainger. Will had been his contact with the Ranger office, but more than that, had been a mentor to Zach—as he had been to Josh before him. He loved the old-timer, and when Pike and Cain had brought in Will's body, he'd wanted to start blasting at them right then and there.

Granted, he'd had plenty of time to admit the truth to her today, but they both had too much on their minds to muddy up the water any more than it was already.

As soon as they were out of this mess, though, he'd set her down and explain.

Knowing Rose, she'd be madder than hell. Zach grinned. The beauty was, she'd get over it just as fast. Because now they were committed to each other. It was a new feeling—one he hadn't understood before.

He'd always been curious about those special looks between his father and mother, but now he understood what they meant: commitment. An unspoken message that said, right or wrong, I'm there for you.

And that was the feeling between Rose and him. It meant he'd put her welfare ahead of his own, as she would for him. Sure, somewhere in the mixture he knew that loving her and wanting her physically was part of it, too; but the feeling went far beyond love, or sex, or the desire to be with her above all others. It was like what they were doing now: riding through the night together, no physical contact of any kind, not even talking—yet having an awareness of each other that comforted.

He'd never expected that one day he'd know this feeling.

And it felt good.

When large raindrops began to splatter the dust, Zach reined in and Rose rode up beside him.

"There's a poncho in my saddlebags. Better put it on."

"What about you?" she asked.

"I'll be okay."

Rose dug the garment out of the saddlebags, and by the time she managed to get it on the storm had moved in on them.

Jagged lightning pierced the darkness, accompanied by earsplitting booms of thunder. Rose jerked in fright every time one of the luminous spears streaked from the sky.

She was scared of lightning—petrified of it. She'd carried the fear in her heart since childhood, when her mother had warned her that lightning was a sign of God's anger for their sins.

Now, helpless and unprotected, Rose hunched lower in the saddle and feared His anger was directed at her. Were her and Zach's sins so grievous to have incurred His wrath?

In no time, the rain began to cascade in waterfalls off the granite summits of the buttes, flowing like rivers through the gulches and narrow ravines below to gorge even deeper into the existing gullies. Visibility had narrowed to a few feet, and conversation was impossible. She felt relieved when Zach motioned to the rocky wall bordering the road. Although it couldn't offer any protection, she figured that standing in the storm was a darn sight better than riding through it.

Shivering, Rose watched as Zach began to check along the base of the rocky wall. After several feet she could no longer see him through the downpour, but he reappeared a few moments later.

Grabbing the reins of her horse, he motioned to her to follow. After about twenty yards he stopped at where his horse had been tethered to a scrub of tumbleweed.

"There's room to shimmy under that layer of rock over there," he shouted, above the thunder.

Rose nodded and crawled under the projecting slab of rock. Zach followed close behind, and she shifted onto her side to make room for him. They were cramped, lying face-to-face on their sides, but at least it got them out of the storm.

Rose was shivering so hard her teeth began to rattle.

"What are you doing?" Zach asked, when she began squirming in an effort to get out of the wet poncho.

"This poncho's wet and bulky." She worked it up

to her waist, then managed to raise her head and shoulders high enough to enable Zach to shove it over her head. Although her skirt was sodden, her bodice was only damp.

Zach pulled Rose closer and she willingly cuddled against him. Gradually the warmth of their combined body heat penetrated through her wet clothing, and she stopped shivering.

"This storm should pass over soon," he said. His breath was a pleasant warmth at her ear.

"Keep talking, MacKenzie. It feels good."

He kissed her until she was breathless. "How does that feel?"

"Even better," she said.

"I have a pint of whiskey in my saddlebags. We could use it right now."

"Don't even think of moving," she commanded. "I'm just beginning to feel a little warmer. Besides, I can't swallow lying down." She attempted a smile.

"Smiling, Miz Rose?"

"Trying to. Sorry, but it's the best I can offer when lying soaking wet under a rock while lightning and thunder are scaring the sass out of me. I've got a confession to make, Zach. I'm scared to death of lightning."

He hugged her tighter. "Honey, I told you I won't let anything happen to you"

"Right now I'm having a hard time believing you. Let's try that kiss again."

He covered her lips, and for a few precious seconds she put everything out of her mind except the pure pleasure of the kiss. But regretfully, all good things had to come to an end.

"Did it help?" he asked.

"Yes, but these wet clothes are a problem. If I had them off, I'd be in good shape."

He slid his hand inside her bodice. She gasped aloud when his cold hand touched her breast, but soon she felt the rise of heat as her body began to respond to the gentle massage.

"I'd say, wet or dry, it feels like your body's in fine shape, Miz Rose."

"I swear you're perverted, Zach MacKenzie. You aren't actually thinking about sex at a time like this."

"I do nothing but think about sex. However, I'm doing this for medicinal purposes: to warm you."

"Under any other circumstances I'd say you're lying, but it *is* helping to warm me, so don't stop."

He chuckled. "It's helping to warm me, too, Rosie."

"Just the same, I hope we can get out of these wet clothes soon."

"Now who's thinking about sex?"

She nipped at his ear. "You know what I mean."

"Once the rain stops, we'll be able to change clothes. I'm sure I can find something dry for you to put on."

"I'm ahead of you on that one. I stuffed some of my clothing into your saddlebags." She yawned and her eyelids began to droop. "I think I'm falling asleep."

"If you're afraid of lightning, how can you fall asleep in the middle of a storm?"

"Because you're holding me, Zach."

"That's sweet, honey." His voice trailed off and

his hand stilled, her breast still cupped in his palm. Then the slight brush of his even breathing on her temple confirmed to her that he had fallen asleep.

She closed her eyes.

Rose was awakened by Zach kicking away the saddles he'd piled across the front of the opening. It was daylight, and more importantly, it wasn't raining.

When Rose squirmed out after him, she winced with pain. The effects of the beating had been exacerbated by sleeping on the ground in wet clothing. She was so stiff and sore she could barely move, and felt as if every bone in her body was aching.

Zach was checking the horses, and she called, "Good morning."

He turned his head and smiled. "Hi. How are you feeling?"

"Like something that just crawled out from under a rock."

"It'll pass. Thank goodness our mounts seem none the worse for the ordeal," he said, continuing his inspection.

"Unfortunately, I'm not a horse," Rose grumbled. She buried her head in her hands to ward off the dizziness that had occurred when she sat up. She'd never felt so miserable, yet he was more concerned about the darn horses than he was about her.

Well, the first thing she'd do was get out of the wet clothes. She pulled the saddlebags over and dug out a change of clothing.

Her legs wobbled so badly when she attempted to stand up that she sank to her knees. She knew she had to force herself to move to work the stiffness out of her body, so she tried again and succeeded in getting to her feet.

When she started to unbutton her blouse, she saw bloodstains. Horrified, she saw some on her skirt, too. "I'm bleeding!"

Frantically, she began to grope all over her body but couldn't find the source of the bleeding. She looked in panic at Zach, who had come over to her side, and froze, staring horrified at his bloodstained shirt and pants.

"Oh, my God, Zach. It's you, not me." Clearly the wound to his leg had not been as trifling as he'd indicated—fresh stains appeared on his pant leg. Just as distressing were the ones on his shirt. He'd never mentioned a wound to his shoulder. There appeared to be new stains there, as well. "Your leg, Zach! Your shoulder! How much blood have you lost?"

"They've been bleeding off and on. But the bullets are out, so they just need some tending to."

"Well, sit down, for heaven's sake, and let me look at them." She took his arm and led him over to lean back against the rock wall. As she pushed him down to a sitting position, she noticed that his body had offered little resistance. Her heart leaped to her throat. He was becoming weaker, which meant he'd lost a great deal of blood.

Gingerly, she slipped the shirt off him. The puckered bullet hole in the front of his shoulder looked small enough, but the exit wound on his back was larger and uglier.

Thinking of how he'd endured such an injury

throughout the night without saying a word tore her apart. The anguish surfaced as anger. How could he have been so cavalier about his injuries?

She rooted through his saddlebags and dug out a roll of gauze. Then she ripped up the petticoat she had brought along and folded several sections into square wads.

"What are you looking for now?" he asked, when she dug into the saddlebags again.

"That whiskey you mentioned last night."

She not only found the whiskey, but a jar of spiced apples. "Bless you, Mrs. Downing," she murmured.

After cleaning the wounds with whiskey, Rose covered each with a compress and tied those on with torn strips of her petticoat.

When she started to pull off one of his boots, he tried to stop her. "I can do that."

"Sit still," she ordered, and removed his boots. "Now the pants."

"You gonna take those off me, too?"

"What do you think?" She wanted to cry when she removed the bloody bandanna tied around his thigh.

"I fantasized about moments like this," he said, when she unbuckled his pants. He shifted so she could lower the pants past his hips.

"Did you fantasize about bleeding to death, too?"

Rose cleaned and bandaged his thigh, and by the time she got him fully dressed in dry clothing, she felt totally exhausted. As she knelt catching a much-needed breath, her heart was aching—all the bandages and disinfectants in the world couldn't replenish the blood he'd lost. And that was the fear that preyed on her mind.

Zach leaned his forehead against hers. "Don't be mad at me, Rosie." There was more amusement than contrition in his voice.

Didn't he know she'd be unable to bear it if something happened to him? She loved him beyond measure—beyond expression.

"It's not funny, Zach. You're old enough to know how serious this is."

He pulled her into his arms. "Honey, I'll be fine. It takes more than a couple slugs to bring down a MacKenzie."

"Is that a family battle cry?" she snapped, but she snuggled closer against him. She wanted to believe it. It felt so good to be in his arms again, to feel the warmth and strength of him. It was the only medicine she needed. She slipped her arms around his neck and kissed him. "You ready for a breakfast of spiced apples?"

"We'd better get moving," Zach said as soon as they finished eating.

She put the empty jar aside. "Not before I put your arm in a sling."

"No."

"Zach, a sling will keep your arm steady and prevent the wound from opening again. You can't afford to lose any more blood."

"I am not wearing any sling."

There was an emphatic finality to the declaration. He picked up his gunbelt and buckled it on. "I'll saddle the horses while you get out of those wet clothes."

A change of clothing and a quick brush of her hair helped to make her more comfortable but did little to ease her worry over Zach. He had just begun to go through Tait's saddlebags when she joined him. "Is there room in there for our wet clothes?"

"Sure," Zach said. "I don't see anything worth saving in here." He shoved their clothing into one of the pouches, then untied the other one.

Suddenly he expelled a long, low whistle.

"What is it?" she asked.

"Look at this." He pulled out a thick handful of greenbacks.

Rose gaped in surprise. "There must be hundreds and hundreds of dollars there!"

"This must be the money Tait stole from Rayburn's safe."

"What are you going to do about it, Zach?"

He shoved it back into the pouch. "Nothing I can do right now. Dammit, this is bad news."

"Why? You didn't steal it."

"But Tait's gang knows I've got it. I figured they might turn back when the rain started, because they had nothing to gain by following us. But now they'll come after us to get this money back. Let's get out of here. We've wasted valuable time."

Chapter 24

Zach had minimized his condition so he didn't scare Rose more, but he could tell he was getting weaker. The sooner he got to a doctor, the better. But if they stayed on this road, Tait's gang would probably catch up with them in a few hours. They'd have to move up to higher ground, where there'd be better cover. It'd be slower and harder going, but there'd be less chance of being seen. He swung off the road and started to follow a narrow climbing trail, and once again Rose rode silently behind him.

A wall of rock formed the inside of the trail, with a sharp drop on the other side. Zach turned his head to glance back at Rose. Her bruised face was pale and tight-lipped as she hugged the wall, as far away from the treacherous rim as she could get. The poor kid was scared to death. She was too inexperienced to be on horseback on the slippery path, where the slightest false step or stumble could send her plunging over the side to her death.

He dismounted. "These horses need a rest. We'd best walk for a while." Rose climbed down cautiously, and the moment she set both feet on the ground, she appeared to relax. "We'll have to lead them up," Zach said. When she nodded, he grabbed the reins of his horse and moved on.

The trail finally widened, opening onto a sprawling plateau covered with cottonwoods and ponderosa pines, thick clumps of mesquite, and clusters of huge granite boulders. He'd traveled this trail several times before and knew where to find shelter and fresh water, which would give them an advantage if they were followed. But the steep climb had drained even more of his strength. He needed to rest or he wouldn't be much good to Rose or himself. Zach walked to the rim of the rocky ridge and gazed down at the flat plain hundreds of feet below. If only he knew how close their pursuers were . . .

His wish was immediately answered as four horseman rode into view below. They were too far away to identify, but it had to be the Tait gang.

"We've got company, Rose." She came over to his side, and he pointed to the horsemen.

"How can you tell it's them?" she asked.

"I don't believe in coincidence. It's them, all right."

"Maybe they'll stay down there and continue to follow the road."

"They'd have to be blind not to see the spot where we left it. The ground was still soft from the rain, so there'll be prints." And if he hadn't been so light-headed from loss of blood, he would have realized that at the time and erased them. Damn!

His suspicions were confirmed when the riders veered off the main road. "Let's get moving. They should crest the ridge by dusk, so we've got a half a day on them at the most." With his waning strength, would it be enough?

They stopped twice to rest and water the horses. Rose gathered up hazel nuts and stuffed them in her skirt pocket at one stop. Though he'd seen plenty of wild game in the area he didn't dare risk the sound of a gunshot, and there wasn't time to try to trap a rabbit or squirrel. So hazel nuts it would have to be.

Bright moonlight lit the trail by the time they reached the spot he'd been looking for. He didn't dare push himself any more or he'd be useless the next day. He dismounted stiffly.

Rose rode up to him. "Are we staying here?"

"Yeah, there's a narrow passage in that wall of boulders. It'll give us good cover for the night."

The passage opened into an area large enough for the horses, too. By now, Zach barely had the strength to lift the saddles off them. When he finished, he sank down on the ground and unbuckled his gunbelt.

Wishing they'd saved a few of the spiced apples, Rose emptied the nuts out of her pocket and came over and knelt in front of him. "Zach, are you okay?" Her voice was heavy with concern.

"Yeah, I just need a little rest. I'll be fine in the morning."

"I want to build a fire so I can check your wounds."

"Too risky. You can do it tomorrow morning." He reached out and gently caressed the bruises on her cheek. "How are you doing, honey?"

"I'm fine, Zach. They don't even hurt anymore."

"It's a good thing Tait killed that bastard, or I would have."

"I was so stupid, Zach. You tried to tell me from the start, but I wouldn't listen to you. Now you're hurt, and it's all my fault." Tears glistened in her eyes.

"I knew what I was doing, so stop blaming yourself. But tell you what, Rosie love—if you feel that bad, I know a way you can make it up to me after I get my strength back."

"Can't you ever be serious? I'm worried about you, Zach."

"Didn't I tell you we'll get out of this?"

She buried her head against his chest. "Oh, Zach, I love you so much."

"I love you, too, Rosie. Lord, how I love you."

He put an arm round her and they lay back. She snuggled against his side and tucked her head in the hollow of his shoulder. Zach put all thoughts of danger and survival out of his mind and let himself enjoy the contentment of just being together for a while.

He thought Rose might have fallen asleep until she murmured softly, "Zach, can't you feel the love in here?"

"Uh-huh."

"Do you suppose this place is enchanted?"

"Could be. My dad and mom once stayed in this same spot, when they were being pursued by Indians. This could be the very place where they fell in love."

"Are you serious?"

"Yeah. That's how I knew about this trail and this place. My mom told me about it when I was younger, and when I had the chance, I came and found the places she'd described to me. This is one of them."

She sat up and began to gently stroke his head. The touch of her hand was a soothing balm. "What a beautiful story. I'd love to hear all of it."

"Well, my dad was what you'd call a loner when he was younger. He wasn't anything like my uncles, and from what I'm told, not much like his father, either. My Grandfather MacKenzie died at the Alamo fighting for Texas's freedom."

"So your roots have always been in Texas," Rose said.

"Yeah, but I never got a chance to know my Grandma MacKenzie, either. She'd gone to the Alamo with my grandpa, but once the fighting got fierce, he sent his family back to the ranch. My Uncle Luke was two years old when his daddy died, my dad was one, and my Uncle Cleve was born six months later."

"Oh, how sad."

"Reckon it gets sadder. Grandma never remarried, and years later, while my dad and uncles were off fighting in the War Between the States, a band of

Comancheros raided the ranch and killed Grandma and my Uncle Luke's first wife. Dad and my uncles spent the next few years tracking down the Walden Gang that did it."

"Was your mother born in Texas, too?" Rose asked.

"No, Mom was born in Georgia. Her name was Garnet Scott. She was a widow and had come West on a wagon train after the war. That's how she met Dad."

Zach always felt a rise of pride whenever he thought about his father. "My dad can read a trail better than most men, so he did a lot of scouting back then. Some for the army, but mostly for wagon trains."

"So he was the scout on the wagon train your mother was on. Oh, how romantic!" Rose exclaimed.

"No, unfortunately. Had he been, maybe everyone on that train wouldn't have been massacred."

"I don't understand. Didn't you say that's how your parents met?"

"Yeah, but at the time, Dad was following the trail of a couple of members of the Walden Gang. He was up on the high ground here and saw a lot of Indian sign, and when he spied the wagon train down below he figured the Comanche were going to attack. He rode down and warned them to turn back, but nobody paid any attention to him except my mom. When he left, she followed him back up here and he had no choice but to take her with him. They still ended up having to fight off Comanche and a couple bad hombres." He chuckled warmly. "Mom told me she was determined to marry him from the start, but Dad had different ideas. By the time he got around to admitting how much he loved her, I was already a bun in the oven."

Rose smiled. "They sound wonderful."

"They are."

"Is your mother pretty, Zach?"

"Can't say I ever gave it much thought, 'cause she's always been beautiful to me," he murmured, yawning. "You remind me a lot of her, Rosie. She's feisty and outspoken—and she's got red hair, too."

"And your father?"

"Just the opposite. Dad's reticent, with a mind of his own. But when they're together, they're a single unit. They worship each other."

"And you worship them," she said, and pressed a light kiss on his lips.

"Reckon I do. Can't think of a time they ever gave me cause not to."

"Zach, I don't understand something. If you love and respect your parents so much, how can you pursue the life you've chosen? I can't believe they approve of it."

He'd never have a better opening to tell her the truth about himself. "That's what we've got to talk about, honey. You see, honor and duty have always run deep in my family. That's the code I was raised to respect."

"Duty to what, Zach? Country?"

"Ah . . . service."

"Service to your country. Of course, I understand." She cuddled closer.

"You're forgetting my family are Texans, Rosie. We also hold a duty to Texas."

"Really, Zach, you talk as if Texas is a separate country."

"We tend to look at it that way; that's why we call ourselves the Lone Star State. When we won our independence from Mexico, we had to protect ourselves against all kinds of enemies: Indians, Mexicans, bandits. So the Texas Rangers were formed to protect our borders and uphold the law."

"So this duty and service you're referring to is to the Texas Rangers."

"That's right, honey."

"Are you trying to tell me that your father is a Texas Ranger?"

"He was. So were my uncles and a couple of my cousins."

She chuckled. "That must make it interesting when you have a family gathering. Lawmen on one side of the room; you on the other."

"Well—I reckon we're all on the same side of the room."

"What do you mean?"

Zach took a deep breath.

"I'm a Texas Ranger, Rosie."

She started to laugh. "Next you'll tell me Jess Tait was one, too."

"No, but Will Grainger was. We were working together."

She looked at him as if he'd just slapped her in the face. "You're serious. You really *are* a lawman."

"I wanted to tell you a dozen times, Rosie. To warn you about Rayburn when I began to find evidence that linked him to the rustling, but—"

"Don't say another word. Not now, Zach." She turned her back to him.

He put his hand on her shoulder. "Honey, you've got to believe me: I never wanted to lie to you."

"I don't know what to believe, Zach. And I don't want to hear any more right now."

"If you believe anything, believe that I love you, Rosie."

She couldn't breathe. The shock of his words was as painful as the physical aches she'd sustained. Her heart felt weighted with anguish. They had vowed their love to each other. How could he have withheld such truth from her? Betrayed her? She closed her eyes and let the silent tears slide down her cheeks.

Rose felt the warmth and opened her eyes. It was lighter in the chamber but there was no sunlight; long shadows deepened the entrance. The heat came from Zach, who was curled against her.

She felt his head and he opened his eyes. They were dulled by fever.

"Zach, you're burning up."

He sat up slowly. "Yeah, I know. I just need a drink of water."

Even his voice sounded weak. She shook her head. "You need more than water, Zach. You can't go anywhere with that fever."

"There's a stream nearby. Once I get some water, I'll be okay. Let's get going."

"Not before I change those dressings on your wounds."

"You can do that at the stream."

Her heart ached for him when he struggled to his feet. For several seconds he leaned against his horse, then bent down and labored to swing the saddle off the ground. She hurried over to give him a helping hand.

When they were ready to leave, Rose reached into her pocket and offered him a handful of nuts. "At least eat these. You can do that while you're riding."

After riding in a downpour, sleeping on the cold ground in wet clothing, no medicine to treat two bullet wounds, and blood loss followed by another day of no rest, it was a miracle that only the entry wound on his shoulder had become infected. But the infection looked bad.

Rose wanted to build a fire so she could try to draw out the infection with hot compresses, but Zach refused. She didn't know what to do. He *had* to have immediate medical attention, yet going on was just weakening him more.

By midday his eyes looked glazed, and he was slumped forward in the saddle. She wasn't even certain if he knew where he was going.

Near dusk, when they finally stopped to rest the horses, he was so weak that he fell to his knees when he tried to climb back into the saddle.

Rose had had enough.

Looking around for shelter, she chose a clump of ponderosa pines that would give them the most concealment. A granite wall behind it would protect their backs, so she'd only have three sides to worry about. Zach offered a weak argument when she led him over to it and made him lie down. Ignoring his protests, she unsaddled the horses, and by the time she hefted the heavy saddles and saddlebags into a pile next to him, Zach's eyes were closed and perspiration dotted his brow. She dug her soiled bodice out of Tait's saddlebags, wet it in the stream, then folded it into a square and put it across his forehead.

Despite the danger, she had to build a fire to get hot compresses on the infected wound. It was still light enough so that the glow of the fire wouldn't be seen, yet dark enough that the smoke wouldn't be observed from a distance.

She wasted several matches trying to ignite the wood, which wouldn't stay burning. Desperately, she looked around for something small to get the fire started. Her glance fell on Tait's saddlebags— which were full of the greenbacks he'd stolen from Stephen.

Hurriedly, she dug out a handful and put a match to them. They immediately flared to flames, and she carefully added small pieces of wood, then the thicker ones. In a short time she was able to put a cup of water on the fire to heat.

Since she could only boil one cup at a time the process was slow, but she managed to change the hot compress four times before she extinguished the fire. By that time her hands were stinging painfully from wringing out the hot strips of cloth.

After putting clean bandages on Zach's wounds, Rose bathed his face with cool water, hoping it eased some of his discomfort. Then she went to the stream and rinsed her aching hands in the water. It felt so good that she did the same to her face and neck. But all the cool water in the world couldn't rinse away her fear.

The fever was consuming him, and he'd begun tossing in delirium. The cool water was doing little to reduce it. What if he never opened his eyes . . . if he died? She tried to shake the thought off—refused to consider it. He *would* get well again. She wouldn't let him die.

Returning to Zach's side, she replaced the cool rag on his brow, and he opened his eyes—his beautiful sapphire eyes that had fascinated her the first time she'd looked into them.

"That feels so good, Rosie," he said.

Rose smiled tenderly, and gently stroked his cheek. "I wish there was more I could do for you."

"I could use a drink of water."

She helped him to raise his head and shoulders, then brought the cup to his lips. He drank it down thirstily, then lay back.

"Rose, there's something else you can do."

"Anything, Zach."

"I want you to get out of here now. I'll catch up with you later."

She shook her head. "I'm not leaving without you."

"Honey, I'm slowing you up. You know what they'll do to you if they catch up with us. Just stay on this road and you'll come to the town of Comanche Wells. You can get help there. The sheriff's an honest man."

"Zach, I am *not* leaving you, so save your strength. Like it or not, MacKenzie, you're stuck with me."

"I love you, Rosie." He tried to reach for her hand, but could barely raise his off the ground. She grasped it and brought it to her lips.

"I love you, too, Zach."

"We wasted so much time trying to fool ourselves."

"I know we did, my love." She hugged his hand against her cheek. "We have the rest of our lives to make up for the mistakes of the past." Her words seemed to hang in the air as a grim reminder of the existing crisis.

Finally, he spoke. "Just in case I don't make it, I want you to go to my folks. Tell them what happened. They'll take care of you."

Her heart was aching so badly she could barely choke words past the sob in her throat. "You can tell them yourself, because we're going to get out of here. Please, Zach, don't give up now," she pleaded. "Don't do this to us. We've just found each other. I won't let you give up. If you love me, you'll keep fighting, because if you die . . ." The anguish gnawing at her heart became unbearable. ". . . I have no reason to go on, either. You're my life, Zach."

"I'm sorry about everything, honey. There's so much I want to say to you: what you mean to me, the things I love about you. I wish I'd been more honest with you from the start.

"It's not too late, Zach. From now on, there'll be no more secrets between us."

"Yeah, no more secrets." His voice began to trail off. "Promise me, Rose. Go to my folks. Calico, Texas."

She recognized the name of the town at once.

"Zach, my friend Emily lives in Calico. Are you related to Josh MacKenzie?" But her question fell on deaf ears: his eyes were closed and he appeared not to be breathing.

She felt a panic like she'd never known before. Pressing her ear to his chest, she heard a faint heartbeat. With a mixture of relief and despair she stayed there, sobbing.

When she was physically spent she went back to the stream, rinsed the tears off her cheeks, then refilled the cup. She had no sense of time as she continued to change the cool compress on his forehead, but sometime later, he began to shiver. His whole body shook with the tremors. She covered him with the poncho, but his shivering did not cease and he opened his eyes.

"Cold. I'm so cold," he mumbled, before slipping back into his fevered sleep.

There were no matches to build another fire. Removing all her clothing, she next stripped Zach of his, then gathered him into her arms and covered them with the poncho.

Hugging him tightly to her warmth, she rocked him gently throughout the night—his Colt nearby at her fingertips.

No man or beast would do further harm to this man she loved.

Chapter 25

Rose glanced skyward. The morning had begun with a gray, overcast sky. She dared not delay their departure any longer.

She saddled the horses and as much as she hated disturbing Zach, she woke him, dressed him, and gave him a cup of water. His condition didn't appear to have improved; he was still feverish and incoherent—but he had survived the night. For that, she was grateful. But he was too weak to control a horse. They'd have to ride double.

After a struggle that left her exhausted, Rose finally managed to get him astride her horse, then tied the reins of his horse to her saddle. Climbing up behind Zach, she curled her arms around him and pulled his body against her. It almost knocked her off, but she managed to grasp the reins, and nudged the horse forward. Tait's sorrel followed behind.

The going was slow, but she managed to keep Zach and herself in the saddle. She feared it was just a matter of time before the Tait gang caught up with them.

When she stopped at a stream to rest the horses, Rose managed to get another cup of water down Zach. Then, desolate and tired, she sank down beside him. Throughout the morning he had slipped in and out of consciousness. But even when he was conscious, he was too consumed by fever to know what was going on around him.

Wearily, she got to her feet and walked over to the outer rim of the trail. For the last several miles the plateau had narrowed into a winding trail descending toward the valley below. Once they reached that valley, they'd be easy targets for their pursuers.

Glancing upward, her heart leaped to her throat as she caught a glimpse of riders on the trail above them. The gang was closing in on them and probably would overtake them within a half hour.

What could she do? She looked around in desperation, and spied the iron thread of railroad tracks snaking along the canyon floor below. The slope down was steep, but offered enough growth to conceal them from a casual glance of any passerby. If they could make it to the bottom unseen, she might be lucky enough to flag down a train.

She was too inexperienced to control a horse on such a steep descent, and Zach was too weak and incoherent to do so, either. They'd have to climb down. With precious moments ticking swiftly away, she dug into the saddlebags and jammed the few remaining strips of cloth into her skirt pocket.

Now she needed something to tie her and Zach together. She cut a long strip off the reins of her horse with Zach's bowie knife, and tied one end around his waist and the other end around her own. Her hand trembled as she picked up his Colt. It was heavy and cumbersome, but she might need it. She stuffed it into her pocket.

With time running out, she untethered the horses. Leaving them meant giving up the only means of transportation she had. Drawing a deep breath, she slapped each of them on the flank as hard as she could and the two horses galloped down the trail.

There was no turning back now.

"Zach, can you hear me?"

"Rose?" he mumbled.

"Listen to me, darling—you have to try and walk. I'll help you. Do you understand?"

He nodded. "Walk."

"Yes. It's going to be difficult and steep." She put his arm around her neck. "Please, Zach, try to hang on to me," she pleaded. Then, with her arm around his waist as added support, they started down the steep declivity.

Under normal circumstances it would have been an arduous task for anyone, and Zach's weight made the descent even more perilous.

She had to carefully gauge each step so they didn't slip on loose gravel or a rock.

Then Zach stumbled, throwing her off balance. She wrapped her free arm around a tree to keep them from pitching forward and rolling down the slope.

After about fifty feet she halted, and they slumped to the ground. She gasped much needed air into her lungs. She had already exhausted her strength, and they weren't even a quarter of the way down. This had been a mistake. Why had she ever believed she could get them down this hellish slope? She should have taken her chances and stayed on the trail, tried to find a place to hide. Or why hadn't she tried to fight them off? She'd have had Zach's Colt and a box of shells. This climb was sure to kill him. If she made it to the bottom and he didn't, what purpose would life have for her without him?

Zach squeezed her hand. Startled, she glanced at him. Had she imagined it? If she was on the verge of giving up, what was he feeling? And how had he ever rallied the strength to go through with this insane idea of hers?

He squeezed her hand again, and she knew she hadn't imagined it. Was he actually coherent enough to offer her encouragement?

Well, if he was willing to go on, so was she. Rose leaned over to him and kissed his cheek. "I love you, Zach." She stood up and helped him to his feet.

After another hundred feet she halted to rest behind a clump of mesquite that clung to the side of the slope as tenuously as she and Zach did.

Rose's breath thumped in her ears like the

pounding of a drum. As soon as it slowed enough to move again, she checked Zach.

He was lying on his back. His face and shirt were soaked with perspiration, and the rasp of his breathing nearly sounded like a death rattle. Rose buried her face in her hands—she was torturing him to death.

"Zach, we're halfway down now. Hold on, darling. Just hold on."

She shifted closer and put her arm across him protectively. Too exhausted to move, she lay still with her cheek against the ground, her tears blending with the dust.

As the clatter of hooves thundered past on the trail above, Rose raised her head and glanced upward.

Then she slumped back down. It was a minor victory, but were they any better off? And what if the gang found their horses and backtracked to find them? She reluctantly tried to rouse Zach.

"Zach, we have to go." When he didn't respond, she leaned over him. "Zach . . ."

He was barely conscious. All she could hope for was that he could get to his feet.

Sheer willpower kept her moving, reaching for anything to cling to, shifting from tree to boulder, sapling to mesquite clump. Her vision blurred, her lungs ached, the ground seemed to spin underfoot, and she grew fainter and fainter.

With less than a hundred feet to the base of the slope, Zach stumbled and fell, dragging her to the ground with him. She slid past him on her stomach, gravel and jagged rocks lacerating her skin. The weight of his body halted the slide and the reins that bound them together became so taut if felt as if she was being cut in half. Groping to free herself, she finally succeeded in releasing the rein. Gasping for air, she crawled to Zach.

He was pale and barely breathing now. And there was a spreading stain bleeding through his pants on his thigh. His wound had broken open.

Rose laid her head on his chest. "I'm so sorry," she sobbed. "I tried, Zach. I tried so hard, but I don't know what to do anymore. Don't leave me now. We've just found each other."

Tears streaked her cheeks as she grasped his hand. And for the first time in her life, she spoke in prayer.

"Dear Lord, I don't know if there's a proper prayer to ask for Your help. I've always believed I made my own luck and didn't need anybody's help—not even Yours. I guess there's no reason why You should listen to me now, except that even though I've never gone to church, I've always held You in my heart."

She swiped at the tears on her cheeks, then continued.

"I've broken your commandments, Lord, and I don't know the words of the scripture. So I guess I have no right now to ask You for anything. What have I ever given You?"

She lowered her head in shame. "But please, Dear Lord, don't blame Zach. He's a good man, though he tries to act otherwise. If I know this in my heart, then surely You do, too. A traveling preacher said that You are the Almighty and know everything . . . that You have power over everyone. Zach was trying to help me, Lord. It's my fault he was shot. So take *me*, if you must, but I beg You to find mercy in your heart and spare Zach. I love him so much. Please don't let him die."

She lifted her head heavenward, and her voice broke into pleading sobs. "Please, Dear Lord, please don't let him die."

Engulfed with despair, she laid her head on Zach's chest and wept uncontrollably.

A sob caught in her throat, choking the flow of sound. She slowly lifted her head. Had she imagined she heard a whistle? Holding her breath, she listened intently. The shrill blast of a train whistle pierced the still valley. She hadn't been mistaken. A wave of hope surged through her.

"Zach, can you hear it? Can you hear it, darling? It's a train, Zach! It's a train! Oh, thank You, God. Thank You!"

She rose to her feet, her tears of despair changing to tears of renewed faith as she rushed downhill toward the track. She stumbled and fell, rolled several feet, then picked herself back up and ran again. Aches, scrapes, misery, despair were all forgotten. Nothing mattered except reaching that railroad track before the train passed. Stumbling and staggering, tripping and falling, she reached the track as the engine drew nearer.

But would they see her? She had to attract their attention, and pulled off her bodice, waving it as she stumbled to the middle of the track.

The penetrating screech of metal grinding against metal grated in her ears. Then her lungs seemed to stop functioning, darkness flooded her senses, and she pitched forward.

"Why did we stop?" Beth Carrington stepped off the observation platform of their private car and joined her sister.

Cynthia Kincaid raised a hand to shield her eyes against the sun as she gazed down the line. "I don't know. It looks like there must have been something lying across the tracks. Here comes Dick now," she said as a young man hurried up to them. "What's going on down there, Dick?"

"Tim and Charlie said a lady collapsed on the track, Miz Kincaid," the brakeman said. "She looks to be in pretty bad shape."

"Oh, my goodness!" Beth exclaimed. "Thia, let's go down and see if we can be of any help."

The two women hurried past the dozen freight cars to the front of the train, where the engineer and fireman were knelt over a young woman lying on the ground.

"How is she, Tim?" Cynthia asked the engineer.

He shrugged. "She came around for a minute. Said there's a guy up on the slope who's wounded and needs help."

"Maybe it's a trick," Cynthia suggested. "Train robbers."

"Why would anyone rob this train?" Charlie asked. "We're not carrying any passengers, just rail-road supplies."

"Look at her, Miz Kincaid," Tim said. "She's in pretty bad shape."

Dick shook his head. "I'd think if it was a holdup, they'd have hit us by now."

Beth nodded in agreement. "We better see if we can help the young man she's talking about."

"I can see a patch of white about a hundred feet up that slope. Reckon that must be him," Charlie said. "If he's as bad off as the lady said, I don't see how we're gonna get him down."

"If she got this wounded fellow down four hundred feet of that slope already, surely you three able-bodied men can get him down the rest of the way," Cynthia declared,

Dick grinned sheepishly. "Reckon so, ma'am."

"We're wasting time," Beth declared, her position as president of the railroad showing. "Tim, we've got plenty of tarpaulin. You and Charlie make some kind of a sling or cot to get him down. And while they're doing that, Dick, you carry this girl back to our car. We'll take care of her."

That said, she spun on her heel and headed back to the private car. When they entered, Beth pointed to the bedroom. "Put her in there, Joe."

While Cynthia got a basin of hot water from the kitchen, Beth hurried to the bathroom and returned with antiseptic and bandages.

"Oh my, the poor dear must have gone through hell," Cynthia said, cleansing the girl's hands and arms.

Beth, who had been sponging off the girl's face, peered more closely at her. "Thia, look at these bruises on her face and that black eye. Those aren't new injuries. From the color, they have to be several days old."

"Yes, I think you're right," Cynthia said, after leaning down for a closer look. "But these cuts on her hands and arms sure are new. She must have slid halfway down that slope on her stomach to scrape herself this much."

"Do you think she might have broken some bones?"

"I can't feel any. Let's get this torn clothing off her and maybe we can tell. I have a robe in my valise; we can put that on her."

They succeeded in getting the robe on the girl and had just laid her back on the bed when Rose opened her eyes and sat up. Dazed, she looked around the room.

"Where am I?"

"Relax, dear. You'll be okay," Beth said.

Rose's eyes suddenly rounded in panic. "Zach? Where's Zach?"

"Is Zach the man who's wounded?" Cynthia asked.

"Yes. Where is he?" she pleaded.

"The crew went to get him. We told them to bring him here," Beth assured her, trying to calm her fear. "What's your name, dear?"

"Rose Dubois."

"I'm Elizabeth Carrington, and this is my sister, Cynthia Kincaid."

"Would you like something to drink?" Cynthia asked.

"Thank you. Water would be fine."

Cynthia poured her a glass from the ewer on the dresser. "Easy, dear," she cautioned when Rose began to gulp it down.

"Are you ready to tell us what happened, Rose?" Beth asked gently when Rose finished.

Rose nodded. "We were—"

Her explanation was cut short by the return of the men.

Rose bolted to her feet, then grabbed the bedpost, overcome by dizziness.

Cynthia and Beth each took an arm to keep Rose from keeling over, and sat her down on the edge of the bed.

"Is he still alive?" Beth asked.

"Barely," Tim said, grim-faced.

Beth motioned to the bed. "Lay him down there."

"He's bleeding from a leg wound," Tim said. "But from what I can tell, he ain't got any slugs in him."

"That's about the only thing that's *not* wrong with him," Dick mumbled irascibly. "He's burning up with fever. Only thing I can figure is that he's too stubborn to die."

"There's a doctor in Comanche Wells," Beth said. "Let's get moving. Full steam, Tim. The sooner we get there, the better."

"Okay, Miz Carrington. We're on our way."

"You need any more help with him?" Dick asked.

"Not right now. We'll do what we can for him. Thanks, boys," Beth said as they headed for the door.

Rose had already shifted over to him. "Zach, can you hear me?" She looked up at them, tears glittering in her eyes. "He's so pale."

"Honey, let us see what we can do for him," Cynthia said, gently nudging her away.

Beth and Cynthia leaned over the wounded man. "My God!" Cynthia exclaimed. She glanced at Beth, who was staring, just as startled, at the man on the bed. "It's Zach MacKenzie!"

"You know him?" Rose asked.

"Know him?" Beth said. "He's our cousin's son."

Chapter 26

R ose was too stunned to say anything. She gaped in shock and watched as Beth and Cynthia worked over Zach. Was this all some bizarre nightmare she'd mercifully wake from in her bed in Brimstone?

Finally, she swallowed hard and said, "You're related."

"Yes," Beth replied. "Flint MacKenzie, who is Zach's father, is our cousin."

"Is Josh MacKenzie Zach's brother?"

"No, Zach and Josh are cousins," Beth said. "Josh is Luke's son. Luke and Flint are brothers, and cousins to me and my sisters."

"Beth," Cynthia interrupted, "if you don't mind,

will you finish the family tree later? I need some help here."

"I'm sorry," Rose said. "I'll help you."

"That's all right, honey. You sit quietly right where you are and let us take care of this." Cynthia reached for Zach's belt buckle. "We've got to get these bloody jeans off him."

"Maybe you should let me do that?" Rose said.

"I don't think so," Cynthia replied. "We just got your hands bandaged. Let's not get them bleeding again."

"Zach's naked under those pants, Cynthia. His underwear was too bloody to put back on him."

Both women stared at Rose for an instant, then Cynthia finally said, "I see. Well, this will be our secret, ladies."

"Why don't you just cut off the trouser leg?" Beth suggested. "I don't think it's necessary to remove his pants."

"You girls are no fun," Cynthia declared.

"You'll have to excuse my sister, Rose," Beth said. "She likes to shock people with outrageous statements like that."

Despite the repartee between the two women, it was easy to see the deep affection between them. Rose also suspected that they were trying to take her mind off Zach's condition.

However, Cynthia paled when she removed the bandage from Zach's thigh. "Oh, my God." She glanced grimly at her sister. "The wound's infected pretty badly, Beth."

"Last night I tried to draw out the infection with hot compresses," Rose said. "But it was very limited. I only had a cup in which to boil the water."

After examining the wound, Beth's pallor equaled her sister's. "I don't think hot compresses will even help anymore. They might do more harm than good at this point. All we can do is clean it up until we get to a doctor."

Rose had struggled too hard to get him this far; she wasn't about to give up now. "At least we can do something to lower his fever."

"I think we have some antipyretic." Beth hurried to the bathroom. Within seconds she was back carrying a medicine bottle and a basin of cold water. "There's only a couple of doses here—but it's enough for now."

"Let's get some cool compresses on him," Cynthia suggested. "That will also help to keep the fever from getting any worse."

Suddenly the car lurched as the train ground to a stop. "What now?" Cynthia groaned.

Rose knew it was trouble. Instinctively she reached for Zach's hand.

Cynthia handed the bottle to Beth. "Here, give him a dose while I see what's going on outside." She went out on the observation deck and returned immediately. "This doesn't look good. Four men on horseback have stopped the train."

Rose was gripped by fright. "It must be the gang that's chasing us. They're the ones who shot Zach."

"Why didn't you tell us you were being pursued?" Beth asked.

"I wasn't thinking about anything but Zach's condition." Rose looked around desperately. "My skirt? Where's my skirt? Zach's Colt is in the pocket."

"Rose, there are four of them. You can't outshoot them," Cynthia said. "We've got to think of something else."

"The first thing we have to do is hide Zach and Rose," Beth said. "They're sure to come in here and search for you, or they wouldn't have stopped the train. Quick, let's get Zach under the bed. Rose, you get under there with him. Don't let him make a sound."

As fast and carefully as they could, the three of them picked up Zach, and by tugging and shoving succeeded in getting him under the bed. Rose crawled under after him.

"Beth, get rid of all these soiled clothes and bandages."

"What have you got in mind, Thia?" Beth asked as she gathered up everything and tossed it all under the bed.

Rose found her skirt and dug the Colt out of the pocket. No matter what Cynthia said, she'd shoot anyone who tried to harm Zach. He began to toss in delirium. "S-h-h-h, my darling," she whispered, and put her hand over his mouth.

"Beth, stuff a pillow under your gown and get into that bed. You're having a baby. And make it good and loud."

"That I can do. Remember, I delivered twins."

"Rose, are you okay under there?" Cynthia asked.

"Yes. Just be careful. These men are evil."

"Don't worry, honey," Cynthia said. "I've faced more than my share of bad men when we were building this railroad."

Cynthia had just dumped out the basin of water when the door was flung open. A snarling menace with pistol in hand filled the doorway.

"Oh, thank goodness!" Cynthia exclaimed. "Are you the doctor?"

"What the hell are ya talkin' about, lady?"

Rose recognized Bull's voice and her grip tightened on the Colt.

Beth began to moan loudly. "Help me, Thia! Please, help me. I can't stand it any longer!" She ended with an anguished scream.

"What in hell's going on in there?" Bull demanded.

"My sister's having a baby."

"Cynthia, I can't stand it. Help me! Help me," Beth cried pitifully.

"Tell that bitch to shut up," Bull snarled, "or I'll put her out of her misery."

Arms akimbo, Cynthia stomped her foot. "Of all the nerve! You, sir, are no gentleman."

"Shut your mouth, lady. Your sister's makin' enough noise for the two of you." Bull went into the bedroom, and Beth moaned at the top of her voice.

Cynthia, who was of the school that a good offense was better than a bad defense, sallied forth with verve and courage as her weapons. "Just who are you?" she demanded. "I do not appreciate your barging in here when my poor sister is in agony; and to add insult to injury you have the audacity to call her disparaging names. Have you no compassion in your heart, sir?"

"Lady, if you don't shut up, I'm knocking your teeth out." He stomped out of the room. Cynthia turned to Beth and gave her an okay sign with thumb and forefinger, then followed after him.

"What are you looking for, Mr . . ."

"Name's Bull." He opened the bathroom door and peered in. "You gals got pretty fancy diggin's here, ain't ya? How come yer the only passengers?"

Cynthia dug into her pocket for a handkerchief and began twisting it nervously. "Because we had to get my poor sister to a doctor, so the railroad attached this car to the freight train." As she spoke, she managed to slip off her wedding ring and bury it in the folds of the hankie. If he was a thief, this brute was not going to steal that. "This was the only train heading this way." Another pathetic scream from Beth rent the air. "Please, we must get going. I don't know how to deliver a baby. Do you?" she asked hopefully.

"You kiddin', lady? I wouldn't go near that screechin' banshee even if I did know how." He headed for the kitchen.

"Just what are you looking for, Mr. Bull?" Cynthia repeated, trying to be heard over another loud scream from Beth.

"For a couple of murderin' desperados. We figure they might've hopped a ride."

Cynthia drew back in alarm. "Murderers! On this train!"

"Yep. Gal killed a rancher, and the guy killed one of the posse."

"Oh, my poor sister. What are we going to do?" She started to cry hysterically.

"Will you stop that wailin', lady? Between you

and yer sister, a man can't think!" He headed for the door.

"Are you just going to leave us here, helpless?" Cynthia cried. "You must stay and protect us, Mr. Bull, in case they attack the train."

"You think I'd put up with that any longer than I have to?" Bull grimaced at the sound of another groaning scream from Beth. "What in hell is she havin' in there? An elephant?"

He stalked out, slamming the door behind him.

Cynthia went out on the observation deck. The other three men rode up to him, and one of them said, "There ain't no sign of them, Bull."

A painful wail from the bedroom carried to the outside. "What in hell is that?" the man asked.

"A bitch from hell. Let's get out of here," Bull said. Cynthia waited until they rode away, then went inside and locked the door. She returned to the bedroom, grinning. "Coast is clear."

"Whew!" Beth said, climbing out of the bed. "Not a minute too soon. I was turning hoarse from all that screaming."

"You came through loud and clear, honey," Cynthia said, giving Beth a hug.

"I know." Beth pulled the pillow out from under her skirt. Cradling it in her arms, she began to rock it. She sighed deeply. "But this was a very painful birth, Thia."

Cynthia giggled. "Mr. P. T. Barnum certainly knew what he was talking about. There *is* 'a sucker born every minute.' "

Beth reached down to lend a helping hand to Rose, who was crawling out from under the bed.

"You girls were wonderful. I don't know how I can ever thank you enough."

"Well, the fun's over." Beth got down on her knees. "Let's get Zach back in bed."

"He's become very restless," Rose said. "He's tossing in delirium again."

They soon found out it was easier getting him under the bed than getting him out from under it. Zach was a big man, and he battled their efforts as though they were the demons he wrestled with in his delirium. But his energy was soon depleted, and they finally succeeded in hoisting him onto the bed.

Exhausted, Cynthia sat down on the edge. "I've never had this much trouble getting a man into bed." She puffed at a stray lock that had fallen across her eyes.

Beth and Rose had slumped down on the opposite side to catch their breath. "Don't feel bad, Thia," Beth said, grinning despite her exhaustion. "Jake always warned me that records are made to be broken."

Ignoring her sister's teasing, Cynthia said, "Rose, I don't see how you ever managed to haul Zach down that slope."

Rose felt near to collapsing. This last effort had drained the little bit of strength she'd had. Now that the threat of danger had passed, she'd lost the surge of energy that had kept her going. Nothing remained now except the fear that Zach would not survive. She pressed her hands over her eyes, which burned with weariness and unshed tears.

Beth slipped an arm around her shoulders.

"Rose, when was the last time you slept or had something to eat?" she asked gently.

Dazed, Rose looked at her. "Ah . . . I'm not sure. I had some nuts. I think it was yesterday."

"Thia, will you put a cool cloth on Zach's forehead, then I'm sure you can find some clean clothes for Rose to wear among our things. I'm going to fix her something to eat, and when she's through, I think a hot bath will do her aches and pains some good."

Beth took Rose by the hand and led her to the kitchen. "Sit down here." She pulled out a chair at the table. "Tea or coffee?"

"A cup of tea would be fine."

"Hope you like eggs; that's about all we have."

"Whatever's the easiest," Rose said. "The two of you have done so much already, I don't know where to begin to thank you."

"Rose, honey, Zach is family," Cynthia said.

"Family or not, I think the two of you would help anyone in need. I just wish Zach could eat something."

"He'd probably choke on it, Rose. We've got all we can do to get water down him."

"I know." Rose sighed deeply. "But I feel guilty knowing he's—"

"Eat, Rose," Beth said cutting off her worried thought. She put a plate down in front of her. Rose stared blankly at the scrambled eggs and piece of toast. "Before it gets cold, Rose."

She began to pick at tiny bites of the eggs and before she realized it, she'd consumed them along with the toast. Smiling sheepishly, she said,

"That was delicious. I didn't realize how hungry I was."

Beth sat down and poured them each a cup of tea, then leaned over and looked her in the eye. "Now, don't you think it's about time you tell us just what in hell this is all about?"

"And don't leave out a single detail," Cynthia added.

Rose took a long look at them. The two women were exquisitely beautiful. There was both delicacy and strength reflected in each face: straight nose, full lips, and the high Celtic cheekbones indicative of their Scottish ancestry. Beth's hair was a deeper auburn than her own, and Cynthia's was dark brown. But the most astounding thing was that both had the same incredible, darkly lashed, sapphire-colored eyes as Zach.

As they listened intently while she related the story to them, she saw the same probing intelligence in their eyes that she'd seen so often in Zach's. It made her as curious about their lives as they were about hers.

There was a long silence when she finished, then Beth smiled and squeezed her hand. "I can tell you love Zach very much."

"I never believed I could love anyone as much as I do him."

Beth stood up. "Well, while Thia and I clean up the kitchen, you take that hot bath. Then I want you to lie down and take a nap."

Cynthia jumped to her feet. "I'll draw the bath for you."

Once Rose was comfortably ensconced in the

bathtub behind a closed door, Cynthia returned to the kitchen.

"Beth, did you notice something very interesting about her story? Rose sounded angry when she spoke about Zach being a Texas Ranger."

"That was my impression, too. I wonder why?"

Cynthia looked pensive. "Maybe she holds Zach's Ranger duties responsible for all they've gone through together."

"Well, if he loves her just half as much as she does him, I'm sure they'll work out whatever the problem may be."

When they finished in the kitchen, Beth and Cynthia returned to the bedroom, changed the cool cloth on Zach's brow, and waited for Rose. She joined them shortly, looking considerably more refreshed.

"Feel any better?" Beth asked.

"Much. I can't remember when I enjoyed a bath so much. I thank you and so do my aching bones. I'm afraid, though, I got my bandages wet."

"Why don't you lie down next to Zach and try to get some sleep now," Beth suggested.

Rose sat down on the bed beside him. "This railroad car has more conveniences than any house I've ever lived in. A bathroom and kitchen with hot water. And the sitting room is so elegant. Paneled walls, gorgeous furniture and draperies. I've heard stories about these magnificent private cars, but this is the first time I've ever been in one. Who owns it?"

"We do," Beth said. "It was our father's before he died. Then Thia and Dave lived in it while they were building the railroad."

"Dave Kincaid's my husband," Cynthia said with a proud smile. "I'm not one to brag, honey, but he just happens to be the smartest and handsomest man in all of these United States *and* continental Europe."

"Oh, good Lord!" Beth groaned.

"So your husband works for this railroad?"

"Yes he does. He's the chief engineer."

"Is he the engineer of this train?"

Beth and Cynthia exchanged amused glances, then Cynthia giggled. "He's not that kind of engineer, honey. He *builds* railroads. Our family owns the Rocky Mountain Central Railroad, and Beth's husband owns the Lone Star Railroad. We merged the two lines after Beth and Jake were married."

Rose was flabbergasted. It had been easy to see that Beth and Cynthia were women of class and fine breeding. But the extent of their wealth was astounding.

"I don't know what to say. Zach never mentioned he had such prominent relatives."

Beth arched a perfectly curved brow. "Rose, dear, did Zach happen to mention his family owns the Triple M ranch?"

"He said his folks have a ranch."

"One of the largest ranches in Texas. The Triple M brand stands for MacKenzie: Luke, Flint, and Cleve."

Rose shook her head. "This is all surprising. Last night Zach told me if he doesn't make it, I should go to his family in Calico and let them know. I recognized the name of the town, because my best friend, Emily Lawrence, married Josh MacKenzie."

"You're a friend of Emily's!" Cynthia exclaimed. "Oh, we adore her."

"Em and I were Harvey Girls together in New Mexico."

"You were!" Cynthia said exuberantly. "We've heard that delightful story of how she ran away from her domineering father and became a Harvey Girl. And then Josh was hired to find her when he was a Pinkerton agent. I loved it! It was so romantic."

"In case you haven't noticed by now, Rose, my sister is a romantic at heart. Her story is just the opposite of Emily's. She chased after Dave until she caught *him*."

Cynthia winked at Rose. "Unlike my sister, I had the good sense to know what I wanted when I saw it. Dave didn't have to coerce me into marrying him, like poor Jake had to do to Beth. Can you believe that a rich, handsome entrepreneur like Jake Carrington, who also happens to have the greatest sense of humor in the world, had to literally blackmail Beth into marrying him?" Cynthia sighed deeply. "My poor little Beth." They looked at each other, then both women broke into laughter.

Once again Rose sensed the deep bond of love and friendship between the two sisters.

"I think Rose has more on her mind right now than listening to us air our family secrets."

Rose smiled. "You and Cynthia aren't fooling me, Beth. I know you're just talking to try and take my mind off of Zach."

Sobering, Cynthia squeezed her hand. "But Beth's right, Rose. You should try to rest."

Rose lay back and rested her head on the pillow. "How long before we reach the nearest town?"

"In about an hour," Beth said.

Rose reached for Zach's hand and brought it to her cheek. "Hang on, my darling," she murmured. She glanced up at Beth and Cynthia. "Zach's a fighter, you know. He's not going to give up."

Cynthia smiled gently. "That's for sure—he's a MacKenzie. Wait until you meet the rest of his family."

Chapter 27

It was dusk by the time the train pulled into Comanche Wells. The town was far different from Brimstone. The main street was bordered with sidewalks, and several of the buildings were faced in stone, among them a hotel, church, and bank.

While Rose and Beth had Zach carried to the doctor's office, Cynthia went to notify the sheriff and send some telegrams.

The doctor's office was located in a two-story clapboard building with a black roof and shutters. A picket fence, clusters of wisteria creeping up the walls, and the sweet scent of lilac created an air of tranquillity, and the shingle read, "DR. JAMES SERENE, DOCTOR OF MEDICINE." Rose took it as a good sign.

The door was opened by a mature woman, who

led them to the doctor's examination room, where the doctor and his orderly took over. After expressing their best wishes, the crew said good-bye and returned to the train.

The doctor was gray-haired and cherubic-looking, and after a few cursory questions he asked Rose and Beth to wait in his office.

Rose was convinced that divine intervention had delivered Zach into safe hands.

Thirty minutes later her confidence had begun to fade as she waited for the doctor to complete his examination. She jumped to her feet the moment he appeared, desperately trying to read his face.

"Please sit down, Miss Dubois," he said grimly.

Zach was worse than she feared! For a few hours she had deceived herself into believing he'd pull through, but the dreadful truth was that he was going to die.

Rose gulped back her sobs as hot, stinging tears trickled down her cheeks, and she slumped back down in the chair.

"May I offer you ladies a beverage?" Dr. Serene asked.

"No, thank you," Beth said. She grasped Rose's hand and squeezed it in reassurance, but Rose was too numb to respond.

"Perhaps a small glass of sherry, Miss Dubois?"

Rose shook her head.

Dr. Serene cleared his throat. "Well, I don't have to tell you that Mr. MacKenzie's condition is very serious."

Just say it! Why was he delaying?

"The wound in his shoulder is a clean one, and fortunately caused no internal damage. But, as you well know, the leg wound is seriously infected. I dug out a tiny scrap of denim, which most likely has contributed to the infection."

Dr. Serene sat back, put his balled fists together, and rested his chin on them. "Unfortunately the infection has spread through his body, resulting in an extremely high fever. I have done what I can for him medically, but I cannot say whether it's too late to be of any good. I don't wish to raise any false hopes, but I do see one encouraging sign."

Rose's head jerked up at once. "What is that, Doctor?"

"Mr. MacKenzie appears to have been in exceptionally good physical condition before he was wounded. Considering the complications I've just described, I doubt most would have survived this long. Even in delirium, he appears to have a strong will to stay alive. I've discovered that can often be as good a medicine as any I can administer."

"Then there's still hope he can pull out of this," Beth said.

His chubby face wrinkled into a smile. "I'm a man of science, Mrs. Carrington, but I still believe in miracles." He stood up. "My orderly, Robert King, is bathing him, and I've given Mr. MacKenzie an injection to enable him to rest more comfortably. There's not much more any of us can do for him except hope for that miracle."

"May I remain with Zach tonight, Doctor?" Rose asked.

"Of course. But only if you allow me to examine the bruises on your face and those lacerations on your hands and arms."

At that moment the housekeeper tapped on the door. "Doctor Serene, there's a Mrs. Kincaid in the foyer asking for you."

A clearly agitated Cynthia brushed past the woman. "They're here," she said breathlessly.

"Dr. Serene, this is my sister, Cynthia Kincaid," Beth said.

The doctor stood up. "How do you do? Please sit down, Mrs. Kincaid."

"Thank you." Cynthia took a seat. "I apologize for my abrupt entrance."

Dr. Serene settled back in his chair. "Perhaps you ladies should tell me just how Mr. MacKenzie got those bullet wounds, Miss Dubois the face bruises, and just who 'they' are?"

Rose briefly related the story.

Cynthia had the last word. "And when I came out of the telegraph office, I saw the gang tying up their horses in front of a saloon."

"Did they see you?" the doctor asked.

"No. They weren't looking in my direction."

"Then it would appear that these gentlemen do not know that you're even in town."

"Believe me, Doctor, they're not gentlemen."

"I'm sure they're not. The solution is simply to inform the sheriff."

"I tried the sheriff before I went to the telegraph office. He's out of town until tomorrow morning."

"Did you wire Zach's folks?" Rose asked.

"Honey, I not only wired Flint and Garnet; I sent

Dave a wire, Jake a wire, and Angie and Giff a wire. They're our other sister and her husband," she added to Rose. "I wired the governor, the Texas Rangers, and even President Harrison. If you can think of anyone else, I'll sneak back and send it."

The doctor chuckled. "You appear to have the situation well covered, Mrs. Kincaid. I think it's advisable for you ladies to remain here. If I understand correctly, this gang has no reason to suspect Mr. MacKenzie was wounded."

Rose was suddenly struck with an appalling thought. "I'm afraid they might know. The last time I changed Zach's bandages, I simply discarded them. They could easily have found them on the trail."

"But they still would have no reason to believe you came here."

"That's true. And they were very stupid," Cynthia agreed.

Beth was less confident. "As long as they're here, I can't believe they wouldn't take the time to check out a doctor."

Cynthia patted Beth on the shoulder. "This might require another performance by our laboring mother."

Rose could no longer hold back her feelings. "I can't expect all of you to keep risking your lives for us. I'll leave and take Zach with me."

"Honey, we've been through this with you before," Cynthia said. "We're family."

"And I, Miss Dubois, have sworn a Hippocratic oath," Dr. Serene said. "I could never release a patient as seriously ill as Mr. MacKenzie."

Beth slipped an arm around her shoulders. "Rose, dear, the sheriff will be back tomorrow. It's more than likely that gang won't even bother us."

"I agree, Mrs. Carrington. Now, will you ladies join me for dinner? It's been many years since I've had the pleasure of such charming company."

"Haven't you ever married, Doctor?" Beth asked.

"My wife died five years ago, and my daughter moved to Washington, D.C., when she married two years ago. So your presence is most welcome."

"If you'll excuse me, I'm not hungry," Rose said. "I'd like to see Zach."

The doctor smiled. "I understand perfectly, Miss Dubois. You may get out of joining us for dinner, but you aren't wiggling out of my examining you." He turned to Beth and Cynthia. "I'll have Mrs. King show you ladies to the dining room while I check my patient, and then join you."

"His temperature has gone down two degrees," Dr. Serene said later. "That's very encouraging, Miss Dubois."

"He's not restless either, Doctor."

"Yes. I'd say the medicine is having a good effect on him. I wouldn't doubt that fever will break by morning."

Rose sighed. "Thank God."

"Now, Miss Dubois, you make sure you eat that sandwich and glass of milk Mrs. King brought you. We don't want you getting ill, too."

Smiling, Rose glanced down at Zach. He looked as if he were sleeping now, instead of unconscious. The orderly had even shaved the stubble off his cheeks. Although Zach still had a pallor, she could see he was getting better.

"Rose—if I may be so bold as to call you that?"

"Please do, Doctor."

"Rose, how much sleep have you had in the last few days? Why don't you take this opportunity to stretch out in a bed and get a good night's sleep?"

"I will tomorrow, when the sheriff returns," she said. "I promise you that once I'm certain Zach is no longer threatened I'll go to bed for a week."

"You won't have much choice if you don't start thinking of your own health." He patted her shoulder. "Mrs. King has brought you a blanket and pillow. Is there anything else you'd like?"

"Nothing, Doctor. I'm fine."

He halted at the doorway. "And you make sure you eat that food she brought you, as well."

Rose picked up the tray. "I promise. Good night, Dr. Serene."

"Good night, Rose."

She sat down by Zach's bedside and took a bite of the sandwich, her spirits considerably buoyed. Unless Zach took a sudden turn for the worse, he would recover. She found herself actually hoping the gang would not leave town before the sheriff's return. Despite her low opinion of lawmen, people seemed to have a lot of confidence in this one. She could only hope their trust wasn't misguided.

"You look tired, honey."

She jerked around at Zach's voice, nearly spilling the milk. His eyes were open, and he was smiling at her.

"How are you feeling, darling?"

"Okay."

She put a hand on his brow. He still felt warm, but not as feverish as he'd been.

"Where are we, Rose?"

"In Comanche Wells. You've been very ill, Zach. The doctor said it's a miracle you stayed alive."

"You mean I was too ornery to die."

"Don't joke about it, Zach. I've been worried sick."

"I'm sorry, Rosie."

She began to stroke his forehead. "But you're getting better. That's all that matters now."

"Lie down next to me, Rose?"

"I don't think the doctor would like that."

"I just want to hold you, sweetheart."

"Once you've recovered, there'll be plenty of time for that."

He grasped her hand. "I love you, Rosie. Why was it so hard to say it before?"

"Because you're a stubborn fool. Let me warn you though, Zach MacKenzie: you better find it just as easy to say once you're out of that bed, because I'll never get tired of hearing you say it." She leaned over and pressed a kiss to his lips. "And I'll never get tired of repeating the same to you, beloved." She rubbed her cheek against his. "Now that those scratching whiskers are gone you look downright handsome, fever and all."

"And you look downright beautiful, black eye and all." He chuckled, and she could tell he was tiring.

"Poor baby. You're still feverish."

He licked his lips. "You taste like mayonnaise."

"It's this sandwich." She picked up the roast beef sandwich Mrs. King had made. "You want a bite?" She held it to his mouth and he took a bite of it.

"Your turn."

She took a bite. "Here, try a sip of milk." She held up his head and he took a swallow from the glass.

"Now you," he said.

For the next few minutes, they alternated taking bites of the sandwich and sips of milk.

Finally, he said, "My head's getting fuzzy again, honey." He drifted off, but this time she knew it was only into sleep.

She gazed down at his beloved face. "I love you more than life itself, my darling," she murmured softly. "But once you're well, there's an important issue to be resolved between us." A tear slid down her cheek. "Why couldn't you have trusted me, Zach?"

Rose dimmed the lamp and curled up in her chair with a pillow and blanket. At the last moment, she pulled Zach's Colt out of her pocket—they still had to make it through the night.

Chapter 28

"**D**ammit!"

Rose jerked up her head. Surely that wasn't the doctor who'd cursed, and she doubted it was the orderly, either.

"Be quiet or you'll wake the whole house," someone hissed. The voice sounded faintly familiar.

She stood up. Her hand trembled as she picked up the Colt, but she felt surprisingly calm. She'd run from these men long enough, and the time had come to face them. She quietly cocked the pistol and pointed it at the door as the footsteps drew nearer.

"Maybe he ain't here either, Josh."

Josh? There was no Josh with the Tait gang, she thought, just as a shadowy figure filled the doorway.

"Don't take another step or I'll shoot," she ordered.

"Don't shoot, ma'am, we don't mean you any harm."

Rose turned up the lamp and her face broke into a smile. "Josh MacKenzie!"

The tall figure in the doorway gaped in surprise. "Rose? Rose Dubois? What in hell are you doing here? And put down that damn pistol before it goes off." His gaze swept the room and came to a halt at the bed. "How is he?" He hurried over to Zach.

"I think he's getting better." Suddenly her legs felt like they couldn't support her, and she sank back down on the chair.

"Rose, this is my cousin Cole."

"Ma'am," said the younger man who had followed Josh into the room. Tall and rangy, there was no mistaking him for anyone but a MacKenzie. The two men leaned over the bed. "He sure don't look too perky," Cole said.

"I can assure you, he looks a hundred percent better than he did yesterday," she said. "He came to earlier, but the doctor's given him an injection to help him rest more comfortably. How did you fellows even know where to find us?"

"My dad. I'd sent him a telegram about where Cole and I were staying for the night. When he got the news about Zach, he wired me back and said that Zach was here, wounded, and needed help. We'd gotten Zach's telegram before, and Cole and I were headed for Brimstone. We were lucky enough to catch a train and double back. When there was no sign of Zach at the hotel, we figured we'd check out the doctor's office."

"I'm glad you're here, Josh. The four men who are trying to kill Zach are in town. They don't know we're here, though."

"I thought the Tait gang was after him. There's five of them," Cole said.

"Zach killed Jess Tait in Brimstone."

"And the others came all this way just to get even? That sure don't sound like the gang I knew."

"Tait had stolen money from a rancher before killing him. We escaped on Tait's horse, and the money was in the saddlebags. They're after the money."

"Where is it now?" Josh asked.

"I burned most of it."

"You what?" Cole exclaimed.

"Zach was burning up with fever, but shivering with cold. I had to make a fire, and I used the money to get it started."

"Miz Dubois, did you ever hear of wood?" Cole asked.

"I was desperate."

"Where is this gang now?" Josh asked.

"I have no idea. Cynthia Kincaid said she saw them ride into town when she was at the telegraph office."

"Cynthia Kincaid is here!"

"Yes, so is Beth Carrington. They're upstairs sleeping. If it weren't for them, we'd never have made it this far."

Josh shoved his hat to the top of his forehead. "Well, I'll be damned!" His warm chuckle was so like Zach's that her breath caught in her throat. "Rose, I don't understand why you didn't ask for help from the sheriff. Ben Morgan is a tough old lawman who runs a clean town."

"Cynthia checked. He's out of town and due back in the morning."

"Maybe we should look up this gang, Josh. I used to ride with them, so I know what they look like," Cole said.

"No, let the law handle this. It's almost daylight. We'll just sit tight right here with Zach until the sheriff gets back. If the gang shows up before he does, then we'll handle it."

"What's going on here?" Dr. Serene stood in the doorway.

Josh and Cole pivoted, their pistols clearing their holsters as they turned. Seeing the irate little man in a belted robe, his gray hair disheveled from sleep, they uncocked their Colts and holstered them.

"Get away from my patient," the doctor ordered.

"Dr. Serene, these are Zach's cousins. They're here to help him."

"Then they can help him by not disturbing him. If you'd all step out of the room, I'd like to examine Mr. MacKenzie. Mrs. King is preparing coffee. I suggest you go into the dining room."

They filed out, and Rose led them to the dining room. By the time the coffee was ready, Cynthia and Beth had come downstairs.

Rose sat with her elbow propped on the table and her head cradled in her hand. Half-asleep, she listened to their chatter. She was glad there was someone else to fill in the details for the new arrivals. Dr.

Serene soon joined them, and Mrs. King brought in heaping bowls of oatmeal and a large platter of scrambled eggs and fried ham.

After a few bites, Rose lost her appetite and shoved back her chair. "Dr. Serene, is Zach awake?"

"He slips in and out, Rose. At this stage it's due to the medication, but I don't want to withhold it, because he needs it to fight the infection."

"He hasn't eaten in days, other than a few bites of my sandwich last night. Should I try to feed him?"

"You might try the oatmeal and some liquid, of course. Liquid is the most important thing, to avoid dehydration. I don't recommend anything much heavier on his stomach until he's able to sit up."

Daylight streamed through the window by the time Rose returned to Zach with a bowl of the cereal and a glass of milk. She shook him lightly on the shoulder and he opened his eyes.

"Good morning. Do you feel up to a bowl of oatmeal?"

"You going to feed it to me?"

"Like I would an infant."

"When do I get the steak and potatoes?"

"When you can sit up."

"I'm ready to do that now."

"Sure you are." She helped him drink the glass of milk, then eat the bowl of oatmeal. By the time he'd eaten half of it, he couldn't keep his eyes open.

As she carried the tray back to the kitchen, the bell tinkled above the door. When the orderly opened it, the tallest man she'd ever seen stepped through the door. He wore a star on his vest.

"Howdy, Robert. Can I talk to the doc?"

"I'll get him, Sheriff."

"Excuse me," Rose said, setting the tray aside. "Are you Sheriff Morgan?"

"Yes, ma'am," he said, doffing his hat.

The man emanated such an aura of dignity, she couldn't help but trust him. His face was tanned and weathered, but whether from age or exposure to sand and wind was hard to say. She guessed him to be in his mid-fifties, but his body appeared to be that of a younger man—solid muscle without a wasted ounce of flesh on it.

His eyes were the clearest blue she'd ever looked into, and never wavered from her own when she introduced herself.

"I was told a Mrs. Kincaid was looking for me."

"I'm Cynthia Kincaid," Cynthia said. She came into the foyer followed by all the others, each one trying to be heard above the other.

"Please, one at a time," the sheriff declared.

When he heard the full story, Morgan let out a long, low whistle. "So these fellas managed to flatten Zach MacKenzie. I'd hate to be in their boots if Flint ever runs into them. If the gang's still in town I'll arrest them, but I'll need you three ladies, who were personally involved, to sign complaints."

"You need any help with that arrest, Ben?" Josh asked.

"You're damn right—I've only got one deputy. You and Cole come with me; I'll deputize you."

"I know the bastards," Cole said. "Bull's the most dangerous, Joe's the least. Pike and Cain are downright mean."

"If they draw on us, I'll take Bull. Josh, Pike's

yours, and Cole can take Cain. My deputy can take this Joe. Let's go."

The three men departed before anyone could even wish them good luck.

Rose joined Beth and Cynthia on the front porch. The men had been gone for fifteen minutes, and Rose waited anxiously for their return. She became increasingly uneasy with every moment that ticked by. If the outlaws had left town, they'd still represent a threat to Zach. She wanted the whole situation to end right now.

A sudden gunshot rent the air, then a stillness settled over the town. A few early risers came out and looked up and down the street, then went back inside and closed their doors.

"What do you think?" Cynthia asked.

"I don't know," Rose replied. "I only heard one shot, didn't you?"

"Here they come now," Beth said solemnly.

They stared as the sheriff and his deputies came down the street with three handcuffed prisoners and turned into the jail.

"Looks like it's all over but the shouting, honey," Cynthia said, hugging her.

"Bull wasn't with them," Rose said worriedly. "I wonder why?"

"Let's go down and sign those complaints the sheriff mentioned," Beth said. "We'll be able to find out then."

Beth and Cynthia each slipped an arm through hers and they marched up the street arm in arm.

The three outlaws looked woefully at Rose from their locked cells. Seeing them behind bars somehow made them appear less ominous to her.

"Where's Bull?" she asked. "Did he get away?"

"Bull wasn't too willing to come with us," Sheriff Morgan said.

"He made the mistake of drawing on Ben," Josh added.

"Was that the shot we heard?" Cynthia asked.

Morgan nodded, and handed them each a paper. "Now, if you ladies will just sign these complaints, our business will be over and these men won't be bothering you anymore."

Rose was anxious to get back to Zach with the good news. She was relieved when they left the jail to go back to the doctor's house.

Cynthia slipped her arm through Morgan's. "Sheriff Morgan, what took you fellows so long to take those men prisoners? We were on pins and needles, not knowing what was happening."

"Well, Miz Kincaid, seems these fellows were spending the night with a few of Comanche Wells's soiled doves. It took us some time to round them all up."

He suddenly looked over to where an engine and several cars had just pulled into the depot. Members of the United States Cavalry were disembarking, leading saddled horses. "What in hell's going on now? Looks like we're being invaded."

Two men who were not in uniform came running toward them. Squealing with pleasure, Beth and Cynthia ran into their open arms.

Perplexed, Rose looked to Josh. "Do you have any idea who those men are?"

"Yep," he said. "The fellow kissing Beth is Jake

Carrington, her husband. And the other guy is Dave Kincaid. He's married to Thia. I figured it wouldn't be too long before they'd show up. When you own a railroad, it's easy to hop a ride."

With her hand clasped in her husband's, Cynthia led Dave Kincaid over to introduce him. Rose's immediate impression was that Cynthia had not exaggerated her husband's handsomeness.

Jake Carrington was equally as handsome. And the love and adoration both men felt toward their wives was evident in their relief over finding them safe and unharmed. They kept their wives hugged to their sides.

"The family will always be grateful to you for what you've done for Zach, Rose," Dave Kincaid said.

"From what Thia's told us so far, it sounds remarkable," Jake Carrington added.

"There was nothing remarkable about what I did," Rose said, blushing. "The remarkable thing was that Zach survived and is on his way to recovering."

"I think you're being much too modest, Miss Dubois," Jake said. She felt overwhelmed when he leaned over and kissed her on the cheek. "Zach means a lot to all of us."

"Speaking of people who mean a lot to us, how are my young darlings doing?" Beth asked. "I miss them."

"Your son and daughter miss you, too, Rusty, and I've promised them I'll never let you out of my sight again. Particularly when you're venturing out with their Aunt Cynthia. She attracts trouble like honey does bees."

"Tell me about it," Dave groaned.

"Lovely as they are, gentlemen, sounds like the town'll be better off if your wives don't visit us too often," Ben Morgan said with a wink. "We've kind of gotten used to peace and quiet around here."

As if to dispute his words, the cavalry, now mounted, came riding up amid swirling dust and snorting horses. A young lieutenant dismounted.

"Wouldn't he have been better off just walking over here?" Cynthia whispered aside to Rose and Dave.

"Who's in charge here?" the lieutenant asked officiously.

"Reckon I am, right now," Ben Morgan said.

"Sir, I'm Lieutenant Keogh. By the authority of the president of the United States, I have been dispatched to the town of Comanche Wells to investigate the condition of Andrew Zachary MacKenzie, and to offer said Andrew Zachary MacKenzie the protection of my command. Can you direct me, sir, to his whereabouts?"

"Reckon I can, sonny, but you might have to shoot the doc to get to him," Morgan said.

"Whatever is necessary, sir," the lieutenant said. "First four troopers dismount," he shouted, then started coughing from the dust when a half dozen riders galloped up to them.

"Are you Sheriff Benjamin Morgan?" the leader asked Ben.

"Reckon I am. What can I do for you, stranger?"

"Sheriff Morgan, I'm Evan Bundy with the marshal's office in Austin. On direct orders from the governor of Texas, my officers and I are to use whatever force is necessary to defend and protect Andrew MacKenzie. Do you know where I can find him?"

"Reckon so, Marshal Bundy, but I'm afraid you'll have to fight the U.S. Calvary here to get him."

"I'm afraid I don't understand, Sheriff," Marshal Bundy said.

"Maybe the lieutenant there will explain it to you," Morgan replied.

Marshal Bundy and Lieutenant Keogh began to talk, and soon their voices rose as they argued over whose authority outranked the other.

"Ten bucks the lieutenant wins," Jake said to Dave.

"My money's on the sheriff," Dave replied.

"I might have known they'd show up," Ben murmured, when six more riders rode up slowly.

Leaning forward, the leader of the latest arrivals casually rested his arm on the saddle horn. "Howdy, Ben. Josh. Cole," he said, nodding at each of them.

"Pete," Morgan acknowledged.

"Heard you quit them Pinkertons, Josh," Pete said.

"Yeah, last year when I got married."

"What brings you Texas Rangers this far north?" Ben asked.

"We're lookin' for Zach MacKenzie."

Snugly secure in the arms of her husband, Beth turned her head and glanced at her sister. "Thia, just what *did* you say in those telegrams?"

Cynthia shrugged, then giggled delightfully.

"What do you want with Zach?" Ben asked.

"Went and got himself shot up by four outlaws wanted for murder and cattle rustlin'. Capt'n figured he might be needin' some help. All I can say is, those fellows better hope we catch up with them before Flint MacKenzie does. Ole Flint won't take too kindly to 'em shootin' his son." The two men broke into laughter over their shared joke.

"Reckon I saved you boys some trouble. I've got those hombres locked up in my jail. Had to shoot one to bring 'em in, though."

"What about Zach?"

"He's here, but hell, two bullets ain't enough to take down a MacKenzie," Morgan said.

How could they joke over Zach's wounds? Rose had heard all she could take of this circus. She went back to the doctor's house.

When she entered the room, Zach opened his eyes and asked groggily, "What's all the excitement out there?"

"You wouldn't believe it if I told you. Go back to sleep, my love." She climbed into the bed. "We'll probably wake up to find the bed surrounded by the U.S. Cavalry, but I'm too sleepy to care anymore."

Zach slipped his arm around her shoulders as she curled against him. "Welcome home, Rosie."

Laying her head on his chest, she closed her eyes and smiled in contentment. Zach was recovering, the Tait gang was no longer a threat to them, and tomorrow . . . tomorrow would be the first day of forever.

Chapter 29

Rose jerked awake. She sat up and looked around in confusion at the strange room, then remembered where she was and glanced down beside her. Zach was asleep. She felt his forehead. He was still feverish, but nothing like he'd been the day before.

Glancing at the clock, Rose realized it *hadn't* been the day before. It was eight o'clock, and sunlight was streaming in the window—she'd slept away most of yesterday, as well as the whole night. What must people be thinking?

She hastened out of bed. She needed to bathe, and wondered if she could prevail on Beth or Cynthia for fresh clothing again until she could get back to Brimstone. Then she was struck by another jarring thought: would she even be able to return to Brimstone without being arrested by that idiot sheriff? Although the Tait gang was behind bars, there still were a lot of issues to be resolved back there.

Slipping out of the room, she hurried upstairs and discovered the bedrooms were deserted. With the arrival of their husbands, Beth and Cynthia would probably have gone to the hotel last night. In the kitchen she found Mrs. King, who confirmed it.

"They stopped by before they departed for Dallas this morning and left you a package and a letter."

"Oh my, and I slept right through it," Rose said, disappointed.

"They didn't want to wake you, dear. The ladies felt you needed the rest," Mrs. King said kindly.

"I wish I could have said good-bye. I owe them so much."

"I'm sure they understand, dear. Would you like some breakfast now?"

"I think I would like to bathe first. Where did you put the package they left?"

"In Mr. MacKenzie's room. Is he awake? The doctor's hoping he'll be able to start eating some solid food."

"He was sleeping when I left him. I'm going back to get the package, and I'll let you know. Where is Dr. Serene now?"

"The doctor was called out on an emergency several hours ago."

"Thank you, Mrs. King."

Rose tiptoed back into the room and checked Zach. He was still sleeping peacefully, so she picked up the package and letter from the table and left the room.

As she drew her bath, Rose read the good-bye note. The sisters assured her they'd see her again—at her and Zach's wedding. And, thankfully, the letter went on to say that besides picking up some toiletries and underclothing for her, Beth had given Rose one of her gowns.

Inside the package, Rose was delighted to see a green-and-white-checked gown and a white snood for her hair, as well as the other items the sisters had been thoughtful enough to purchase.

For the next thirty minutes she luxuriated in the hot tub, soaking the soreness out of her aching body. Then she washed her hair to rid it of the trail dust, and while it dried, she cleaned off her boots.

After donning the clean clothing she gave her hair a good brushing, then gathered it into the snood pinned to the back of her head. After she'd applied face powder, the black eye and bruises on her cheek were barely discernible.

She felt like a new woman.

In the hallway she met Dr. Serene, who told her that he'd examined Zach. His temperature still wasn't normal, but the wounds appeared to be healing, and at the rate he was improving, the doctor felt Zach would probably be out of bed in another week.

Her day turned even brighter.

Robert had just finished cleaning up Zach when Rose entered. "Mornin', miss," the orderly said, and winked at her on his way out.

Zach was propped up with pillows. As soon as he saw her, he broke into a broad smile. He still didn't have his color back, but just seeing him sitting up smiling sent a warm glow of happiness through her.

She grasped his hand. "You look wonderful."

"And you are the most beautiful sight I've ever seen. I want to get out of this damn bed and take you in my arms."

"Rather than risk a relapse, MacKenzie, I'll see what I can do." She bent down and kissed him.

"You just shot my temperature up a couple degrees," he said when she pulled away.

"I hope you're hungry."

He grinned. "Glad to see we still think alike."

"I'm talking about food, MacKenzie."

"I guess we *aren't* thinking alike."

She gave him an indulgent look. "Dr. Serene said you're ready to eat something. Anything in particular you'd like?"

Just then, Mrs. King tapped on the door and entered carrying a tray. Rose hurried over and took it from her. "Mrs. King, you don't have to wait on us. I'm used to carrying trays of food."

"It was no trouble, my dear. Enjoy your breakfast."

"Hmmm, this looks good," Rose said, sitting down on the bed. She put the tray on her lap. "Oatmeal and corn muffins." She slathered butter and jam on one and took a bite. "Mmmm, they're still warm." She licked a spot of jam off the corner of her mouth.

"Why are you doing this to me?" he asked plaintively.

"Doing what?" She had no idea what he was talking about.

"That damn thing you're doing with your tongue."

"I'm sorry; you're probably very hungry." She handed him the rest of the muffin.

"I wasn't referring to any damn muffin, and you know it." He took a bite.

She grinned. "Open up." She spooned oatmeal into his mouth, and they continued sharing until it was gone. Then she took a bite of a canned peach. "Oh, this is delicious. I bet Mrs. King canned them herself." She fed him a piece.

"It is good. My mom does a lot of canning. Can you cook, Rosie?"

"Probably not as well as your mother. What about you?"

"I can warm a can of beans and fry a hunk of salt pork when I have to."

She laughed. "I'm pretty good at cracking nuts."

"You sure are." He reached for her hand and squeezed it. "I've never trailed with anyone better." He sobered. "I'm grateful to you, Rosie. I'd never have made it without you."

"I'm the one who's grateful, Zach. You saved my life in Brimstone. Now, let's not talk about this anymore."

Gratitude was not an issue. Whatever she'd done was instinctive, out of love for him. She hoped that had been his motive, too.

"There's tea and coffee. Which do you want?"

"Coffee," he said, his gaze never leaving her face.

* * *

Later that day, she was reading Kipling's *The Light That Failed* to Zach when Dr. Serene came in accompanied by an older couple.

The woman rushed across the room, and Zach raised his hand to grasp hers. "Hi, Mom."

So this was his mother. Tall and graceful, Garnet MacKenzie appeared to be in her late fifties. Moisture glistened in her green eyes as she gazed at her son.

She sat down on the edge of the bed and leaned over and kissed his forehead. "How are you, Zach?" she asked. Her soft tone bore the traces of a Southern accent.

"I'm fine, Mom. The doctor said I'd probably be up and around in another week."

The man now stepped forward. Rose could see where Zach got his height and broad shoulders. Flint MacKenzie's profile showed an inherent strength, and although his dark hair was streaked with gray, he had the sinewy body of a man half his age.

"Son," he said. The single word expressed more than a dozen others could have done.

"Hi, Dad." As the two men shook hands, Flint covered their grasp with his other hand.

"You gave us a scare, boy. I told your mother a couple of slugs wouldn't keep you down."

Zach grinned at him. "Like father, like son. Right, Dad?"

"Which will be the death of me yet," Garnet said. "When can we take him home, Doctor?"

"I'd say by tomorrow, if you keep him off his feet," Dr. Serene said. "But I'll be able to tell better in the morning. I have patients waiting, so we'll talk later."

"Mom and Dad, this is Rose Dubois," Zach said, as soon as the doctor departed.

For the first time since entering the room, the couple turned their full attention on Rose. His mother's gaze was curious but warm; Flint Mackenzie's was enigmatic, with no hint of what lay behind his sapphire gaze.

Garnet came over and hugged her. "It's such a pleasure to meet you, Rose. Thia and Beth told us all about you. We can never thank you enough for what you did for our son."

Rose was at a loss. She knew she should say something gracious, but, unintentionally, the couple intimidated her. Or was it the change in Zach? That could be the reason, because she was used to seeing Zach, the reckless outlaw. Zach, the adored son, was unfamiliar to her. She felt like an outsider—like she didn't belong.

Rose managed a polite greeting, then backed out of the room. "I'm sure you'd like some privacy, so I'll leave you alone."

"No, stay, Rose," Zach said.

"I, ah . . . have some things to do."

Once out of the room, Rose leaned against the door and took a deep breath. She felt so alone. She was the stranger among these people. Even the town's sheriff was close to them.

They were all kind, good, and caring people, but that didn't make her belong.

Not even to Zach—the adored son.

Desolate, she stepped outside. Josh and Cole

were in conversation with a woman. At the sight of Rose, Josh nudged the lady and she turned her head to look.

Joy surged through Rose when she saw Emily MacKenzie rush toward her with outstretched arms. Squealing with joy, they hugged each other, stepped back, and looked at one another, then they hugged again.

"Let me look at you," Emily declared. She took a long look at Rose's face. "Oh, Rose! Josh wasn't exaggerating: you and Zach must have gone through hell. I couldn't believe it when Josh told me you were with Zach. You never mentioned you even knew him. Your last letter said that a rancher named Stephen Rayburn had asked you to marry him."

"It's a long story, Em."

"I don't care how long it is; I want to hear every word. I want to know just how you got that black eye and all those bruises and scrapes, and how Zach ended up with two bullet holes in him." Emily linked arms. "Come on, we'll go have a cup of tea, and you can tell me all about it."

Rose smiled happily. Just being with her dearest friend again somehow made all those events seem like an eternity ago. She wasn't alone anymore.

Arm and arm, they walked to the hotel and sat down in a corner of the dining room.

As soon as the waiter brought them a pot of tea, Emily poured them each a cup and settled back. "Now remember, Rose, don't leave out a thing. I want to hear every detail."

"Well, the worst of it began the night Stephen gave a party to celebrate our engagement."

"You always vowed you'd marry a rich man."

"I know. But by that time, I was in love with Zach, even if I didn't want to admit it to myself."

Emily grew somber as Rose related the events after she'd told Stephen she couldn't marry him. By the time she finished, Emily's eyes were misted with tears.

"You're so brave, Rose. Zach would have died if it hadn't been for you."

"I had a lot of help. I prayed on that hillside, Em. I've never done that before. And I believe my prayer was answered."

At that moment Garnet MacKenzie came into the dining room and sat down with them.

"How is Zach feeling?" Emily asked, filling Garnet's tea cup.

"He's sleeping right now. Josh and Cole are in the bar, so Flint joined them." She took a sip of the tea, then sighed deeply. "I feel so much better now that I've seen Zach. The doctor thinks we might be able to take him home tomorrow."

"That's wonderful news, Aunt Garnet," Emily said.

Garnet reached over and squeezed Rose's hand. "We're indebted to you, Rose, and we're expecting you to come back with us."

Rose hesitated. "I don't know, Mrs. MacKenzie. My clothes and everything I own are in Brimstone. I was planning on returning there."

"Perhaps I misunderstood Zach? He said that the two of you were planning on getting married."

Rose swallowed hard. "We, ah, actually never had time to discuss marriage, Mrs. MacKenzie.

There's a lot of loose ends to tie up before I can even consider that. I may still be wanted for murder."

"Oh, Rose, that can all be cleared up easily. I know you'll love the Triple M," Emily said, her face shining with exuberance. "I couldn't believe it; it's almost a town in itself. We all have our own houses, grouped around a central location. And Rose, they actually have a sort of store for everyone's convenience, where they stock food, canned goods, condiments, and general household items. If you need a bottle of Heinz ketchup or a peck of potatoes, you just go there and get it. Kitty, who is Josh's sister, is in charge of the inventory. And not all the merchandise is necessarily practical; there's hand cream and other personal items a woman needs. It's so convenient, and it's maintained with Triple M profits."

"You mean you don't have to pay for anything you take?" Rose asked.

"That's right," Garnet said. "The store was Cleve's idea. When he and his brothers came back after the Civil War, the Triple M was just a couple thousand acres. When they all married and started families, they kept expanding the ranch as land became available. Now their children have started families, so there are a lot of mouths to feed."

"How big is the ranch?" Rose asked, flabbergasted.

"It's between three and four hundred thousand acres."

Rose's eyes popped open. "What!"

"One of the largest in Texas," Garnet said.

"The Triple M's got everything except its own post office," Emily added. "Just think, honey, we'll be neighbors! Maybe not as close as roommates—since we've both found new ones," she added with a grin—"but our houses will be within sight of each other. We're all together, but each household still has its own privacy."

"It sounds too good to be true," Rose said. "It's a wonder the boys would ever want to leave."

"All our sons had to test their wings," Garnet said, "just as their fathers did. But once they're ready to settle down, they come back."

"If they're still alive, you mean," Rose said, recalling the events of the past week: murders, Zach's near death, her own injuries, the desperate flight to stay alive, and the heartache of betrayal—Zach's failure to be honest with her.

She stood up, suddenly feeling overwhelmed. "You'll have to excuse me. I have to get back."

"Rose, wait," Emily called out to her.

"I'll talk to you later, Em," she said, and literally ran out of the dining room.

She didn't stop to check Zach, but went straight to the bedroom. His deceit was too big an issue to discuss until he was well. But how could she keep up a pretense that it didn't matter until then? It would be wiser just to tell him she was going back to Brimstone to get her clothes. He'd have no reason to doubt her.

When Rose joined Zach's family for dinner, she received another shock. The body of Will Grainger was arriving on the morning train, and the MacKenzies were taking him to the Triple M for burial. Everyone would be leaving on that train—Zach included.

With time running out, she went into his room and told him her intentions.

She might just as well have struck him. "Rosie, don't do this to me, please. I need you," he pleaded.

"Zach, you don't need me. You have a devoted family who will wait on you hand and foot."

He grabbed her hand. "You don't really think that's why I need you, do you? Waking up and seeing you beside me heals my body and soul. That's why I need you, Rosie. That's why I'll always need you. As soon as I'm back on my feet, we'll get married and go back to Brimstone to get your things. Or you know Kate'll pack up your clothes and ship them to you. Okay, Rosie?" he asked, looking at her hopefully.

He was doing it to her again. Mesmerizing her with those sapphire eyes, that irresistible little-boy look. Making her forget everything except how much she loved him.

The next morning, when the train pulled out of Comanche Wells, Rose sat beside Zach's berth. He held on to her hand as if he'd never let go, and she wondered just when she'd lost control of her own life.

Chapter 30

The trip had tired Zach, and he was put to bed as soon as they arrived. While he slept, Rose had a chance to look around at the compound. Emily had not exaggerated; the Triple M resembled a little village.

And it was the ideal place for a man and woman to raise their children.

She paused by a fenced-in graveyard, and was surprised to see that, despite the hired help, Josh MacKenzie was digging the grave for Will Grainger.

"You're working hard, Josh. Can't you get someone to help you?"

He wiped his brow. "It's the least I can do for Will. Besides, everyone works hard on the ranch. In the years I was gone, I'd almost forgotten just how hard it is, but it's a good life. I was ready to come back."

"What about Emily?"

"Em loves it. She soaks up work like a sponge does water. You wouldn't believe it, but she and my mom canned pickles last week. Emily Lawrence MacKenzie, canning pickles." He chuckled. "What a woman."

Rose smiled at the vision of the wealthy Eastern heiress canning pickles, and she thought of their shared giggles when they were Harvey Girls. Good Lord, it had only been a year ago. It seemed like centuries.

"This certainly is a big ranch," Rose said. "I imagine it does keep everyone busy. It's a cattle ranch, right?"

He nodded. "We run about forty thousand head and sell ten to fifteen thousand head a year, depending on the demand."

"No wonder it takes so many people for the operation."

"We grow all our own vegetables, too. With few exceptions, everything eaten on the Triple M has been raised on it."

"You sound pretty proud of this place," she said, smiling softly.

"The ranch wasn't always so successful, especially after my grandfather died at the Alamo. Then it was just a little piece of land, but my dad and uncles turned it into what it's become today." Josh hesitated, then said, "And the women they loved toughed it out with them. I've got a lot of good memories, Rose, and you'll grow to love the Triple

M the same as Em has. She calls it Utopia, Texas."

"That's a far cry from her opinion of Long Island, where she was raised."

"We both know what she thought of that place. Would you believe her father has even come down here and visited? He's talking about building a house in Dallas."

"It's strange what courses people's lives take. Zach and I once had a discussion on that very subject." Suddenly, without any intention to do so, she blurted out, "He came so close to dying, Josh."

"But it's over, Rose. Put it behind you and look toward the future."

"I'm trying to, but I'm not sure I belong here. I don't think I can live up to the other MacKenzie women."

"I think you can, Rose, and obviously Zach believes it, too. You've been through a rough time, but you can relax now. Zach will soon be up and around, and if it's any comfort, you're not alone anymore, honey: there isn't a person on this ranch who's not gonna look out for your welfare. Trust us—and stop doubting yourself." He put aside the shovel and climbed out of the hole. "I reckon I better get back to the house. You okay, Rose?"

"I'm fine," she said.

"You sure you don't want me to send Em down?"

"No, I'm on my way back, too."

For a long moment she sat there, staring at the stone crosses that marked the graves.

"Are you thinking how one of those markers could so easily have had Zach's name on it? I know I have."

Rose jerked up her head to see Garnet MacKenzie standing nearby. "Oh, forgive me, Mrs. MacKenzie, I didn't realize you were there." She turned back and stared at the crosses in the gravesite. "It's very sad. There are quite a few of them, aren't there?" She started to read the names aloud. "Kathleen MacKenzie. Sarah MacKenzie."

"Flint's mother, and Luke's first wife. They were brutally killed during the Civil War while the boys were away in the army."

"Maude Malone. Was she a MacKenzie?"

"You might say that." Garnet smiled in memory. "Maude more or less adopted the MacKenzies. She'd been a close friend of Kathleen and Andy, and watched the three boys grow up. Our husbands loved her; our children adored her. She was the grandmother they never had."

"And those graves marked Matthew and Linda?"

"Matthew was Luke's and Honey's son. The precious little one died of consumption in infancy. Linda was Cleve's and Adee's daughter. She was stillborn. Flint and . . ." She suddenly stopped and drew in a deep, shuddering breath.

"What is it, Mrs. MacKenzie?" Rose asked.

"Flint and I have been fortunate; we've never lost a child. I can't bear to think of what it would be like." Garnet MacKenzie turned her head and stared right into Rose's eyes. "But I know that part of us would have died with Zach if he hadn't survived." Her eyes were moist as she grasped Rose's hand. "Forgive me, Rose, but I overheard part of your conversation with Josh. Between Cynthia and Zach, my husband and I have pieced together what you did. You weren't struggling to save your own life—you were fighting to save Zach's. Don't believe for a moment that you don't have the mettle to be a MacKenzie wife. You belong here, my dear. And we'd welcome you with open arms."

After a soft squeeze of Rose's hand, she left as silently as she'd arrived.

The next morning, Rose sat on the wagon seat beside Zach for Will Grainger's burial. She glanced in sympathy at the Rangers and the MacKenzie family, who stood with bowed heads and saddened faces as they said this final good-bye to their comrade and friend.

With stark awareness, she realized that every man present was serving or had served in the Texas Rangers. And his offspring were sure to follow in that same tradition. Despite Garnet MacKenzie's words of assurance Rose knew she wouldn't be able to mourn this stoically. How could she bear it if it had been Zach who'd fallen in the line of duty, instead of Will Grainger?

She stole a glance at Zach. He looked so pale, and his stricken countenance was a grim reminder of the anguish he was suffering. Though his wounds were healing, this funeral was taking a toll on what meager strength he'd recovered.

Maybe it was a reaction setting in, but whatever the reason, she had to get away to think the whole thing through. To try and understand what his motives for deceiving her had been. As much as it did not—could not—lessen her love for him, the deception made her heart ache. She had to go away and make peace with it; she knew she couldn't do that at the Triple M. She'd be surrounded by people who loved him too much to be objective.

Although she'd vowed to never leave him again, she had to go back to Brimstone. Zach was past any danger, so she could leave with a clear conscience. And when he was well, she would come back and hear his explanation.

But she'd have to do it quickly. If Zach even suspected her intentions, he'd talk her out of leaving again.

If she was lucky, she could get to Calico before the northbound train came through, but she would have to borrow the ticket fare from Emily.

When they retured to the house, Zach went to bed and Rose went straight to her bedroom to get her few possessions. Removing Zach's Colt from the pocket of her skirt, she stared at the pistol for a long moment. His life revolved around the use of a gun; hers, a Harvey Girl uniform. Could it be true they were as far apart as these symbols of their chosen lives indicated? Sighing deeply, she folded her clothing and tied it up in a package.

When she stopped to express her thanks to his parents for their hospitality, the couple was astonished.

"Rose, I don't understand," Garnet said. "Does Zach know you're leaving?"

"It's an emergency. There's something I must do in Brimstone." At least that wasn't a lie. "Zach's sleeping, and I don't want to wake him. The funeral was very difficult for him. I'll return as soon as possible."

"Is there anything we can do to help, Rose?" the reticent Flint asked. His words were few, but Rose doubted he ever missed a sight or sound around him.

"No, sir. It's something I must do myself."

"Reckon you'll need a ride to town," he said. "I'll hitch up the team and drive you."

"I'd appreciate that, Mr. MacKenzie. I want to say a quick good-bye to Emily." She hugged Garnet. "Thank you again, Mrs. MacKenzie. I love Zach. I'd never hurt him, and I'll be back as soon as I can."

Garnet cupped Rose's cheeks between her hands, and stared deeply into her eyes. "I know that, dear. Have a safe journey."

It took every bit of Rose's willpower to leave the house without stopping for one final look at Zach, but her courage and determination remained steadfast. She went straight to Emily's house to seek her aid.

"I have a favor to ask of you, Em," Rose said, when Emily came to the door.

Emily frowned. "Come on in, Rose. I've seen that look before. You're about to do something that you know I'm not going to like."

"I need twenty-five dollars."

"Oh, is that all? You had me scared for a moment." She dug into a sugar bowl in the kitchen cupboard and handed Rose the money. "If you're going shopping, I'll join you."

"I'm not going shopping, Em; I'm going back to Brimstone."

"You mean now?"

"Yes. Zach's father is driving me to the depot."

"Rose, what's going on? Did you and Zach have an argument?"

"No, he doesn't even know I'm leaving."

"Rose, he's going to be devastated."

"I haven't much time, but I'll try to explain," she said. "There are some things I have to think over, and I need some time alone. Away from Texas Rangers, sheriffs, outlaws, the United States Cavalry, and . . . forgive me, but, away from Mackenzies!"

"Think about what, Rose?"

"Em, I don't know if I belong here."

"I thought the same thing when Josh brought me here, Rose. But this family embraced me, and they will you, too. They already adore you for having saved Zach's life. So, there's something more than that. What aren't you telling me?"

Rose fought the tears that threatened. "Zach lied to me, Em. He never told me he was a Texas Ranger until he thought he was dying. Until then, I believed he was a drifter. I don't know the real Zach MacKenzie; I only know the make-believe one. He didn't even tell me he was related to Josh. I asked him when I first met him, and he knew you were my best friend, but he still didn't admit it. I just don't know what to think anymore, Em. I have to get away."

"Oh, honey, I know how you must feel. Remember, I had to struggle with my love for Josh when I knew he was pretending to be someone he wasn't. Why don't you confront Zach and hear what he has to say? He must have had his reasons for keeping the truth from you."

"I'm sure he did. But I bared my soul to him, Em. Why didn't he tell me he was a Texas Ranger? Why didn't he tell me his family owned a zillion-acre ranch? Instead, he let me go on believing he was a penniless drifter—a member of an outlaw gang. He might have gone to his grave with me believing that."

"Rose, I'm not trying to make excuses for him. I'm sure he loves you. He's told the whole family he wants to marry you. As long as you love each other, nothing's so bad that you can't work it out. Believe me, I'm speaking from my own experience. What else matters?"

"I'm so confused lately I'm not even sure he really loves me. At one time I believed it, but I'm no longer certain, Em. Maybe he's just grateful to me for helping to save his life."

"Oh really, Rose! Now you *are* talking foolish. If Zach was just grateful, he'd say thank you and that would be it. He wouldn't marry you out of gratitude. MacKenzies are too fair-minded to do that to anyone. At least go tell him good-bye."

"I don't have the willpower to say good-bye to him, Em, so you have to do it for me. Tell him I'll be back. I'm not leaving forever; I just have to make peace with it myself."

Flint rode up with the buggy, and the two women walked outside. Emily grasped her hands, and her voice broke. "Rose, are you sure this is what you want to do?"

"I don't want to do it, Em. But I have to do it."

Holding back her tears, Rose hugged Emily. "Remember, tell Zach I love him. Tell him I'll be back." She climbed into the wagon.

"When, Rose? When?" Emily ran beside the buggy as it moved away.

"I don't know. But it will give him time to think things out, too."

Rose turned her head and waved good-bye to the lone figure standing on the path. Garnet MacKenzie walked outside and stood next to Emily.

Chapter 31

Brimstone

Rose was utterly miserable. The weight in her chest seemed to be getting heavier, rather than easing with the passing of time. It was impossible to make any rational decision when her treacherous memory kept reminding her of his engaging grin, the sound of his warm chuckle.

Time and time again in the past two weeks, Rose had questioned why she was doing this to herself. In the final scheme of things, did it matter if she might love him more than he did her? So what if he thought he loved her out of gratitude? At least she'd be with him.

So why prolong being away from him? Though she'd believed it was good to get away and clear her mind, she hadn't realized how much her heart had a say in it. All she was accomplishing was denying herself the pleasure of being with him, of seeing him, of tasting his kiss. Oh, how she longed for just the touch of his hand. Hadn't she learned by almost losing him that every shared moment was a gift to be cherished—not forsaken?

She had come to understand why he hadn't told her he was a Texas Ranger sooner, but it hurt, to think he hadn't trusted her enough to be truthful with her.

Rose stood up and put on her apron, thinking aloud. "Could it be because he'd intended from the beginning to leave me when it was over?"

She'd just see about that! Like it or not, he was stuck with her. Tomorrow she was heading back to Calico. She'd rather be miserable with him than without him.

Rose went to the mirror to pin the bow on her hair. "But if he *really* loved me—"

"He does, darlin'."

She spun around and there he was, climbing through the window. The familiar grin. The irresistible mischief in his eyes. And in that instant the yoke of doubt lifted, shattered by the pulse-pounding certainty of their love.

She gloried in that certainty as he walked over to her and cupped her face in the warmth of his palms. His gaze devoured her lovingly.

"I've told you in a dozen different ways, Rosie. But if you want, I'll say it again. I'll shout it to the world. I love you."

Then he kissed her, and she came alive again, a Sleeping Beauty awakened by the kiss of her prince.

Lord, how she loved this man! It had seemed forever since she'd felt the thrill of his touch, the
warmth of his love. Any doubt, any reservation, any
misconstrued notion she might have harbored became meaningless.

When breathlessness forced them apart, he held
her for a long moment, reacquainting their senses
and bodies to the feel of each other. To the peace of
mind of being together, their hearts beating as one.

"Rosie, why did you leave?"

The moment shattered, returning her to reality.
She stepped away and stared at him with eyes
widened in shock.

"You can ask me that? Have you forgotten how
you lied and deceived me from the time we met?
You were practically on your death bed before you
admitted to me that you were a Texas Ranger, and
not the drifter you pretended to be."

"Rose, I had to do that. I was undercover."

"What does that mean—a license to lie? It only
proves my point: lawmen can't be trusted. I don't
know if I can ever trust you again."

For the first time, she saw him angry. "You
know, Rose, you've got a couple of pretty twisted
values: you could trust me when you thought I
was an outlaw, but you can't now because I'm a
lawman. So Sturges was a son of a bitch, and
you've met up with a couple of rotten lawmen.
Well, for evey *one* you can name, I can name ten decent ones, including my dad, uncles, and cousins.
Rangers like Will Grainger, marshals like Pat Garrett, and sheriffs like Ben Morgan. The West is dotted with the graves of honorable lawmen who

have died bringing law and order to this country. I'm damn tired of listening to you ridiculing them."

"Don't you try to put me on the defensive, Zach MacKenzie. I'm talking about you and me—truth and trust between *us*."

"Then believe this: there's a simple explanation why I wasn't entirely honest with you. In the beginning I couldn't tell you—I was working undercover. Then it became too late because you were going to marry Rayburn, and he was my prime suspect."

"So you didn't trust me."

"Why should I have trusted you? I had Will Grainger's life to consider. Secondly, you were adamant about marrying a rich man. *And* you sure as hell made no secret how much you hated lawmen. And for your own good, it was better you didn't know the truth: if those bastards suspected you knew anything, they'd have tortured you to get it out of you. All I could do was warn you away from Rayburn, but you wouldn't listen. You thought I was doing it out of jealousy."

"I figured out for myself why you kept the truth about Stephen from me. It was one of the doubts I had to come back here and work out alone."

"I have to know, Rosie: are you unsure . . . that you love me?"

"How could you ever think that? If I didn't love you, nothing you said or did would have hurt me."

"I'm sorry, honey. I never meant to hurt you. And I tried like hell not to fall in love with you. Reckon I failed at both. I almost went crazy when I woke up and you were gone."

"I always intended to go back, Zach. Didn't Em tell you?"

"She told me, but I didn't know . . . I couldn't understand why you left."

She shook her head in helplessness. "It made sense at the time. I just needed to get away from everyone and settle it all in my mind. Everything had been so hectic. I was hurt that you'd lied to me about your past, and wasn't even sure how you'd feel about me when you recovered. We'd gone through a lot together, and I thought you might have convinced yourself that you were in love with me. My leaving would give you a chance to think it out, too."

He snorted. "You've got that right, Rosie. I did a lot of thinking— *thinking* that I'd go out of my mind before I could get out of that bed and come after you."

His expression sobered, and he raised his hands to her cheeks. "Rosie . . ." The words seemed to catch in his throat. "Rosie, how could you do that to us?" Heartache glimmered in his eyes, tears in hers.

Sitting down, he pulled her down on his lap. "I want you to listen carefully—and believe—everything I'm about to tell you, because it's probably the longest speech I'll ever make, and talking about myself's never come easy to me.

"Something happened to me when we were running from that gang. I always had a pretty cavalier attitude when it came to my own death. But when I actually believed I was going to die, all I could think about was not wanting to leave you. The night you said we'd have the rest of our lives together, that your life would have no purpose if I died, was when I quit feeling sorry for myself. I thought about what your grief would be like. Your pain. And that thought just about broke my heart. That's what kept me going, honey."

"Because you felt sorry for me?" she asked.

"Because I *love* you! Dammit, Rose, aren't you listening to anything I'm saying? Your love got me through it."

She stood up and walked over to the window. For a long moment, she remained silent. Then she turned and smiled slyly. "Well, were you?"

As always, he understood her perfectly. "I'd never have let you marry that son of a bitch, Rosie."

"I've already figured that out. But that's not what I asked you, Zach. No secrets, remember?"

He couldn't hide his grin. Getting to his feet, he walked slowly toward her. "*You* are a witch, Rose Dubois. A seductive, soul-stealing, redheaded witch." He slid his arms around her waist and pulled her against him. "Whom I adore."

Leaning into him, Rose slipped her arms around his neck. "Yes or no, MacKenzie?"

"You know damn well I was jealous. But I was right about Rayburn, wasn't I?"

He kissed her so soundly she felt it all the way down to the tips of her toes.

"Now I have a question for you. Do you still hate all lawmen?"

"I met one I'm crazy about," she teased.

"Is that right?" His cocky smile made her glow.

"I bet he feels the same way about you."

"Well, I don't think it will do me any good. I understand Sheriff Morgan is a confirmed bachelor."

"Lady," he groaned, "you're eating me alive. You burrow under a man's skin and just kept chewing. How do you feel about Texas Rangers?"

"I think the Texas Rangers are very courageous and admirable, but I'll be honest with you, Zach: I'm going to be miserable married to one, wondering if the man I love will be shot and killed in the line of duty."

"I figured as much. The Tait gang was my last assignment. I didn't reenlist."

Rose's happiness bubbled over. "Do you mean it, Zach?"

"I mean it. I did my duty and upheld the family tradition. But you and I have a much more urgent problem to settle. If I don't make love to you soon, I'm going to burst. Let's go to bed, Rosie."

She looked sorrowful. "I have to go to work now."

He groaned. "You have to go to work!" Grasping her by the shoulders, he stared down at her. "Tell me, Rose, since I gave up the Rangers, are you giving up the Harvey Girls?"

"We'll talk about that as soon as I get back." She gave him a quick kiss and headed for the door. "I'm late, Zach. I must go."

He caught her as she reached the door, and turned her around to face him. He cupped her neck in his warm palm and tilted her head back. "Forget about it tonight and stay here with me." His kiss was long and persuasive. "Rosie, it's been so long. I need you," he whispered, between soft kisses to her face and eyes.

"I need you, too, Zach," she said, yearningly. "But I'll only be gone for a couple hours. I'll come back as soon as the train pulls out, and we'll have all night to make up for lost time."

"Lost time is lost forever, love. This is here and now. Let's not lose any more time than we have already."

His kisses became longer and hotter, his stroking tongue sending exquisite shivers spiraling through her. "Don't make me beg, Rosie," he whispered. "I can't look at you now without wanting to make love to you."

She curved into him instinctively, and he traced down her spine and rested his hands on her derriere, then crushed her against his throbbing, swelling erection. She sucked in an ecstatic gasp and closed her eyes.

"Feel my need, Rosie. Feel what you do to me. Two more hours is an eternity."

She knew he *would* stop if she insisted. But the damage was done. His every kiss—his every erotic plea—had escalated her passion beyond any hope of walking away from him now.

"Rosie?" He waited expectantly, with the look of a little boy caught with his hand in the cookie jar waiting to hear his punishment.

A wisp of a smile tugged at the ends of her lips. "It would be an eternity for me, too, my love."

He pulled her to him. "Rosie, I love you. I love you," he murmured.

His kiss was so tender she didn't realize she was

crying until he gently brushed the tears off her cheeks. Then he picked her up in his arms and carried her to the bed.

"This is so irresponsible of me," she murmured as he removed her clothing. "Inconsiderate, unforgivable, and . . . and . . ." He laid her on the bed, then lowered himself to her.

"And so-o-o divine," she murmured before his mouth captured hers.

"What time is it, honey?" Zach asked.

Rose rolled over and looked at the clock. They'd been together for over two hours.

"It's seven o'clock. The dinner train's come and gone. What am I going to tell Mr. Billings?"

"So long, it's been good to know you," he said.

Rolling back, she leaned on his chest, her silky hair feathering his cheek as she gazed down at him. "That's not funny, Zach. I'm going to miss him and the other girls. In addition, since Sheriff Bloom and most of the outlaw element have moved on to greener pastures, Brimstone isn't such a bad town now. There's a new sheriff, and he seems to be a pretty honest man."

"A kind word about a lawman coming from the mouth of Rose Dubois? I never thought I'd live to see that day."

She dipped her head and kissed him. "You look much better than the last time I saw you." Her gaze automatically swung to the ugly wound on his shoulder. "How does it feel?"

"A little stiff, that's all. In another couple of weeks you won't even know it's there."

"I'll always know," she said solemnly, and lightly traced her fingers over his thigh. "And this leg wound?"

"Never felt as good as it does right now, honey." He wove his fingers into her hair, pulled her head down, and stroked her lips with his tongue. "You're all the medicine I'll ever need, Rosie."

She parted her lips in a sigh, and their mouths found a fit. It was meant to be a quick, light kiss, but as always their hunger for each other controlled the moment. Pressure deepened, emotions intensified, light banter became sighs and groans, and desire became a floodtide.

Afterward, Rose eased herself out of his arms and sat up on the edge of the bed.

"What are you doing, Rosie?"

"I'm going to the restaurant and make my apologies."

"I'll go with you."

She turned her head and looked at him over her shoulder. His long body was stretched out in relaxation. "That's not necessary, Zach. I'll come back as quickly as I can."

"Not on your life." He sat up. "I'm not letting you out of my sight." He kissed her on the back of her shoulder, then got up and peered out the window.

Rose slipped on her combination, then went over to the mirror and put her hair in order. When she started to put on her black uniform, Zach glanced up from pulling up his pants and looked at her in surprise.

"That's what you're wearing?"

She arched a brow. "Why, yes. Why not?"

"I, ah . . . thought since we just got engaged, we ought to celebrate. Why don't you wear that ruby gown, Rosie? You look so beautiful in it."

It wasn't like him to care what she wore. Confused, she glanced again at him. He sure was acting strange. "Zach, are you still on some kind of medication?"

He pulled on his shirt. "No, why?"

"Just curious," she said, and reached for her stockings and shoes. Then, to please him, she put on the ruby gown.

When they were ready to leave, he walked over and peered out of the window again.

"I know old habits die hard, Zach, but why don't you try leaving by the door this time?"

Slapping on his Stetson, he gave her a light swat on the rear as he followed her out.

Chapter 32

Rose was happy for the first time in two weeks as they walked hand in hand to the depot. She was surprised to see an engine and several cars parked on the siding.

"Looks like a train broke down."

Zach cast a quick glance at it. "Ah, Rosie—before we go inside, there's something I didn't tell you."

He looked so guilty, she knew it was bad news. "Worse than your being a Texas Ranger?"

"Maybe."

She glanced at him warily. "You mean there's another way you took advantage of my trusting nature?"

" 'Fraid so," he said. She paused with her hand on the restaurant doorknob. "Rose, don't go in there yet."

"Why not?"

"Remember how you said coming back here seemed like a good idea at the time, but it really wasn't?" She nodded. "Well, I did something, too, that seemed like a good idea at the time. Now I'm not so sure."

"So that's the reason you've been acting so strange."

"Let's go back to your room, Rose, and I'll tell you all about it."

"All right, just as soon as I talk to Mr. Billings," she said, and opened the door.

Rose froze on the spot and stared, dumbfounded. The room was full of smiling faces—*familiar* smiling faces.

Emily MacKenzie rushed up, hugged and kissed her, then stepped back. "Oh, Rose, this is so exciting."

Stunned, Rose looked at Zach for an explanation.

Emily's green eyes rounded in sudden comprehension. "She doesn't know?"

Zach looked sick. "I haven't had time to tell her."

"Tell me what?" Rose asked warningly.

"You'd better tell her, Zach," Emily murmured.

But it was too late. Several others descended upon them, Zach's parents among them.

"Rose, dear, I'm so happy for you and Zach," Garnet said. She gave Rose a hug and kiss. "I couldn't hope for a more loving wife for my son."

"Same with me," Flint said in his typical reticent fashion.

Cynthia Kincaid and Beth Carrington came over, accompanied by a lovely, dark-haired woman.

"Rose, honey, this is our sister Angie," Thia said.

Angie hugged her. "I'm so happy to finally meet you, Rose. I've heard so much about you. I want you to meet my husband Giff." She grabbed Rose's hand and led her over to a tall, tanned, blond-haired man. If it weren't for the tiny lines at the corners of his eyes, he could have passed for a youthful Adonis. Rose recalled Em telling her about Peter Gifford, who had been the ranch foreman on the Colorado ranch where the MacKenzie sisters had been raised.

Soon Rose had Zach's aunts and uncles, his cousins, and their offsprings around her. The room was full of MacKenzies. From what she could tell, the Harvey Girls and Mr. Billings were the only outsiders in the crowd.

Then the bell tinkled over the door, and the Reverend and Mrs. Downing entered the restaurant—and it suddenly became very clear what all these people were doing there.

Stunned, she looked at Zach.

He at least had the conscience to look sheepish. "That's what I had to tell you, Rosie."

Rose turned away and forced a smile to lips that felt as if they were glued together.

"Will everyone listen, please?" she said, raising her voice to be heard above the drone of noise in the room. All conversation ceased, and everyone turned their heads toward her.

"It's a pleasure to see all of you again, but I'm sorry you've all come so far, *because there's not going to be any wedding tonight.*" It had not been her intention for the ending to come out in a screech, but somehow it did.

Having said that, she pivoted on her heel and strode to the kitchen.

Zach followed her.

"Does this mean you've changed your mind and won't marry me?" he asked as soon as the kitchen door swung shut.

With arms akimbo, Rose turned and glared at him. "I said *tonight*! How dare you invite all of your relatives to a wedding I knew nothing about? I presume that *is* all of them."

"Every last one of 'em."

"Well, you can get 'every last one of 'em' out of here right now."

"Shhh, Rose, they'll hear you."

"Good! It's time they're enlightened to the fact that you are the worst lying, sneaking, lowdown nogooder I've ever met."

"I only wanted to surprise you."

"Surprise me? Surprise me!" She felt almost out of control. "You can surprise a woman by asking her to marry you, but you don't *surprise* her with her own wedding. Don't you know a woman dreams of her wedding day? She plans every detail of it. A string quartet playing soft music, the fragrance of orange blossoms in the air—*not* the smell of roast beef," she declared, sniffing the kitchen odor. "She sees herself on the arm of her husband, surrounded by loving family and friends, and she's wearing a beautiful white wedding gown with a long veil and satin bows like those in a catalog."

"You're as beautiful to me in that ruby gown as you'd be in any fancy white gown, honey. And I can guarantee you'd be surrounded by a loving family. My family all love you. I'm sorry there's no orange blossoms, but my cousin Kitty made you a lovely bouquet of Texas bluebonnets. And we may not have a string quartet, but we do have a vocal one: my Aunt Honey's agreed to play her guitar, and Thia, Beth, and Angie are going to sing with her."

"When you were making all those arrangements, I don't suppose you happened to remember a wedding ring."

"Of course I did." He dug a ring and a gold locket out of his pocket. "My mom wants you to have this locket. It's her only keepsake and belonged to her mother. Mom hopes that one day it will be passed on to our children. She thought it could be the 'something old' for you to wear." He fastened it around her neck.

Having vent her initial anger, now, try as she might, she couldn't sustain it. He was so adorably contrite. And everyone seemed to have gone to a lot of trouble to make it special. But he was still wrong not to have discussed it with her before bringing his whole family to Brimstone. In a way, it was kind of sweet. *Sweet but stupid.*

"I'm sorry, honey. All I could think of was getting you roped and hog-tied so you couldn't run away again. I didn't stop to think that naturally you'd want to plan your own wedding. I'm an inconsiderate, stupid fool."

"That you are, Zach."

"I'll go in and tell them the wedding's off until you can plan it right and proper. We'll make this an engagement party."

"No, we won't," she declared as he started to leave.

He turned to her with a questioning look. "You mean you don't want that, either? Rosie, even Billings went to a lot of trouble for this."

"Mr. Billings was in on it, too?"

"Uh-huh. Can't you smell it cooking?"

"So now, after everyone has gone to all this trouble and has come all this way for a wedding, your whole family's going to think I'm rude and ungrateful."

"No, Rosie, they'll understand. They're all great people, and they already love you, because they know I love you. That's probably difficult to understand, but that's the way we MacKenzies are—every last one of us. Once we're married, you'll see that for yourself."

Confused by conflicting emotions, she'd already begun to falter. "Then that makes me appear even *more* ungrateful for their love and loyalty."

"Honey, it's your privilege to have the kind of wedding you want without worrying what my family thinks about it. I want our wedding to be the happiest day of your life. We'll hold off until we can arrange the kind of wedding day you've always dreamed about.

"Well . . . I suppose it doesn't really matter what a woman wears when she gets married. It doesn't make her any less married, does it?"

"That's beside the point. A bride should have the kind of wedding she's always dreamed about."

He was really beginning to irritate her. How had the rogue turned the tables on her? Now she was the one trying to convince him. "Dammit it, Zach, I'm the bride. I ought to know what I want. I've changed my mind."

"You changed my mind, too, Rosie. The more I think of it, the better it sounds. I can imagine how beautiful that red hair of yours will look against a white veil."

"Too late, Zach—because the gown I'm wearing is the one I'm getting married in. *Tonight. This* is my wedding."

"It's mine, too, isn't it? Don't I have anything to say on the subject?"

"We'll just see about that!" She surprised him by snatching his Colt out of the holster. "You aren't going to make a fool of me in front of your whole family, Zach MacKenzie. They came here for a wedding, and they're going to see one."

He suddenly broke into laughter.

"What's so funny?"

"History repeating itself—except it was my dad who forced my mother at gunpoint to marry him."

Rose couldn't help grinning. "The little I've seen of your parents, I doubt it took that much *forcing*."

He took the Colt from her and slipped it back into its holster. Then he cupped her cheeks in his hands, and stared down at her with that little-boy earnestness that always made her want to hug him.

"Are you sure this is what you really want to do, honey?"

Rose looked up at him. His eyes were warm and compelling, his mouth softened in a smile. "Sweetheart, those things I mentioned—like fancy gowns and veils—were just trimmings. I never told you what the most important thing was in my wedding dreams."

"What is it?"

She slid her arms around his neck. "To marry the man I love."

"Even if he's not a rich man?" He slipped his arms around her waist.

"Ah, but the man I love is very rich: he has the richness of a loving family."

Zach smiled down tenderly. "And even greater fortune he has your love, Rosie. No other man has that wealth." His kiss was unbelievably gentle, and said so much about this man she loved.

Joy bubbled in her laughter as he swept her up in his arms. "So what are we waiting for, Rosie love? We're holding up the wedding."

Laughing, Zach burst through the kitchen door carrying his future bride.

The mix of voices ceased instantly, and all stared with surprise and confusion.

Garnet MacKenzie was the first to grasp the meaning. With a smile tugging at the corners of her mouth, she exclaimed, "Oh, my! It would appear Zach has inherited his father's tactics when it comes to getting a woman to agree to marry him."

Flint's usually impassive face broke into a wide grin of approval.

"Yep, that's our boy, Redhead!" he said, swelling with pride.

"With one difference," Luke said beside him, and winked at Cleve.

"And just what would that be, Big Brother?" Flint asked.

"What he means, Brother Flint," Cleve replied, "is that at least your son doesn't have to use a shotgun to get the bride to say yes."

Flint cast a droll glance at his younger brother. "It was only a Colt, Little Brother. Just a li'l old Colt."

The MacKenzie brothers broke into laughter, and Honey, Garnet, and Adriana MacKenzie combined their lilting laughter with that of their husbands.

Cynthia MacKenzie Kincaid added hers as she looked up into the brown eyes of her husband, David, who'd begun whistling and applauding.

Angeleen MacKenzie Gifford's laughter blended with her beloved Giff's, and she snuggled contentedly against his firm body. He kissed the top of her head and tightened his embrace.

Elizabeth MacKenzie Carrington blushed with pleasure as her husband, Jake, ceased cheering long enough to bend down and whisper an intimate message in her ear.

Clapping and hooting, Josh shouted, "Way to go, cousin!" He winked at his younger cousin Cole, then slid an arm around Emily's waist and drew her closer.

Cole MacKenzie added his whistle and applause and hugged his cousin, Kitty.

Squealing with happiness, Kate, Melanie, Aubrey, and Andrea hugged each other, each hoping that one day she, too, would experience such a happy moment.

Everett Billings dabbed a sentimental tear from the corner of his eye, then glanced anxiously at the clock and hoped they'd get on with the ceremony before the beef roast overcooked.

Zach gazed with adoration at the woman in his arms. "See what you're getting into, Rosie?"

Rose, her eyes sparkling with happiness, whispered back, "I love you, my darling." Listening to the sound of the heartfelt jubilation that filled the room, she added, "And I love the whole MacKenzie family, too."

She looked up into the adoring gaze of the man she loved. "Every last one of them."

Epilogue

*L*egend has it that to this day, the streets of the town still echo with the joyous laughter from that extraordinary August night in 1892—when the MacKenzies came to Brimstone.